From the Notebooks of Doctor Brain

"Minister Faust's gleefully surreal approach to story lines, wonderful word-play, and offbeat, faster-than-a-speeding-bullet wit make [this] a marvelous read." —Eden Robinson, author of *Monkey Beach*

The Coyote Kings of the Space-Age Bachelor Pad

"A joy to read."—*The Seattle Times*

"Minister Faust brings [*The Coyote Kings*'] world alive in a jumpy, hold-nothing-back style. . . . Faust anatomizes [the Edmonton setting] with the same loving care Joyce brought to early-twentieth-century Dublin. . . . Faust's debut novel is a fresh and stylish entertainment." —*The New York Times*

"Quite simply stunning."—*Cinescape*

"Writes like Kevin Smith as if he'd grown up in an African immigrant neighborhood—just as comic- and pop-culture-obsessed but with a dose of righteous ethnic minority fury." —*Hollywood Reporter*

"Unique." —*Ebony*

"Faust's novel explodes with exuberant ideas, creepy adventure, intense emotions and linguistic derring-do. Every page is pure pleasure." —*Montreal Gazette*

"I feel quite comfortable in saying that there's never been a book quite like this one . . . [which] fairly teems with dark corners. . . . A stylish, accomplished first novel. Alternately laugh-out-loud funny, deeply tender and downright chilling . . . Filled with pop culture references, modern philosophy and subtle thoughts on the nature of human relationships. A first-rate novel from all angles; one can only hope it's the first of many." —*January magazine*

BY MINISTER FAUST

The Coyote Kings of the Space-Age Bachelor Pad
From the Notebooks of Doctor Brain

From the Notebooks of Doctor Brain

From the Notebooks of DOCTOR BRAIN

Minister Faust

BALLANTINE BOOKS
NEW YORK

A Del Rey Trade Paperback Original

Copyright © 2007 by Minister Faust

Published in the United States by Del Rey Books, an imprint of The Random House Publishing Group, a division of Random House, Inc., New York.

Del Rey is a registered trademark and the Del Rey colophon is a trademark of Random House, Inc.

ISBN 978-0-345-46637-2

Printed in the United States of America

www.delreybooks.com

2 4 6 8 9 7 5 3 1

Designed by Stephanie Huntwork

For my very own Mary-Jane Watson,
my beloved wife, Michelle

BY DOCTOR BRAIN

Seven Habits of Highly Defective Teams

Why Do Bad Villains "Happen" to Good Heroes?

Evil Geniuses Who Hate Humanity and the Women Who Love Them

Sacred Identity: Reclaiming the Demi-God in You

Secrets from Menton's Brain: Using Two Lefts to Make Yourself Right

Being Super-Mom in Today's Multiverse

Side-Kicked! When the Alpha-Hero Treats You Like Omega

Bulletproof, Schmulletproof

Secret Origins, Starring: Your Miserable Life

Unmasked: When Being a Superhero Can't Save You from Yourself

UNMASKED!

WHEN BEING A SUPERHERO CAN'T SAVE YOU FROM YOURSELF

Self-Help for Today's Hyper-Hominids

DOCTOR BRAIN

BALLANTINE BOOKS
NEW YORK

HEY!
YOU IN THE CAPE!
Why Are You Reading This Book?

You can wrap a steel I beam around your neck with your bare hands and wear it like a tie. You can swim so quickly that you can go back in time to offer Columbus correct directions to India. You can climb the outside of a building, regurgitate the ton of paper you've eaten, and weave a beautiful multilevel hive while not paying a cent in downtown rent.

But are you happy?

There was an innocent time not so long ago when most people assumed that the flamboyant adventurers whose stories emblazoned the front pages of our newspapers and whose exploits ricocheted across the six o'clock news must really have had it all: fame, good looks, public adulation, and seemingly godlike powers.

But as our society has matured, many of the greatest heroes of our time have come to the numbing epiphany that invincibility and immortality simply aren't enough. The war of Götterdämmerung was finally concluded in victory, the worst ultra-menaces were locked inside the maximum-security force fields of Asteroid Zed, and the rest of the misguided offenders are being cared for by the finest psychiatric facilities for the atomically insane.

But while superlawbreakers are being profiled in movies of the week, fêted for their (sometimes literally) ghost-written autobiographies, and cared for to the price of millions of tax dollars, who will care for *you*?

Who will care for you, the brave men and women who put the menacing malefactors away? Who will care for you, the courageous crusaders who risked your headquarters, your magic bracelets and diadems, your proprietary technology, your connection with your subdimensional xeno-souls and even your lives? Who will care for you, who jeopardized every relationship you were forced to put on hold or which you allowed to wither while you were fighting to preserve our freedom?

Far too often, the sad answer has been *no one.*

You men and women who kept our world safe from the likes of the Infinity Farmer and his Time Tractor, from X-Stacy and the Ravers, or from the technopurges of Robot-Stalin, have too often defined yourselves solely by the existence of your foes. But what are you supposed to do now that those foes are gone and the ungrateful world no longer applauds from the safety of its decorative balconies?

What are you supposed to do now that you're trapped in a safe world of your own making, a world that offers you no challenge, no role, no identity, no external enemies?

Yes, the supervillains of old are gone. But there's a new group of them around today. And they're *psychic.* No, not psychic like Sarah Bellum, Menton the Destroyer, or the Specially Relative Einstein Baboons.

Nor are the poisons of these villains green glowing crystals hidden inside lead strongboxes or poisonous prions murdering you one DNA helix at a time. Instead these poisons are locked inside your head and your heart, revealing themselves as depression, paranoia, rage, guilt, performance anxiety, psionic decay, dimension-shifting, impotence, imomnipotence, or any number of other impairments of the soul.

Perhaps now you're forced to recognize that *hyperhominidism* is equal part curse to the blessing of your glory days.

But if you've been suffering due to HH, the time to suffer without help is no more.

Meet Your Mentor

My name is Dr. Eva Brain-Silverman, but to thousands of superpowered individuals like you I'm simply known as Doctor Brain. For twenty years at my Hyper-Potentiality Clinic in the refurbished Mount Palomax Observatory in sunny Los Ditkos, I've been helping the extraordinarily abled to adjust to a life beyond heroics, and to feel alive again even when there are no more neutron bombs to defuse inside the UN building and no more Treemasons to burn out of our forests, banks, and government offices.

The book you're holding in your hands is the summation of two decades of advice I've dispensed as balm to heroes across North America at lectures, seminars, and clinical sessions.

But it's more than that. It's also the case study of the most spectacular group session of my career, whose destructive dysfunction culminated in the diabolical July 16 Attacks, which are even now reshaping our world.

When first contacted by the board of directors of the Fantastic Order of Justice to assist its six most contentious and confused members in conquering their intercommunal conflicts, I leapt at the opportunity to assist. Which heroes among Earth's foremost fighting force for freedom, I wondered, were so bent on antagonizing one another and destroying themselves that their own leadership was threatening to terminate them unless they solved their problems in group therapy?

To my astonishment, my lineup was a list of legends *among* legends:

- *Omnipotent Man,* AKA Wally W. Watchtower, seventy-one-year-old refugee from the destroyed planet Argon, and Earth's mightiest man,
- *Flying Squirrel,* AKA Festus Piltdown III, seventy-year-old billionaire industrialist and scourge of the criminal underworld,
- *Iron Lass,* AKA Hnossi Icegaard, the immortal Norse warrior-goddess and the planet's leading martial strategist,
- *Brotherfly,* AKA André "P-Fly" Parker, twenty-six-year-old wall-crawling, wisecracking, bluebottled ladies' man,
- *Power Grrrl,* AKA Syndi Tycho, the nineteen-year-old dynamic diva and pop music sensation, and
- *X-Man,* AKA Philip Kareem Edgerton, the thirty-four-year-old detective supreme and militant rabble-rouser from the ghettos of Los Ditkos.

While numbering only six, these individuals had afflictions galore: SID (Secret Identity Diffusion), narcissisism, Savior Complex, ODI-CFFB (Obsessive/Defensive Ideation and Compulsive Fight-or-Flight Behavior), Icon Trap, Mortiquaeroticism (death-seeking urges), and RNPN (Racialized Narcissistic Projection Neurosis), among others. Added into this miasma of mental maladies were group dysfunctions: Rudolphism and the Uranus Complex. And pervading all their disturbances, the leading malaise of our times among hyper-hominids: MILD (Mission-Identity Loss Disturbance), also known as PPSD (Post-Power Stress Disorder).

My Mission . . . and Yours

By examining the three-week travail-to-triumph odyssey of the most extraordinary assembly of patients—or as I prefer to say, "sanity supplicants"—I have ever treated, you will put yourself on a trajectory out of the magma pits of mediocrity and into the metropolis of mental health.

Unmasked! When Being a Superhero Can't Save You from Yourself will give you back the ultravision you once had—but stronger, so that you can perceive not only threats like Micro-Crip and his Nanogangstas, but also the ennui that destabilizes the superego ions of your self-respect.

Reading this book is the first step in rearming yourself with the ultrapower necessary to rescue the only innocent person you've so far failed to save: *yourself.*

CONTENTS

PART THREE

APPEALING TO A HIGHER POWER

PART ONE

VERY BAD CONDITION

CHAPTER ONE

OPERATION:
COOPERATION!

FRIDAY, JUNE 30, 1:43 P.M.

There's No "I" in Team, but
You Can't Spell "Teamwork"
Without "Me at Work"

"**O**mnipotent Man," shouted Iron Lass, "help me knock ziss monster off balance!" Her cloak exploding like coal dust and transforming itself into huge black wings, the Valkyrie streaked into the sky with Omnipotent Man behind her as a red, blue, and white flash.

The rest of the team scrambled in the badlands sands, narrowly escaping being crushed. With ever-increasing speed, the mile-high metal wheel of mayhem rolled its juggernaut path northwest toward the ten million people of Los Ditkos.

"What *is* that thing?" screamed Power Grrrl.

Buzzing above us and almost silhouetted by the flaming sunset, the Brotherfly whooped, "Muss be Codzilla's hula hoop!"

"Don't either of you know a kot-tam thing? That's Cyclo-

Tron!" yelled the X-Man, gaping at the terror wheel rolling its long arc to merge onto the interstate toward its target. From this distance, Cyclo-Tron's twirling lights resembled an ultramassive Ferris wheel, but only for a carnival of destruction in which the cotton candy is made of pink insulation and the corndogs have sticks of dynamite inside them. "Nearly destroyed Houston in '78," yelled X-Man, "until—"

"—until Captain Alamo and the Confederate Wrecking Crew turned it into the world's largest spare-parts yard," said the Flying Squirrel, focusing his Squirreloscope on the retreating spectacle of Iron Lass and Omnipotent Man failing to knock over the unicycled behemoth. "Well, X-Man? We need a vehicle!"

The X-Man closed his eyes. Slowly, carefully, he enunciated the word *au-to-mo-bile*.

A geometry of shadows—onyx curves, lines, and planes—congealed in front of me, composing themselves into the finned sleekness of a shining 1955 Ford Fairlane. X-Man and his elder jumped inside, rocketing down the cracked and splintered highway. Meanwhile, Brotherfly wrapped his arms and legs around Power Grrrl to fly her away, scraping the ground occasionally with her dangling boots from bearing the additional weight.

Clicking forward several miles, I found Iron Lass and Omnipotent Man swirling like chaff in a dust devil, desperately dodging deathbeams from the sinister spokes of the Cyclo-Tron. The wheel's blinding neon rays slashed mile-long smoking scars into the badlands, the rubble reeking of sulfur. Omnipotent Man was virtually invulnerable, but Iron Lass lacked the protection of her impregnable wings while airborne, and was ignitable as a chicken breast marinated in ethanol.

After witnessing Cyclo-Tron nearly incinerate the Brotherfly and Power Grrrl, Iron Lass swooped down to where they were flying mere inches above the badlands floor of cactus and purple sage. "Get her out uff here, you *verdammt* ik-noramus!" she yelled.

"Like, we have every right to be here?" shouted Power Grrrl, clinging to the Brotherfly's midsection like a baby possum to its mother's belly. Even while furious, she intoned her statements like questions, as if expressing uncertainty or seeking the permission of some unknown agency.

"You cannot do any goot here, Broderfly!" yelled Iron Lass. "Get aheadt to Los Ditkos—get ze civilians out of ze way!"

"But damn, Lass," said the Brotherfly, "you c'n fly faster than I can, specially with this lil girly-girl weighin me down!"

"Omnipotent Man unt I vill slow Cyclo-Tron down—now you get her out uff here!"

Off flew the two youngest members, and Iron Lass shouted to her partner to follow her lead. Zooming miles ahead on the highway and then hovering low, she swung her black longsword *Darkalfheimsdottir* toward the road. *Muspells*-fire belched from her blade, turning a hundred-yard stretch into a hundred-foot-deep flaming crater.

Streaking back another mile, the valorous Valkyrie dragged her white *Grendelsmuter* shortsword with her, the entire distance crackling into ice in her wake. "Vally, rip it up!"

Sweeping low like a stealth bomber, Omnipotent Man dug his arms beneath the skin of the road, ripping it into the air like grass clippings.

Cyclo-Tron rolled right through their speed bump, slowing slighty but not stopping.

Iron Lass: "Odin damn it!"

Omnipotent Man: "Hnossi, I unnerstand y'upset, but there's never any need for that kinda language, even if y'are invokin' your heathenish blasphemy again—"

"Vally, for ze love of fuckink Loki, just *do* sumsing!"

"Roger that, Iron Lass, ma'am," he said, streaking off.

Clicking over to Route 22 on the outskirts of Los Ditkos, I found the Brotherfly and Power Grrrl struggling to evacuate a Squirrel Burger drive-in franchise.

"Yo, my peeps," yelled the Brotherfly, crawling along the ceiling and yelling down toward the customers, "you gots to get your Squirrelly Fries and Nut Shakes on an turn yo highways to bye-ways, cuz danger is biz-anging on the door and briz-anging hell with it, kwamn sayin?"

Apparently none did know what he was saying, for staring back at him were nothing but blank eyes, while mouths kept chewing and seam-popping polyestered legs remained motionless beneath the bright pink furry tables.

"I got this one, Brotherfly!" said Power Grrrl. *"Hear ye, hear me,"* she called out, disco lights streaming out of her bustier, a dance track thumping out of her Power Pumps. She sang:

"You got to get the move on, your groove on!
It's time for PG's smooth song, the lube song!
And o-o-o-O-O-uh-uh-UH-UH-UH—"

she intoned, rippling in her trademarked R&B/gospel trill,

"—can you think! slink! and JINK like ME?"

In a Squirrel Burger blink, sixty diners of all ages, body shapes, races, and genders simply disappeared.

Replacing them instantly, in the same chairs and the same poses, were threescore uniformed Power Grrrls, "booty-shaking" their way behind the original as she dance-beat them to safety outside and away.

A moment later, a gray-haired man in plaid slacks shuffled his way out of the restroom, reclasping his eagle-shaped "Elvis" belt buckle. Swooping down on him, the Brotherfly plucked him up and out of the restaurant an instant before

Cyclo-Tron flattened the diner into an inch-high greasy crust of flaming rubble and burning food products.

Burning Bridges

hecking my display, I clicked myself over to the fringes of mainland Los Ditkos where the X-Man and Flying Squirrel were speeding at 160 miles an hour over fractured highway right behind the thundering Cyclo-Tron. Lacking any real opposition, the hurricane wheel had ceased aiming its particle beams—otherwise X-Man and Flying Squirrel would have been reduced to nothing but costumed puffs of smoke.

"Omnipotent Man, Iron Lass," shouted the X-Man into his comm, "what in the hell're you two doing in southeast Los Ditkos? We've gotta stop this thing out *here*!"

"Wellsir," crackled back the voice of Omnipotent Man, "we can't let this here monsterosity cross the Centurion Bridge over to Bird Island. If downtown Los Ditkos is destroyed, th'whole free ennerprise system of the state could be at stake!"

"So you're gonna bring down that big metal bastard in *my* neighborhood? So what if all the coloreds buy it, so long as you can save Ivory Town?"

"Son," snapped the Squirrel, "this isn't the time for your Zulu goddamned nationalism, do you hear me? For once in your life, *listen* to people who know what they're actually doing and let them bring down this giant steel cocksucker like they know how to!"

"Old man, we can clear the path to Centurion Bridge, destroy the bridge, and drown this motherfucker in the river, we can destroy Cyclo-Tron here while we still can, *or* I can personally rip you to pieces and fry you into hot wings. Now either shut your caviar-hole or help me blast this freak—or better yet, both!"

"And how do you suggest we do that, Rochester?"

"What's its power source?"

Even behind the mask, the Flying Squirrel's eyes glinted. "Get me as close as you can to that super-colliding sonofa-bitch!"

As if he were piloting a ship in a tsunami, X-Man ripped at the steering wheel, hurtling along in the ditch at station-keeping with the giant wheel's hub, all the while dodging the storm of crushed cars, spinning street lamps, and flying trees pouring down on them. Dialing his comm, the Flying Squirrel waited for his connection and then unleashed thirty seconds of fury at the person on the opposite end.

Instantly Cyclo-Tron's lights went black. Slowly, the peak of its rotation dipped left, and the device fell straight for the Ford Fairlane.

X-Man cranked hard to the right, arcing 180 degrees east. Behind him, the entire mile-high apparatus that was Cyclo-Tron plummeted. From that height, the distance to fall was so great that the descent appeared to be in slow motion, until the wheel clapped the earth with a sound like God backfiring His truck, turning every window within four miles of the shock wave into a mutilating hurricane of slivered glass.

"I can't be*lieve* you pathetic bunch of cripples!" snapped the Flying Squirrel, ripping off his Event Helmet, unstrapping himself from the Event Chair, and storming out of the Id-Smasher® before I could call him back.

I tapped my panel, releasing all my sanity-supplicants from their Event Chairs. Each one detached him- or herself, stretch-ing and groaning, before exiting the techno-pinnacle of my analytical career. At more than three stories tall, the neuro-dimensional Id-Smasher® was a glittering titanium tower of nine hundred terabits of cognintegrated processing power. I held back a moment, admiring the technology which interlaced

the psychespheres of my patients via the long, slender trans-
duction rods through its two black processing bulbs.

"Looks just like a giant shrimp, Doc," said the Brotherfly,
observing me observing. "Come to thank of it, I'm hongry for
some takeout now that we up outta there! Brotherfly be sayin
'ka-pow!'—or should it be 'kung-pow'? *Bzzzt!* Somebody, anybody, can I get a witness?"

Laughing at his own joke, he looked around for approval,
holding out a hand palm-up for slapping reinforcement. He received none.

"Thank you for sharing, André," I offered.

"Now could somebody fill me in on something?" said Omnipotent Man, rubbing a dried trail of drool from the side of his
mouth. "How exactly did we bring down ol' Cyclo-Tron, anyway? Cuz I think I mighta missed how that happened."

Festus shook his head. "Since you people couldn't destroy
it, I went after its power source."

X-Man snorted. "Only because I told you to!"

The Flying Squirrel rippled an eyebrow in my direction,
then said, "When we were driving alongside that mangler, I
called the Defense Department, which is what kept Cyclo-Tron
operational. I got them to yank its funding." He harrumphed,
fluttering his flaps. "Hell of a simulation you've got there, Doctor, to've actually arranged a simulated DOD for me to talk to.
Do you have a Hoover in some other section of that program,
too?"

"I'm glad you approve, Festus. The program improvises according to the essential logic of any gambit you take, responding accordingly."

"Hmph. Anyway," he said, "that's how it's supposed to be
done. Analyze the situation first. That's what Hawk King taught
us—those of us who bothered to learn. Forget the brute-force
idiocy. That's for amateurs. We're the professionals."

"Now," I said, "if you'd all like to get dressed, we'll pick up in the Group Dynamics Verbalarium."

Back to Base, and Back to "Base Sicks"

All teams, super or otherwise, function and dysfunction like all families do: having to cope with intergenerational misunderstanding, birth-order clusters of privilege and disfavor, brutal grudges, pathological codependencies, tragically "scripted" behavior loops, pathogenic levels of neglect and abuse, and phony displays of affection and loyalty.

This catalog of psychological cancers forms what I call the "base sicks," the bombed-out foundation of every human being which is the source of all adult misery and the terror of every "inner child." Because these *base sicks* are buried at the deepest-level programming of any group's origin, they're as invisible to the individuals they're poisoning as a rainbow is to Dog Man.

It's Easier to Change One's Uniform Than One's Mind-Set

Emerging from the changing room, Power Grrrl stumbled, falling into me. I helped her along while she regained her "reality legs," noting the extraordinary change in her appearance. Gone was the black and silver Sensosilk Event Tunic, replaced by one of her more restrained uniforms: a dazzle of sequins, a lace vest with garters, and thigh-high leather boots whose skyscaper heels had no doubt contributed to her tumble.

"Like, Eva," she asked me, "could we have, like, *died* or something in that simulation? Because I am totally not cool with that?"

Behind us, Iron Lass ground her teeth so loudly that for a moment I thought she was chewing ice.

"No, Syndi, not to worry," I said, intercepting the Valkyrie's objection. "The release form you signed cleared me of any liability in the unlikely event of your mental incapacitation, grievous bodily harm, or life-cessation, but while you could experience the *illusion* of pain inside the Id-Smasher®, your bodies couldn't be killed, even if your somatic simulations could be."

"It's precisely that kind of cowardice," grumbled the man waiting for us inside the Verbalarium, "that's destroyed this organization."

Sitting already in the ring of chairs, the Flying Squirrel almost glowed from the sunlight streaming onto him, the fur of his world-famous mask gleaming with its oversized animal ears, snub nose, long white whiskers, and giant, pink-rimmed black eyes. With his Olympic build, tight skin, and laserlike stare, he looked more like a young Brian Dennehy than the seventy-year-old he was. But no one could mistake the power throbbing inside his clawed and furry gloves for that of anyone else.

"Cowardice, contempt for chain of command, lack of discipline," sneered the Flying Squirrel, "and a hundred other maladies of character forming a toxic cocktail that has shaken, not stirred, everything that Hawk King spent decades building. If he'd seen how you invalids performed in there today—"

"O-kay, we get it?" said Power Grrrl, snapping her bubble gum. "You *know* Hawk King, you, like, *worked* with Hawk King, you used to *fetch coffee* for Hawk King—I got it the, like, *first* thousand times?"

"Aw, man, Squirrelly," said André. "Brotherfly say girly-girl just put the *Bzzzt!* on you—"

"Quiet, you," said Festus Piltdown III. He paused to scrub Power Grrrl with his glance. "And as for you, your juvenile blandishments which reduce every statement to an interrogative don't erase the simple fact that your performance was subfarcical!"

"Oh, now jess tether yer ponies a sec, Festy," said Omnipotent Man, making a "whoa" gesture with his hands. "I'ont think we was all s'bad in there. We set 'er up, an you an th'X-Man knocked 'er down. That's the hokey-pokey, right?" He grinned and winked at the ravenish woman in the winged helmet. Iron Lass's ivory faced flushed. He sang, "Now we turn ourselves around . . . that's what it's all about!"

"Ah, poor, pathetic, possum-fried Wally," said the Flying Squirrel, shaking his head minutely. "Would you be giving that moonshine-and-stained-overalls assessment if Hawk King were here? Did you happen to notice that your so-called *settin' 'er up* amounted to virtually zero role in the mission's success?"

The X-Man spat, " 'Success'?"

All faces turned to Kareem Edgerton, HKA the X-Man, before flitting toward my hand, which I kept poised above my whistle, like a gunfighter fingering his Colt.

Kareem leaned back in his seat, letting out a breath while reconsidering his tone. "If today's 'combat' had been real, there would've been a hundred thousand people lined up outside of hospitals looking like bleeding pincushions from the flying glass. 'Success'?" he repeated, catching his voice just as it spiked. He glanced toward my whistle, looked down, loosened his fists, and stage-whispered, "You call that success. . . . I'd hate to see failure."

The Utility of Aggression-Aversion Therapy

Festus Piltdown said, "If you'd been in this business as long as I have, Edgerton, you'd know that sometimes tough decisions—executive decisions—are required when the professionals take on the hard jobs no one else is qualified for—"

"Professionals?" said the X-Man, extravagantly sweeping invisible lint from his black blazer and pants. "Mr. Squirrel here said 'professionals' like that's something to be proud of. But there're professional *killers,* too. And those two"—he wagged his chin across the circle, first to Omnipotent Man and then to Iron Lass—"were willing to *professionally* liquidate everyone in Langston-Douglas to protect the borough of Bird Island. Don't the people in Stun-Glas have the right to life, liberty, and the pursuit of not being blown to kot-tam hell?"

I moved my whistle toward my lips.

"Excuse me, Doc," said Kareem, "blown to golly-gee-whiz-gol-dang *heck.* Or was it just that not enough 'professionals' live over in mainland Los Ditkos?"

Hnossi Icegaard shifted in her chair. "It vuss only a simulation, Kareem," she sighed, adjusting her gleaming silver-gold breastplate and black-feather cloak. "No actual human beingks vut haff been harmedt. Just like in ze moofies."

"So why not—!" Kareem stopped, lowered his volume and tempo. "Why not . . . just let Cyclo-Tron hit the island, then? When we were inside the simulation we all believed it was real. And yet you and Wally had no hesitation to sacrifice how many of *us* to save how few of *you*?"

"Oh, Kareem!" snapped Power Grrrl. "That's, like, not even—"

"That didn't take long, did it?" said Festus. "Have we gone

to simulated Las Vegas now? Because once again Kareem is playing his race cards!"

"You know, in my experience," said Kareem, caging his fingers and drawing out his words, "the jokers . . . who talk the most about 'playing the race card' . . . are the people who own all the diamonds . . . who've picked up the clubs . . . to beat down the spades . . . because they've got no heart."

The Brotherfly laughed, slapping his knees in exaggerated delight. "You gots to admit, Squirrelly-man, Kareem just put the *Bzzzt!* on y'all!"

Kareem switched his gaze to Omnipotent Man and Iron Lass. "Five times more people live on the mainland than on the island. I even told you two to clear a path for Cyclo-Tron to get onto Centurion Bridge so we could sink it there. Did you even *consider* moving into position?"

"For all you know, Kareem, even if ve'd destroyt ze bridch, Cyclo-Tron vut haff continuedt rollink out of ze vaater. Dit you sink about zat?"

"X-Man, hold up there a minute," said Wally. "What if Bird Island got flattened, and then th'entire economy crashed? Then all the mums and dads in Langston-Douglas woulda lost their jobs! Well then how they supposta pay their mortgages?"

"Wallace, have you ever even set foot in Stun-Glas? You think the people there have mortgages? You think half the people there even have *jobs*?"

"Now jess round up yer rangers a spell, Kareem. Jess last week I got a ball off the roof at one a them Langston-Douglas midnight basketball dealies. And don't be saying they don't have jobs, no sir. I saw lots a fine automobiles there with some very shiny, expensive-looking hubcaps, an that means hardworking folks, car loans an auto dealerships fulla happy employees. Gracious jiminny, th'folks down there even try t'dress like superheroes—evra-one wearing red or blue—"

"This monolithic level of ignorance about life in Stun-Glas," said Kareem, imploring the ceiling itself, "is *exactly* why the F*O*O*J lost its HUD contract to police the neighborhood in the first place, and why the L*A*B picked it up and protected our homes, reduced crime to almost nothing, and earned the loyalty of the people there—"

"Maybe, Kareem," said Festus, "if your L*A*B wasn't such a bunch of spear-sharpening, whitey-hating, race-fixated reprobates, they would've kept in HUD's favor. But then they wouldn't be the League of Angry Blackmen anymore, would they?"

"You hear that, Doc? Where's your whistle now? Festus, those sheets you ride around in at night—they made of satin, or silk?"

"I don't have to take that from you, Edgerton!" said Festus.

I blew my Mind Whistle™, and the bickering ceased as quickly as the migraines sucked everyone's hands to their skulls.

"Ladies and gentlemen, we went over the rules yesterday," I reminded them, while resentment skittered across my group's faces like silverfish across a dinner plate.

"I'd thought we might go a few *weeks* at least before the whistle first had to be used, but . . . well. While controlled venting is a necessary part of the therapeutic process, aimless unleashing of antihappiness merely blasts psychemotional shrapnel into the vulnerable underbelly of our healing community. Your real task inside the Id-Smasher® wasn't tactical training, of course, but to prepare you for postsimulation self-observation of how you are decapacitizing the life-potentials you seek.

"Your board of directors—pardon me, your Fantastic Order of Justice Leadership Administrative Council—was quite specific with me, and with all of you. Unless you six can resolve the problems that are making you, and I quote, 'contentious in the extreme, dysfunctional, and impossible to work with,' end quote, the F*L*A*C will terminate your employment with and membership in the F*O*O*J."

I let the weight of my words rest like rhetorical cement blocks upon their psychemotional fingernails. Each hero was also still wincing from the beneficial operant conditioning of the Mind Whistle™.

"Now, while some of you are unconcerned at the prospect of losing your benefits and pension, either due to your personal fortune," I said, nodding to the Flying Squirrel, "or due to your immortality," I continued, nodding to Iron Lass, "I assume the real threat is that of dishonorable discharge from the Fantastic Order of Justice.

"And while such scandal might be a temporary boost in the 'no press is bad press' mode, dishonorable discharge from the F*O*O*J could severely damage a young heroine's outside commercial endorsements," I said, nodding to Power Grrrl, "distance oneself from the command of dedicated soldiers," I said, nodding again to Iron Lass, "or from a community of friends and admirers," I said to the young black man with the floppy transparent wings, blue-bottled bug-eye goggles, and hairy antennae.

I finished by nodding to the thirty-four-year-old black man in his conservative black suit and tie. "And it would annihilate an ambitious man's career aspirations."

Everyone finally took their chairs in the circle, leaving the X-Man as the last man standing, since he'd been jockeying to avoid sitting near either Power Grrrl or Festus. Finally he sat on the opposite side of the circle from his implacable adversary, the Squirrel.

Perhaps ironically (for those untrained in psychoanalysis), the quietest of the group stood out the most. He'd made neither fuss nor folly during the just concluded mini-fracas, and he sat serenely resplendent in his blue suit, golden epaulets, red necktie, and cape. Were I not a highly perceptive practitioner of the healing arts of psychotherapy, I might have believed this man had no worries at all, with his massive brawn and his hands folded in his lap so immaculately they appeared to have been carved by Michelangelo himself.

But I did know better. For Omnipotent Man was as wracked with self-destructive pain as any of his comrades beside him.

Every Superstrength Is Also a Superweakness

As you just saw, conflict on a hyper-hominid team is virtually inevitable. That's because careers self-select for personality type. The irony, of course, is that success during the workday can mean severe interpersonal and psychological dysfunction at night.

Take Clifford David Stinson, HKA the Blue Smasher. His heroism demanded his willingness—indeed his eagerness—to smash anything, anywhere at any time. But during domestic disputes, he also smashed several of his own homes and vehicles as well as those of his neighbors in Los Ditkos's upscale Royal Arch district. In 1988 he so flattened Bucksome Hills that the city council had to rename it Spinster Flats.

Eventually Clifford Stinson's personal failings became professional ones. In 1983, when the Gasteroids threatened to infest the intestinal tracts of the entire population of Crystal City, Arizona, Stinson reduced its city hall, Jewel Museum, and 40 percent of its downtown to shards. No one doubted that smashing had its place—but never in Crystal City.

Similarly, Magna's magnetic-seduction was powerful enough to sway even the Iron Eunuch and the Cobalt Castrati. But her overreliance on her erotipathic powers to the exclusion of all her others tossed her off the peak of her celebrated career and into a sewer of sexual addiction, facedown in the lap of *the capes,* the niche-porn market of ex-heroines and -heroes.

The chief social advantage of the Götterdämmerung had been its demand from all citizens, and certainly from the college of heroes, for self-sacrifice—that is, the development of the *superego.* But lacking an overriding threat, many in our society, including its former champions, had by now developed overactive ids. Such was the case with nearly everyone in my team.

Who's That Whispering from Your Shoulders?

Selfish desire and highest ideal—in the cartoons, they're represented by a miniature devil and angel perching on our shoulders. In rare cases, these voices are literal, as with the tiny wizard Mage Mogdobnag and Lord Lizaard on the opposite epaulets of Noble Man.

But for most of us, these "voices" are expressions of our id and superego, our respective sub- and supercognitive urges toward selfish, violent gratification and altruistic self-actualization.

Our id isn't evil. Its self-interest fuels our self-preservation and individual advancement. The id's social defect is its incapacity to value the needs of others. And while the superego's lofty goals might seem almost saintly, if left unmoderated a superego-controlled individual could starve to death from refusal to harm animals or plants, or be so possessed by her idealism as to slip out of our reality and into the Platon Dimension of pure Ideals.

That's where the ego comes in. The ego balances selfishness and selflessness. But because the superstrength of most heroes comes from the interaction between super-ids and super-superegos, destabilization occurs when one capacity becomes stronger than the other. Unfortunately for several members of my team, a post-Götterdämmerung world has starved their super-egos, letting their ids grow unchecked, like black-dripping toadstools on a yellowing psychemotional lawn.

Failing Checks and Balances Among Super Powers

Festus," I asked the Howitzer of a man after he'd stopped grimacing from the effects of the Mind Whistle™, "despite the simmering soup pot of rage which has just bubbled over onto your behavioral stove, you haven't walked out. Why not?"

He leveled his eyes on me like twin turrets, silently.

"As one of the country's wealthiest men," I probed, "you're at the head of a corporate empire of mass media, defense contracts, surveillance technology, and fast food. You've led a distinguished career as one of the nation's finest investigators—"

"The World's Greatest Detective®," growled the black-haired septuagenarian. "Period."

Brotherfly: "Damn, Squirrelly. Takes balls to be trademarkin y'self as the world's greatest dick, knawm sayn? *Bzzzt!*" Everyone ignored André while he laughed. "C'mon, y'all! All y'all can't be that uptight, can ya? Who gon leave a brother hangin like that? Syndi-girl, snap me a *bzzzt!* from them bad girls!"

Syndi smirked and shook her fortified cleavage in tardy acknowledgment of his jape.

"That's what I'm talkin 'bout! *Bzzzt!*"

"Kot-tam, André," snapped Kareem, "would you please, for just five minutes, QC?"

"Whuzzat, Exxy?"

"Quit cooning!"

"Festus," I refocused, "you've never been one to follow orders meekly. So why haven't you defied the F*L*A*C and marched out the door?"

Festus Piltdown III sat back in his chair and crossed his gloved forearms over the flying squirrel silhouette emblazoned on the tunic covering his massive chest.

X-Man: "I can tell you why, Doc."

"Kareem, ze doktor dit not ask you."

"And the Squirrel didn't *an*swer her, Hnossi!"

"Gawd, Kareem, would you, like, shut up?" said Syndi, stamping her boots, one-two, and putting one hand on her hip-strung backlash. "You want her blowing her, like, whistle-thingy again?"

Finally Omnipotent Man put up his hand.

"See now, ma'am-doctor, maybe Festy's a might modest, but as y'all probably know, he's fixin' to run in th'upcoming election for Director of Operations. You knew that, din'tcha?"

"I think I recall having heard it somewhere, Wally, but as I don't follow politics, it must've slipped my mind."

"Wellsir, an as y'can pro'ly guess, if the F*L*A*C shows ol Festy out through the F*O*O*J saloon flappers, he caint run for D.O.O. Then his dreams're hooched, knowuttamean?"

"I, uh . . . I think so, Wally."

"An Festy pro'ly figures, an I agree with im, that he's earned this goldang job. He was in the F*O*O*J almost since the beginnin, he's served almost evra other p'sition on the F*L*A*C—Director of Personnel, of Finance, of Investigation—he was even Chair once. So y'can unnerstan if the F*L*A*C sendin im to your woodshed an threat'nin to turn im loose altogether has got his fur up an hackled."

I asked Festus how he felt about Wally's remarks.

He glared back at me with all the glowering, terrifying, predatory intimidation of his mammalian namesake.

On the Receiving End of F*L*A*C

For a group of men and women who had devoted their lives to saving others, my six psychemotional journeyers were stunningly incapable of saving themselves. That many of them despised one another was obvious to anyone; that each one despised him- or herself was unknown to all of them.

And that is why the F*O*O*J's F*L*A*C had ordered them into my care and analysis, since the infighting and dysfunctionality generated by their mutual- and self-loathing threatened to vaporize their organization at a time when the F*O*O*J was particularly vulnerable: election time. Three of the six directorships were up for grabs, and for the first time since the F*O*O*J's inception, so was the post of Director of Operations.

In theory the most powerful position on the F*O*O*J Leadership Administrative Council, the DOO was responsible for setting long-range mission goals, determining strategy and vetting tactics, outlining long-term needs for staff and matériel acquisition, and, potentially, reforming the obese F*O*O*J bureaucracy. The retirement of Colonel Strom Flintlock from his grandfathered, unelected position meant that the F*O*O*J was poised for potentially massive change. And while many people had assumed that Festus Piltdown III, HKA the Flying Squirrel, was destined for the DOO post which was the de facto commander-in-chieftancy of the F*O*O*J, there was a surprise buried beneath the election field like a land mine in a miniature golf course.

If the F*O*O*J had been a vehicle for national and even global change, the F*L*A*C was the front axis of that vehicle's wheels. So the candidate—or candidates—in our therapeutic sessions were in desperate need of a good greasing.

Back Issues:
The Origins of the F*O*O*J

Forged during America's now mythical Golden Age of Heroism to counter the threats of rum-running, communism, juvenile delinquency, and marijuana, the (then) Fraternal Order of Justice was Earth's foremost and finest fighting force of fury. Delivering the decisive blow against the German war machine following the Soviet invasion of Berlin, the F*O*O*J became a planetary icon for justice and freedom. Its founding members' names are synonymous with glory: *Omnipotent Man, Iron Lass, Lady Liberty, Gil Gamoid and the N-Kid, Captain Manifest Destiny,* and their brilliant, mysterious, mystical mentor, the incredible *Hawk King.*

Returning to America and the expansive East Coast metropolis of Seagull City, the F*O*O*J moved into its first legendary headquarters, the Mando Mansion, and began recruiting among the nation's growing ranks of costumed avengers.

Thus began the F*O*O*J's Silver Age, whose new stars would shine as brightly as the originals—*Siren, the Evolutionist, Flying Squirrel,* and *Chip Monk*—defending our country and our planet against some of the worst scourges imaginable: Nemesaur, the Leninoids, Codzilla, Black Mamba, Standing Buffalo, Cosmicus and the Hordes of Entropy . . . truly an unlimited series.

But in the goggled eyes of some, the atomic-powered America of the Silver Age was mutating into something unrecognizable. Gone were the neat pleats and fedoras of the founding era of the F*O*O*J. Now rock and roll, the Civil Rights and women's movements, miniskirts, hippies, and drugs were bubbling out of the gutters and recoloring the splash pages of our country.

Like most institutions, the conservative F*O*O*J resisted

any change until change was forced upon it, mandated not only by the pervasive influence of altered American mores, but by legal action. Gone was the adjective *fraternal* because of the Siren's embittering lawsuit; the word was replaced by *fantastic,* so the F*O*O*J's heralding acronym could be preserved.

Other changes—some with far more sweeping outcomes— were on the way. Warlock War II saw the magical relocation of Seagull City to the West Coast and its integration into the city of Los Ditkos. The war's destruction of Mando Mansion led Festus Piltdown III to construct a replacement F*O*O*J headquarters, the glittering gold-silver Fortress of Freedom, which remains the leading tourist attraction of downtown Bird Island in Los Ditkos. Perhaps most contentiously, as a recipient of federal security contracts under President Nixon, the organization could not by the early 1970s continue to receive such funding if it remained all-white. Racial integration of the F*O*O*J introduced America to such now-classic crimefighters as the Spook and La Cucaracha.

Colossal figures were undergoing colossal change.

The Bitter Aftertaste in the Chalice of Victory

But there's only so much change any organization can take before its primary-colored tunic begins washing out and splitting at the seams.

Integration, popular demands that the F*O*O*J apply itself to new threats such as environmental devastation and domestic abuse, and increasing public concern about due process and the legal loopholeism that allowed superheroes to operate meant that the legitimacy of the F*O*O*J's mission—if not its very existence—was in question.

But no one, least of all the F*O*O*J's founders, could have dreamed of the devastating impact that America's and the world's two major victories would have: the almost simultaneous collapse of communism and victory in the Götterdämmerung, the global war against supervillains.

Suddenly, for more than two hundred active F*O*O*Jsters, several hundred affiliates, and the public they were sworn to protect (and whose taxes funded them), the F*O*O*J no longer had any reason to exist.

Fortunately for the F*O*O*J, drugs continued to plague America's cities, but the battle against this epidemic lacked sufficient drama to inspire a generation and the media, and it initiated as many awkward questions as it answered.

Inheriting a lugubriously legendary legacy impossible to leap above, but no longer possessing a substantial-enough organizing objective (or "mythic narrative"), the F*O*O*J's workplace dysfunction soon became a matter of public record. Bickering among heroes transformed itself into publicized personal attacks and escalated into lawsuits, public brawling that shattered whole city blocks, and finally criminal charges against legendary heroes in front of a mortified America.

RELEASED: Jack Zenith's sensational *Two Masks of a "Hero,"* the era-shattering tell-all and the very first investigative book on the F*O*O*J with a credible inside source—Clifford David Stinson, HKA the Blue Smasher.

REVEALED: Decades-old internal conflicts; lurid allegations of harassment, assault, and perversion; cases of heroes gambling on the outcomes of their own superbattles; countless tales of substance abuse, power-fixation and dimension-shifting; and most shocking of all, the outing of dozens of secret identities.

REDUCED: Dozens of heroes who had traipsed across our globe like gods above the Trojan War were revealed as the lawyers, scientists, industrial magnates, romance novelists, major imprint editors, husbands, wives, and robots they actually were.

For a world weary and wary of secrecy among the powerful, *Two Masks of a "Hero"* was an electromagnet for the alloy of public scrutiny and popular outrage. Demands exploded for the full disclosure of F*O*O*J mission records and especially its financial accounts. On the advice of managers, attorneys, and PR agents, some heroes preemptively revealed their own identities in order to shape perception about themselves and their careers and thereby limit the damage from ongoing and future investigations.

The shattering of the old paradigm was loud enough to cause permanent damage to the ears of some heroes, and just as the ear is the center of balance, the psychological disequilibrium that followed cast many costumed crusaders upon the grimy, vomit-streaked barroom floors of their careers and personal lives. Golden Age icons and F*O*O*J founders such as Gil Gamoid and his sidekick the N-Kid, implicated in a heinous conspiracy and revealed at trial to be suffering from paranoid schizophrenia, were sent to languish in the psychic detention facilities of Asteroid Zed. And although rumors of sightings persisted, since 1975 the immeasurably masterful Hawk King had withdrawn to his mysterious Blue Pyramid, accepting only a rare audience for his cosmic counsel.

If Golden Age greats such as Gil Gamoid and the N-Kid could disintegrate, and if visionary founders such as Hawk King could abandon the world of men, then surely the epoch of the invincibles was as done as that of the dinosaurs.

The resulting shock wave through the hero community saw not only the inferno of more published tell-alls, but a tornado of resignations, divorces, self-exiles, and even suicides. And so the new generation of 1980s and '90s crimefighters, the so-called Digital Age warriors, was all dressed up . . . but with no place to go.

America not only didn't need heroes anymore—it no longer believed they existed.

Hyper-potentiality Is First and Last a State of Mind

Such a private and public crisis of confidence was the situation as the F*O*O*J stared into the new millennium.

Lacking a substantial external threat around which to create a new mission but teeming with internal contradictions that threatened its cohesion, the Fantastic Order of Justice found itself in a crisis that could only be resolved by looking within, especially for two generations of its most conflicted members.

Adding to this instability was the imminent power vacuum of an oncoming election. And except for the fanatical conspirators involved, no one could have guessed how that election would lead directly to the July 16 Attacks.

Facing this complex interconnection of social, political, and psychemotional chaos, none of which could be resolved by teleportation, spirit-gems, kraton beams, or an old-fashioned "dustup," I charged my six sanity-supplicants with a new mission. That mission was for them to come to terms with the very ordinary, very fragile defining human experience: fundamental emptiness and limitless fear of meaninglessness, or what I call the "Crisis of Infinite Dearths." If your own identity is mission-rooted, and your mission is now complete, how could you *not* be confused as to who you really are?

Directed to me by the winding country lanes of their own

confusion, my patients arrived at my Hyper-Potentiality Clinic yoked to wagonloads of psychemotionally dysfunctional produce. Other than this group's toxic mutual antagonism, chief among the disruptive behaviors reported to me by the F*L*A*C were:

- *the questionable competence and unrealistically un-flappable optimism of Omnipotent Man*
- *the bullying, aggression, and rage of the Flying Squirrel*
- *the micromanagement devolving into nanomanagement by Iron Lass*
- *the social inappropriateness bordering on sexual harassment of the Brotherfly*
- *the narcissism and self-absorption of Power Grrrl*
- *the insubordination and racial antagonism of, and unapproved investigations by, the X-Man*

Even during those first sessions, I had recognized an encyclopedia of psychosocial crises besetting the group—unmanaged anger and guilt, sexual confusion, the Uranus Complex, Secret Identity Diffusion, and the Savior Complex chief among them.

Clearly, ahead of us lay a Trojan struggle to resolve the problems of such great powers. But of course, with great power there must also come great psychoanalysis.

And just as it was my task to help the F*O*O*Jsters accurately envisage their own contraefficiencies, so is it your mission to recognize your own. Periodically throughout this book I'll be asking you to write down *your* answers to the generation-appropriate questions I posed to my "Big Six" throughout our explosive time together. Write your brief (ten words or fewer) responses in a journal, and then reflect on how they change depending on the varying exercises and processing you're experiencing each time.

For Golden and Silver Age heroes: *What will it mean for your life, and your view of yourself, if the glory days never return?*

Omnipotent Man: "I'm good. America's good. And being good is great."

Flying Squirrel: "Given these pathetic invalids, America needs me more than ever."

Iron Lass: "Never was it glory, but ever justice that I sought."

For Digital Age heroes: *How will you face knowing that you will never exceed, or even equal, the accomplishments of your predecessors?*

Brotherfly: "Brotherfly be fine. Always has been. He's a survivor."

Power Grrrl: "They never looked inside themselves. I won't make that mistake."

X-Man: "Who are *they* to be equal to? *Deserve* victory. Period."

Gazing into the Dusk

Mere demi-moments into our reconvened session in the Verbalarium, I was summoned by my secretary to take a call. Knowing that only a true emergency could have motivated Ms. Olsen to have disturbed the sanctity of a session, I took a call from the Spectacle, the F*O*O*J Director of Investigations.

I listened to the Spectacle, and the world as I knew it shattered.

And while none could have then known, the information conveyed in that call led directly to the abomination of the July 16 Attacks.

xerting every erg of professionalism at my command, I reentered the discussion chamber with a visage of calm detachment.

As I continued around the circle, the Brotherfly glanced up at me anxiously. For the first time since I'd met him, his face and posture betrayed an emotion other than flip playfulness or hyperscrotal lust. Perhaps his legendary "fly-feel" was tingling, hinting to him the horror of what I was about to reveal.

"My friends," I said finally, clearing my throat, "I have . . . some very difficult news . . . to share with you."

"What, Doc?" asked the Brotherfly.

"The man . . . the hero . . . you knew as the incredible Hawk King . . . is dead."

Everyone stood, their faces focused on mine.

Jaws unlatched, relatched.

"Vut?" said Iron Lass at last. "You caan't be—Frau Doktor, zat's impossible—Hawk Kink *caan't*—"

"Now ma'am-doctor, you musta gotten yer facts wrong on that one, cuz ev'rabody knows that ol Hawk King can't—"

"Miss Brain, I do believe you've flipped your substandard lid. Master Hawk King is an Egyptian deity—dying, by definition, is one of the few deeds *beyond* his potential—"

"How?" yelled X-Man, standing, the sole voice of non-denial. "How? Kot-tammit, how?"

"The call came directly from the F*O*O*J," I explained. "Major Ursa had an audience scheduled at the Hour of the Ninth Gate last night . . . but the Ka-Sentinels at the Blue Pyramid never showed up to let her inside the retaining wall—"

"Ze Kingk never missed an appointment," said Iron Lass. "Not in over fifty yearss, for any reason—"

"When there was still no response by ten A.M. today, Major

Ursa and the Spectacle led a team back to Sunhawk Island. The gate was open, the Ka-Sentinels were in a state of stupefaction . . . The Pyramid portal was open . . .

"They found Hawk King lying on his back inside his Duat Chamber, gripping his crook and flail."

They stood silently, but their eyes were screaming.

"The Spectacle's preliminary call," I concluded, "is natural causes."

" 'Natural causes'?" spat the X-Man. "Closest thing to invincible, closest thing to omniscient, and suddenly, just like that, dead by 'natural causes'?"

While the rest of us stood impotently, Kareem lowered himself back into his chair, his face ripped by rage, and then suddenly, horribly blank. And incongruously in that expressionless void, tears seeped from his eyes.

"No way. No way was this natural causes," he muttered, staring at the seam where one wall crashed into the next. "Hawk King was *murdered*," he said. "And if someone could kill *him,* that means all of us, and the world . . . are in for shit beyond anybody's reckoning."

Into Battle: But Where— and Who—Is the Foe?

Ironically, at the exact moment that global peace has triumphed, the gravest threat to superheroic mental health has become paranoia.

Although supercitizens now can bask in the summer sun of safety, the hypervigilance of their careers has cast them into a winter of ODI-CFFB: Obsessive/Defensive Ideation and Compulsive Fight-or-Flight Behavior, much in the way that a satyr or nymphomaniac, if placed in solitary confinement, may fall into chronic masturbation with attendant carpal tunnel syndrome.

The death of a loved one or a revered icon such as Hawk King is often a trigger for paranoia, but that paranoia speaks to a deeper drive than fear. Paranoia is a defiant charge to a cold, unfeeling cosmos: "Hear me! I exist! I'm important!" Because after all, if someone is actually orchestrating the chaos of the universe against you personally, then you do matter. When no one seems to care anymore, at least "enemies" give you the comforting illusion that you count.

As we'll see throughout *Unmasked! When Being a Superhero Can't Save You from Yourself,* above all other psychic threats, paranoia holds more destructive potential than even Cosmicus, the Digester of Worlds. As the old saying goes, paranoia can indeed "destroy ya."

CHAPTER TWO

FACING THE ULTIMATE ARCHENEMY

SATURDAY, JULY 1, 9:30 A.M.

Stages of Grief

Although as a hyper-hominid you've spent your entire career risking your life, there's only one task as difficult as facing the unresolved scandals and unsightly scars of your secret origin. And that is facing the deaths of others, especially that of a fellow hero.

After all, you've spent your professional career beating the odds, continually cheating the grim reaper at his own card table. But Death plays the ultimate trump card and is the only archenemy guaranteed to cash in everyone else's chips.

The morning after such an epoch-shattering event as the death of Hawk King, it would have been predictable for my team of sanity-seekers to skip out on therapy at my Hyper-Potentiality Clinic. That's because they, like everyone else, were falling up and down the escalator of the nine stages of the **Brain-Silverman Grief Scale™** (Revised):

1. *Confusion*
2. *Obsession*
3. *Lust for vengeance*
4. *Self-pity*
5. *Boundless contempt*
6. *Reckless adventurism*
7. *Depression*
8. *Paranoia* and
9. *Hollow acceptance*

Regardless of each hero's sadness, the F*L*A*C's orders were emphatic: even at this moment of global mourning, any of my F*O*O*Jsters who failed to attend therapy and achieve measurable improvement would be summarily removed from the ranks of Earth's most celebrated superteam.

And thus, in the bright sunlit Saturday morning of the Anger Room, my heroes sat in a circle of morbid moroseness.

In their fumbling individual attempts to bear the psychemotional weight of their legendary mentor's death, each F*O*O*Jster shared something with the group to ease individual and collective sorrow, and offered a few halting remarks met by sodden silence. In doing so, each one evoked aspects of his or her personality which had until that point remained hidden—tenderness, nostalgia, melancholy, compassion, and more—a stunning departure from the factionalizing and fractious fracas factory of the previous day.

Wally W. Watchtower brought with him a pharaonic crown given to him by Hawk King, an interroyal gift from an ancient Egyptian king to the surviving prince of the doomed planet Argon; Wally explained how that gesture, in late 1944, had helped him rise from confusion as a wandering, super-powered Jehovah's Witness farmboy from Kentucky to his grand destiny as Omnipotent Man. The Flying Squirrel distributed free advance copies of two books from PiltdownPerennial: a coffee-table book of the most famous photographs of the Egyptian deity, plus a small, black, clothbound volume of wisdom-quotations called *The Utterances of Hawk King;* even Festus Piltdown's perpetual gadfly, the X-Man, seemed impressed and moved by the gift.

André supplied a sumptuous collection of delicate confections he'd baked personally, from flans to mille-feuille, and while serving them to everyone uttered not a single *bzzzt!*; Syndi distributed advance CD singles of the dance-beat eulogy she'd rushed into production the previous night called "Hawk On (Long Live the King)." And during a moment of intense quiet, Iron Lass produced a gleaming silver ram's horn she'd brought from Aesgard more than a millennium before, from which she elicited a sound like Louis Armstrong on a muted trumpet, rendering in tear-trickling agony what she later informed me was Duke Ellington's "Solitude."

Only one of my sanity-supplicants came empty-handed: the X-Man. But even he would nonetheless later share something—a situationally inappropriate but entirely predictable paranoid rant.

Stages of Grief: Confusion

How do you all feel," I said, looking for anything to get our discussion started at last, "about . . . oh, the media coverage of Hawk King's passing?"

Getting no response, I held up a couple of newspapers. *The Los Ditkos Sentinel-Spectator* carried the headline NATION MOURNS FOUNDING F*O*O*JSTER. *The Los Ditkos Sun* announced HAWK KING: DEAD AT 7000+. *USA Today* blared "AVIAN AVENGER" DEAD/"NATURAL CAUSES" RULES F*O*O*J CORONER.

Each front page displayed iconic photographs of Hawk

King, two of his classic portrait and the third an image of him seated in a golden woven-wicker throne. From the portrait beamed his golden beak and gold-rimmed black eyes, his black-feathered face topped with golden pharaonic crown. In the seated image, his black body gleamed, bedecked in golden Egyptian skirt and sandals; his hands clutched a golden crook and flail, and his black-golden wings were spread as if to devour the seven winds.

I clicked on the television; PNN was broadcasting aerial shots of tens of thousands of people gathered on the mall of the F*O*O*J's Fortress of Freedom and at the gates of the ferries over to Sunhawk Island and the mysterious Blue Pyramid. At both places, mourners deposited offerings of handmade Egyptian mortuary *ushabtiu* figurines, pipe-cleaner and tissue-paper lotus flowers, and small bottles of milk and beer. According to the reporter, arrests for public drunkenness and lactose-intolerant public vomiting had skyrocketed.

"And the radio call-in shows," I said, further prompting them while shutting off the TV, "are equally wrenched by misery."

To my group's silence I added, "Perhaps it would help if people shared their own memories of Hawk King. Their personal experiences of him."

The Flying Squirrel sucked in a big preamble breath; since he tended to dominate discussion, especially by name-dropping Hawk King and verbally footnoting his every connection with him, I immediately prompted Iron Lass, the only person Festus Piltdown III seemed never to interrupt.

Her eyes shifted toward me dully, the glint from their cold metal apparently rusted over. She was actually *slouching*—this, despite routinely targeting me and her teammates with comments about our posture during our previous sessions.

"Hawk Kink," she said at last, putting down a piece of André's baklava onto a coaster, "vuss ze greatest of us all."

After a pause, I asked her to continue.

"Alzough, *ja,* I am a goddess, I felt, perhaps becoss he is an even olter deity from a more ancient panseon . . . venever I vuss in his presence, I could unterstaandt vut mortals felt when zey met Odin, ze lordt of Aesgard. Hawk Kink inspiredt . . . ze only vurt I can sink uff iss . . . *awe.* I vuss alvays in awe of him. He vuss a brilliant scientist, a brilliant alchemist, a brilliant leader, *ja,* all of zat. But more. He vuss . . ."

She stopped, looked down, cleared her throat.

Festus Piltdown sucked in another preelocutory breath, but Iron Lass flashed a glare at him until he let it out wordlessly.

"I vurked viss Hawk Kink for fifty years. I haff liffdt two sousand," she said. "Zere vill never be anuzzer like him."

I waited for the pathos of Hnossi Icegaard's words to permeate everyone's thoughts.

When Festus looked ready to speak again, I asked Wally to share his feelings. At that moment he was leaning his head toward his shoulder, as if the weight of his grief exceeded the strength of his neck. His hair, flattened, lacked its usual gloss and front-row e-curl. When I called his name, he perked up momentarily, his ever-present, generally unrealistic optimism seemingly recharged. But just like that, the lightning in his expression grounded itself in the deep, dark rings beneath his eyes.

"Wellsir, ma'am-doctor," said Wally, "the King recruited me. Hnossi, too, an Lady Liberty, an, well, all of us in the original team—course ev'rabody knows he foundeded the F*O*O*J. Don't know . . . I mean . . . it's like, let's say if suh'm came up, an ya didn'know what to do about it, y'd just ask him, y'know? Djunnerstann what I'm sayin?"

He scanned the faces of his two older colleagues, but neither met his eyes.

And in words so childishly pathetic I will never be able to forget them, Wally W. Watchtower looked imploringly at his comrades, his hands upturned and empty on his knees, and, with voice cracking, asked, "And now . . . what're we sposta do if suh'm goes wrong . . . *an we don'know how t'fix it?*"

Saturday morning sunlight fell into Wally's eyes, twinkling wetly. Wally leaned over and picked up André's entire uncut apple strudel. As soon as he sank his teeth into it, the strudel began crumbling over his suit and cape. He blew on the dessert, crackling the entirety of it into a strudel-cicle, crunching chunks between his teeth in mournful mastication.

"Good fritter, Br'erfly," he said, looking at the floor and chewing. "I should show y'all m'recipe for fried peanut butter–banana–and–candy bar samwidges."

By then, not even the younger heroes would look at him.

I asked Kareem to share his thoughts.

"Since there's no reason to believe Hawk King could have died of natural causes," he said without hesitation, his voice as raw as an abrasion, "we're dealing with a murder."

Stages of Grief: Obsession

All eyes clutched Kareem, like a loan shark's hand on the neck of an overdue lendee.

"The murder of the world's smartest man, by the very nature of such a crime," said the X-Man, "indicates threat on a scale we may never have seen before. Despite my persistent warnings, this organization has been overconfident, stuffing its belly with its own myths. And we've been acting as if *all* our enemies were dead or locked up on Asteroid Zed, as if all the ones up there now have been rendered totally harmless—"

"This is not the time for your postseason quarterbacking, Edgerton!" said Flying Squirrel. "Difficult F*O*O*J decisions were being made on a daily basis by heroic men facing death for decades before you were *born*. You're going to choose a time

of planetary mourning to let loose your astigmatic recrimina-
tions?"

"Look, Festus, unlike some people around here, *I* actually
cared about Hawk King, which is why I'm putting my energy
into investigating, not mourning. Now look at this."

Kareem closed his eyes, enunciated the word *suspects,* and
a rotating rogues' gallery glistened blackly into shadow-shapes
above us.

"These," said Kareem, pointing to the lower ring and the
upper ring in turn, "are the Beta- and Alpha-level foes of the
F*O*O*J who are still unaccounted for. The Heavyweights,"
he said, gesturing to the lower ring.

Although the images were devoid of any color save black,
we could make out the forms as Kareem announced their
names: the glinting man-lizard called the Crystal Crocodile, the
oversized crushing hands of Key Grip and Best Boy, the robed
and lightning bolt–excreting Shockrates, and the obviously
shaped Specially Relative Einstein Baboons.

"And the Superheavyweights," said Kareem, pointing to the
nuclear-armored dictator Baron Von Drako, then to the horned
head of the star-consuming titan Cosmicus and his herald
the Gold Glider, then to the swirling miasma of horror called
L-Raunzenu, then to the aardvark-faced sociopath Warmaster
Set, and finally to the shambling mass called Ymir the Planet-
Corpse.

"How is it possible," asked Kareem, while his audience
gazed up at the rings of terrors orbiting above their heads, "for
someone of Hawk King's power to have been killed? And how
could he have failed to see such an attack coming in the first
place?

"His *Udjat*—that's what you people call the Eye of Horus,
what should be the Eye of *Heru* if you could bother to learn the
Afro-Egyptian name—should've alerted him. So what we're

looking at is someone with soular-invisibility, dimension-shifting, or counter-remote-viewing.

"On the Heavyweights list, it's *possible* Shockrates could've generated a strong enough electrical field to disrupt the Eye . . . and the E-Baboons *might've* been able to use a string-dimensional tunnel to get inside the Blue Pyramid. But neither should've had the power to kill him.

"Of the Superheavyweights, Cosmicus seems unlikely—we would've detected his Nebulanaught approaching, just like we would've seen Ymir's iceberg fleet if he'd reconstituted himself at the north pole. Warmaster Set's vendetta is seven thousand years old . . . but there's been no sighting of him or anyone else on that list since the Götterdämmerung. Of course, there's always the possibility of L-Raunzenu."

A monstrosity of pure terror described in the *Encyclopedia of F*O*O*J Adversaries,* Vol. III (Revised) as "a cosmic culmination of a billion horrors, personified and transmogrified into a universal force of unstoppable, ravaging evil," L-Raunzenu, in the most literal way possible, was everyone's worst nightmare.

But despite media fireworks about the threat posed by L-Raunzenu, fewer Americans were killed by that entity during its entire existence than the number of people in the same time period who died from rattlesnake bites or choking on chicken bones. And the L-Raunzenu death toll was simply insignificant when compared to, say, the annual human and financial cost of alcohol- and tobacco-related illness and morbidity.

But, blinded by grief-induced obsession and paranoia, Kareem was oblivious to such basic logic.

"Of course," continued Kareem, "there's also the matter of those supervillains who *are* accounted for. Who are on Asteroid Zed right now. *Menton*—"

Everyone glared at him. He shut his mouth, realizing the enormity of his breach of etiquette.

"Ve don't speak his name . . . so *idly,* Kareem," whispered Hnossi, narrowing her eyes. "Unt need I remind you zat he's been in a Psionic Impotence Helmet for five years?"

"I'm aware of that, Hnossi," he said slowly. "But Ment—the *Destroyer's* abilities were off the scale. Do we really know if a P-Imp hat could stop him?"

Iron Lass rolled her eyes at Kareem's abbreviation. He continued without regard for her disdain. "And on that exact same topic—"

Knowing where he was going, the older F*O*O*Jsters reacted instantly.

Hnossi: "Zere are certain lines zat even *zey*—"

Wally: "Now, Kareem, I know what y'all're about t'say, but lemme tell you suh'm—"

Mr. Piltdown: "I don't care what they were *alleged* to have planned—even you can't seriously accuse them of striking out against our greatest—"

"They went bad. *Very* bad," said Kareem, too loudly. Then he whispered something inaudible.

Behind him, massive shadow-sculptures, like a miniature Mount Rushmore, oozed into existence. Even in black, the busts were unmistakable: on the left, the elder, Gil Gamoid, with his thick neck, wild beard, wild eyes, and spike-teeth; and on the right, junior with his ram's horns and flowing mane, the N-Kid. The two titans from the distant world of Ur-Prime, orbiting the mysterious quasar Q-939.

"Yes, they were founding members of the F*O*O*J. Yes, they were great heroes. Once upon a time. But now they're locked up wearing P-Imp hats on Asteroid Zed. Because they're paranoid schizophrenics. Who were conspiring to commit mass murder."

"Zey were foundt not guilty—"

"On account of being criminally insane, Hnossi? You call

that a defense?" he sneered. "Hell, I rarely grok brain-to-brain with you people, but on this issue . . . you not only floor me, you *basement* me. Those two 'heroes' were planning to massacre all of *you*! You Stone Agers aren't exactly the most forgiving freaks in the circus, so why all this sympathy for Gil Gamoid and the N-Kid?"

"Listen to me, Edgerton," growled Festus. "And this will be more complex and nuanced than your minstrel show ever apparently gets, so listen closely—"

"You hear that, Doc? Aren't you gonna censure him? Well, if you're not reporting him to the F*L*A*C for *that* cracker-ass crack—"

"Listen, sonny, those two heroes—yes, *heroes*," said Festus, "were wounded terribly in the line of duty. Mentally poisoned, probably by the Destroyer—but possibly by L-Raunzenu. But even given the awesome extent of their mental damage, they would never, I'll say that again, *never* plot against our Founder."

"Even though both of them plotted to kill the rest of you—"

"Even *if* they did, which was never proven in court—"

"Come on! Hawk King recruited them into the original F*O*O*J, and he used the *Udjat* to uncover their plot! He built 'em up and he took 'em down. Don't you think that in their current state they might just want revenge?"

"Why now, Edgerton? Can you answer me that? Why would they or anyone else want to move on Hawk King *now*?"

"You're the self-proclaimed World's Greatest Detective. Why don't you tell me?"

"Damn, dawg," said the Brotherfly, *"fuck this."*

Stages of Grief:
Boundless Contempt

ven Hnossi Icegaard's lips parted at that outburst. Even more than Power Grrrl, André Parker, HKA the Brotherfly, was the most fun-loving, unflappable, and glibly superficial member of the group. Because no one could have expected his reaction or even his capacity for deep feelings, no one spoke—not even Kareem or Festus, at whom the intense psychemotional verbalization was targeted.

"André?" I asked. "You just psychemotionally verbalized intensely, targeting Kareem and Mr. Piltdown. Can you tell me about that?"

"I mean, *bzzzt,* Doc," said André. "Look, I'ont know about them fools, but fuh real, the King was the shit, knawm sayn?"

"So . . . you disliked him, then?"

"Naw, Doc—*the shit,* see, that means 'good'—"

The Flying Squirrel: "Then for the love of Greenspan, could you simply goddamned *say* that?"

"Festus, please. André, continue," I said. "You were saying that in your view, Hawk King was 'the shit.' "

"Damn skippy, Doc," he said. "I was actually blessed to *meet* the King when I was just a shorty, like, back in '82? I was one of twenny-fi schoolkids—our class won a contest for essay writin—'Why would you like to meet Hawk King?', you knawm sayn? I mean, he'd already been up in his self-imposed exile an shit for, like, seven years by then—ain'no kids getting to go t'see the King no how, but, like, *we* was, son. Just about to turn thirteen, an *I* get to meet the King!

"So us an Miss Jackson, we take the ferry over to Sunhawk Island, his Ka-Sentinels guiding us through the gates, then through the portal of the Blue Pyramid, down the shafts, up the shafts, right up into his Celestial Chamber . . . all them turquoise hieroglyphics on them black-silver walls, movin like they alive, like they talkin to each other an the stars.

"An he sittin there right in the middle, right on his Sapphire Star Throne, like a sunrise in space, knawm sayn? Golden beak, black body, hands holdin on to his maces an shit . . . but the eyes. Never forget them eyes. Whole room was hummin, vibratin, an them eyes, like radio transmitters beamin inside my spine.

"Changed my life, dawg, goin there. I *still* dream about it, every week since I was a kid for like thirteen-fourteen years, of havin the chance, the blessin, you knawm sayn? to go back. But . . . y'know, thangs don'always work out how we want."

He cleared his throat.

"Anyway, I made up my mind right then—" he said, crackling an electrical charge between his antennae for emphasis without even saying *bzzzt!,* "I was gon be a superhero. Man changed my life. I owe him. We all owe him.

"An now . . . he's dead. An my aunt, she's, she just—look, it's like, after my . . . my uncle died . . . the King was the one thing in the world she could count on that would always make things right, knawm sayn? But now she caint stop cryin. You hear me?"

He shook his head, then jutted one antenna each in the directions of Flying Squirrel and X-Man.

"An these two fools is gon sit here ying-yangin bout some muhfuckin unknown, unknowable, invisible 'conspiracy'? King's body ain'even cold, funeral still three days away an them superbrains caint shut up outta respect for a coupla kottam hours? Tryin t'get my *grieve* on here, knawm sayn? Should be honorin his life, not squawkin like vultures over who gets to autopsy the muhfuckin corpse!"

Kareem shifted forward, facing his younger teammate.

"Listen . . . André." I'd never heard Kareem's voice contain such—I won't say gentleness, but—lack of antagonism for

André, or for anybody else. "It's absolutely essential that right now, we—"

"No, *you* listen, dawg," said André, standing up and shouldering his thick, lobed, translucent wings behind him. "The man aint no 'debate topic,' knawm sayn? People die. You got that, son? They just die. An aint nuthin you can do about it, not with all your theories an your Afro-ballistics an your muhfuckin *maāxeru* magic words, knawm sayn? So stop stickin an stabbin the man's body with your Detecto-Junior Crime Kit an let im have some muhfuckin dignity, my *'brutha'*! "

Kareem's jaw muscles bunched.

"André," he gritted, "we're all. *Tense.* Now. So I'm gonna let that—"

"Whatever-whatever, Mista Mystery. Right now whyonchu let us feel the sadness and regret we all gots to feel. Specially since y'all don'know the meaning of the words!"

At that, André unfurled his proboscis, snapping at the rotating rogues gallery, and three of the Superheavyweights smashed into obsidian shards. Then André hopped over to the window and proceeded to *tap-tap-tap* his head again and again against the glass.

After Festus finally suggested wielding a can of Raid against the noise, André stopped, putting his hands and feet against the wall and with a *splippetty-splabbatty* sound, crawled up toward the ceiling and stuck himself, glowering down through his two complex and three simple eyes.

Kareem whispered, and the shadow-sculptures of Gil Gamoid, the N-Kid, and the remaining rotating supervillains and the shards of André's tongue casualties dispersed into dark mist and disappeared.

Wally excused himself to go to the restroom.

I suggested we move on. "Would others like to discuss their own experiences of Hawk King?"

Syndi snapped her gum, raised her hand halfway.

"Like, I didn't really know Hawk King? An like, hel*lo*-o, I *get* it: 'sad!' But does the whole city have to go spaz-mode? Like, I couldn't even get a table at Chez Guevara because they closed early last night? And I was gonna take my crew to Dance-Tronics, but, yeah, cl*o*-osed!"

I asked her how she spent her night in lieu of her usual frolicking.

"I, like, stayed home, cut that Hawk King single, and answered fan mail."

"You—!" choked Iron Lass. "You awnser *fan mail* vile all uff Midgard cries out viss agony unt tears?"

"Like, n*o*-o. I had my PA do it. I am so like *stressed,* you know? So I got Brianna to do me—you know, massage? But now, today, the stress is all back! Thank God for André's strawberry tarts—they're better than Prozac." She craned her neck and smiled up at him sweetly. "Thanks, P-Dawg."

"Babydoll, when ain'nuthin funny, eat what's sweet. That's my philosophy," said André from overhead. "Glad everybody liked em. Cept Kreem, who aint tried pastry-one. Shoulda made him suh'm with cherry, chocolate, an kiwi. Only red-black-and-green for the great Marcus Garbage. My man wouldn'even *dream* of eatin no angel food cake, knawm sayn?"

Kareem reached for the plate, popping into his mouth a piece of crystalized ginger covered in nougat and chewing defiantly.

"And yet, Syndi," I said, "despite listing rather trivial issues such as answering fan mail or being denied access to trendy restaurants, perhaps to imply that you're entirely unmoved by the death of Hawk King, you *did* 'cut that single,' as you put it, which means—"

"Which means she exploitedt ziss great beingk's passink to make a qvick morbid buck!"

"I think it means more than that, Hnossi, although perhaps Syndi wants us to think otherwise. How about that, Syndi?"

I looked between the two women, waiting for either of them to respond.

Facing their silence, I resolved to put the two together for a later session, to spelunk the depths of the psychemotional stalactites and stalagmites they perpetually aimed at each other. But at that moment I changed directions.

"You've been rather quiet, Festus," I said. "How did you spend yesterday evening?"

I expected him to unleash a blistering denunciation of Syndi, but instead Festus Piltdown III delicately swept ladyfinger crumbs from his tunic pants. "Like Hnossi," he said quietly, "I went to my post."

He irradiated everyone with his glare.

"The F*O*O*J Fortress. Scanning for threats. Doing my duty to our country. Our planet. When a champion of such magnitude falls, criminals become an opportunistic infection poised to contaminate us all."

"Festus vuzn't simply vaatching ze monitors in ze Situation Room, Frau Doktor," said Hnossi Icegaard, smoothing her raven mane. While speaking to all of us, she looked only at Mr. Piltdown, who stared at a part of the ceiling where the Brotherfly wasn't then crawling. André was removed from our sight-line; the only indication he remained in the room came from a soft, high-pitched buzzing near the lamp.

"Festus spent last evenink unt all last night comfortink ze heroes unt heroines who'd assembult at ze Fortress, like a vize unt gentle faazer or feutal lordt, offerink his shoulder or knee for zeir tears. Unt vile shelterink our soldiers viss his . . . his *moral* leadership, he spoke viss everyone, softly. Uff honor, unt diknity, unt true heroism, from a life devotedt not to self, not to glory, not to personal revardt . . . but to *justice*." She sighed lengthily. "Unt sroughout all ziss, vhere vere you, Kareem?"

Kareem stiffened in his chair, goggling at her.

"Where was I, Hnossi? I was in Stun-Glas! Walking the

streets, talking to my people! *My* people, the ones *you* people always seem to forget about, the ones you were gonna let Cyclo-Tron crush. I was down with the people praying in the AME Church on the corner of Cowan and McDuffie, down with the folks stuffing fried mock-chicken and corn bread down their mouths at Dark Star, down at the QRIB with the League and pa-trolling Stun-Glas to keep people cooled out and safe! What I *wasn't* doing was pulling any fake Churchill act, covertly cam-paigning for DOO on the grave of a *real* hero!"

Mr. Piltdown: "Why you invidious, usurping, cork-faced hypocrite, accusing *me* of exploiting the death of our leader!"

"Nothing stabs like truth, does it, Goebbels?"

"You are out uff line, Kareem!"

I held up my whistle until the combatants stood down emo-tionally, and then asked Festus to explain his claim that Ka-reem was being hypocritical.

"Miss Brain, I'll tell you this just once: Whatever your mawkish, liberal, multicultural self-delusions, you cannot trust this individual. He's already launched his plot to exploit Hawk King's death by seeking the post of Director of Operations for the F*O*O*J."

All eyes fell on the X-Man.

His mouth opened silently.

Stages of Grief:
Reckless Adventurism

Well, deny it, Edgerton," said Festus, "if you can!"

"Kareem, is ziss true?" asked Iron Lass. "You're standink for election after beingk a F*O*O*J member for only two years? You don't sink zat's presumptuous?"

"Hnossi—" Festus chuckled "—this fraud couldn't get him-self elected head of a chain gang."

"You shoulda told that to Hawk King, Fester," said Kareem. "Because I'm submitting nomination papers signed by him!"

Silence settled on the room like fog.

And then came the lightning.

"You're a goddamned liar, Edgerton!" yelled the Flying Squirrel. "How dare you, you *blaspheme* the holy name of our departed mentor like that!"

The X-Man closed his eyes and whispered the word *pamphlets.* Instantly, rectangles of darkness congealed in each of our laps.

I had difficulty reading what Kareem had given us; the logogenic tracts were black only, with empty space where the letters went. I spread his literature out over the thighs of my pantsuit so the pamphlet's holes could be read in contrast (fortunately I'd worn beige that day).

Above a shadow cutout image of the white-shirted, black-tied and -suited X-Man exhorting an implied, adoring crowd beyond the picture frame, were the block letters

ELECT

X-MAN

DIRECTOR OF OPERATIONS

A BETTER F*O*O*J

FOR A

BETTER WORLD

On the next panels of the material was Kareem's "Five-Point Platform for a New F*O*O*J":

1. *Shift the F*O*O*J's investigative focus to corporate crime, now that the Götterdämmerung is over*
2. *Rewrite the Concord of Heroic Duty to prevent the F*O*O*J from intervening in the affairs of sovereign states*

3. *Defend and extend quality-of-life security for ordinary
   citizens—security from predatory corporations, landlords,
   polluters, etc., not only in disaster relief but in prevention*
4. *Deploy F*O*O*J technology toward public service and
   job creation*
5. *Liaise with schools, community organizations, and other
   nonsupergroups to promote safety, freedom, and public
   responsibility*

"Damn, Kreem!" said the Brotherfly, fluttering down to
snatch the pamphlet from Power Grrrl's lap, then laughing once
he was stuck back on the ceiling. "You gots to be insane in the
hindbrain if you think you gon win gainst Squirrelly-Man! He
gots the money, the experience, the money, the money—"

"I'm more concerned," I said to Kareem, "by your campaign
literature's lack of attention to the very problems that brought
you and your colleagues here in the first place. Nowhere in
here do you acknowledge the importance of confronting the *internal* supervillains, such as the Crisis of Infinite Dearths, id es-
calation, depression—"

Kareem rolled his eyes.

"Your delusion is truly tragic, Edgerton," said the Flying
Squirrel, "even beyond this nonsense about Hawk King having
'endorsed' you. Even if, due to some thermodynamic miracle
combined with an unforeseen alignment of the voodoo chicken
bone stars, you actually somehow got elected as DOO, you'd be
nothing but a legless mule. Piloting the F*L*A*C means navi-
gating the interpolitical high seas relationships of six highly
willful—"

"Six positions, plus Chair," said Kareem, counting them
off on his fingers. "Chair, Merry Mac, AKA Mitchell Morgan
McDonald, age sixty-three. *Retiring.* Director of Personnel, the
Manipulator, AKA Emory Dogstale, age fifty-nine. *Retiring.* Director of Finance, the Downsizer, AKA P. Martin Klein, age

fifty-eight. *Retiring.* Director of Operations, Colonel Strom Flintlock, age one hundred seventy-three. *Retiring.*

"That's the old guard. They're gone.

"But there's a new crew up in this election, Festus. Gagarina Girl's vying for D-Personnel against your girl, Major Ursa, I believe—"

Festus spluttered. Kareem breezed on.

"—and she's got a better chance than does Earnest Beaver. Dynamiss is going to take on your boy Dow-Man for D-Finance—"

"Neither of those nattering neophytes stands a chance against Team Squirrel!"

"Be that as it may," said Kareem, smirking, "three positions aren't up for election this round. The Spectacle's D-Investigation, age forty-three. Periodic Man's D-R&D. He's forty. Shockra's D-External Affairs. She's thirty-six. That's a young bunch, Festy. Digital Age heroes looking for change, looking to deal a better hand than they were dealt. And even if neither Gagarina Girl nor Dynamiss wins, the three incumbents plus me'd make a majority on the F*L*A*C. Wouldn't even need the Chair to break ties. You and the rest of the old motherF*L*A*Ccers're history, Squirrel!"

Iron Lass: "Kareem! *Langvicht!*"

Everyone quivered in their chairs anxiously, clasping their hands about their ears in anticipation of my blowing the Mind Whistle™ either at Kareem's epithet or to circumvent the inevitable Flying Squirrel retaliation.

But apparently retaliation was not inevitable. Festus simply sat silently staring at Kareem, hurling neither invective nor his chair. Instead, he methodically bent and tore the logogenic *Elect X-Man* pamphlet into a primitive origami squirrel.

Dissecting the Flying Squirrel

estus," I probed, seizing the moment, "shredding that tract isn't helping you to focus your psychemotional microscope upon the slide of your pain. What, precisely, do you feel—you personally—right now?"

"What do I 'feel'?" he sneered. He tore at the remains again, erecting two snubby ears on the paper squirrel's head. "Did you actually ask me what I 'feel'? I 'feel' I'm surrounded by morons!"

"Festus," I said, tapping my whistle. He grimaced and shoved his palms against his eyes, rubbing hard enough to make me wince. "I'm asking not for your assessment of the rest of the group, but of your psychemotional state. Try using an 'I-statement.' "

"An 'I-statement'?" he snorted. "If I use an 'I-statement' you're just going to sic that goddamned dominatrix whistle of yours on me!"

"No, I'm giving you permission, because right now we're not in a free-for-all. You have the floor."

Festus glared. Grunted. Glowered.

Finally: "I *feel* frustrated. There. Have I satiated you?"

"That's good, Festus. Talk about that."

"It's good I'm frustrated?" he said. I raised an eyebrow at his playing dumb.

"I *feel* frustrated," he begrudged, "because I've devoted my entire adult life to this organization, tending to it like a Shinto priest to a desktop grove of bonsai, cherishing it, protecting it . . . and now that I've arrived at the correct time, the appointed time, the right time for me to lead it . . . a—a goddamned dilettante lindy-hops his way in here with lies about a Hawk King endorsement and a sense of entitlement bigger than his Afro and acts as if he has a right to lead. I *feel* nobody has the 'right' to lead. You earn that goddamned right by investing decades of service—not milliseconds of presumption—earning interest and building capital of public confidence, collegial respect, and heroic loyalty, which I was intending to reinvest right now, in the traditions of our noble fraternity originally enacted by Hawk King."

Wally returned from the rest room. Perhaps because of the anxiety level in the Verbalarium, the air seemed almost to tingle. "Excellent, Festus," I reinforced. "You've done a fine job of—"

"I'm not done, Miss Brain. Bad enough to have our election turned into a midway freak show, but since the end of the Götterdämmerung to have to bear witness every day to what the slugs in the slime-trailing liberal media are saying about us—"

"*Bor*-ing," said Syndi. She got out of her chair, turned on her hip-speakers to the *thump-whump*ing tune of her spring Top 40 hit "Boom! I Hit It Again," and, activating her Power Pumps, began high-speed rocket-skating/dancing around the room.

Festus: "Turn that goddamned jungle music off and sit down!"

Wagging my whistle, I warned Syndi to return to her chair, but I was reluctant to risk the whistle's overuse because my patients might habituate to its stimulus. Wally, snapping his fingers, conceded that he found the tune "kinda ketchy, though a mite Jezebellish." I asked Festus to continue, but more loudly.

"—I *feel* humiliated!" he seethed above the bass line and drum snares, "*vi*olated because the papa-goddamn-razzi are trailing around a bunch of teenybopping costumed incompetents who're here because our F*L*A*C insists we have to change our image 'to suit the times,' forcing us to incorporate mattress-back pop tarts who're here because they want to be famous, not because they know or care one whit about protecting people or national security or what it means to have fought a war every day for the last forty-five goddamned years of your career while they're flitting away their mayfly existences preening and prancing around and having their highly publicized perverted little 'sexcapades' and publicly dragging the name of this organization through a urinal, making a mockery out of what real heroes—men like Hawk King, women like Iron Lass—have sacrificed!

"*I,*" he shouted, gripping his chair by the arms so hard his glide-flaps and whiskers shook, "*feel furious!*"

Stages of Grief:
Lust for Vengeance

estus Piltdown III panted, grimaced, blinked—I couldn't tell whether from exhaustion or embarrassment. Finally, after regaining his breath, he said simply, "That's it."

"Don't hold back, Squirrelly," yelled a voice from the ceiling. "You might still have some spleen or pancreas left up in there to spit up—"

"André, please. Let's positively reinforce Festus's commendable first foray into self-revelation."

"And that's another thing, Miss Brain," said the Flying Squirrel. "In my day, people didn't call their elders or their superiors by their first names. One said Mister So-and-so and Miss Such-and-such. Would you go around calling Hawk King 'Hawk'? No. It's called respect. Propriety. And maybe if we had a little more of that, our Fraternal Order wouldn't be swirling down the toilet right now."

"Can I say something, Eva?" Power Grrrl reverse-rocketed to a stop and raised her hand as if she were a schoolgirl.

"Only if you turn that music down, Syndi."

She wagged her hips, and the music ceased. "Why is it okay for *Mister* Piltdown to be sitting there judging us and insulting me? If he wants to be respected, doesn't he have to, like, treat the rest of us with some respect?"

"*Bzzzt* for me too, girly!"

I openly fondled my whistle, but, lost in their escalating id-confrontation, my F*O*O*Jsters raged on obliviously. "Treat you with respect?" spat the Squirrel. "I'll treat you with respect when you goddamn start acting like you deserve some respect! What would Hawk King say if he could see—"

"Festus—Mr. Piltdown, please. Please. Look deeply. You spoke a moment ago about propriety. Don't we need to model the behavior we wish to have others emulate? Focus on how you feel instead of what other people are doing. That way you can take ownership for your own feelings. Remember, you're a stockholder in the exchange of your own emotions, but only your own. You can't control other people."

The Squirrel crossed his arms, leaned back. "That's the god-damn problem. These children *need* controlling!"

Syndi wagged her hips and the music resumed. "I don't have to take that!"

I blew the whistle.

But nothing happened. As soon as my team realized that they were not paralyzed by behavior-modification migraines, they waded back into their swamp of invective. I raised my voice. "All right, now—which of you did this? Who used their powers on my whistle?"

They met my interrogative with stares of faux innocence.

"I see. Presumably, had only *one* of you sabotaged my whis-tle, someone else would have revealed his or her name out of vindictiveness. Since no name is forthcoming, I have to assume all of you attempted to or succeeded in using your powers against my whistle. That's disappointing. And I'll have to re-port that to your F*L*A*C."

They raised a chorus of objections against me, but none was willing to lay the blame at another's feet. Either they were all guilty—a bad sign indeed—or they were protecting one of their confederates, which meant there might, indeed, be hope for reducing the toxicity of their interrelationships.

Yet on they raged, led by Kareem. "This is just what we were already facing, times ten!" said the X-Man. "A power struggle! Cept without Hawk King, there's no ref, the gloves are off, and the brass knuckles are on—"

From behind the furry mask and snub ears: "How dare you incite a riot at a time like this, Edgerton!"

From the buzzing ceiling: "Kreem, dawg, you always stirrin shit, like some Nat Turner–Mandingo plumber!"

"André," spat Kareem, "I notice you aren't eating any of the cream-puffs you brought. Afraid of cannibalism?"

"Fuck y'all!"

"André," I began, "regardless of my whistle's status, you know the rules about swearing—"

"You see this, Doc?" said Kareem. "Hawk King was the only thing left holding this screwfreak museum together. Now that he's gone, the kot-tam F*O*O*J is gonna collapse at the precise moment there's someone out there powerful enough to whack *him*. Someone lit fire to the house while we were all asleep, an they're probably staked out across the street for us to start runnin out so they can shoot us down one at a time!"

"Emotions," I said, standing to face the maelstrom, "are at critical energy, everyone. And I understand that. All of you held Hawk King in the kind of regard in which the public holds you. Right now you're vulnerable. You're afraid. You're passing through the nine stages of the Brain-Silverman Grief Scale™, Revised. And you're not here by choice but under orders from the F*L*A*C to participate in these sessions. So I understand you're feeling especially pressured.

"Therefore it's time now to disengage and reflect, and resume later. You have some choices on how to spend our remaining hours today: in the Id-Smasher®"—a suggestion greeted by groaning—"with Direct Writing time in the Neuro-Demonstrative Cerebiographer®"—more groaning, and louder—"or individual talk sessions with me."

The groaning ceased instantly, as did Syndi's music.

While they mumbled their assent to choice 1 or 2, Iron Lass reminded everyone of their duties, including preparation for Monday's funeral for their fallen founder.

What will it mean for your life, and for your view of yourself, if the glory days never return?

Omnipotent Man: "I feel like a blinded horse with three busted legs."

Flying Squirrel: "We'll defend this planet. It's what the King would've wanted."

Iron Lass: "With the greatest of us gone . . . glory has no meaning."

How will you face knowing that you will never exceed, or even equal, the accomplishments of your predecessors?

Brotherfly: "We have no choice. It's live or be killed, right?"

Power Grrrl: "Same old story. Elders abandon you. I'll shine without them."

X-Man: "A world without Hawk King . . . frightens me. Especially now."

Facing the Ultimate Archenemy

Nothing is more terrifying than facing the ultimate archenemy, Death, and its horrifying henchman, Grief. Maturity means recognizing the inevitability not only of combating these foes, but of our inevitable defeat at their hands. Even if we live long enough to evade their grasp for a century (or in the case of Iron Lass, two millennia), our reward will merely be to see all of our loved ones cut down one after the other.

Because you are a hero, your identity is based on exceeding limitations; therefore, the awareness of such inescapable defeat is a mental kidney stone that not even you can pass during the urination of your psychemotional processing. Death is a barrier even you can't smash down, fly over, phase through, or disintegrate with your maservision. Consequently, dealing with death means invoking the most vile curse word ever to contaminate the tongue of any champion: *surrender.*

But paradoxically, it is only in surrender that you can achieve victory, for without your acceptance of eventual vanquishment, you will perpetually be running away from reality. As Carl Jung said, avoidance of legitimate suffering is the root of all mental illness. And one truth you must suffer is that everything and everyone you love will eventually die.

Even gods.

No one wants to die feeling they failed to achieve their dreams, or that they failed to employ their powers to their full extent. So free yourself by recognizing that you only *thought* you wanted those dreams, and that you didn't fail to live up to your power because you were never really as powerful as you'd made yourself believe . . . certainly, never possessing the power to cheat death permanently.

Ids, Gods, and Death

Rooted in every sentient being is the id-centered yearning to outshine all others. The fate of anyone with the lust to be such a luminous being—or to employ the ancient name, a *Lucifer*—is clear.

Even for the most powerful and spectacular heroes, the

quest to outshine everyone else will ultimately fail, and for everyone else beneath the paramountcy of power, the mission is a failure before its first sortie.

If all you want is simply to be the best, why not roll up the world's largest ball of string? If you want to be the best skater, why not break your competitor's ankles? You could be the world's most accomplished excretor, entering hot dog–eating championships after consuming a gross of Ex-Lax tablets. Clearly such an aim—merely being "the best"—is empty on its own terms.

But even if victory were possible, it still couldn't provide meaning or genuine happiness, because saying "I want to be the best" is simply the polite way of saying "I want everyone else to be worse."

Selfishness is the very heart of your glory, the same impulse which caused the mid-1950s wave of superhero-on-superhero battles to see who was bigger, stronger, or better. Yet not one of those battles to be the brightest produced anything of value (especially not for those heroes' insurance companies), and every last one of those champions and their comrades has already died or one day will. Even deities like Hawk King.

What you must do is decide how you want to live *now*. In fear? In rage? In competitive hamster-wheeling? Or in acceptance?

To avoid wasting your remaining time and relationships with ever-more destabilizing distractions, *surrender*. Surrender to this truth: that a life devoted to scaling the mountain of your own pride does not mean you can build a palace at the peak. Like everyone else, you'll still have to erect a sod house on the flatlands of your own mere existence . . . and that, too, will eventually crumble.

Visualizing such an erection can be a powerful means to escape the awful anticipation of your own demise. If you've never employed visualization before, go beyond the suggestions of *Unmasked! When Being a Superhero Can't Save You from Yourself* and employ the approach I detailed in *Secrets from Menton's Brain: Using Two Lefts to Make Yourself Right* (also available on audiobook and holodisc). Your greatest power over emotions such as pride and fear is your imagination. So use it.

But as my F*O*O*Jsters were about to discover, the only path to escaping hubris and mortal terror is deicide.

CHAPTER THREE

CLASH OF THE ICONS

SUNDAY, JULY 2, 9:12 A.M.

Voyage into Iron Lass's Brain

dols. Gods and goddesses. Icons.

They're the embodiment of any society's perspectives on the pinnacle of human achievement. Whether representing beauty, intelligence, strength, science, combat, industry, eroticism, or religion, icons serve as foci of mass attention and mass emulation.

But to the same extent, they serve as implements for mass emasculation. When hyper–role models exist on a plane far higher than we can safely fly, our desperate attempts to touch the hems of their garments will eventually knock us down the staircase of humiliation and into the depths of abasement.

So what happens to one who both *is* an icon and *has* an icon, especially when his own icon fails? Can anyone survive the pincering punishment that is the iron mandibles of the Icon Trap?

Icon to Generations

She sat across from me, the only illumination inside the echoing darkness, radiant in her raven-feather hair and flashing amethyst eyes. In one way it was hard to believe that it had been only two days since she learned of the death of Hawk King.

On the other hand, she'd exchanged her electrum-plated iron armor for an elegant black skirt and a mandarin-collared powder blue cardigan, and her ubiquitous black-and-white feathered cloak was hung neatly elsewhere.

But if she was attempting to affect a *schule-frau* appearance, it wasn't working; her six-foot-four feminine muscularity couldn't be contained by pleated wool. In the 1950s, more than one Hollywood scribe compared Lauren Bacall to her. Half a century later, she still looked an athletic thirty-nine when in fact, she'd seen two millennia. Yet by some accounts, she'd changed more during her twentieth-century career than she had over the previous two thousand years.

This woman knew better than almost anyone what it meant to be an icon. Because for centuries, Iron Lass–AKA Dr. Hnossi Icegaard, UCLD professor of Military History, Political Economy, and German and Scandinavian Literature—was literally worshiped as Hnossi of Aesgard, daughter of Queen Frigg of the Norse gods.

Since our sessions began, I'd noted her extreme reluctance to share her feelings; rather she hoarded her words and thoughts in my presence as if they were a mound of Hostess Twinkies and I a projectile bulimic. Hoping for better results that day, I shifted into a new approach as the two of us sat alone inside the temporal lobe of her brain.

"I'm sure that over the last forty-eight hours, Iron Lass,

you've been reflecting mostly on Hawk King and your relationship with him, probably to the exclusion of pretty much anything else.

"But today, I'd like to touch on an outstanding issue at the core of why you're here—namely, why *are* you here?"

Purple lightning crackled overhead along a neural pathway, the synapses pulsating in echoing thunder like throbbing stars.

Hnossi Icegaard revealed nothing but a flicker of one eyebrow.

I remained undeterred.

"Frankly, Hnossi," I said as the cerebral thunder diminished into distant rumbles, "I'm surprised that the F*L*A*C required you of all the F*O*O*Jsters to attend our sessions."

Her eyes, like a cobra's, dilated and scoped on me as if I were a mongoose.

"After all," I continued, "on several occasions you've played the role of lawgiver with your colleagues, *unto* them, if you will, maintaining order, decorum. Hardly a disruptive behavior, it would seem."

Her chin tilted up, slowly shifting to the right; her eyes remained locked, like glinting safes.

"Does ziss mean my presence is unnecessary, Frau Doktor? Becoss if so—"

"It means your presence is *highly* necessary, Professor Icegaard. Necessary for your teammates in providing limits, and necessary in providing a role model. Given all that, why in your opinion would the F*L*A*C suggest you're a disruptive influence in the F*O*O*J?"

She pursed her lips, maintained her stare at me. "You vud haff to ask zem."

"You've obviously had time to form your own analysis of the F*L*A*C and their decision."

She was silent. Behind her, the temporal lobe shimmered, but there was no lightning.

"So according to your analysis, what is the F*L*A*C's rationale for ordering you here? Where have they miscomprehended you and your work?"

"Ze F*L*A*C . . . unt ze FOOCH itself, fails to unterstandt . . . ze significance uff self-discipline unt reevaluation . . . durink difficult times . . . or uzzervise."

"And that refers to you how?"

"I haff providedt guidance, Doktor. Guidance zey apparently belief is no lonker reqviredt. Alzough, perhaps *now,* sadly, in light of Hawk—"

"You're an icon, Professor," I said, changing directions again to prevent her clambering into her psychemotional bunker to escape the falling shells of my inquiry. "Not only as a Norse deity and as a twentieth-century superhuman, but in the academy—author of *Women Who Fly with the Valkyries, The Frigga Mystique,* and *The Buri Myth,* among others—"

"Ja?"

"You broke down doors, sometimes literally, to gain entrance to traditionally male domains. Dozens of female heroes entered the F*O*O*J because they were inspired by you, and they've sung your praises in interviews, books, and the motivational speaker circuit. And, of course, the fact that you've been worshiped for centuries—"

"*Ja?*"

In the northern sky of her brain's emotional center, blue lightning flashed; the thunder lagged by seconds. I motioned for her to stand and walk with me, which she did, and we headed off toward the nexus of her divine motor function.

"That's quite a burden," I said above the thunder finally rolling in, "having to live up to all that. Never being allowed to falter. To be vulnerable."

"Burtens are a part of life in ziss vurlt. Hawk Kink . . . taught us all zat."

"A *part* of life, yes. You think they're the entirety?"

"I didt not say zat."

"A burden you've borne for twenty centuries. And now, even with the Götterdämmerung over, you're still having to hold yourself up as an example of what people can achieve if they have the will and honor, if they're devoted to what they consider right. It must be . . .

"Well, I won't tell *you* how it feels, but beholding a generation of younger heroes, younger *women* heroes, who comport themselves as if all the privileges and access they have weren't fought for and struggled for by the women who preceded them, most of whom never got such opportunities . . . opportunities that they're—some would say—squandering? You must find that absolutely galling."

She drew in a huge breath through her nostrils, but even with her mouth closed I could hear her teeth grinding against one another as if she were chewing the metallic sweetbreads of the mythic iron goat Scyldscrotgnashhunt.

We were close.

Iconsternation: Iron Lips

I aimed my neuron probe up into the cerebral "sky" of memory, the zone to which my Id-Smasher® had mapped and routed the segments of Hnossi's actual flesh-and-ichor brain.

Inside her virtual cerebrum, the sky warbled at my neuron probe's beam. I then tapped a sequence on my belt controls, stimulating the sensory-memory lobe, and around us IMAXed the remembered sights, smells, sounds, and wind-rushing tactile impression of flying over snow-clutched Scandinavian mountain peaks. Neurally connected to her as I was, I felt the strain at my shoulders of wings surging through the stratosphere, felt the cold rush across my body.

"Your other powers," I said, aiming my probe elsewhere, "include the ability to summon this, correct?"

Instantly we were standing in a bald, gray valley; a gleaming iron chariot appeared, connected to a train of tiger-sized iron cats. I clicked again: across the sky, we looked down at two massive projections of Hnossi's hands, into which materialized her two magic iron swords, one short, one long.

"Iron chariot; iron cats; iron swords. You can turn your wings into iron, you can occasionally turn your body into iron, you have gold-and silver-plated iron armor, your *name* is—"

"Your point, Doktor?"

"That's a lot of iron, Hnossi. You tell me. What's the point?"

"Mm, *ja*," she sneered. "Don't you sink zat's just a *bit* too . . . mm . . . pre*cise*, Frau Doktor? Too purfectly pat unt pristine? Zat my carryink uff iron implements unt various transformations viss iron connote a hardness or hard-heartedtness uff my character, Freudianly suggestink furzer some sort uff pursonal or family dysfunction?"

"I didn't say a word about your family, Professor Icegaard."

She stiffened, blinking at me, looking like a sleeping cockatoo whose perch had suddenly collapsed beneath her.

"But the way you reacted to my question, Hnossi, is interesting. Have you found in your career or your mothering that shame is an effective means of silencing people when they question you or your decisions?"

Her lips flattened like spatulas, her eyes nailed onto me like eviction notices. The giant projection of hands and swords flared and then turned to black smoke, while the entire sky erupted in flame.

The two of us stood crisping in the violent orange light of the inferno. But because I refused to look away from her face, Hnossi finally spoke.

"Vell, first uff all, you're mistaken ven you say—it's inaccurate to, totally incorrect to suggest zat I—zat I *shame* people,

Doktor, vezzer professionally or pursonally. Unt even if, unt I punctuate *if,* vut I said to you vuss 'shaming,' zen zat's only becoss zat's vut you'd just been doingk to me!"

"Why are you choosing to think I was trying to shame you?"

"You, you just—you vere just tryink to somehow make me feel ashamedt uff my ferric powers! Vich I've been using for centuries in your vurlt, savink people like you, people who caun't take care of zemselfs!"

"So you admit that you did try to shame me as retaliation for what you perceived as me shaming you, and you just attempted to shame me *again* by saying people like me can't take care of themselves."

The firestorm emitted what can only described as a confused light, diminishing into vast, belching fields of smoke which I waved away with my hands. Hnossi removed her mandarin-collared powder blue cardigan, and from her back her wings emerged in a burst of snow and black ash. Standing, she flapped her vast black falcon wings to clear our air.

"So in which ways, do you think," I said, coughing, "has this belief of yours that two wrongs make a right led to professional or personal problems for you?"

She sat agape, finally squeaking out, "I caun't belief your shoddy, scattershot, disjointed—you're not even listeningk to me! I don't *haff* any professional or pursonal proplems!"

"Not even denial?"

"So if I defendt myself against untrue accusations, I'm in denial?"

"You're divorced—"

An image of her ex-husband, the Mexican superhero Strong Man, in his cape, mask, and wrestling tunic, glimmered behind her. He smiled broadly. "Yes I am, as are about a hundred million uzzer vimmen viss soughtless husbands in ziss country—"

"You've been sent to therapy with me—"

An array of caricatures—dwarfish versions of the F*L*A*C

officers—sprouted from the "floor" like toadstools. "Because an assembly of scaredt, jealous, foolish, myopic *untermenschen* on ze F*L*A*C is afraid of vut I represent unt how tiny zey feel ven zey're forced to evaluate zeir own lifes in comparison to—"

"You're estranged from your children, Hnossi."

Her mouth stopped. Shut.

A wall of hewn stone appeared behind her, soaring back left, right, and upward, and with a thunder-smack concluded its construction as an impenetrable fortress.

From behind narrowed eyes, she said, "You don't know ennysing about my children."

"Tell me."

"I come from a culture, a generation, zat said private matters are *private*. Unt ve do not discuss our problems viss just vutever professional gossip-junkie happens to troll ze back alleys looking to . . . to score."

"But you just said you didn't have any personal problems."

Her eyes snapped open, her lips opening for a breath. But if she had a sentence waiting to fly, she never surrendered its passport. By then, Hnossi Icegaard was beginning to see that neither my office nor the Id-Smasher® permitted the use of denial as an avoidance technique.

"Prove me wrong," I said. "If you don't have any personal problems, then tell me about your children, why your emotional-memory center has metaphored a psychic fortress around any image of them, and why your not seeing them doesn't indicate or constitute a problem."

"Ve're not estrangedt! Ve see each uzzer all ze time!"

"When was the last time you had a meal together? Actual family time, sitting around the table for roasted wild boar, tankards of Jotun ale, recitations from the *Poetic Edda*?"

"Please spare me your painfully passetic attempts at cultural sensitivity, Doktor."

"So. When was it? The last time?"

She looked to her left, looking "east," and the glittering Bifrost rainbow bridge raced up toward the mountain rising from the black plains of memory. At its peak glittered into existence the silver and golden meadhalls of Aesgard.

I ignored her attempt to hide in her "happy place."

"Married to, let's see," I said, clicking a projection of my IRON LASS file after Hnossi's prolonged refusal to speak, "married May 1962 to Hector 'Qetzalcoatl' El Santo, HKA Strong Man." The life-size smiling image of the caped-and-tunicked hero and Mexican screen idol reappeared beside Hnossi. She moved closer to it as if automatically, then forced herself to step back and look away.

"Two children: Inga-Ilsabetta, born October 1962, and Baldur, nicknamed Lil Boulder, born June 1964."

A tall girl and a shorter boy, both dark-haired, appeared at Strong Man's hips. Both looked up toward their father with the power of the sun in their smiles.

"Separated from El Santo, 1974; children chose to live with their father. El Santo eventually filed for divorce in 1981."

The family triad diminished into blackness and disappeared. I paused, looking at the woman staring at the fading footprints of shadows.

"Later that year, you drafted a paper entitled *Toward a Practical Götterdämmerung: A Logistical Analysis,* ghost-rewritten and repackaged to the public as the paperback bestseller *Time to Ragnarok!* It became the clarion call that initiated the War."

I glanced away from my file projection to see Iron Lass's eyes attempting to carve me into individual slices of luncheon meat.

"The same year your husband tells you that your marriage is truly finished, you, essentially single-handedly, declare a global war that changes the planet. A war whose logistics you chart. A war you lead to victory."

"Ziss is absurdt," she said, her left hand glowing white, her right hand shadowing into black. "Vut ridiculous, patronizing, reductionist nonsense, to claim an entire geopolitical hyper-hominid conflict can be explainedt avay as merely *a vuman scornt*?"

"To go from leading your fellow Valkyries into battle for centuries, being literally worshiped as a deity of iron—to open-ing yourself up to simple, mortal love, meaning you'd've had to've made yourself soft and pliant and vulnerable to humans, bearing children for a mortal man, even . . . and then after all of that, to be rejected? That's iconoclasm, Hnossi! The shattering of an icon . . . you!

"So rather than being 'patronizing' or 'reductionist,' I'm try-ing to get you to integrate everything you've gone through into a postwar logistical analysis of your*self*."

Her eyes, aflame, dimmed; her body, rigid, melted by a de-gree. Her hands resumed their normal state, no swords having appeared in them.

"My muzzer," she finally muttered, "alvays saidt to me, she saidt, 'Brünhilde, you're too smart by half.' " She lowered her voice further. "She never remembert my name."

What will it mean for your life, and for your view of yourself, if the glory days never return?

Iron Lass: "I never sought glory. Basic respect would suffice."

Iconditional Love

Blobs of Day-Glo color oozed and swirled around me as if I were standing inside a giant lava lamp, and the air smelled like a mixture of bubble gum and the cosmetics depart-ment at a Target store.

"So, Syndi," I asked the only other person with me inside

the Id-Smasher®'s neuroscape, "how do you feel about the F*L*A*C ordering you into counseling?"

"Like, as far as I'm concerned," said the young pop star, once again and in quick succession yawning, stretching, snapping her virtual gum, and rolling her eyes, "*everybody* should be in counseling."

Power Grrrl had manifested from her memories the leather sofa from my Verbalarium and had draped herself across it, her back wedged into one of its corners, one thigh hiked up over the sofa's arm, her hair dazzled along the sofa's back as if she were awaiting her paparazzi. Mentally clad in black-and-silver leather dominatrix garb and swaying her torso to the dance beat seeping from her bustier-speakers, she was, that day, unusually low-key.

"Tell me about that, Syndi. Why should 'everybody be in counseling'?"

"Isn't it obvious, Eva? These F*O*O*J-feebletons really need you, and one day I'm sure, like, they'll thank you?" she said in her usual question-intonation, smiling sugar all over me. "But just look at the world, you know? Everyone's, like, crazy—all this negative energy they're beaming? These F*O*O*J-fogies need to fix them*selves* before they start invading everyone else's proximity, you know? Gawd!"

"So you think they're being hypocritical, Syndi?"

"Like, yeah!"

"Aren't superheroes supposed to be involved? Helping others?"

"How're you supposed to help people if you should really be under round-the-clock observation on a coupla hundred meds?"

"You seem to get along fine with the Brotherfly."

"P-Fly? He's cool," she said, while behind her drifted an image of the Brotherfly gazing at her adoringly. "He knows how to have fun. He's not afraid to live, y'know? The others, like, need to get over themselves. 'Legendary heroes'? Right!"

"Not even Omnipotent Man?"

Brotherfly disappeared, replaced by an Omnipotent Man half his correct size, and old beyond his years. "Just a sad old man who's, like, totally lost in his own rep."

"The Flying Squirrel?"

Omnipotent Man disappeared, replaced by the image of an actual flying squirrel wearing a black top hat sitting atop a pile of virtual money and screeching. "Just an angry old tightass who can't deal."

"Deal with . . .?"

"My orientation?"

"Yes. Let's discuss that momentarily. And X-Man?"

She paused a moment with a look on her face that suggested she was chewing a uniquely dreadful species of sushi. The top-hatted squirrel was replaced, oddly, by an image of herself wearing a white shirt, black suit, and tie. The image appeared to be gasping for breath before it disintegrated.

"Gawd," she said, "he's, like, the most uptight of all of them. Everything's about *race* for him. He *se*riously needs your help, Eva. Like, if he didn't have his job and his politics and his religion, he wouldn't even have an identity!"

"And how about Iron Lass?"

She stopped her sofa-swaying, looking at me for the first time, while above us towered a giant, rusting iron-fleshed Iron Lass like a Norse Statue of Liberty, glowering down from the clouds with such intense disappointment that the virtual ground beneath us split open.

Rolling her eyes, Syndi blew a bubble. Made it larger.

Larger still.

Popped it.

She sucked it back inside her mouth and chewed.

She rotated the twin volume knobs on each cup of her bustier. The *thump-bump* pumped louder, and only then did I recognize the song—one of her hits from the previous summer: "Thong Power."

"She's just a depressed, tired, worn-out, broken old woman, Eva," said Syndi, getting up from the couch and amble-dancing around the discotheque that had sprung up around us to shield us from the iron giantess. Syndi glanced at numerous mirrors and portraits of herself, then examined objets d'art and bookshelves her memory had manifested here from my office. She pulled books halfway out of their slots on my shelves, glancing at them before leaving them.

"She's always daggering me with her eyes, always making these, like, snide remarks about how I dress, about my relationships with, like, Cathode Girl and Billi Biceps and Beast Mistress . . . saying I don't have any focus or purpose or direction . . . I mean, who does she think she is? My, like, mother?" She snorted. "I already have one of those, and she supports me every step of the way!"

Beside her, a full-size Bianca appeared, a woman in her late forties, overtanned and leather-skinned, wearing a bustier and white pants that would be called chic on a woman two decades younger.

"Yes, I remember after that openmouthed kiss with Media Medea on the Golden Tunic Awards on ABC. There was a lot of controversy. Your mother backed you completely."

"Yeah. Bianca's cool," she beamed.

"You call your mother by her first name?"

"Like, why not? We're not hung up with society's 'rules.' Plus she's like not only my best friend, she's my agent. She got me *in*to the F*O*O*J, got me my Sony deal. If old Iron Ass wants to be someone's mother, maybe she should start with her own kids?" My bookshelves disappeared, replaced by a floating array of gold and platinum records—Syndi's, I assumed. "I hear neither of them even talk with her . . . I even heard one of her kids even tried to like kill herself or something? Some role model. Iron Gash could like learn something from Bianca. Gawd! I hope you *can* help her out . . . for her kids' sake, if no one else's."

"I noticed, in the simulation against Cyclo-Tron, you and Iron Lass certainly seemed to clash. And you never speak to each other in front of me."

"Like, I just told you? She hates me."

"Well, Syndi, I've certainly never gotten the impression she—"

"No, she hates me, Eva, I'm telling you?"

"Don't you think you might exag—"

"*She disapproves* of me intensely, then? Happy now?"

"What's interesting to me is how much you two are alike."

She spun back around to face me.

"You have *got* to be, like, riffing."

"No, Syndi, I'm not 'riffing.' Look . . . you're both icons to women. You're both symbols of femininity and feminine power. From the 1940s through the 1980s, Hnossi inspired women superheroes and ordinary women to break into male-dominated professions and stand up for themselves, and now you're inspiring a generation of young straight and nonhetero-sexual women and girls to believe in themselves, to be proud. Surely you can see the connection."

"We're like totally different! She's all like 'Do it zis vay' and 'Diknity! Honor! Sacrifice!' It's all about trying to get everyone to be just like her!"

"But Syndi, what about your HEAT Ray?"

She gaped indignantly. "That's like *to*tally not the same!"

"You used it in the Id-Smasher® simulation. You've used it in the small number of melees you've been in during your brief crimefighting career, and you even use it in your concerts. Your . . . what's it called, now? Hyper-Emulation—"

"Acquisition Transmission Ray, yeah, yeah—"

"Syndi, you turn people into duplicates of yourself. *Literally*. And literally under your control. Not to mention your highly successful line of Power Grrrl's Grrrl Guides™ . . . *Power Grrrl's Grrrl Guide™ to Yoga, Power Grrrl's Grrrl Guide™ to Diamond-Hard Abs, Power Grrrl's Grrrl Guide™ to Buddhism,* the *Grrrl Guide™ to Yoga Writing the LSAT*—"

"So I know something about marketing. With all your books and videos, Eva, I'd think you of all people could appreciate that!" Suddenly the discotheque reformatted itself into what must have been a Barnes & Noble, to judge by the wafting smell of lattés.

Syndi wandered off, disappearing amid all the shelves of her own CDs, DVDs, *PG!* magazines, and books. Just before I located her again, I finally found copies of something other than her work: a battered hardcover of Professor Icegaard's *Toward a Practical Götterdämmerung: A Logistical Analysis,* and a few copies of my own self-help series. They were on the remainders table.

"Well, despite what you think, Syndi," I said, "I *am* impressed by how much you've accomplished—and not just for someone your age, but for anybody of any age. Your LSAT manual is apparently the most effective one on the market, and my own agent said your editor swears you wrote every word of it, even though you're only nineteen and you've never been to law school—"

"Of course I wrote it! I wrote all my books!" she said, climbing onto a display case next to a standee of herself. "Why's that so hard to believe? People are, like, always underestimating me just because I express myself on my own terms!"

"So you don't see your manuals as an attempt to make other people live like you do?"

"I'm, like, *help*ing them?" she said, vaulting from the display case onto the top of a decorative pillar. Miraculously, despite her heels she did not fall. She stood up straight. "That's not controlling them!"

"Yes, but don't you think Iron Lass sees her actions the same way?"

"I don't care what she thinks, Eva! Whose side are you on, anyway? I don't exactly feel supported here!"

"Syndi, my job isn't to be on anybody's side. It's to be on *every*body's side."

"Gawd, what good are you then?"

"Syndi, did you ever think that using your HEAT Ray on others might be a violation of their rights?"

She chewed her gum furiously for several seconds, as if hoping her mastication might provide clarification. "Their rights?" she said finally. "What are you talking about? Because I included them in my *me*ness?"

"People have a right to freedom, to individuality—"

"Eva," she said from atop her pedestal, "why wouldn't anybody want to be *me*?"

Iconquest: Id-dentity Crisis and the Power of Narcissism

art of the id's purpose is to assert its host personality onto the world to ensure its host's continued existence. *If I get enough,* says the id, *I will exist another day.*

But unlike the narrator from the classic disco song "I Will Survive," the id isn't satisfied with "enough," because enough is never enough. The id always needs more, or specifically, *more than anybody else.* So "enough" becomes "more than" which becomes "all." And even then, the id fears that all can be taken away; therefore crushing the capacity of others to resist becomes paramount.

Narcissism is the id's assertion of itself, not just over its host but over others as well. It is the illusion that one's own needs are not only more important than other people's needs, but that one's own needs *are* other people's needs.

Because Power Grrrl was a highly narcissistic personality, she could not understand that my role as therapist was to aid everyone from her team and not to be her own personal ally or avenger. Nor could she understand that her paranormally overdeveloped id was the true power source of her HEAT Ray and that her use of it fundamentally abused the people whom she dominated.

Most of all, perhaps, narcissism blinded Syndi to her true reason for disliking Iron Lass: their similarity. Both iconic heroines sought to control others, believing such control was a boon rather than a bane.

But while Iron Lass was overbearing, her attempts at control were manifested through blame, guilting, and manipulation, all of which still provided some chance for resistance. Power Grrrl's HEAT Ray provided no such chance for escape . . . a reality that led, indirectly but inescapably, to the July 16 massacres.

Clash of the Icons

You come from a large family, isn't that correct, Hnossi? And royalty, too?"

Iron Lass's gaze flickered over to Power Grrrl before she looked back to answer me. She'd done that several times since we'd reconvened inside a neutral Id-Smasher® mindscape both their brains had selected, a badlands grove of buttes at sunrise.

"*Ja-a-a-a . . . ?*" she said slowly.

Power Grrrl coughed into her hand, except it wasn't a

cough—she'd barked the word *phony,* eliciting a glare from Hnossi.

"Syndi? Is there something you think we need to attend to?"

"Like, aren't we supposed to be *hon*est here, Eva? Because I happen to know one or two things about this 'icon' over here. And they don't square with what she's been saying?"

Staring back at the young woman, Hnossi's face looked as coldly cutting and metallic as the grille of a 1955 Pontiac. I asked the elder woman to respond, but when she said nothing, I pushed further. "Hnossi, am I missing something? You're Hnossi, daughter of Odin and Frigg, the royal family of—"

"Oh, Eva," sighed Syndi, "I thought you had a better built-in BS detector—I can't believe you fell for Hnossi's 'royalty' shit."

"Vatch your langvidge!"

"Watch *this,*" said Syndi, cupping her pudenda.

"Ach, Kvasir's bowl! Vhere's your vhistle now, Frau Doktor? I shouldn't haff to stand here unt take ziss—"

"Please, ladies—let's deal with this properly. Syndi? You said I fell for an untruth. So what is the truth?"

"Like, there's more than one Frigg in the Norse pantheon, Eva? People always think that the other Frigg, also known as *Freyja,* is Frigg, the wife of Odin. And Iron Lassy there just lets 'em think that. Like, isn't that deceit or something? Doesn't that violate some sort of Aesir honor code-thingy or something?"

"So, Hnossi, you're not related to Frigg, wife of Odin?"

Iron Lass: ". . . *Nein.*"

"So why have you let people believe—"

"If people make ziss mistake on zeir own, am I suppost to take all my time to correct zeir misconzeptions? I have a life, Doktor, of teachink claasses, gradink papers, providink guidance in ze F*O*O*J—"

"Lying . . ."

"Syndi, please. All right, Hnossi. We can get back to family of origin later. Let's see here . . . you became a Valkyrie, correct?"

"Ja."

"Why'd you join?"

Her eyes were like switchblades, swinging their glinting tips between Syndi and me. When she spoke, the indignation of her words grated like the fingernails of the damned on a blackboard in hell.

"I vaanted," she said, "to be part of sumsing devoted to ze greater goot. Vhere honor vut alvays vanquish self-indulchence. Vhere clarity uff vision decisively defeatedt ze false promises uff moral relativism."

Syndi rustled in the scrub grass, about to interrupt. I intervened.

"And you felt you weren't getting that at home?"

Syndi laughed, snidely enough to spoil yogurt. "I bet that wasn't the only thing she wasn't getting at home."

"You're a disgraceful lout!" said Hnossi. She looked furious enough to knock down the buttes around us. "Everysing for you is sex, sex, sex! Do you have a sinkle uzzer sought in your headt? I've devotedt my entire life to—"

Syndi mouthed the words along with Iron Lass. "Justice, honor, diknity!"

"Yes, zat's right, little girl. Mock me all you vaant! But for centuries vimmen haff looked up to me as an example—unt now, sanks to people like you, I look aroundt unt find a generation of tarts more devotedt to diamond tongue studts unt causink media scantals zan achieving power in politics, in ze vurkplace—"

"Your problem, *Hnossi,* is that you not only don't like men, you don't like women, either! You *liked* being the only woman in the F*O*O*J! How long was it after Lady Liberty, like, *died* that the F*O*O*J got its third heroine? Twenty-five years? And that was only after a lawsuit? What walls were you breaking down then? Oh, almost forgot—you were too busy getting ready to break down your marriage!"

"You know nussink about ziss! You're a disgraceful, disrespectful—you'd be better off viss a little more Germaine Greer unt a lot less Camille Paglia, young lady!"

"And you'd be better off with a little less Ayn Rand and a little more Frigg! The *real* Frigg, like, your mother?"

"You're only in ze FOOCH to milk it for marketing, for synergy tovard your next album, your next product line, your next *Grrrl Guide on Tantric Flute Playink* or vutever, or to launch a movie career! You haff no more devotion to ziss organization zan a tapevurm hass to a stomach! You need to straighten out your priorities! You need to chainch your life! You need to—"

"*You* need to remember you're *not my mother*!"

Both women fell silent.

A hot breeze blew through the neuroscape, tugging at each woman's hair, and the dust grew thick enough to choke on.

Syndi's simple statement of fact seemed to have sliced through the argument like a dull ax through a forehead. And it was the last sentence I could wrangle from either of them for the rest of the morning.

CHAPTER FOUR

ICONOCLASTIC MEANS "I CAN!"

SUNDAY, JULY 2, 1:45 P.M.

Iconversion:
Art for Heart's Sake

Your task," I told Hnossi, Syndi, Kareem, and Mr. Piltdown inside the Aesthetics Laboratory of the Hyper-Potentiality Clinic, "is to construct with the materials in this room a three-dimensional model of your own personal icon."

"Good God, 'Doctor,' " said Mr. Piltdown, "is there any floor past which you cannot sink? The finest flame of the Age of Heroism has just been extinguished, and meanwhile you want us to pretend we're in grammar school so we can *drawr pitchers*?"

"Art therapy, Mr. Piltdown, is a highly reputable and effective means through which the subconscious mind can release its repressed fears, anxieties, grief, and yearnings. And during the psychemotional turbulence of having lost a figure of such importance to you all, to the country—"

"So the answer is yes, then," said the brawny septuagenarian billionaire. "This is pointless. And if I'm to be subjected
to this pointless inanity, why aren't Wally and that dung-crawling
tap dancer here to be punished alongside us?"

"Festus, please," sighed Hnossi. "Let's just get ziss over viss.
Can ve do zat?"

He paused, finally nodding to her. "For your sake, Hnossi."

"Sank you. Continue, Frau Doktor."

"Thank you, Hnossi. To answer your question, Mr. Piltdown, André isn't feeling well—"

"Either a hangover, or a ho-over," muttered Kareem, possibly louder than he thought (or possibly not), "number seven
hundred and thirty-eight."

"—and Wally said he'd be here, so I'm sure he's just running
behind."

Flying Squirrel: "Running *some*thing, I'd wager."

I looked to Mr. Piltdown, expecting him to elucidate. He
said nothing.

I continued. "You have all afternoon. Look around the Aesthetics Laboratory. Use anything, from felts and crayons to
swatches to minerals to industrial cast-offs, and employ whatever powers, skills, or talents you wish. All I want you to do is
to evoke through art what moves you most about the person,
group, or place that embodies your highest ideals. The point
here, especially during this period of bereavement-processing,
is to connect yourself with the power source of your emotional-
intellectual nexus.

"While you're working, I'll ask you some questions about
what you're doing and why and how, and then at the end we'll
have some conclusion-and-contemplation work. So, go to it!"

Power Grrrl raised her hand.

"Yes, Syndi?"

"Is there any of André's baking left from the other day?"

"No, Syndi."

"Like, could you call him and ask him to bring—"

"Just focus on ze verdammt assignment, Fraulein 'Grrrl'!"

"What-*ever*!"

Iconograffiti

Because actual icons—the type held in museums—represent our most esteemed virtues, we might assume they must be constructed exclusively from genuinely precious materials such as marble, gold, or achillium.

But during Europe's Middle Ages, a thriving trade in faked icons saw horse molars sold as the teeth of Saint Paul, splinters sold as shards of the True Cross, and bear's hair sold as clippings from the beard of Solomon. Clearly, the composition of an icon is irrelevant to its purpose—that being the focal point for our contemplation.

So if you're prevented from confronting your own inadequacies because you're prostrate in front of a golden calf that's been thrust upon you, or if you're stuck inside a narcissistic id-loop of worshiping yourself, then right now, put down *Unmasked! When Being a Superhero Can't Save You from Yourself,* and take whatever random materials you have in your apartment, headquarters, cavern, or hideout and build an icon of your own.

When you're done, resume reading the chapter and follow along with my heroes. Write down your own answers to the questions I ask them, and take part in our final exercise. What you discover may put you much closer to freeing yourself from the cold clutches of your own psychic supervillains.

Iconstruction

My team quickly surveyed the room, each seeker securing the materials necessary to build his or her own icon, or in Mr. Piltdown's case, seizing the resources he thought others might require for their work.

I noticed that the dynamic detective was also depositing pamphlets around the room—red-white-and-blue glossies whose covers featured his own cowled scowl beneath the slogan RETURN TO HONOR, PRIDE, & GLORY and above the phrases ELECT FLYING SQUIRREL and DIRECTOR, F*O*O*J OPERATIONS. No one so much as glanced through one, not even Kareem, even though the tract was a direct challenge to him.

But while Mr. Piltdown tried to spark Hnossi's interest, to his obvious disappointment she was much more concerned with the three-yard-wide broken slab of granite she was hefting from the industrial cast-offs section of the Aesthetics Lab and laying across the floor of her workbay. Syndi had dragged over a mannequin and gone back for armfuls of cloth scraps and cans of spray paint, while Mr. Piltdown began by flipping through a stack of magazines, constantly casting looks over his shoulders (whether from angry suspicion or embarrassment, I'm not sure).

X-Man, however, was standing at his workbay without tools, without materials, without scraps. His eyes were closed, and he remained motionless.

From behind me was a simultaneous rush of frost and heat—Iron Lass had manifested her white and black swords, alternately freezing and melting sections of her vast granite slab before shearing them away.

I noticed Mr. Piltdown had become completely still—not due to gazing at Iron Lass but because he was fixated on the inside of a 1979 issue of *Time* from which he'd been tearing out images and text.

He stood staring at a full-page photograph of a beautiful, slender-muscled young Asian man in tight green shorts, a tight red leather vest, a short yellow cape, and a shiny black mask with stubby, furry gopher-style ears. His legal name, which had not been revealed when the article was written, was Tran Chi Hanh.

Back then he was known to the world as martial-arts ingenue and Flying Squirrel sidekick Chip Monk, North America's first Buddhist superhero. And its last.

"*You* were once *his* icon," I said as quietly as I could to Mr. Piltdown. "Before . . . before he left you."

He looked down at me, his eyes burning like piles of discarded hospital waste. "That was before he ended up in therapy," he hissed, "with the likes of *you*."

"Looking up to anyone as much as Tran did to you can be very destructive to one's ego integrity—"

"The word *therapist*, Miss Brain," snarled Mr. Piltdown. "You put a space after the third letter, and you get *the rapist.* Chip fell into therapy, like any street junkie falls into smoking *maki.* That's what ruined him, not—"

"I can't imagine the burden you carry, Mr. Piltdown, of having to be an icon, always having to be perfect, never being able to make a mistake. Because the distance to the pinnacle that people believe you're perfect, it's to the same depth they'll be furious when they inevitably discover you're not."

"Tran's betrayal, Miss Brain," he said, "wasn't because of any perceived imperfection on my part. You brain-shredders! Devoting your lives to splitting marriages, ruining families and organizations, digging up depravities that *should* be repressed and reanimating them in front of a crowd—"

"Perhaps the real problem, Mr. Piltdown, is being some-one's icon within a close relationship. It's inevitable that worship decays into contempt, because worship is ultimately about being trapped, being a slave."

"The only slavery I see here, Miss Brain, is your cultish, psychopathologizing claptrap!"

He returned to his *Time,* tearing the picture of Chip Monk down the middle and glancing at 1979 entertainment coverage of *Ragnarok Now!,* the Oscar-winning film about superheroes suffering from Post-Power Stress Disorder. "Tran Chi Hanh, the boy I raised as if he were my own son, betrayed me. Betrayed me because of a very sick and very evil little man."

He turned his burning glare on me, then on everyone else, but no one was looking back. Had they heard him, they all would have instantly understood his reference—to the premier scandal of Reagan-era superheroics.

In 1980, after rumors of an ever-degenerating relationship between the senior hero and his sidekick, Chip Monk resigned at his first, brief, and final press conference.

And then he disappeared for more than four years.

Surfacing in 1985 under his legal name and fresh out of law school, Tran began his new public identity as an intern at Human Citizen, the premier anti-superhero public-interest law firm headed by the archnemesis of the Flying Squirrel—Jack Zenith, author of *Unsafe in Any Cape* and *Two Masks of a "Hero."*

" 'Betrayed' you?" said X-Man from his workbay, his eyes still closed. Apparently someone had been listening to Mr. Piltdown after all.

"Interesting wording, Festus." He chuckled. "You sound like a lover scorned. Of course . . . that's exactly what everyone said actually happened, now isn't it?"

Festus was crossing the distance to X-Man's workbay and reaching for the weapons in his utility pouches before I could intervene. X-Man barked the words *"Arms and armor!"* and with the snap and stench of gunpowder he faced the Flying

Squirrel in a battle stance and wrapped in the gleaming black armor of a fifteenth-century Benin warrior, mace in one hand and lance in the other.

"You filthy-mouthed carpetbagger!" said the Squirrel. "I'll beat the black off you!"

"I'm not your sidekick, Festy." Kareem laughed. "You won't be beating off anything around me!"

Suddenly there was a deafening *CRACK,* and a ten-foot-high wall of blinding white ice crisped into existence between the two would-be combatants.

"I vudn't touch zat if I vere you, Frau Doktor," said Iron Lass, her white shortsword *Grendelsmuter* pointing toward the barrier she'd just constructed. "Unt you needn't vorry about melting or mess, since ze vall's at least vun hundret dekrees below zero. When all ziss nonsense is done, I'll turn it into steam unt be done viss it. Unt I suggest you get a new Mind Vistle as soon as possible, *ja*?"

She turned back to her bickering fellow F*O*O*Jsters. "Now, shut up unt get back to vurk, you two, or I'll put you bose in briefs I'll make ze same vay I made zat vall."

Iconflict

ell you suh'm, Doc . . . gonna be some *big* changes when I get on that F*L*A*C," said the X-Man, standing in his workbay behind the ice wall.

After my warning to him and Mr. Piltdown that I'd immediately place a call to the F*L*A*C if there were ever again a hint of violence between them inside the Hyper-Potentiality Clinic, Kareem launched into a fifteen-minute lecture to me on why he should not be made to remain in therapy when he should have been investigating full-time the "suspicious" death of Hawk King.

But finally both his eyes and his mouth were shut, his armor was gone, and his body was perfectly still, back in its uniform of white shirt and black suit and tie.

I was very conscious how intensely dry my mouth was, probably because Iron Lass must have sucked all the moisture out of the room's air to make so much ice. Licking my lips to keep them from cracking and wishing I had not only a psych-emotional but an epidermal balm, I told him, "You sound very confident about your chances of winning, Kareem."

"It's not a matter of confidence, Doc. It's allies. It's strategy. It's having done the due diligence." He breathed in deeply, let it out in a long rasp as if from the bottom of his soles. *"Legs and feet."*

Like a prairie sky coning into twin tornados, dust and shadow condensed in front of me into two columns. Supple muscles puffed up like Ball Park franks, feet arching and toes curling inside golden sandals whose straps wrapped themselves like snakes around the calves of the disembodied legs.

Kareem opened his eyes, inspecting his work. "And it doesn't hurt being up against a Ku Klux Klown like the Flying Fart. He really thinks he can get more than two percent of the electorate onside? That old allosaurus is probably the most hated member of the F*O*O*J—and not just by the public, I'm talking about F*O*O*J members themselves here."

"If he's no threat to your candidacy, why are you even talking about him?"

"Because even the idea of that filthy old fascist becoming the DOO is offensive to me. Nothing but a northern cracker. A caviar cracker. A canapé. He's everything that's wrong with the F*O*O*J. He's—you know what this man is? The perfect metaphor for him is that ice wall right there. A cold, white barrier too tall to go over, and lethal to the touch."

He closed his eyes, tilted his head back slightly.

"Now, what we should've been doing, especially after the

end of the War, is using the power of the F*O*O*J to clean this country up for real—and not going after freaks in tights, either, not that there're many of them on the *out*side of the F*O*O*J these days, anyway."

"But how do you think that—"

"Hold on a minute." He concentrated, closed his eyes. *"Pelvis."*

Condensing into existence atop the two legs in three-dimensional block letters was the word PELVIS. It wobbled, fell to the floor, shattered.

The X-Man opened his eyes. "Damn it," he growled. *"Khaibtu kher."* The shards *popped!* into dust, and then even the dust disappeared. "Look, Doc, I've gotta concentrate on this—"

"Sounds to me like you were just about to say something rather important about what you feel is wrong with your organization."

He sighed. "First of all, it's not 'my' organization. *The* organization is nothing but a bunch of mercenaries in rainbow lingerie. Decades of taxpayer money funneled into DOD contracts for overseas ultraviolet ops or HUD contracts to 'stabilize' inner cities? Which it has always failed to do? What is *that*?

"F*O*O*J headquarters are right here on the West Coast, but where was the F*O*O*J during the *maki* epidemic when the DIA and the Office of Naval Intelligence were shipping in coelacanth-weed to sell to Southern California gang-bangers to finance their terrorist army to overthrow the government of New Atlantis? Suddenly every black or Hispanic neighborhood on the West Coast had a *maki* house on every block and enough automatic weapons to fight a war!" he railed in a single, indignation-powered breath. "Where was the kot-tam leadership of the F*O*O*J during all that? I'll tell you where—Lying Squirrel was lunching with Kissinger and Reagan on how to destroy New Atlantis and Wally Watchtower was posing with Nancy on his lap on a CBS Christmas Special telling kids to just say no. Meanwhile, you know what old Wally was doing on the sly?"

I waited for an answer, finally having to prompt Kareem with a "No, what?"

Kareem looked furtively around the room, his head hunkered turtlelike into his collar.

"Never mind," he said, snarling.

This was the first time I'd seen Kareem censor himself. Whatever he was hiding, he obviously had no plans to discuss it around these colleagues whose ratification votes he'd need to ascend to the F*L*A*C.

"Well," I said, "that's a, a fascinating *the*ory, Kareem, but in terms of your feelings—"

"Jeez, Doc, you don't even try to hide when you're patronizing me, do you? You ever talk like that to Festering Squirrel? 'Fascinating theory'?"

"Kareem, I assure you, I treat all my—"

"—all your colored hero patients the same, yeah, I know. Look, don't you get it? It's not about 'theories' or 'feelings,' it's about what we can do. The F*O*O*J has patents on all kinds of technology, tech it licenses out to the government, to corporations. If all we did was take a cut of that and create some jobs, we could rebuild these inner cities we're being paid to protect— and failing to protect—from the *maki* gang wars our own government's actions created!

"Instead," he said, gesturing to the space between his cupped hands as if he were holding donkey dung, "the F*O*O*J hands over its returns on licensing fees to a bunch of kot-tam parasitic investors! That's what the *f* in F*O*O*J stands for, Doc. *Financial.* And *failure*! And *fascist*! And completely fu—"

"Brilliant campaign slogan, Rochester," said Mr. Piltdown from across the ice wall.

"As opposed to yours, Facedown? *'F*O*O*J über alles?'* "

"You're a disgrace to this entire organization!"

"That's not what Hawk King thought," said X-Man across the ice wall.

I could see it in Kareem's body language: He was making a decision. He made it, then stepped forward. "I'm gonna wait one week after the funeral—out of respect—and then I'm holding a press conference to announce the contents of a papyrus Hawk King wrote and gave to me."

Mr. Piltdown: "Hawk King never gave any papyrus to the likes of you!"

"I'm announcing," continued Kareem, "that what Hawk King wanted all along wasn't for the F*O*O*J to be some kind of kot-tam enforcer, the police-mafia in spandex, but to break down walls and build up halls, to shake the powerful and re-make the power*less*. And when he got roadblocked, steam-rollered, and presidentially knackered, he couldn't take it anymore, and *that's* why he went into exile!

"But he was ready to start all over again, smash the jail they built around him and be reborn with a new mission. And I'm going to reveal what else he said in his papyrus . . . which included endorsing me as Director of Operations. And I'll hold up that papyrus for the world to read!"

All work in the room ceased.

"Edgerton, good goddamnit, you're nothing but a ghastly, ghoulish little phony who's prostituting the corpse of our finest hero to foist your inadequacies upon Hawk King's finest crea-tion! There's no papyrus—you're a fraud!"

"I'm a fraud? If that aint the fridge calling the stove white. If Americans knew even ten percent of the truth about you, you'd be on *multiple* death rows right now, Fespus—"

"Well, Kareem," I cut in, "congratulations. You must be very happy."

"Happy? Happy that the King wanted me—*me*—to guide this group? Happy 'cause he left me an endorsement, which is the closest thing to God writing me a reference letter? Happy that I'm gonna lead this sad group into the twenty-first century and remake it into a hammer for justice?" he said in his rhetorical crescendo. "Kot-tam right I'm happy. I'm slap-a-*cracker* happy!"

"The King would never've endorsed you!" yelled Mr. Piltdown from over on his side of Hnossi's ice wall. "Not in ten million years! Not if you were the last biped on this planet! And you'll be laughing out of the other side of your watermelon-hole when I put a voting-day thrashing on you that'll make Hiroshima look like a campfire!"

I expected Kareem to materialize armor and weapons despite my warning, but instead he grinned triumphantly. "Alzheimer's," he stage-whispered to me, "has robbed America of its richest moron reactionary."

"I heard that!"

Icondescension

Anyway," said Kareem, "what we need is more than just sweeping out the old guard fascists. We also need to clean out the new generation *fashionists*."

"Meaning?"

"Have a look," he said, thumb-pointing toward Power Grrrl and the mannequin she was working on, to which she'd affixed cloth scraps and wiring in a rough approximation of tassels, G-string, garters, and stockings.

Tension between these two had been obvious since the beginning of our sessions together. The X-Man did anything he could to avoid sitting next to Power Grrrl, and most of the time he wouldn't even look at her or acknowledge her remarks. Given the comments he'd aimed at the Flying Squirrel about Chip Monk and made about Power Grrrl's iconic status as the lesbian "it" girl, homophobia clearly informed at least part of

Kareem's antipathy. A common cultural trait in the inner city, homophobic neurosis was obviously as strong a component of the X-Man's id-crisis as his racial neurosis.

Such racial antagonism had publicly marked the X-Man's career from its inception. Prior to developing his full logogenic powers, Kareem had employed rudimentary pictogenesis in his burgeoning crimefighting career, noteworthy for his corruption-crackdown on the moguls of African American Network Television and the hip-hop/rap industry. Several years earlier the prestigious *Los Ditkos Inspector* magazine carried a four-page feature on a younger Philip Kareem Edgerton, shortly after he'd switched his alias from "Mac Rude" to "X-Man." As a rising star in the League of Angry Blackmen, which had drastically reduced crime in the Los Ditkos inner-city neighborhood of Langston-Douglas, Kareem had been invited to speak before a $500 per plate dinner for the liberal West Coast philanthropic group the Dream Foundation.

After disparaging the AANT executives in the crowd as well as hip-hop/rap artist-producers P. Bowels and the Nefarious N.I.G., Kareem, according to the *Inspector,* proceeded to tease, taunt, and ultimately terrorize the elite dinner audience with a self-righteous, condescending harangue that allegedly included him grabbing his crotch and inviting the crowd to sample "these nuts" after their soup. The *Inspector* concluded that such behavior ultimately cost the L*A*B its HUD security contract for Langston-Douglas.

Knowing his F*O*O*J political ambitions, I asked Kareem how he expected to advance his career when his reputation was so rife with racialized rage.

"I've got a right to be hostile, Doc," he said after a long pause in which he finally managed to logosynthesize an actual pelvis above the two legs he'd formed earlier. "My people are being persecuted."

"Kareem, I've read that *Inspector* article about the dinner you attended—"

"The *Inspector*'s a piece of crap, and ninety percent of what that punk wrote never even happened—"

"—and based on your behavior at that dinner, it's clear that you *wanted* those people to dislike you. As if you were afraid of them."

"Afraid? What *are* you talking about, Doctor?"

"Afraid of their acceptance."

Dropping his jaw with faux-shock, he said, "Let me tell you about these people 'accepting' me, Doctor. That dinner, it was about half Day-Glo long-john types, a quarter media muckety-mucks, and the rest wealthy superhero groupies. Some of that meringue mafia like to pretend to *like* people like me. It spit-shines their white liberal credentials. The rest don't even bother pretending.

"But you know who else was there? F*O*O*J punks like the Beaver Brothers, who were the number one source for that rat-gut reporter. And just two weeks ago I found out that Carrol Beaver's been spreading rumors about me. That I'm a sexist! Me! What kind of fecal fungus is that? You see how I treat Iron Lass. Is that sexist? And I never had anything but com*plete* respect for the Supa Soul Sistas—"

"Yet you won't even acknowledge Syndi's presence, Kareem," I said. "And every time she speaks, you either roll your eyes, cross your arms in judgment, or get a look on your face like you're sipping from a bucket of something turgid."

"That," he said, immediately jabbing a finger toward me before catching himself, "that's an entirely different . . . which's got nothing to do with gender, Doc."

"Is it because of her orientation?"

He rolled his eyes, crossed his arms, and got a look on his face as if he were sipping from a bucket of something turgid.

"Trust me," he said, "it's got nothing to do with her 'orienta-tion.' "

"Then tell me what it *is* about."

"This is all a joke!"

"What's all a joke?"

"This!" he said, sweeping the room with his chin. "Being in this laboratory, completely cut off from the real world . . . How's this high-tech chicken coop supposed to reveal anything about how we actually function out there? The real reason we're here isn't because of *our* fears, Doctor, it's because of *yours*. In here, you're safe. You're boss. You're in control. The way you like it.

"You claim you want to understand us, to understand *me*? I'll believe that the day I see you walking the streets of Stun-Glas. And *I* should be out there investigating the murder—*assassination*—of the greatest hero of our times, instead of facing expulsion from the F*O*O*J for failing to attend this psycho-sycophantic suckfest you've got us starched into!"

"Well-played, Kareem." I smiled, nodding at my young pa-tient. "Very skillful."

"Meaning what?"

"Turning the conversation to someone else's supposed shortcomings and away from your antagonism toward Syndi."

"Look, Doctor. You want me to finish your assignment or not?"

Being one of the country's most insightfully attuned psy-choanalysts, I recognized when it was time to reel in a patient, and when it was time to release him. There would always be time later for the net.

Iconfusion

After calling in my secretary for some lip balm, I found Hnossi Icegaard at the next workbay listening to music on her Q-bot player. "I trust zere's no rule against ziss?" she said, gesturing to her small silver cube.

"Not at all, Hnossi—this is art therapy, after all. Ella Fitzgerald, right?"

"Ja. She won ze Grammy for ziss. 'Mack ze Knife.' Even zough she forgot ze vords, her improvisation vuss genius . . . a true warrior of song." She gestured with her shortsword to the granite slab she'd transformed into a stunningly elaborate scale-model replica of a walled fortress, complete with towers, armories, mead halls, stables, and bridges—the mountain-peak home of the Norse war gods. Aesgard. I asked her to tell me about her icon.

Offering a description that differed somewhat from my recollection of the legends, she focused on the Hall of Valkyries, the fortress of the sisterhood to which she used to belong. Yet none of what she said was in the least personally revealing.

"You know, Frau Doktor," she said confidentially, changing tone and direction, "alzough youngk Kareem can be undisciplinedt, you are too qvick to dismiss his legitimate concerns about Master Hawk Kink. I've spoken wiss him at length about ze prima facie case he's been developingk—"

Recognizing her diversion for what it was, I realized it was time to reel Iron Lass in.

"I'll take that into consideration, Hnossi. But right now, I'm curious about something that came up in our dual session with Syndi. After that conversation, I did some further reading about your life . . . and your mother's."

She turned to me, and I was suddenly acutely aware of the

power in the unsheathed swords clutched in her armored hands.

"Unt vut," she said quietly, "haff you discoverdt, Doktor Brain?"

"Well . . . I . . . uh . . . I discovered that there is indeed quite a difference between Frigg, wife of Odin—the goddess-queen most people assume is your mother—and Frigg/Freyja, your *actual* mother." I cleared my throat, choosing my next words as carefully as I would the steps on a rickety bridge across a gorge. "Whereas Frigg, wife of Odin, had an, an ill*ust*rious career as an Aesir warmaster and symbol of virtue . . . the *other* Frigg, your mother, was . . . she was . . ."

"A whore," she stated. "Is zat ze vurt you vere lookink for, Eva?"

"It's, uh, the word *you've* chosen," I said, swallowing. "Tell me why."

She stared at me with her cold eyes of hot fury, a look that made me feel like a mouse crisping in a child's Easy-Bake oven. The song on her Q-bot, meanwhile, changed to Patsy Cline's pathetically innocent rendition of "Tennessee Waltz." The juxtaposition only intensified my anxiety.

She continued staring at me, unblinking, unmoving, until the second verse in which Patsy lilted, *"Only you know how much . . . I have lost . . ."*

I finally broke our gaze, flipping through my file until I found another angle to pursue.

"You're, um, highly lauded, not only among, uh, the public, but, ah, among F*O*O*J members. As a symbol of the very best in superheroism. Since the F*O*O*J's founding, you've enjoyed the highest consistent approval rating among civilians and heroes of anyone except for Hawk King and Omnipotent Man. Ball Buster said in a 1989 issue of *People* that if it weren't for you, she'd've committed suicide, and that she knew of at

least two other heroines you'd gotten through similarly traumatic times."

"*Ja?*"

"You have enormous public regard, endless testimonials in
your favour . . . yet, in 1974, after your daughter is hospitalized
under mysterious circumstances, you separate from your husband, and your daughter and son choose to live with him."

I lowered my voice, kept my eyes on the contents of my file
folder, forcing myself to take a step toward this sword-wielding
woman with eyes of death.

"You've given of yourself to hundreds of thousands of people across the centuries, but the two people in the universe
whom you would most logically want to regard you as *their*
icon . . . they rejected you. And your own icon . . . it isn't a person of flesh and blood or even divine ichor . . . but a group of
cold stone buildings atop a mountain."

Her eyes were ominously huge, like twin amethyst bowling
balls full of dynamite, threatening to drop and crush my skull
and explode in my brainpan.

"My *children,* Doktor—"

"Sorry I'm late, ma'am-doctor," said Omnipotent Man too
loudly, stumbling in and scanning the room to deduce what we
were doing and why. The arctic fury in Iron Lass's face melted
into something softer but far sadder. Wally tripped over his
teammates' work materials while finding a workbay of his own,
laughing at himself self-consciously and whistling the theme to
Bonanza.

"C'n I work over here, Doc? Sorry I'm late—rough night'n
all. I'm sure y'all unnerstan—I aint th'o'ny one what's ever had
one a them. Hey, Syndi, that's quite the . . . Now, whatcha
puttin on her—now, I ain't sure that's an appropriate kinda . . .
Say, Doc, juss what're we doin, anyhow?"

I went over to Wally, explaining to him the task while ob-

serving his dishevelment: his hair was all a-shag, the bags beneath his eyes were big enough to shop with, and his body
reeked of ozone. Reexamining earlier remarks about Wally by
Mr. Piltdown and Kareem, I began to suspect a looming scandal
which, during this time of crisis, the F*O*O*J and the country
might not be able to withstand.

"So I can use anything in the room, ma'am?" he asked before I could inquire about his stench and his shabbiness, not to
mention his tremendous tardiness.

"That's right, Wally, but first, I think we need to—"

"Wellsir, ma'am, gotta get started. Time is money, penny
saved, early worm gets two in the bush," he said, gripping the
sides of the ice wall and ripping it up from the floor, hauling it
off to his workbay and immediately carving it with his super-
fast digits. And with the protective wall between Mr. Piltdown
and Kareem gone, their conflict inflamed immediately to the
verge of vengeance.

They'd both constructed images of the incredible Hawk
King.

Iconfrontation

I expected a volley of insults, but each man was silent, stupe-
fied with rage, each hero's contempt for the other intensified
by a jealous, proprietary fury.

With both heroes motionless in their contest of wills, as
if the one who moved first would prove himself the lesser
worshiper, I was free to inspect their work, which the other
F*O*O*Jsters did as well.

Kareem had employed his logogenic powers to sculpt a
masterpiece, a six-and-a-half foot tall gleaming black hawk-
headed man, adorned with pharaonic double crown and kilt,
arms stretched forth, hands clutching crook and flail, and

wings spread wide as if to encompass the world. One might easily imagine Egyptian peasants and priests prostrate before this statue. Everyone—except Mr. Piltdown, of course—was impressed.

The Flying Squirrel's work, while lacking the artistry, sophistication, and three-dimensional grandeur of Kareem's, was nonetheless fascinating. Since Mr. Piltdown could neither draw nor sculpt, he'd hewn a primitive collage from pictures, logos, and other text he'd torn from his stack of magazines. On a large sheet of Bristol board, a Frankenstein's monster of a Hawk King had been cobbled together from the body parts of various subjects; the figure stood in front of an undersize Blue Pyramid made from blue stretches of automobile, cleaning products, and perfume ads. Radiating from Hawk King's crown like the sun's rays were corporate logos clipped into words and phrases such as "HeRo" and "GETting the JOB doNE Right" and "Master your WORK place" and "MISSion acCOMPlished."

"Fascinating presentations, gentlemen," I said. "Who'd like to tell me about his work first?"

The X-Man, without breaking his stare at his adversary, reached up and behind himself to his icon's face, which moved slightly. I noted with fascination that Kareem's icon featured limited articulation.

He rasped, "Care to look under the mask, Festy? Or you afraid what you'd find?"

"Well, I'll be a pigeon's whiskers, Kreem, but that's a gosh-durn fine piece a work! *Fine* piece!"

The X-Man, eyes still chained to Flying Squirrel's, said, "Thanks, Wally. Glad you like it."

"Kareem," I said, "tell me about this detail here."

He didn't budge. "Which one?"

"This one where I'm pointing, right here."

Reluctantly breaking his glare, he scowled at me when he found me pointing at nothing and realized he'd been had.

"I just wanted you and Mr. Piltdown to break out of your testosterone-enflamed id-escalation. And now that you have, please take a few minutes to reflect on your icon so I can ask you about it."

"Hey, Doctor Brain, ma'am, look at mine! Look at what I done!"

Despite his late arrival, Wally had already transmuted Iron Lass's ice wall into an admirable ice sculpture, a ten-foot-tall man with star emblems across his jacket and DNA brocade trimming his cape. The figure stood gazing toward the ceiling as if reading the mysteries enshrouding the ends of the universe.

"That's m'daddy, Jobuseen-Ya," said Wally, "th'late an greatest defender of th'late an greatest planet." He looked around for support, then offered, "*Argon*. Y'all knew I meant Argon, right?"

"Beautiful craftsmanship, Vally," said Hnossi. "Impressive vurk viss my ice. But, mm, perhaps you should freshen up, ja? Haff a coffee or sumsing? You're looking a tad . . . overvurked."

Iron Lass fooled no one. To the extent that Wally's icon was masterful, Wally himself was a sluice-floor hackwork: unshaven, straggle-haired, mud on his suit, rips in his cape, and the even worse reek of ozone since his last trip to the rest room. "Tell me about your icon, Wally—"

"Eva, like, you haven't even looked at *my* icon yet?"

I was about to ask Syndi to wait her turn, but when I beheld what she'd built, I was both shocked and shocked at myself for being shocked.

Syndi's mannequin-based icon, with its dominatrix-inspired attire, was an image of herself.

Having anticipated someone's possible failure to notice her icon's identity, Syndi had glued gold glitter into the forms of the letters *P* and *G* around the nipple spikes of the black breast cups of her monument to herself, and AUTOGRAPHS HERE in the same gold glitter across the mannequin's buttocks and GRRRLS DO IT BEST upon its crotch.

"And, like, I gave myself dreads," she said, pointing to the sections of rope festooned from the mannequin's skull, "cuz, like, I've been thinking about getting some?" She tilted her head with her trademarked coquettishness. "What do you think, Eva? They look good, don't they?"

The X-Man swore.

Syndi tilted her head the other direction. "Kareem, if you, like, use the word 'appropriation' even once, you can talk to my, like, autograph dispenser?"

With everyone's work complete, I moved them out of their workbays to their datapads on the table and had them type out why they'd made their icons, what these images meant to them, and what they'd learned from what they'd made. But as important as their answers were, my real purpose was to prime the pump for phase two.

"All right, everyone. You've completed your answers," I said. "Now it's time to destroy your icons."

Iconoclasm Means "I Can"

The F*O*O*Jsters stammered and sputtered with outrage, demanding to know why I would ask them to put such effort into their artwork if it existed only to be smashed. After reminding them that nothing real lasts, I told them one of my favorite Zen stories.

A monk had been walking through the jungle for several weeks on his way to a grand pagoda, when he encountered the Ganges. Where he found himself, the river was too deep and too wide to cross by walking or swimming, so he wandered downriver for half a day or more in

search of a narrower, shallower point. The river grew
only deeper and wider, and throughout his search, his
unease grew that each step was taking him farther from
his destination, which he could see above the canopy in
the sunset, glittering golden atop a mountain.

The monk finally realized that his only means across
was to build a raft. Never having done so, he worked past
sundown experimenting with construction methods and
then spent the entire night lashing together logs with
vines, weaving a sail with fronds, and fashioning an oar.

When morning came, the monk tentatively ventured
upon the river, not knowing whether he'd drown or be
eaten by piranhas and crocodiles. But to his amazement
he reached the other side of the Ganges in less than an
hour, his unsurpassable barrier conquered easily.

Alighting upon the shore, he surveyed his work with
pride. But he couldn't imagine abandoning the craft of
his craft. So he gathered vines, hoisted his heavy raft
upon his back, and trudged through the jungle and up
the mountain toward his pagoda.

"Why did the monk haul his raft with him?" I asked.

"Because he was obviously intending to sell the vehicle
after he left the goddamned monastery. Or trade up, at least."

"Becoss he vanted neizer to litter nor to vaste."

"Cuz he had hisseff a nice lil ol boat, an he probably wannid
to take er out fishin when he was done monkin for the day."

"Because he didn't want anyone to, like, rip it off?"

"Because he was too blind, too self-delighted, or too afraid,"
said Kareem, "to accept that something useful had become a
burden."

"Precisely, Kareem."

A small smile—not insincere—crawled onto the X-Man's

lips, and I saw him then as he once must have been: the smartest student in the class. I tried to imagine him at a time before his awesome bitterness, when that smile would have been broader and more frequent, but it was difficult to picture.

And yet, despite myself in that moment, I found myself liking Philip Kareem Edgerton, and the impish twist of his lips suggested the feeling was slowly, surprisingly, becoming mutual.

"And the same is true of your icons," I continued, building from Kareem's solution to my wisdom-riddle, "not the artifices you've constructed this afternoon, but the ones that hold hegemony over your hearts and mastery over your minds.

"Especially during this id-crisis that's crippling your work environment, it's critical for each of you to examine how you are exploiting your ideals and your idols to excuse yourself of your own dysfunctional behavior."

The F*O*O*Jsters' arms were crossed, their faces dour. Except for Kareem's. Perhaps he chose to believe I wasn't including him in my description. Or perhaps it was something else entirely.

"Consider this, you men and women whom the world calls 'heroes.' By maintaining an icon, you are permanently placing yourself below someone or something which you consider to hold greater wisdom or intrinsic merit than you do. Icons, therefore, are 'virtual parents' situated inside your psyches, *indefinitely infantilizing you.*

"If you want to terminate your internal id-loops and deactivate your interpersonal dysfunction, you need to escape your Icon Traps. And doing so is as simple as proving to yourself that you need no more false idols in your life. Ultimately idols can only fall down and crush you. You need to start to take care of yourselves, and not be dependent on others or hold unrealistic opinions of your 'elders.' So go ahead. Smash your external icon. To do so isn't blasphemy. It's to be born again."

All five F*O*O*Jsters stood motionless, confused if not still upset.

"Like, does this even ap*ply* to me?" asked Syndi. "I mean, like, I'm obviously not in this icon-thingy like them, right?"

All but Wally rolled their eyes. "No, Syndi, not exactly like the rest of them—"

"Good, cuz I wanna keep mine."

"Wellsir, if she's keepin hers, ma'am-doctor, c'n I keep mine?"

"It's made of ice, you clod. You're familiar with melting?"

"I c'n keep it frosted, Festy."

"Bickering, my friends," I said, "is a self-constructed off-ramp from the freeway to mental health."

"Fine," grunted the Flying Squirrel. "If the only way to escape the Sisyphean nightmare of this 'therapy trap' and Miss Brain's meningococcal metaphors is to do as she said, let's be done with this rubbish and get the Sam Hill out of here. I don't have time for this hog-sputum—I've a eulogy to write for tomorrow."

And with that, Mr. Piltdown ripped his bristol board Hawk King icon into two large pieces, then four medium ones, and then decreasingly into a flurry of Hawk confetti. "You see? Painless. Done. Because it's meaningless anyway, Miss Brain."

An earsplitting *CRACK* forced our gaze upon Iron Lass. Micro-Aesgard lay in rubble at her feet, her iron hand still in chop-pose before her and *ringing-inging-ing* like a temple gong.

"It is done, Frau Doktor. Unt now, O unexpected cosmic bounty, I'm breassing sanctified air viss ze clean lunks of a mentally liberated purson. Oh, I feel so much freer unt better unt more joyful. Vunderbar. You truly are a miracle vurker, ja. Now can I go?"

"Doc, if it's all the same with you," said Wally, "can I let mine melt? Don't seem right to mush down m'daddy."

"Wally, you won't be 'mushing down' either your father or

your love of him, because your father isn't controlling your life. Only your idealization of him is."

"So can I, then?"

"No, Wally."

Hanging his head, his shoulders fallen, Wally looked like an intensely guilty gigantic child. He pulled up his dress shirt and lowered his trousers an inch, exposing his navel.

There was a blinding flash, and suddenly everyone's hair was drooping from the steam saturating the room. Although visibility was nearly nil through the ice-fog, Wally's icon-father was no more.

I found my next charge in the fog while Wally tucked in his shirt.

"Syndi?"

She pouted. She stamped.

When I insisted, she dropped her arms as if they weighed tons, then started ripping the materials off her mannequin.

I found Kareem in his misted workbay, his back turned to me.

"Khaibtu kher," he whispered.

With a sound like sifting sand, the X-Man's shining black idol fuzzed into black and silver smoke, faded to shadow, and was gone.

I touched Kareem's arm. He jerked away, still averting his face. I softly asked him the meaning of his magic words.

" 'Shadows . . . shadows fall,' " he sniffed, before reaching a palm to his eye.

What will it mean for your life, and your view of yourself, if the glory days never return?

Omnipotent Man: "What's the point anymore?"

Flying Squirrel: "The King would've wanted us to build a New Age."

Iron Lass: "Götterdämmerung is the end of the *gods,* too. We're there."

How will you face knowing that you will never exceed, or even equal, the accomplishments of your predecessors?

X-Man: "We have no choice . . . but to become our own kings."
Power Grrrl: "Who are *they* to be equal to?"

Icomposting:
Enrich Your Mental Soil

ronically, the very people who are icons to millions are often the most icon-worshiping of all. In many cases, such idolization was the impetus for young heroes to challenge death on a daily basis. For hyper-hominids, idolization led to emulation, emulation to overidentification, and overidentification with an elder "superior," paradoxically, to infantilization.

No matter your intentions, when you wrap your superego inside the tunic of your icon, you're not wearing a cape. You're wearing a diaper.

Believing in anyone more than you believe in yourself causes you to suspend your own judgment, which leads to counter-self-actualization, or self-deactivation. And while Power Grrrl's exaltation of herself is certainly the cause (and effect) of many of her problems, that very exaltation frees her from the maleficent manhandling of the Icon Trap.

Most important, no one—and therefore no idol—is perfect. Inevitably you will discover your idol's imperfections. And when your idol falls, its final act will be to crush you.

Iconsciousness:
Time to Take Off Your Diaper

Adulthood means taking care of yourself, not psychic dependence on others or clutching on to unrealistic opinions of our elders. It's time to unchain yourself from your mentor. And while you might think that your idol is made of gold, it's really just made of garbage.

It's time to toss your idol into the composter. It might stink for a while, but at least it's transmuting into something useful . . . and fit to walk on.

But if you don't dispense with your empty idol, in all likelihood you'll be setting yourself up for the very chaos you are about to witness among the F*O*O*J.

PART TWO

MISSING NUMBER ONE

CHAPTER FIVE

LIMITED SERIES

It's Ironic That Funerals Are Sad

Funerals and superheroism are a natural combination. Each involves uniforms, oaths of allegiance, declarations of virtues, and connection to superhuman power under circumstances of high drama frequently performed to theme music.

But despite these abundant affiliations, hyper-hominids are notoriously psychemotionally mismatched with the requirements of funereal deportment. Consider the following cases:

- The pustulent eruption of grief from Tempest and Pyromanny at the laying to rest of Lady Liberty was a popped pimple on the face of the 1945 funeral scene, resulting in no less than a flash flood and an instant inferno (which thankfully cancelled out each other without loss of life—but not before transforming the contents of a nearby grocery market into a giant stew whose lingering aroma kept neighborhood animals in a frenzy for months).

- The 1973 service for Doctor Patho saw the evacuation of forty square city blocks after her sidekick Dea Coli wept tears of pure anthrax, which a sobbing Cumulus Maximus accidentally dispersed into the atmosphere.
- Hyper-hominid funerals have produced freezings, mutations, growth of vestigial organs, virgin births, impotence, chimpotence, shrimpotence, spontaneous macrophagocytosis, and interdimensional neuroflatulence.

As we saw in the previous chapter, because you as a hyper-hominid believe in the myth of your own invulnerability, facing death is even more difficult for you than it is for "mere mortals." Therefore no experience—outside of death itself—is more traumatic (and dramatic) for you than the funeral. And that is because facing funerals means discarding our idols and becoming, for the first time, independent.

And, fundamentally, more alone.

MONDAY, JULY 3, 8:00 A.M.

Independence Day

Despite the grief-stricken plans that the Pathetic Fallacy announced in *The Los Ditkos Sentinel-Spectator,* the weather at the sunrise funeral of Hawk King on Sunhawk Island could have dazzled a pharaoh. The disk of the sun glorified the horizon like a divine disco ball, drizzling gold along the eastern face of the distant Tachyon Tower, while the sky

above us melted from orange to azure like a child's crayons left
on a hot stove.

Media outlets from FOX and ABC to Mutant TV and
CAPES had been camped outside the wall of the Blue Pyramid
complex since the previous night, drinking from the stream of
primary-colored celebrities marching into the grounds since
the dawn.

That day's costumes were the rarely glimpsed dress uniforms
and dress tunics reserved for funerals, replete with gold brocade,
left-breast mission tags, ceremonial wands and scepters, gilded
armor, and formal capes. Traditional bagpipes, taiko drums,
and throat-singers intoned the eschatological atmosphere amid
the silent witness of obelisks, the giant Ka-Sentinels, and the
radiance of the Blue Pyramid. Everything combined to say that
we were truly at the end of an era, the exit of an epoch, the
egress of an age.

Even before the service began, it was already clear that the
gathering was the largest such funeral in history, exceeding
even the final services of the Götterdämmerung. Silver Agers
such as the Monolith, the Evolutionist, and the gladiatrix Dynamiss were assembled, joined by Civil Rights–era stalwarts
such as the Spook and La Cucaracha, and Digital Age up-and-
comers such as the Beaver Brothers, the Cyberpunk, and Bag-
Fulla-Asswhuppin. Even the oldest living F*O*O*Jster had
arrived, the 173-year-old outgoing Director of Operations and
Civil War veteran Colonel Strom Flintlock, floating in his
hover-throne with the regalia of oxygen tanks and IVs like
a modern-day Charlemagne. Only two people were notably
absent—two living founding F*O*O*Jsters, Gil Gamoid and
the N-Kid, imprisoned on Asteroid Zed.

Smaller supergroups such as the Merry Men were there, in-
cluding Dazzle Man, Fabulous Man, Original Fabulous Man,
Simply Fabulous Man, Rainbow Man, and Man Boy. The Bold
Bots 0001 through 0110 were arranged and buffed to gleaming;

the Blue Collars, the Supa Soul Sistas, the League of Angry Blackmen, the Asian Invaders, and the Mohawk-Aztec-Mayan Brotherhood Organization were joined by hundreds of unaffiliated heroes from Alpha Dog to Zed, the Living Phoneme.

Of course, the outpouring of mourning extended beyond the superheroic profession. Government and the international community were represented by President Bill Clinton, UN Secretary-General Kofi Annan, and New Atlantis Comandante Uno Umboot Pinolawi among many others.

Suddenly everyone's quiet reverence was ripped apart by a media tornado at the entrance of two men: Tran Chi Hanh, FKA Chip Monk, flanking his replacement mentor and the head of Human Citizen, the unrelenting watchdog on the hypercommunity, Jack Zenith.

A reporter who'd sneaked in disguised as a fire engine with siren epaulets shoved a microphone into the face of the Flying Squirrel, demanding to know how he felt about Gil Gamoid and the N-Kid being prevented from attending Hawk King's funeral, while Jack Zenith, the Squirrel's sworn enemy, was allowed to walk in without even being jeered.

Mr. Piltdown growled, "It's a disgrace, a travesty," before hissing a canister of Squirrel Spray into the reporter's eyes and nose. The man hit the ground vomiting before being scooped up and tossed outside the wall by the elongated arms of Extraneous Man.

No one had any clue that within minutes, two bombs would be detonated that would rip apart the F*O*O*J as we knew it.

Pavanne for a Dead Prince

Never one for brevity, and id-charged by such highly public moments into grandiosity, Mr. Festus Piltdown began his address by thanking Liberty Lady and Captain Manifest

Destiny, martyrs of the original F*O*O*J, and then spent the next forty-eight minutes citing every conceivable connection between himself and Hawk King.

". . . which is why this city, this state, this country, this planet, yea, even, dare I say, likely this very galaxy, joins me and us this morning in mourning a man-god of such magnitude, might, and magnificence.

"Because this honorable king of hawks embodied all that my gloved hands clutch at the epicenter of my heart: nobility, wisdom, determination, and unflinching defiance in the face of despots, demons, and the depraved defilers of all that is decent, right, and good!"

Mr. Piltdown put his hand over his heart, just to the left of the black-on-bronze squirrel emblem of his dress uniform. Looking up toward the milky moon in the brilliant sky, his eyes glistened.

"And I promise you, sir, my comrade, my liege, my *King*, wherever you are . . . that I will follow you into whatsoe'er battle you so will for me, for now and ever after, that perpetually will I hold fast my shield and hold high my spear, and that I will never, ever slip from this crusade divine whose fire you ignited like the sun in the space of my soul!"

Applause spattered up from many of the younger heroes in the crowd, unaccustomed as their generation was to the etiquette of such events. As Mr. Piltdown left the platform, he stooped to lay his hand on the Egyptian sarcophagus of Hawk King and then straightened up to salute before sitting down in the front row.

I expected to see Kareem scowling, but the X-Man's face was a charcoal portrait of unreadability.

I was less surprised to see the Brotherfly looking as he did, tears leaking from beneath his Fly Goggles. A week earlier I could never have imagined that such an aimless, hyperactive, socially inappropriate, and vain young man could experience loss at such a depth. But from André's explosion in therapy two days before and given his absence until now, he'd begun revealing himself as a more complex person than anyone could have deduced.

When the Greatest Defenders
Are Rendered Defenseless

Throughout the morning's speeches, the anticipation in the crowd thickened like smog on a hot Los Ditkos day, awaiting the words of the man whose name was synonymous with *hero.*

"Afternoon, y'all," said Wally. "Or, I mean, g'mornin. This . . . this was a day . . . wellsir, a day I . . . I ain'never spectid t'see in, well . . . not in my lifetime, anyway."

Wally stood awkwardly at the podium, the eastern sun gilding one side of his face, the reflected sun from the Pyramid blueing the other side of his visage. He tugged at his white collar, straightened his black tie, pulled at his black jacket and white cape, rearranged his black epaulets, hunched his shoulders in his famous manner, while the sole camera crew allowed inside—from Piltdown News Network—sent the image of the world's mightiest fidgetter to an estimated audience of three billion people.

"I never knew anybody like Mr. King. He was powerful smart. Powerful wise. Powerful *power*ful. He recruited me. Taught me how t'use m'powers. Always kept my compass pointin north. An so for me, t'be, t'be *stand*in here in fronta y'all like this, without im. . . ." He looked down to the sarcophagus. "Well—"

He stopped to clear his throat into the microphone, a sound like a walrus yelp, then began clasping his hand and yanking at his fingers as if he could detach them.

All around me, I saw the faces of people expecting to be comforted by Omnipotent Man's wisdom shifting from morose to anxious, anxious to angry, and angry to confused.

"See, times like these, now," said Wally, hunching his shoulders ever more hunchedly, as if he were being transformed into a panda bear, "they tell a man, even when sometimes he in't inclined to be listnin, that suh'm . . . suh'm's . . . *wrong*. The Gooterdimmerang's done been over for years. The villains is all retired, beaten down, locked up, or dead. An here we are . . . I mean, alla us . . . like a big ol slumber party messin around in our finest three-color peejays . . . an meanwhile we jess found out—"

Wally's voice caught in his throat, like a mouse bisected in a trap.

He dehunched his shoulders and took a breath, then let it out shudderingly.

". . . jess found out . . . thet Daddy's dead."

Wally bowed his head to his raised cuff, dabbing his cheeks and eyes. Across from me, heroes such as Atomic Giraffe, Chloro Phyllis, and King's English immediately did the same.

"So . . . well . . . t'be honest, I jess don'know anymore. Who I'm sposta be. What the world thinks is right if fellers like ol Hawk King c'n jest up an die. Maybe th'world should figger its own way outta troubles from now on. Looks safe enough from where I'm sittin."

He took a quick breath, visibly making a decision.

"An so, ffective immediate-like, I am resignin as the world's mightiest man an retirin to private life."

Shock smashed through the crowd like a wrecking ball through a tea party.

"So, uh . . . thank y'all, 'Merica, planet Earth. Nice knowin yuh."

And with that, Omnipotent Man rose like a humanoid zeppelin above the anger and wailing, up, up, and away from Sunhawk Island.

Just before the second bomb exploded.

Sublimating Grief
Doesn't Make It Brief

Brothers and sisters, ladies and gentlemen, friends and . . . enemies," said Kareem after the furor had died enough for him to take to the podium. "I greet you in the ancient manner of the splendor-power-and-triumph of the Forty-Two Chambers: *Dã'f xu, us em maãxeru.*"

Members of the L*A*B and some of the Supa Soul Sistas intoned their response: *"Maa-ten neferu-f."*

"And I also greet you in the name of other great and fallen heroes, such as the Son of Nat Turner, killed by Kyklos the Imperial Grand Dragon in 1991; the Brother from the HOOD, killed in a nightclub in 1992, and the man who was an inspiration to me and all of Stun-Glas, who inspired all of us who joined the L*A*B; Maximus Security"—scattering of applause, *mm-hm!*s and *A-men*s from the same area—"who was killed in Reagan's war against New Atlantis back in 1984." (Grumbling from other areas of the crowd, especially from the coterie around Mr. Piltdown.)

"This morning, I'd like to say a few words about the hero whose life we're here to honor, because just as I and many others are increasingly convinced—yes, that's right, I'm saying it—con*vinced* that we aren't being told the truth about Hawk King's death, I know that practically nobody has been told the truth about Hawk King's life."

Grumbling surged, joined by ejaculations of *Preach, brother!* and *Break it down.* X-Man waited for both grumbling and support to subside, then leaned into the silence to proceed.

"First, I'd like to acknowledge the League of Angry Black-men, who are here in full effect. Every Brother in the League, I'm sure, is taking this as hard as I am. Because after Maximus Security died, it was Hawk King who stepped up, who inspired every last one of us, to be what we are. Protectors. Defenders.

"Everybody here knows the official story. Hawk King was Heru, who those who don't know better call Horus—the avenging son of Lord Usir, the Egyptian savior Osiris. As Hawk King, he intervened seven thousand years ago in the world of men—and women, yes, sorry, Sisters—to wage his ongoing battle on Earth against his evil uncle, Warmaster Set, or out amongst the stars against the cosmic serpent Ãâpep, and to pursue the cosmic mysteries that consumed his incalculable intellect. And when he came back in 1937, he helped save Europe from the Nazis, and later on from threats such as the Specially Relative Einstein Baboons and Cosmicus, Digester of Worlds. He returned to his role in our realm as our greatest thinker. As our greatest teacher. In the ancient sense of the word, as our Master.

"Now, everybody always thought Hawk King was Hawk King only, without any secret identity. But everybody was wrong."

The crowd fluttered and whispered at X-Man's implication of secrets about to be scattered, like a swarm of pigeons squawking in anticipation of ripped-up hoagie buns.

"As a celestial being," said Kareem, "Hawk King was physically powerful. But when he lived among us in his hidden role as a human, he did so in a frail body. Withered. Old. An aged invalid in a motorized wheelchair who in the last few years of his life couldn't even talk. Had to have a voice-synthesizing computer do it for him.

"The man inside Hawk King was a brilliant scientist and professor—an archeologist, a cosmologist. Taught at Robeson College in Langston-Douglas for the last forty years. His name was Dr. Jacob George James 'Jackson' Rogers. He was my mentor.

"And Dr. Jackson Rogers—Hawk King—was a black man."

Gasps and guffaws shot up like spontaneous sprinkler sprays on a golf green, with one man in the front row a geyser.

"How *dare* you!" shouted Mr. Piltdown, standing and aiming his finger at the X-Man as if it were an avenging foil.

"Hawk King wanted big changes," Kareem sped on, "*huge* changes in the F*O*O*J! He gave me all his final papyri—specific directions on how and what to do, to overhaul the F*O*O*J and change the direction our planet's going—"

"Shut your mouth, you reprobate rascal! We are here to honor our greatest hero, not listen to your crack-induced bafflegab—"

"—seeing what the F*O*O*J had become broke his heart, and he had a plan, a plan to completely revolutionize the group! One week from today I will reveal the contents of *The Instructions of Hawk King,* his final papyrus, detailing—"

"—*dare* you sully this holy day with your selfish, delusional election grandstanding and your bizarre negroist fantasies?"

"Don't be accusing *me* of electioneering, Mr. Two-Hour 'I Was Hawk King's Bestest Friend Ever' Eulogizing Cryptofascist, who *owns* the only TV network allowed to shoot in here! And don'be doubting who Hawk King was, Pilly, 'cause I've got proof! Including the fact that Dr. Rogers went missing the day before Hawk King was found dead!"

Mr. Piltdown hustled onto the platform and toward the podium. The PNN cameras moved with him. "Get off there, now! You're done, Edgerton, you hear me?"

Kareem held up his hands, fingers splayed, saying something inaudible while the Flying Squirrel kept rushing toward him. X-Man leaned into the microphone, saying, "What, you gonna throw down right here in the middle of a—"

Mr. Piltdown's left fist slammed into Kareem's belly hard enough to double him over, whereupon his right fist smashed

X-Man's face upward and back. Reeling from the uppercut, Kareem swung blindly, missing Mr. Piltdown's cheek by half a foot, but his second fist connected with the older man's throat. The PNN cameras caught it all.

All around me, men and women were scrambling into action, battle lines gashed by race and/or generation. Members of the L*A*B, the Supa Soul Sistas, the Asian Invaders, MAMBO, and the Merry Men were deep-ending into the melee against F*O*O*Jsters such as the Beaver Brothers, the Newt, the Evolutionist, and independent heroes such as Ivory Giant, Smithing Wesson, and the fifty-three-year-old Kid Kombat, Sr.

Folding chairs and chunks of burning sod ascended and descended like a convention of locusts; Messers Clinton, Annan, and Pinolawi were escorted out under guard through a chorus of swearing, screaming, and pleas for calm, with Jack Zenith leaving under the protection of his civilian-clothed protégé, the former Chip Monk.

Countless heroes waded into the dustup, trying to separate the combatants. Extraneous Man and Cumulus Maximus formed a fog-and-flesh barrier while the sickle-and-hammer-caped Son of Soyuz flew left and right, biting people's bottoms, wagging his little tail furiously and barking at them to stop—

When suddenly the sky collapsed from an embolism.

Raging overhead, blotting out the sun, were what must have been millions of hawks, their screeching choir sounding like the world being buzz-sawed apart, their wings somehow transforming the remainders of the sky into an awful anguished violet saturating the earth and everything else beneath them.

And then three bolts of lighting—amber, ruby, and emerald bolts of dazzling energy—pulverized the stage and the podium into smithereenlets.

All combatants jumped back from whomever they were pummeling or rolled away from whoever was pummeling them, crouching and quivering at the sight of the lightning, which had struck and remained in place. The bolts snapped and twisted and finally congealed into the black-light forms of three titans: a giant with the face of a jackal, another with the face of a flamingo, and a female giant holding what looked like a massive feather.

The Jackal stooped, gently picking up the sarcophagus of Hawk King and cradling it like a baby. The Woman pointed her feather like a lance, panning it across the crowd.

And then the Flamingo took each comrade by the hand, and the triumvirate transmuted themselves back into lightning.

And disappeared.

Peace Is Not Simply the Absence of War

Funerals are emotionally dynamic experiences, and even nonpowered humans may find themselves reacting in ways that frustrate or embarrass themselves and others: excessive sobbing, laughter, panic attacks, and incontinence, among many other overreactions, are common.

But for you in the super-powered community, careening through high-stakes careers and hobbled by overactive ids and the Icon Trap, outbursts and even violence at funerals are practically an occupational hazard.

To get a better understanding of how my sanity-supplicants were faring during this uniquely stressful time, I chose to observe them outside the clinical environment, seeking them out on their own turf where they'd be more able to process and safely/appropriately externalize/verbalize their psychemotional disturbances.

While a few of my patients retired postfunereally to the Fortress of Freedom, most made their way to a well-known eatery in midtown Bird Island, a cramped enclave on Bustle Avenue famous for its head-high smoked meat sandwiches and its heart attack–inducing cheesecake. Just as New York actors roosted at Sardi's, Los Ditkos hyper-hominids congregated at Soup 'n' Heroes, an old-fashioned two-story deli dwarfed by surrounding skyscrapers and owned by brothers Jan and "Stack" Leeby, who still squabbled daily over who invented which soup and which sandwich. And almost as famous as Soup 'n' Heroes' founders was its manager, the eye-patched and affable S. Bruce Pippen.

Sadly, Soup 'n' Heroes was no stranger to funeral receptions, and that day was crowded even more than usual. Its trademarked howling waiters merely whispered above the crowd's murmurs, while the diner's jukebox sat mutely, unplayed. Draped with black cloth monogrammed with golden letters spelling HAWK KING, the deli's mirrors reflected only shadows.

Despite my obvious capelessness, no one questioned my presence as I nudged my way through the overcapacity; I'd treated enough of these men, women, and cyborgs to have been accepted silently into their community.

Regret: the Ghost That Haunts the Living

There were almost as many heroes on the walls as there were between them: framed and autographed black-and-whites from the Golden Age to the Glitter Age, including shots of Gil Gamoid and the N-Kid. Despite complaints from some diners and even a few hyper-hominids, manager Bruce had always refused to take them down. Regardless of Gil's and the N-Kid's poisonous paranoia and murderous, malevolent madness, old-time hero-watchers still adored those two F*O*O*J pioneers from Ur-Prime, the planet orbiting the distant Quasar Q-939.

Among the assembled mourners, only quiet clucking over the brawl remained, mixed with awe over the phantasmagoric apparition of Hawk King's divine relatives. But then that soft conversing was crushed into absolute silence, enough to seem as if it had been the braying of an army of donkeys.

But after all, how could anyone utter a word when the world's mightiest man ambled in after having announced his own self-imposed exile?

Mr. Piltdown could.

"Well, well, well—if it isn't the world's mightiest quitter," he rumbled, not even in a mock-whisper. "To what do we mere mortals owe this anticlimactic farce of an honor?"

Despite his white dress cape with black trim and epaulets, Wally looked like a broken man, his shoulders hunched beyond even their usual enhunchment, like a show pony struggling beneath a morbidly obese rider.

"Jess wannid . . . to . . . I'ont know. Say g'bye t'folks? Properlike. I didn'mean to have all that come out like it did at th'fun'ral."

Mr. Piltdown, perhaps in irony, made a sound very much like the word *harrumph*. "No, of course not. You certainly didn't intend to steal the funeral's spotlight any more than that logos-powered lawn jockey did." (Outside the therapeutic environment, it was clear that whatever inhibitions Mr. Piltdown might have had against unleashing his anticompassionate behavior were negated.) "No, your grandstanding just . . . 'happened,' is that right?"

"What? I didn'—"

"No, of course you *diddin*," sneered Mr. Piltdown. Reaching toward his boot, he removed his Squirrel Screen from its utility sheath. He unfurled it like a scroll, then plucked Wally's framed photo from the wall and hung the screen from the now-free nail. Tabbing concealed buttons on his left long glove, he brought the screen to life and sifted among television channels.

Nearly every image was of Wally at the funeral dais uttering his resignation until finally cleaving skyward. The images were all identical. Evidently PNN had opted to sell the lucrative rights for the footage over maintaining the journalistic honor of an exclusive.

"Look, Festy, I never spected t'have m'speech all over th'TV like that—"

The image on Channel 101 switched to another event: Mr. Piltdown heckling Kareem before storming the platform; Mr. Piltdown racing toward Kareem who was yelling back "what, you gonna throw down right here in the middle of a—"; Flying Squirrel decking X-Man, only to be throat-punched in return before the melee of a thousand capes and tights burst out.

"This is outrageous! How in the hell did—?" said Mr. Piltdown. "Filthy goddamned media whores! There was *another* camera smuggled in there?"

The image then switched to a howling pack of journalists outside the wall of the Blue Pyramid complex.

CBS reporter: With the impending F*O*O*J election and this special relationship you're claiming to have had with, uh, with Hawk King, not to mention the, the "fracas" allegedly begun by the Flying Squirrel during the funeral, do you think either of you will be disciplined by the F*L*A*C, or do you think you're now a shoo-in for the post of Director of Operations?

X-Man (grinning): Well, Sheila, if there's one thing I learned today [gingerly touching his belly], it's that you can't ever know for sure what's gonna happen—

Reporters: (laughter)

CBS reporter: What about this scroll, this papyrus you men-
tioned? What's it about?

X-Man: It was—*The Instructions of Hawk King*—it was Hawk
King's final analysis of what's wrong with the planet and how
to fix it before—

Second reporter: How will you be able to verify its authenticity?

X-Man: Trust me. Everyone'll see. Everyone'll know.

Third reporter: Why are you waiting a week to reveal its contents?

X-Man: The country, the world, needs time to grieve. But as
soon as the grieving's done, like ol' Joe Hill said, "We've got
to organize—"

"Can you *believe* the nerve of that nattering negro nimrod?"
said Mr. Piltdown to no one and everyone. "He's exploiting the
death of our leader to advance his own political career! He's a
goddamned polyp inside the colon of propriety!"

CBS reporter: Following release of this violent amateur video
smuggled out of this morning's funeral, an unscientific CBS
phone-in poll found a majority of callers supporting the
X-Man's Five-Point Plan for F*O*O*J Renewal, favoring the
so-called X Slate of candidates over the Squirrel Slate, and
indicating that if the vote were today, and by a ratio of eight
to one, they would support the X-Man over the Flying Squirrel for the post of Director of Operations—

Stabbing the keypad on his glove and listening to his earbud,
Mr. Piltdown paused a moment before hissing into his wrist:
"Yes, tell him—I don't goddamned *care* if he's meeting with
the affiliates, I own the goddamned network! You tell Finch-
beck to get up footage of those Egyptian goddamned gods

exploding into the funeral—that's the most spectacular apparition ever recorded, should've been leading the news every
five—

"What do you *mean* the footage was blank? All of it? How
can it all be . . .? Fine, then just get up a poll—one of *our* polls—
to answer this CBS swinewash before the beginning of the next
commercial or the presidency of PNN will be open by the end
of it!"

He stilettoed his finger into his hang-up key, then switched
his screen back to PNN.

PNN was showing the same footage—some of it, anyway:
that of Kareem hitting the Flying Squirrel, but not the strike by
Mr. Piltdown which initiated it. Mr. Piltdown clicked through
a dozen other channels; on all the stations owned by Piltdown
Corp, the X-Man was the aggressor.

"See, Festus?" said Wally, his eyes like dead bulbs. "They
done forgot about ol Omnip'tent Man an hour anna half later.
I'm done. Yesterday's man. Y'all were worried bout nuthin."

Mr. Piltdown sneered again, turning his back on ever-more
shoulder-hunched Wally. Behind him was the famous photograph of Omnipotent Man hovering beside Mount F*O*O*J-
more, where the last son of Argon had used his legendary
chisel-vision to carve the giant busts of the F*O*O*J's founders
following victory in the Götterdämmerung. Beneath their
gazes, he'd hewn the phrase ENDURING TRIUMPH.

I called him over and drew his attention to the picture.

"This's been a tough day for you, Wally, hasn't it?"

"Yessir, ma'am-doctor."

"You know, Wally, looking at that famous photograph, reflecting upon all the pain and loss and the sense of *lostness*
that you're feeling now, with your resignation in this age of
peace you helped create . . . I wonder if you can see how the
slogan you carved might be ironic?"

He looked at the photograph, squinted. "Whaddaya mean?"

"Well, *enduring* doesn't only mean 'lasting.' It means 'getting through' or 'surviving despite.' "

He chewed his lip. "I . . . I'ont follow ya, ma'am."

" 'Enduring'—see, it means . . . Okay, that's fine, Wally. Look, where are you going now?"

"Back to An'ar'tica."

"Antarctica? Why Antarctica?"

"I'm retirin . . . so I'm gon retire to my Stronghold of Standing-on-My-Own-Two-Feetitude. T'live out my days. 'Merica don'need me no more."

"Wally, I think you're making a mistake, leaving like this before you've processed all your unresolved issues . . . but all I ask you to do is come see me at least once before you go, okay?" He looked doubtful. "Please, Wally. I'm worried about you."

He breathed in, his chest inflating to its fridgelike volume and grandeur. But he was still looking at the floor.

"Kay, doc. But on'y for you." He tilted his head up, looked me in the eye. "Know why?"

"Tell me."

"Cuz you wannid to hep us. To hep me. I's always sposta be th'one savin evrabody. An th'on'y person other'n you who ever tried savin me . . . was that man we done laid to rest t'day.

"An even with all m'pow'rs, m'dadblasted, planet-shakin, worldifyin *pow'rs*," he said, the corners of his mouth curling down as if he'd sucked up rotten milk, "I cain't bring Hawk King back anymore'n I can grab a coupla fistfuls a yesterday."

He sniffled, touched my arm gently with his massive hand, and then pushed open the door before walking out, out and away.

When Heaven Shrivels,
Whither the Earth?

For Wally, the death of his icon was only at that moment becoming truly real. While nonpowered citizens live daily with the reality of their powerlessness and have no choice but to make their peace with it, for you as a hyper-hominid, facing the fact of your own ultimate powerlessness can be devastating. I asked Wally to come see me to ensure that he, a savior suddenly bereft of his own savior figure, wouldn't plunge perpetually into the jackbooted tentacles of the slavering mouth of the black hole of despair.

Others, however, were legendary for their capacity to slough off the slivery yoke of mourning to don the newly dry-cleaned uniform of self-actualization.

Mr. Piltdown was not one of them. Hampered by his own over-glorification of his mentor and pinned to the mat of political intrigue by his contempt for Kareem, Mr. Piltdown was haranguing anyone who would listen—in this case, Dow-Man, the Downsizer, and Smithing Wesson—with his diatribe about the day's events. I took a seat within hearing distance, signaling S. Bruce Pippen for a piece of Original Leeby's Cosmic Cheesecake.

"—nerve of that knot-muscled blunder-boor to come here, just for the sake of appearances. Watchtower hasn't stepped foot inside this establishment in years. Yes, Soup 'n' Heroes might be cramped, run-down, with passé blue-collar kitsch for cuisine and blue-haired biddies named Madge and Eunice serving low-end coffee, but for those of us who honor *tradition*—"

"I haven't seen you here once in the last year, Squirrel," deadpanned Original Fabulous Man, swiveling around on his counter stool.

"Maybe if you didn't spend all your time here in a men's room stall," said Mr. Piltdown, his cohorts snickering viciously at his riposte, "you would have."

"I still have my membership card, Squirrel. I'm still fully paid up. And I'll remember what you said on ratification day."

"You do that," said Mr. Piltdown. "Assuming you can tell the difference between a voting box and what I believe you people refer to as a 'glory hole.' "

"Right now, Squirrel!" said Original Fabulous Man, standing to his full six and a half feet and shoving his rainbow flag off of his immense biceps.

"Somebawdy here wanna get banned?"

It was S. Bruce Pippen speaking, his non-eye-patched eye alternating glowers with both men. "Cuz I am *itchin* to ban somebawdy! Snappin and fightin in here, on the day a Hawk King's fun'ral, like a coupla dawgs out in the street. Samatta witchu guys?"

"Sorry, Bruce," said Original Fabulous Man. "I'll stop if he stops."

"I've already stopped," said Mr. Piltdown, turning back to his own group while Pippen monitored a moment for compliance before putting my cheesecake on my table. "Can't you do sumthin about these mugs, Doc?"

"I'll do my best, Bruce," I reassured him. He winked, then glared at the would-be combatants before limping back to the kitchen.

"Anyway," said Mr. Piltdown, "Watchtower's a fraud and a liar. Always hinting about his pathetic secret identity as some unnamed intrepid metropolitan reporter—"

"You mean he aint?" asked Smithing Wesson.

"Hardly. He's actually the 'acclaimed' advice columnist of 'Ask Aunt Edna' in *The Blandton Gazette-Dispatch*."

"An advice columnist? You kiddin me? What a sham artist!"

"Indeed. It's one thing to lie to the public, but to us? So what does this 'resignation' mean, anyway? Nothing but a failed publicity stunt."

"From what I heard," said the Downsizer, leaning forward and checking each man's face in turn, "this is for real. I heard Wally's so depressed he's thinking about getting the ol' snip-snip."

"Naw, no way!" said Smithing Wesson.

"Yeah. Depoweration."

"Hah!" sneered Mr. Piltdown. "Well, regardless, he may as well've done so decades ago for all the good he's ever done. Certainly with his . . . mm . . . *problem*—"

"Oh, y'mean," said Smithing Wesson, "with the . . .?" He crushed his fist repeatedly, a mysterious gesture.

"Wait, you mean with the—?" added the Downsizer, flicking his fingers at the side of his eyes with equal mystery.

"I thought those was just rumors," said Smithing Wesson.

"Far from it, gentlemen," said the Squirrel. "And while I hate to give credit to any lunatic utterance of that refugee from the Laboratory of Apoplectic Baboons, we are now in a dire security situation. Much as I'm loath to concede the point, brainpower aside, Wally was our ultimate line of defense. Combine that with Hawk King's intellect, and our planet was safe. But now . . ."

"So whaddaya sayin, Fess?" said Wesson. "You sayin the King really was murdered?"

"If he was, my friend, then I suspect the mastermind behind it will attempt to bury several more hatchets in the livers of our individual brothers . . . before he drives a combine over us all."

"You think it's Warmaster Set? Or," whispered the Downsizer before he gulped, *"Menton?"*

The name, uttered even in a hush, chilled the already quiet room, drawing icy glares.

"I think I'd rather not say," said Festus, "just yet."

"Now wait a second, Squirrel—back up to Wally," said Wesson. "What's with this Wally stuff you guys were hinting about? Are you talking about those rumors a him bein like Fabulous Man and them?"

"No, not specifically," said Mr. Piltdown, "though it wouldn't surprise me. Wally's never been married, never had a girlfriend to anyone's knowledge despite that sham of a high-profile relationship with Ticker-Tape Girl in 1947 and then Princess Astra in the early eighties. The nickname *Impotent Man* didn't get whispered for nothing—"

"Festus!"

Mr. Piltdown looked up into the eyes of the ravenish woman standing in front of him, draped in black. All whispering around the deli died.

"Our King iss *dett,* Festus," said Iron Lass, glaring at him from behind her veil. "Iss zis respect? Unt Vally, however flawt he might be, vuss vun of us. Unt now . . . now our two mightiest are gone . . . unt neizer vun even set goodtbye . . . to me."

A metallic tinkle splintered the silence, a sound like dimes dropped on a tile floor. And for the first time since I'd seen him in Soup 'n' Heroes that day, Festus closed his mouth, his jaw muscles powered by an emotion almost certainly new to him: shame.

Iron Lass strode through the sclerosis of the crowd without pushing, since a path opened before her. Once she was at the dimmed jukebox on the wall, S. Bruce Pippen limped quickly toward her, kneeling to plug in the music player before putting a quarter in it for her.

"Danke schoen," she whispered, touching his shoulder like a queen bestowing a knighthood on a commoner. She pressed keys for her selection, then walked back through the crowd. No one met her gaze except me.

Perhaps that's why she sat with me, her face smeared between outrage and relief at what she no doubt regarded as hubris on my part. It was the first time she'd volunteered to speak with me about anything.

But she didn't speak, not immediately; we sat silently listening as a jukeboxed Patsy Cline twangingly explained the single greatest mistake of her life.

"Ah ha!" whispered Mr. Piltdown over at his table, scanning his Squirrel Screen, which blazed with graphs, numbers, and two images: a swelling face shot of the Flying Squirrel and a diminishing one of the X-Man.

Gloating over his requested poll, Mr. Piltdown watched while the PNN anchor explained that X-Man's racial allegations about Hawk King had driven support for the X-candidacy down to 50 percent. Support for the Squirrel had rocketed up to 25 percent, strongest among white male churchgoing Republican NRA members.

"Mr. Piltdown," I called to him softly, "clearly you're heartened by the PNN poll results. Nevertheless, surely you must be concerned about how the F*L*A*C will respond to your bout of fisticuffs with Kareem at this morning's funeral."

He walked over to our table, stood in front of me like a barricade of squirrelly muscle.

"Are you *threatening* me, Miss Brain?"

"Mr. Piltdown, I'm asking you a legitimate question about your feelings—"

"—because I'll remind you not to exceed your mandate, which is limited to what transpires inside that brain-beautician's salon you call a clinic. You are here, just as you were at this morning's sacred commemoration, solely at the sufferance of the men and women of the F—"

"Mr. Piltdown, the F*L*A*C has given me broad authority to conduct my analysis wherever I choose, and base my report and recommendations on *all* observable behavior. So I repeat my question: How do you think the F*L*A*C will respond to your actions this morning?"

He breathed in, leaned down, spoke to me inches from my face.

"Given the current instability caused by the death of our king and the resignation of our atomic-powered jester," he whispered, "regardless of this farce you call therapy, the F*L*A*C wouldn't dare take action against me right now. Not when the alternative would be to hand over the election and Operations to that racialist rabble-rousing Reichstag-torching Rwandan."

He straightened up, turned around, and returned to his seat while Patsy Cline sung lamentations to the lover who deserted her during a performance of the Tennessee Waltz.

I remember that night
And the Tennessee Waltz

Suddenly I heard more metallic clanging. Shining on the glass tabletop in front of me were droplets of metal, hissing steam and cooling.

Iron ingots.

Hnossi Icegaard dabbed her fingers beneath her veil. If what Jack Zenith wrote in *Unsafe in Any Cape* were still true, no one in history had ever seen Iron Lass cry.

Until that day.

"You're—" I began, when suddenly something crystallized for me. "Those . . . aren't just for Hawk King, are they?"

She stared back at me from behind her veil, motionless, silent.

"It's a lot to take, isn't it, Hnossi? To lose both your mentor and someone else so important to you in the same day?"

She waved her hand in dismissal. "Vy are you so surprised, Doktor? Becoss at a moment of dire crisis, when everyvun's spirits are at stake, a husbandt valks out unt—I mean, a hero, *Vally* valks out unt simply abandons us at our time of greatest neet?"

"That's an interesting slip, Hnossi."

She rolled her eyes. "Ymir's blutt, Frau Eva," she sneered. "Surely you can access better clichés zan Freudian slips."

I stared into her twin amethyst ices, waiting for her to own her admission.

And so we sat like that until she finally got up and walked out, leaving everyone else to their quiet elegy of cheesecake and beer.

What will it mean for your life, and your view of yourself, if the glory days never return?

Iron Lass: "The death of the father is the death of life."

Trauma: the Enemies Within

Of course, Iron Lass was not the only hyper-hominid grappling with the grieving process and ending up in a full nelson, facedown on the rank gym mat of denial upon the dingy floor of despair.

Trauma always reactivates the entire unexamined repository of unprocessed misery in the psychemotional cache, much in the way that the flatulence of a diseased colon is particularly fetid given the abundance of undigested organic material in its crevices.

When you engage the grieving process, you're not sobbing simply for the sadness at hand, but for every sadness you've ever suffered, from dropping your ice cream cone when you were four to the humiliation of vomiting from anxiety at your senior prom to soiling your tunic during a particularly frightening melee with a superfoe.

While I'd been able to observe some of my sanity-supplicants firsthand to assess their postfuneral psychemotional degriefing, I also noticed that the grievers had split along the same lines as those in the funereal battle. Not a single active or former member of the L*A*B (or any other nonwhite crimefighters with the exceptions of Sanford Cowl, HKA the Spook, and Gustav Gorditas, HKA La Cucaracha) had assembled at Soup 'n' Heroes.

After making a few inquiries I took the subway. Leaving behind me the mourning silence of downtown Bird Island, I crossed the Mantlo River over to mainland Los Ditkos and the borough of Langston-Douglas, cheekily known by its residents as "Stun-Glas." From there, the only sign of the upscale Bird Island I'd left was the erect grandeur of the Tachyon Tower in the distance.

Negotiating the borough's crumbling streets, graffiti-scarred buildings, and urine-soaked bus benches, I navigated along a depressing procession of gun stores, pawnshops, nail shops, beauty shops, barbershops, rib shacks, chicken shacks, martial arts schools, and Squirrel Burger franchises, until I eventually found the seedy red, black, and green soul food restaurant called the Dark Star.

Self-Delusion: Grief's Superpowered Sidekick

Entering the dark and dust-choked interior, I beheld a myriad of black men dressed in colorfully elaborate native costumes and fezzes decorated with arcane symbols and icons.

All of them turned to stare at me silently.

The only sound was the blare of a clanging, bass-bursting reggae instrumental with electronic bleeps echoing as if into the depths of space. A man behind the counter glared at me. I found myself momentarily hypnotized by his handlebar mustache and the sculpture of his pectorals and biceps beneath his tight white T-shirt before I noticed him nodding to his right, directing me to sit.

Around the corner sat the X-Man, drinking tea with a smooth-skinned Asian man in a suit—Tran Chi Hanh, FKA Chip Monk and, briefly, as my patient.

Their cups emitted ghostly trails of steam into the dark air. Kareem looked up at me narrowly before rolling his eyes and whispering something to Tran. Both men stood, and Tran excused himself to walk past me with only minuscule acknowledgment before he was out the door.

I asked Kareem if I might sit with him. He grimaced, finally pointing to a chair for me and motioning toward the counterman before sitting himself.

"What're you doing here, Doc?"

"Well, Kareem, in therapy yesterday, weren't you the one who told me I wasn't making accurate observations because I was only seeing all of you in the clinic? That I had to get out of my comfort zone and see you in your natural habitat?"

"I don't think I'd ever've used those words—"

"Regardless of the semantics, I'm here."

"Doesn't this violate confidentiality," he hissed, leaning forward, "you coming here like this? And how'd you know I was here in the first place?"

"A good therapist always knows where to find her patients. And as to confidentiality, these people don't know who I am—"

"Yeah, you're only the most famous tunic-shrink on the planet—"

The man with the handlebar mustache brought me a cup of

coffee. After he departed, I told Kareem how much the man resembled African American CNN anchor Bernard Shaw. Anger flashed across his face before Kareem stashed it behind the barrier of a cold smile.

"That's quite the set of facial reactions, Kareem. Tell me what they mean." He said nothing. "By any chance were you going to tell me that I think all African American men look alike?"

He almost smirked, then ripped the expression into the shreds of a scowl.

"You were, weren't you?" I said. "Except I was right, and you think I'm right, too, don't you?"

"Some people say he looks like the lead singer from Cameo. That's a funk band." He paused, smiled against himself. "I'll give you this, Doc . . . you've got a real pair of meteors, coming here like this. Anyway, could we get to the point, here? What do you—"

"Kareem, I'm worried about you, how you're handling the passing of Hawk King. First your claims that someone conspired to do away with him, then your claims that he was an Afro-American, and then getting into a brawl at the funeral—"

"Number one, I haven't 'claimed' any conspiracy—I'm *investigating* the likelihood. Two, I didn't 'claim' Hawk King was a brother—I asserted what I knew from direct experience. Third, I didn't 'get into' a brawl. I was attacked! What, you think I should've just stood there and let him beat me like I was Rodney King?"

"Well, as I recall, Rodney King *did* fight back—"

"What? How can you—"

"—but that's not the point, Kareem. Surely you have to know how all these things will affect your electoral ambitions with the public, not to mention your membership status, which the F*L*A*C could—"

"The public wants to know, Doc. They're sick and tired of

being lied to, and sick and tired of *being* sick and tired. People want somebody who isn't afraid to speak the truth. And as far as the F*L*A*C, well, just *let* 'em try to throw me out now, after I revealed the truth about Hawk King. People'll be in the kottam streets they try that foolishness now!"

Rather than engage Kareem's delusions of popular support, I gestured to the decor: wicker chairs, a zebra-skin rug, what looked like a Masai shield, and finally a wall of framed pictures. The only face I recognized was that of dietitian Dick Gregory.

"That's Marcus Garvey," said Kareem, picking up on my curiosity. "That's the Mighty Sparrow, Bob Marley, Son of Nat Turner, Paul Robeson, Rakim, Steve Biko, Redd Foxx, Fela, Sun Wosret, Richard Pryor, the Brother from the HOOD, Maximus Security, James Brown . . . and that's Dr. Jackson Rogers—"

"The man you claim was Hawk King."

"I don't *claim* anything. I assert the truth."

"Interesting that there's not a single picture of a woman on the walls. And other than me, no women in here at all."

Kareem appeared startled, as if he'd never thought of that before, and then startled further that he'd let slip his startlement. Finally he shrugged. "There *should* be pictures of strong sisters on the wall. I'll mention that to Brother Larry."

"These other men—they're your old comrades from the League of Angry Blackmen, correct?"

He nodded, pointing them out where they stood or sat in front of murals of pyramids, primitive art, and African idols. "In the long black coat, almost see-through in the shadow, that's the Grand High Exalted, Never Faulted, Rock of Gibralted, Atomic Sucker-Breaker, *the Dark Fantastic*."

"That's his name? All of that?"

"Yeah. We all had long titles in the L*A*B. Part of our mystique."

"So what was yours?"

"The Kinetic Kemetic Magnetic Mystic Majestic."

"Very colorful! And the rest of these gentlemen?"

He scowled, as if he mistook my delight in the L*A*B's poetical (if juvenile) fixation for condescension. But he continued anyway. "In the pyramid hat over there, that's the Pyramidic Gikuyu Mau-Mau Hip-Hop Master Blaster, *Ahmed Q.* Wearing the suit with the badge over his breast pocket, that's the Universal Stimulator and General Overseer, *the Black Lieutenant*. Loves to yell—he was always saying how we'd 'gone too far this time'—kind of our coordinator.

"In the cape, carrying the double-headed axe? That's the Cosmic Soul Controller and Planetary Roller, *Shango*. Guy with the glowing knife is the Hyper-Gravitic Invincible Convincer, *Eldritch Cleaver*. Obviously the brother in the locks is the Political, Poetical, Polemical Dreadnaught, the *Dreadlocker*."

"His hairdo is alive? Like Medusa's snakes?"

"Yeah, but they don't turn you into stone. They're like tentacles. Over there with the ankh-staff, ankh-fez, and the black ankh turtleneck is the Star-Breathing, Hyksos-Crushing, Sucker-MC-Smiting Mystical Militant, *Professor Grim,* HKA *Grimhotep, the Living Ka.* In the bowler hat and the Edwardian coat, that's the Righteous, Tonighteous, Fool-Smackin, Punk-Attackin, Preachifyin and Testifyin Upbraider, *the Player Hater.* And finally, the tiny dude next to him in the suit is the Litigious, Pernicious, Troublemaking, Shit-Shaking *Arnold Drummond,* HKA *Mofo Jones.* Brother clerked with Johnnie Cochran. He was the one who got us our HUD contract to protect Stun-Glas—"

"—before you lost it."

"Before *some*body 'lost' it for us."

"And who 'lost' it for you?"

"It's a Black Thing": RNPN (Racialized Narcissistic Projection Neurosis)

The X-Man snorted. "That *is* the question, isn't it?"

"So you don't think it had anything to do with the L*A*B's antiwhite rhetoric?"

"Being ac*cus*ed," he sneered, "is *not* the same thing as being guilty. But in your line of work, I suppose that's difficult to understand—what with Freud blaming mothers, sexual perversion, and everything else for causing the planet's problems except for the white power system and the people who own it—"

"And you don't regard that as antiwhite rhetoric?"

"Hey, if the hood fits . . ."

"It's exactly that kind of language, Kareem—"

He held up an index finger, yelled toward the counterman. "Brother Larry, can you turn that up?"

I looked behind me at the television that had caught Kareem's eye. According to the news report, now that word of Omnipotent Man's resignation had become widespread, tributes were piling up for him outside the fence of the F*O*O*J's Fortress of Freedom—thousands of bouquets, drawings, cards, and action figures, and tied to the fence, red-white-and-blue ribbons and capelike flags with the letters OM on them.

The images were followed by a shot of dozens of tiny Egyptian statuettes in tiny cardboard boats set adrift by citizens across Eaton's Bay toward Sunhawk Island.

"Disgusting," growled Kareem. "Hawk King's death is world news, right? So why is it when that steroid-popping bozo up and quits for reasons I wouldn't buy on an expense account, suddenly everybody forgets the King and starts celebrating the kot-tam jester?"

"How does that make you feel, Kareem?"

"That the best you can do, Doc? 'How does that make you feel?' Maybe it's time to buy a new CD, y'know?"

"Why are you afraid to discuss your feelings?"

"*Afraid*'s got nothing to do with it. But didja ever consider that maybe what people *think* is more important than what they *feel*?"

"Don't overthink, Kareem—that's where you'll get blocked—"

"What I *think* is that the day I announce that Hawk King was a brother, grieving for him dries up from millions to dozens. But when some brain-canned putt-nuts submits his decades-overdue resignation, he suddenly gets the honors due a genuine hero!"

"So all of this is about race for you? Omnipotent Man has been a celebrated hero for decades, cofounding the F*O*O*J back in the forties—"

"Man's a fraud—even the fascist Squirrel said so. You ever read Zenith's *Unsafe in Any Cape*? If Wally'd been named Kwame, Ali, Juan, or Sanjit, you think the press would've overlooked his Peter Sellers routine all these years and crowned him 'world's greatest hero'?"

"What makes you think the public even accepts your claims about Hawk King's secret identity? Enough that they would actually reject him posthumously?"

"What've I just been saying about the tributes drying up?"

"The resignation of Omnipotent Man *matters* to the public, Kareem, whether you respected him or not. And if you think others believe your racial claims about Hawk King, I'd suggest that's more a matter of projection that observation."

Kareem snorted. "In all his papyri and public statements of the last ten years, Hawk King called the ancient Egyptians 'Brothers on the Nile.' You think that was an accident? You think it was coincidence that after he went into exile in the Blue Pyramid, the only domestic Hawk King sightings were in black neighborhoods? That he—"

"There are also sightings of Elvis, the Gold Glider, and Poe-Bot around the country every year. Surely *those* aren't evidence of anything other than wish-fulfillment and self-delusion?"

"What about breaking exile to destroy Hutu militias in Rwanda after the F*L*A*C refused to intervene? Think that's nothing?"

"If you're right, then why didn't he intervene more often? Overthrow apartheid or something like that?"

"Because Hawk King wasn't simply living out a self-imposed exile in the Blue Pyramid! He was living more and more of his life as Dr. Jackson Rogers, trying to understand the struggles flesh-and-blood human beings have and how we can fix our planet without the 'help' of a bunch of phonified freaks hyped up on their own zap-powers. Dr. Rogers, he was old and sick, even depressed. He spent the last twenty years in a wheelchair, the last three unable to speak without his Data-Vox. I don't think he had the energy to transmute himself back into Hawk King very often anymore—"

"Then even if you're right, doesn't that suggest he *wasn't* murdered? That this 'Dr. Rogers' simply died of natural causes?"

He raised an eyebrow. "Look, I was in touch with Hawk King *reg*ularly, and while he wasn't well, he wasn't dying—"

Suddenly I became aware that Kareem's former gang had been staring at us throughout our discussion and was even then menacing in upon us like a fleet of gaily spotted leopards.

"World's smartest hero," yelled the Black Lieutenant at me, "dies of 'natural causes' but fails to predict his own death? Get the hell out of my office!"

"And the planet's strongest 'hero,'" rumbled Grimhotep, his voice like the unmuffled motor of a dump truck, "up and re-signs only a couple of days later, with no previous indicators?"

"And all of it happening," said the Dark Fantastic, a shadow in voice as well as form, "when the man's F*O*O*J is in a leadership and membership crisis?"

And then another voice rose up barkingly from behind their dark phalanx, amused and vicious at the same time, like that of a disgruntled carny vowing vengeance against every townie on the midway: "Which one a you buncha ignant-ass negroes gots to be blown fore the Fly can get hisself some service round here?"

The Rudolph Syndrome

The wall of men parted down the middle, revealing the Brotherfly standing behind them.

Despite the darkness of the interior, André was still wearing his tinted Fly Goggles. He'd retracted his wings, and instead of his usual tunic and its fly-with-afro emblem, he was sporting a tight black T-shirt glittering with a sparkly disco-font logo announcing him as BABY DADDY.

"Fuck you want, fool?" asked Ahmed Q.

"Why, you gonna take the order?" laughed André. "In that case, give Mista Brotherfly a Cristal-an-cream-soda anna bacon double cheeseburger."

"Figures you'd be eating the devil's hound," growled Ahmed.

"We don't serve alcohol and we don't serve meat round here," said Larry the counterman. "Specially not no pig."

"Swine," said Ahmed. "One third rat, one third cat, and one third dog."

"Must be the new biology," said André. "Never realized y'all could do genetics in thirds. Somebody gots to tell Mendel he screwed the mock pooch, knawm sayn? Kay, then, Mister Chef—gimme a plate of goat roti, with a extra shell."

"Like I said, this establishment," said Larry slowly, "is veg-e-*tar*-ian: tofu cutlets, bean pies, parsnip smoothies. Dig?"

"Brotherfly hafta dig *two* latrines if he ate that shit! *Bzzzt!*"
André howled, shifted his hand left and right, palm up, as if expecting someone to put something pleasing into it. "Can Brotherfly get a *bzzzt*? People, people, can a Brotherfly get a *bzzzt*?"

Even from where I was sitting I could smell André, a reek like apricots and cleaning solvent: *maki*. He must have been chewing it ever since he left the funeral, if not during.

"So Brotherfly's flyin over here," said André, strutting and waving his arms as if they were his wings, "an he's thinking, on this most auspicious day when we is all sposta be layin to rest our greatest hero an teacher, when we sposta be payin homage, keepin it real, pouring out the first spurt of the forty an sendin props to the other side, knawm sayn?—an André's thinking, what would the hyper-righteous Zulucentric QRIB negroes be discussin inside the whitelessness of the soulified Dark Star?

"An what do he find here but all you intellectual ultra-mandigoes speculamatin on y'all's conspiracies! What a surprise! Feelin all important bout y'selves cuz y'all is crackin the case of the millennium, bigger than 'Who shot Crispus Attucks?' Bigger than 'Who killed Uncle Ben and Aunt Jemima?' Bigger than—"

"André, you come here shit-talking us," said Kareem, "when you are so fucked up on *maki* you smell like you've been lying in a bathtub of Lysol and apricot jam, and you think *you're* the one showing respect?"

"So who's behind this grand-ass plot to kill Hawk King, Kreem-pie?"

Before Kareem could speak, Eldritch Cleaver, fingering the edge of his luminescent soul-blade, cut him off. "Kyklos," said Cleaver, "the Imperial Grand Dragon. He killed SONT. If he found out 'bout the King being a brother—"

André's laughter stopped him. "Even if Kyklos did know, that double-amputee gots to be seventy years old, not to mention tough as Cool Whip by now. Brother from the HOOD ripped *both* his cross-burners off, remember?"

"He could be in a conspiracy with Warmaster Set," said the Player Hater. "Or Set could be acting alone."

"Dam*n*ation . . . it could've been Omnipotent Man himself."

The accusation hit like a bird into a bay window.

Everyone turned, waiting for the Dark Fantastic to explain himself.

"Think about it. He's one of the only beings on this planet powerful enough to be able to kill the King. And with his 'problem'—dam*n*ation, if Hawk King tried to intervene—imagine how OM might've reacted. And the resulting guilt . . ." he said to his crowd's knitted eyebrows and nodding heads, "that could explain the sudden resignation—"

André kissed his teeth. "Should I come back when y'all worked out your story together? Maybe *y'all* did it, cuz the man wouldn't eat y'all's bean pies—"

"It's Menton," said the X-Man.

The name ground the butt of the conversation into the floor.

Even a decade after the butchery of the Destroyer was brought to an end by the combined might of the F*O*O*J and its unaffiliated allies, the name *Menton* still poured liquid nitrogen down the slacks of everyone in the hyper-hominid community.

"Unless you aint heard," said André, "Menty done got his ass thrown in the clink way the hell up on Asteroid Zed ten years ago. Kinda hard to kill anybody from up there."

"Really, André? Then why to this day are people still afraid even to say his name? Knowing that he used to be able to use just the *cognition* of somebody vocalizing his name as his portal? You ready to bet your life he's no danger anymore?"

"Y'all is too hilarious, quivering like the babies of Dorothy and the Cowardly Lion. Can't even work up a *bzzzt!* for all y'all scaranoid niggity-knights—"

"Maybe that's cuz pork-suckin house negroes like y'self don't care," said Ahmed Q, "if the Destroyer's huntin down an killin off the brothers."

André snorted extravagantly.

"Snort all you like, Hyksos-muthafucka," said Ahmed. "Brother from the HOOD, Maximus Security, Lou Mumba, SONT . . . now Hawk King. Two weeks ago in Cripton somebody almost took out Pimp Man. Got beat-down to half a fuck from death—"

"Uh, actually . . ." said the Player Hater, "the Pimp Man thing . . . that was me."

Everyone turned on him. Ahmed howled, "You crazy? The man personally paid to build the on'y decent playground in Cripton!"

"What, Players' Paradise over on Smalls Street?" cried Player Hater. "Place's a disgrace—kot-tam 'merry-ho-round' an all that shit! An don't be lookin at me like that—fool was holdin back the race! And Fried Chicken Man better watch *his* ass, too!"

"*Hell* yeah!" said someone.

"All you self-righteous, sanctimonious negroes," sing-songed André, "accusing anybody you don'like, beatin em down, drawin up enemies lists *almost* longer than my dick— y'all a buncha perfectest, holy rollin, no smokin, no drinkin, no fun havin, no dancin, no sexin, impotent, limp-dickin Thirty-Six-Chamber-havin, monkey-ass—"

"This ain'no kot-tam Wu Tang album," snapped Ahmed. " 'Baby Daddy' shirt–wearin ho-ass trickety-split nigga! This shit's fuh real, *Forty-two* Chambers, word, not thirty-six! Somebody call nine-one-one on the *pre*emptive fuh this Dead Fool Walkin fore I sweep out the john with this fool's conk!"

"Y'notice, breddren," said the Dreadlocker, his hair-tentacles writhing like a gang of cobras at the sight of a squadron of mongeese, "how dis ere sellout naa even join hour side durin di FRAcas at di fun'ral? How 'im slink out di BOCK widdout even trowin a single punch in hour MUtual diFENSE?"

"Like a byatch!" said somebody.

"Too busy 'swinging' to do any swinging," said X-Man. His line got the laugh he was looking for. Whatever his flaws, Kareem was a gifted verbal improviser, as he continued to demonstrate: "Telling everybody how he's 'the shit' and never realizing just how right he is. So busy chilling, he's completely frost-bit—a slack, slick, loose-dicked, willingly-no-self-control, no-zipper tan-man who *mak*s out his mind to convince himself he isn't a senseless, thoughtless, shiftless, aimless, brainless, oversized pants–wearing, forty-ounce-loving, penis-fixated, self-underrated supreme cham*peen* of galactic niggativity!"

"And you, *Philip*," said André to Kareem, "the biggest hypocrite of them all! You think I don't know why you 'left' the L*A*B? When's the last time you were welcomed here at the Dark Star, huh? You're what, *half a degree* more welcome than *I* am?"

I was shocked, bearing witness to this transformation of André's vernacular (and even his accent) into something I'd never heard from him before—clipped and pristine, like Bryant Gumbel's.

"But now that you're pimping Hawk King's corpse," André railed on, "the L*A*B's got no choice but to deal with you, am I right? So why don't you tell 'the brothers' here what you've told the doctor about you and the L*A*B and your secret scandals? Or should I tell them myself?"

"I aint told her shit, you kot-tam liar, and these brothers don't doubt that for a second!" yelled Kareem, scanning the faces around him for the doubt I saw wriggling like maggots in the corners of their eyes.

"Don't say another word, Kareem," yipped Mofo Jones from down below, before turning to André. "And *you* say one more word, you bluebottled wigaboo, and I'll sue your slandering ass into the Stone Age!"

X-Man: "Better get the hell outta here while you still can, Super-Tom—"

"Motherfuck all y'all!" yelled André.

And just as the L*A*B moved against him to rip him wing from wing, André zipped out of the way with the proportionate speed and agility of a fly and was out the door, yelling *"Bzzzt! Bzzzt! Bzzzt!"* and howling a manic, deranged sobbing laugh as he flew away.

Understanding RNPN and Rudolphism

Whereas racial discrimination was once a daily fact of American life for many, legislation and social progress have ensured that what was only a dream on the steps of the Lincoln Memorial a few decades ago has become a reality for all.

Yet for many heroes of color, the collective memory of that discrimination—and the habits secreted into our culture around commemorating it—have produced a rabid, slavering Cerberus whose heads are Self-Defeat, Self-Fulfilling Prophecy, and Pervasive Expectation of Exclusion.

If you're an ethnic crimefighter who believes everyone is against you, you may find yourself caught in a manifestation-cycle of overt or passive-aggressive behaviors that drive away your colleagues and potential friends. Constantly supercharged by your own antisocial aggression, you are so aswim in your conviction that "discrimination" exists that you remain convinced that everyone else is wallowing in that "awareness" with you.

The belief that everyone shares your worldview, while imputing your own aggression to others' motives and self-servingly transferring back to yourself the victimhood you impose on them, is a toxic mind-set known as "Racialized Narcissistic Projection Neurosis." This delusory perspective, rather than supervillains, is the leading cause of injury among heroes of color, because the distraction and poor judgment the neurosis engenders lead to irrational choices, needless danger, and fruitless fighting.

Of course, people who *believe* they are victims of exclusion frequently become excessive excluders themselves. This is the "Rudolph Syndrome." The atmosphere I observed inside the Dark Star was clearly one of hostile competition, one-upmanship, alpha-doggery, and vicious pecking-orderism. Outsiders, even "outside insiders" such as the Brotherfly, must be attacked bloodily (in body or in spirit) to satisfy the need for a scapegoat. Without such a sacrifice, the self-defeating community would dissolve into civil war; to "riff" upon an African American proverb, the crabs in the bucket would be forced collectively to jump into a boiling pot.

Examine your behavior patterns closely. Are you constantly crying victim? Do you perceive the world as composed of antagonistic institutions whose "propagandized minions" are wittingly or unwittingly "oppressing" you? Do you ever find yourself using expressions such as "the system," "the Man," "our people," or "further evidence of the vast conspiracy against us/me"? If so, you may be suffering from RNPN. And if you are punishing others with the very exclusion you claim afflicts you, you are probably enforcing the ruthlessness of the Rudolph Syndrome.

To deal with your RNPN, begin by recognizing that you are an individual, not a social abstraction. Your destiny belongs to you, not to history, and whatever successes or failures you experience are of your own making. Take responsibility for your own happiness, rather than claiming telepathy you don't have (unless you are telepathic) or ascribing to others ugly thoughts you can't verify, and aiming endless, nonspecific blame for your mediocrity at the Trilateral Commission, "the media," SKULL, the RAND Corporation, the long-disbanded Treemasons, the MAN, the Black Helicopter Legion, or the perennial favorite of paranoiacs, "Them."

Finally, if you're the victim of a Rudolphian attack, remember that it's neurotic to desire the company of those who loathe you. And remember also the lesson of Rudolph, the legendary luminescent crimson-proboscised reindeer: if you continue developing your own abilities and doing what fulfills you without anxiety over other people's judgment, eventually even those who despise you shall be constrained to honor you. It's a paradox, but only by abolishing your craving for your critics' respect will you ever achieve it.

When a QRIB Is Only a Crib: Victim-Identity as Self-Infantilization

ager to expel me from his former hang-out spot, Kareem "offered" to escort me to a gypsy cab or the subway. I was just as eager to probe his perspectives and self-delusions while he was still in his native environment, so I persuaded Kareem to take me on a walking tour of Langston-Douglas, including the headquarters of the League of Angry Blackmen, the QRIB.

A couple of blocks away from the Dark Star loomed a renovated building that had once been a bank but had taken on an entirely different purpose under an entirely different appearance. This near-legendary edifice was sometimes called "the

underground shrine," despite the fact that the slightly trape-
zoidal fortress stood aboveground and five stories tall: the
Quarters for Revolutionary Intelligence, Blackified. The QRIB.

Its architecture vaguely suggesting the Grand Temple of
Luxor, the QRIB boasted wraparound murals crawling with hi-
erograffiti and giant native black African figures dressed like
Ramses gripping sundry white characters by the hair while
smiting them (including caricatures of select U.S. presidents
and members of the F*O*O*J itself). The display was nothing if
not a vast, three-dimensional incarnation of the Racialized Narcissistic Projection Neurosis which undoubtedly helped cost the
L*A*B its HUD security contract to protect Langston-Douglas.

Kareem paused to look up at the images, and even with his
eyes masked by his black "G-man" sunglasses, his face was
darkened by the unmistakable soot of melancholy. I proceeded
gently, asking him what André meant by saying that Kareem
was hardly more welcome than he was at the Dark Star.

He cut me off, pretending he hadn't heard my question, listing instead a myriad of L*A*B miscellanea such as how an
artist named Emory Douglas helped design the QRIB's murals;
how the QRIB was built on the border with Cripton (the most
dangerous part of Langston-Douglas) as a warning to the gangs
that infest it; how independent crimefighters had been shattered by the death of Maximus Security in 1984 and finally
formed the L*A*B in 1987 to continue his work; how those
same L*A*Bsters only later realized that each of them had
gained his powers from being exposed to the contents of mysterious hieroglyphic-inscribed containers called canopic jars,
which, said Kareem, they "found in obscure corners of places
like libraries and the Special Collections Rooms of the Schombro Museum."

Eventually Kareem and his comrades came to believe that
the jars were the divine gifts of Hawk King.

"He interceded in the affairs of Stun-Glas to raise up among us a generation of heroes," said Kareem, his sentence creaking beneath its own obese grandeur, "so that his people—our people—could save themselves. Now maybe we didn't have the deputized supra-legal exceptionalism of the F*O*O*J, but we gave a damn about Stun-Glas. Protected it. Against gangstas, racist cops, and supervillains alike."

As soon as we resumed walking, Kareem pedantically listed and explained the L*A*B's Forty-Two-Point Platform (subdivided into "What We Want" and "What We Believe"). And once again I tried to steer Kareem toward examining what must be for him an unbearable truth, that his awesome rage against white society, contained in his words and his racially fixated delusion about a supposed secret identity for Hawk King as a black, were contributing to a buildup of his paranoia, and that this paranoia could have only dreadful results for him if he refused to resolve it and integrate true reality into his awareness.

His grin grew colder every second I tried to persuade him; when I asked him why he was smiling, he said mysteriously, as if he hadn't understood a word I'd said, " 'Integrate'? You people think integration's the solution to everything."

"Kareem, I'm talking about *psychemotional* integration—"

"I know what you meant," he sneered. "And I don't expect a damn shrink to understand a kot-tam thing about the real world. The only two *ation*s I'm interested in are *lib*eration and *investi*-gation. There are suspects we can't even find—Warmaster Set, Cosmicus, the Einstein Baboons. But we've got three up in orbit I want some answers from, and I intend to talk to em as soon as I can arrange it."

"You mean Gil Gamoid, the N-Kid, and . . ."

"Yeah," he said, "and Menton."

Kareem didn't even flinch when he said the name. Indeed, he seemed to enjoy uttering those fearsome phonemes.

We were only a block from a subway entrance when Kareem stopped with his arm out, holding me back. He pointed along both sides of the street toward the boarded-up faces of half a dozen businesses, one after the other: Ruby's Ribs, Deacon's Gumbo, Junior's Jerk Palace-an-Ting, Down Home Chicken, 'Bama-Ass Chicken, and Git-Yo-Chicken. Finally he pointed to the far end of the street, and the bustling business enjoyed by the Squirrel Burger franchise enthroned there.

Because of my access to F*O*O*J files, I wasn't surprised that the X-Man would single out the burger business. Indeed, the battle between the young Philip Kareem Edgerton and the Squirrel Burger Corporation had nearly prevented Kareem's membership in the F*O*O*J and had ensured a hatred between Kareem and the ultimate master of Squirrel Burger, a division of Piltdown Edible Products International—Festus Piltdown III.

The Black Quixotes Toward Windmills of Color

In 1986, when he was still operating under the hypernym Mac Rude, Kareem and several other proto-L*A*Bsters went to war with every Squirrel Burger outlet in Langston-Douglas. Arnold Drummond launched dozens of frivolous lawsuits against franchise owners, the Dark Fantastic used his shadow powers to make every restaurant so dark that the kitchens were unusable, and Kareem deployed his rudimentary logogenic ability to manifest 3-D graffiti above Squirrel Burger restaurants declaring such phrases as "Squirrel Burger Is Destroying Black Business."

When that campaign had minimal effect, Kareem changed his slogans to urge ghetto residents to "Stick It to the Squirrel— Buy Black." That campaign's failure prompted Kareem to develop his power further, creating mobile "word swarms" or "tags" that followed Squirrel customers after they left the restaurants. Diners found themselves returning to school, home, and work with 3-D phrases such as "I Licked the Squirrel's Nuts" and "I Drink Nut-Shakes" orbiting their heads. Squirrel Burger business plummeted, and local restaurateurs rejoiced.

But eventually Squirrel Burger Corporation regrouped with its franchise owners by offering free burgers, Squirrelly Fries™, and Chocolate Bushy Tails™. Exhausted and overstretched, Kareem and his comrades couldn't maintain their crusade with its homophobic slogans against the sheer numbers of new Squirrel diners; eventually they surrendered completely.

"Makes me sick," said Kareem, glaring at the giant scowling squirrel mascot as if he were Dante in the Pit staring up at the Beast, and then at the people waddling in and out of the fast-food outlet. "But it takes a nation of millions to keep us fat. And stupid. And that nation's us."

"Don't you think people should have the free choice to eat where they want, Kareem? Do you think you should have the authority to tell everyone what to do, how to eat, what to think? To say nothing of depriving local people of jobs?"

"Shit, Doc, are you kidding? Don't get me started on jobs—minimum wage, no benefits, swing shifts? How about down here in Stun-Glas we get some of that high-tech investment from the dimensional research contracts they do up there in the Tachyon Tower and all the spin-off jobs that go with that? That'd be some jobs!

"Can you even see what's in front of your eyes? Look across the street! Fools weighing three hundred and fifty pounds ordering a mega-meal Kilo-Burger, a gross of Squirrelly Fries™, and a Half-and-Half Shake thickened with Crisco? You see that man right there—that one! Can barely walk, but he's walrusing around like an NBA star in his Adidas sneakers and Nike track pants—I mean, they *must* be knockoffs cuz Nike doesn't make size infinity—but this mad-ass madness of tryin to look athletic when you're lethally stuffing yourself with the filthiest foods on the planet? Diabetes, heart attacks . . . used to be poor people starved to death. Now we overeat to death! Killing us off with low-quality, high-fat food, obesing us all into the grave. And Squirrel Burger isn't just a name, Doc. That shit-shack *serves actual squirrels!*"

"Now, Kareem . . . we both know that's not true."

"Isn't it?"

"You're telling me the FDA has approved the sale of wild rodent meat to the general public?"

"You think the multibillion-dollar Piltdown Group doesn't get whatever it wants, whenever it wants it? FDA's a three-dollar-an-forty-two-cent ho, Doc! Wake up! And the squirrels aren't wild . . . Piltdown's got huge factory farms down in Alabama, Kentucky, Arkansas, everywhere Piltdown pulled out his high-tech manufacturing and moved it to Mexico or New Atlantis. Got all those downsized crackers working his squirrel ranches, billions of squirrels in teeny-tiny cages force-fed ground-up rats that were fed ground-up roaches that were fed ground-up brains of all the mentally retarded prisoners they execute down in Dixieland! You heard of the China Syndrome? A nuclear reactor burning all the way down to China? This is Piltdown's Syndrome—burning us all down to nothing. To *nothing.*"

He threw up his arms, aiming his tirade like a wrecking ball at all the empty buildings.

"But people are deaf, dumb, and blind. You can scream the truth in letters ten miles tall, and still the only thing they'll notice is *nothing.* Whole reason Brother Larry opened the Dark Star was so people'd have suh'm tasty and healthy to eat after Squirrel Burger drove everybody else outta business. You know you can buy and get stoned from a whole bag of *maki* in this neighborhood easier and cheaper than you can buy a kot-tam *salad*? But if it weren't for the L*A*B and a few others, Larry wouldn't even be able to keep his doors open."

Slicing Through the Gordian Knot

Kareem's rant veered wildly, even into how the L*A*B operated its own "social programs to counter white influence," including "Free Breakfast for Shorties," "Africa Medallions for Homies," and "Free Fades, Flat-Tops, and Afro-Picks for Soul Brothers," the last of which was undermined by something Kareem called "the Jheri curl plague," which left what he claimed was "Jheri bags and activator empties lying in the gutters of the MLK Boulevard of dreams deferred."

Suddenly Kareem turned on me with accusation burning in his eyes like lit cigarettes.

"I sure hope you aren't planning to turn this conversation or any of our sessions into one of your books, Doc!"

"Well, Kareem, I'm sure if you actually were to read any of my—"

"I checked out your stuff after we got sentenced to your therapy. All of it. I pity the poor mopes you psychocatalyzed. I read what those suckers said—although I had to read between the lines to deduce what you'd cut out since the way you edited everything was so self-serving—and then I'd read your diagnoses and speculations and bizarre psychosuperstitious slop. *Damn.* The least insightful, most outrageous conclusions, like you couldn't see cute on a puppy—"

"Be that as it may, Kareem—"

"I mean, in the dictionary, next to the definition of 'unreliable narrator,' there's gotta be a picture of your degree. I hate to think how you'd be framing anything I've ever said. You take one little word of what people say, then psychopontificate the hell out of it until you've got readers thinking the afflicted are the afflictors, and the afflictors are the afflicted! No different than the F*O*O*J helping destroy New Atlantis while protecting the people bringing *maki* into our neighborhoods—"

It was time to cut through the Gordian Knot of Kareem's white-persecution complex. "If everything you're saying is true, Kareem, why did you even join the F*O*O*J? Why not remain in Stun-Glas full time, fighting alongside the L*A*B?"

"What, remain ghettoized, cut off from the reach that only the F*O*O*J has, unable to effect change past my own neighborhood, prevented from joining a wider cause? *Then* you'd accuse me of—"

"Did the L*A*B expel you?"

He stopped, his jaw half-open.

He closed it, then opened it again only long enough to say "No." He shook his head. *"No."*

"André said you weren't welcome at the Dark Star. You didn't rebut him. What did he mean?"

"Look!" he yelled. "We are in serious danger, Doc—can you get that through your head? Omnipotent Man's resigned! Hawk King's dead by causes unknown! The F*O*O*J is a kot-tam disaster! This morning, at the funeral, the appearance of the Netjeru—that was a warning to us all, a harbinger that if we don't—"

"The what? Natcheroo?"

"*Netjeru,* Doc! Don't you know anything? The so-called gods who took Hawk King's sarcophagus away! They haven't appeared on Earth in five or six thousand years. You think they don't want his killer caught? What do you think they'll do if we don't avenge his death?"

"Are you saying that these gods are inferior as detectives to you?"

"I'm *saying* that . . . Look, even if they don't, I dunno—whatever—what do you think's gonna happen if we don't bring his killer to justice? Who's next, and how many after that? Because if you can kill someone of Hawk King's power, then nobody's safe! How can you not see that?"

"All right, Kareem."

"All right, what?"

"You believe that Gil Gamoid, the N-Kid, and/or the Destroyer could be behind this alleged crime, correct?"

"Yes, for the ninth time!"

"Then let's go ask them."

"What're you talking about? Thanks to you jailing me in therapy, my investigation's barely started! And a detective doesn't tip his hand to a suspect until he's—"

"I'm worried that you're manifesting a vast, disabling paranoid fantasy, Kareem, and *that's* what's jailing you. I'll go to Asteroid Zed tomorrow to interview them myself, if you won't, so we can rule out Gil Gamoid and the N-Kid as suspects—"

"You do that and you're gonna destroy the element of surprise and blow the one chance I've got with them!"

"So I'm going to Asteroid Zed, Kareem, to speak with your triumvirate of terror myself. Unless you want to go with me to rule them out yourself."

He flailed his arms, yelled at me, explained his case a dozen times, pleaded with me not to go. I wouldn't budge.

Finally, after haranguing me for a full ten minutes, he fell silent, his shoulders drooping while his gaze scoured the weeds creeping out of the cracks in the concrete.

He shook his head, chewed his lip. "When?"

"First Space Elevator up. Five A.M., if memory serves."

"Kot-tam. *Fine.* Five A.M. lift to the kingdom of the damned."

How will you face knowing that you will never exceed, or even equal, the accomplishments of your predecessors?

X-Man: "Catching this superassassin is all the glory I need."

The Face of the Foe
Is a Crystal Ball

Whether I chose to combat the RNPN of the X-Man and his comrades or the end-of-epoch ennui of the mainstream F*O*O*Jsters, an ascent to the orbital penitentiary where the worst supercriminals in history were entombed alive seemed at that moment to be the only path toward mental clarity. The death of Hawk King had so damaged the already fragile psyches of my group that unless they engaged in a mythopoeic descent to an Underworld, my sanity-supplicants would find themselves lost in the sewers of self-delusion until finally drowning in the downspouts of depression.

Perhaps it would take the horror of staring into the face of the villain who had murdered so many heroes—or into the faces of two founding F*O*O*Jsters who went mad and came close to murdering them all—for my team to pull back from the brink of self-destruction and be reborn from the psychotherapeutic womb of self-redemption.

CHAPTER SIX

UP IS DOWN:
THE PATH INSIDE
IS OUTSIDE

TUESDAY, JULY 4, 5:27 A.M.

Mirror, Mirror, Above Them All

To know one's enemy," wrote Iron Lass many years ago in *Toward a Practical Götterdammerung*, "is to know oneself."

To test that theorem, I gathered my patients together to voyage into that inferno of foes, Asteroid Zed. And indeed, since in space as in psychotherapy, there is no true up or down (only centeredness and dissociation), it is just as legitimate to say that we *descended* that morning into orbit, because in a relative universe, any place on our planet can be the bottom of the Earth.

Rising (or falling) inside the StarCase™ Space Elevator at sunrise, we slipped the surly bonds of Earth to dance the skies on laughter-silvered carbon nanotube Herculon™ filaments. I was struck how at that altitude even the titanic Tachyon Tower was shrunken into little more than a pepper shaker and how the gridwork of Los Ditkos's streets was reduced to an Eggo waffle. From there in that high, untrespassed sanctity of near-space, it seemed impossible that down inside the city's golden pockets, the cholesterol-laden butter of dysfunction and the sweetly seductive syrup of neurosis were drowning citizens in a chaos of psychemotional condiments.

But in leaving behind our big blue marble of childhood, we were venturing toward a far more dangerous zone wherein we all were to put out our hands to touch the face of madness.

Everyone in the group was upset about our trip and its timing. Two hours before dawn I illuminated the Psych Signal above my Mount Palomax laboratory to draw forth my team. Each member complained bitterly upon arrival—Iron Lass argued that our mythopoeic journey was not to a psychic Underworld but to a technological overworld; Power Grrrl repeated *ad nauseam* (and with many expletives) that she didn't appreciate being ripped away from a warm and triply occupied bed; the Brotherfly, apparently under the influence of some substance(s), issued a slang-soaked diatribe against mornings in general ("André don't do A.M.s, knawm sayn?"); and the Flying Squirrel railed against using a vehicle from the rival StarCase™ Corporation to achieve orbit when either his Squirrel Shuttle or an Allosaurus-Class rocket from Piltdown Dynamics would have been faster (if more ecocidal).

The team's verbal complaints camouflaged the true animal of their anxiety. Obviously nothing upset each teammate so much as the prospect of facing the sociopathic sadists—including former friends—who had hunted, haunted, and attempted to slaughter them.

But sanity is a demanding master, and it insists we seize our traumatic experiences so as to integrate them into our daily consciousness, where their psychic "charge" can be grounded and thus neutralized.

Of course, one doesn't have to be a therapist to deduce from my patients' repetitive gestures, scowls, and agitated body language that morale inside the Space Elevator had become a quicksand of terror swallowing them whole, especially at the thought of standing in a room to breathe the air exhaled by Menton the Destroyer.

Strapped in next to the only F*O*O*Jster who wasn't complaining, I observed Kareem preparing for his imminent encounter with former F*O*O*J friends and foes. He was *literally* absorbing the text from hundreds of hard-copy pages, holding his right hand over an open book and "scanning." The letters flew off the page in a black stream, only to replant themselves in place. According to his file, he called this process *medu gi-orema,* or "word-eating." He was absorbing one page approximately every ten seconds.

Interrupting his studies, I gently warned Kareem that if he were still intent on interviewing the Destroyer, he'd have to save that villain for last and keep his interrogation as brief as possible to minimize Menton's ability to unleash his mental horror-hold.

"It doesn't take a rocket surgeon to figure that out, Doc," whispered Kareem. He flashed me a smile, but it was a warning. "Howzabout this: You don't tell me how to conduct an investigation, and I won't tell you how to head-shrink?"

I reminded Kareem that he had, in fact, told me numerous times how to "head-shrink."

He smiled brittlely, but I sensed it was less from anger than from anxiety. "I guess I hafta write you a check made out to 'touché'."

He folded up his papers and flicked on a satellite monitor, flipping feeds until he found a Pacifica station running a program called *Democracy Now!* It was the tail end of an archived interview with a black, wheelchair-bound cosmologist and archeologist named Dr. Jackson Rogers, discussing the relevance of ancient Egyptian astronomy to recent telescopic discoveries in the galaxy. He looked like an old, withered version of calypso singer Harry Belafonte or TV's Sherman Hemsley.

The archived segment ended, and the screen then switched to a female anchor and a bespectacled, gap-toothed African American guest in a too-tight suit and a long, untamed, graying Afro.

Host: So what do you think, Professor West? Could Dr. Rogers actually have been a secret identity for Hawk King?

Guest: I think, Amy . . . the *possi-BIL-i-ty* that he could have. *Been.* The incre-di-ble Hawk. *King.* And the-resulting-dichotomous-reactions-of-the-American-people-and-the-backlash-against-Brother-X-Man-raises-some-important *QUES*-tio-o-ons . . . Amy . . . Questions. About the fundamental re-FU-sal of certain segments in our soc-*I*-e-ty . . . to ac-KNOW-ledge . . . the-inherent-capacity-of-African-American-people-living-under-white-supr—

The feed clicked to another channel on its own. When Kareem spied Mr. Piltdown clicking the controls on his glove, an argument erupted that only intensified when X-Man and the Squirrel overheard the panelists on the next news station. Those panelists were discussing how, following the loss of two F*O*O*J icons, X-Man had become the vanguard of the new hero generation, deriving legitimacy from his Hawk King connection and credibility from his forward vision; these same panelists dismissed Festus Piltdown III as "yesterday's man."

At that point Mr. Piltdown shut off the satellite feed completely and launched an invective against affirmative action in general and the L*A*B in particular (citing its lost HUD security contract), finally referring to the L*A*B as the Lout-house of Australopithecene Bastards. Only seconds into Kareem's rebuttal, Iron Lass threatened to depressurize the compartment and kill everyone unless the bickering stopped. Mr. Piltdown dropped his voice, muttering about my alleged breach of professional ethics by "coercing" them into an imminent reunion with their murderous ex-nemeses.

For me, Mr. Piltdown remained a fascinating figure, an omelet of a man, rife with the green onions of bitterness yet held together by the tangy Velveeta of integrity. Despite the Squirrel's cantankerous persona, in the wake of Hawk King's death and Wally's resignation, much of the F*O*O*J had coalesced around Mr. Piltdown's inspirational words (if not presence). In general Mr. Piltdown seemed fearless. Yet he, perhaps more than any of the group, appeared horrified at the prospect of setting foot on the prison planetoid.

Then we all saw it through the window, a few dozen miles away, little more than a black space blotting out stars. As we rotated slowly around it, we beheld its sunlit face, and it seemed to me that the silvery steel facility planted upon the dark rock resembled a Zippo lighter stuck into a soot-encrusted skull.

Asteroid Zed.

Our elevator *thunk*ed into the "top floor" Space Elevator terminal, and we unstrapped ourselves, cycled through the airlock, and floated through the station to board the Space Bee transport over to Asteroid Zed.

As I gazed back, the StarCase™ glinted in the darkness like a child's tin can telephone, taut on its string. If anything were to go wrong, if the Destroyer were still the menace Kareem feared him to be, if he were indeed free of his mental restraints only to have assumed dictatorship over the asylum, then that tin can telephone would have transmitted our final conversation to our lost home and life itself.

The Legacy of Mental Dis-Ease

Asteroid Zed had hardly changed since I first visited it in the early 1980s: a cold, gleaming, white-walled and steel-barred environment, sickly with the stench of boiled cabbage and baking soda. Walking its tiers, one had the impression of being entombed inside a giant refrigerator.

The prison's very existence was a layer cake of irony, iced with the stale frosting of our society's failures. An emblem of the triumph of superheroism in the Götterdämmerung, the Asteroid was originally conceived, designed, and constructed in 1971 by none other than Gil Gamoid and the N-Kid. Fourteen years later, those two champions would find themselves interred in their own creation after the F*O*O*J foiled their conspiracy to blow up the Fortress of Freedom and murder all the heroes inside it. Asteroid Zed, refitted in 1985 by Piltdown Dynamics to prevent an escape by its own designers, would soon house countless villains who'd once fought against Gamoid and the Kid.

Our guide through the tiers of the technological Tartarus was Warden Dr. Rudy Wells. On our way through the various holding units, Warden Wells pointed out to us the many prisoners put there by my own patients. In the Fish & Reptile Villains Unit were Codzilla, Monitor Lizard, Black Mamba, and Nemesaur, all captured by Iron Lass; in the Technovillains Unit were MicroCrip and his Nanogangstas and Robot-Stalin, defeated by the Flying Squirrel, as were incarcerees of the Crime Lord Villains Unit such as Pauli the Living Mafia and Tong Triad and the Iron Eunuch. Biovillains such as the Desiccator, the Devolver, and Zee-Roks the Imitator required special containment, Wells explained, which was why they were kept in Unit X on the other side of the asteroid, so as to minimize contamination of the orbital biocosm.

The only unit no one ever saw, of course, was the one that was invisible to the eye, the Metaphysical Villains Unit. The MVU was an upper-string-dimensional confinement zone at a right angle to our reality, specially designed by Hawk King himself for nemeses such as the Infinity Farmer and his Time Tractor. Technically, we were walking through it at the very moment its existence was being explained to us—but then again, we were always walking through it, and we never were, as it was everywhere and nowhere.

I had no idea if the F*O*O*Jsters were pondering that intersection of physics, philosophy, and psychopathology, but it was clear that walking the ultra-bright corridors between cell rows of such monsters was exacting a psychic toll on my team. Iron Lass projected a gaze even colder than usual, surrounded as she was by the prisoners of the war she'd declared and led; Power Grrrl had resisted turning on the speakers of the most somber bustier I'd ever seen her wear; glowering at every cell door we passed; the Brotherfly flicked his gaze flylike from cell to cell, seemingly scanning everywhere for either spiderwebs or Venus flytraps (understandable, given that Spiderbyte and Venus the Fly-Trap were both incarcerated there), as if he feared he'd be dragged inside a cell and ripped apart, antenna from antenna; X-Man's jaw was clamped tightly enough that I could see his mandibular muscles bulging up along the height of his skull and disappearing into his short hair. His fists were clenched so tightly that his knuckles were rendered beige.

But no one looked more agitated than the Flying Squirrel, who was gunfighter-flexing his fingers beside his utility pouches, as if expecting to unleash any of his numerous high-tech weapons at a moment's notice. Combined with the sweat glistening on his upper lip, he resembled no one so much as Humphrey Bogart's immortal Captain Queeg, quivering with increasing paranoia at every second.

"Should've just put down the lot of them," snapped Mr.

Piltdown, cutting off Warden Wells in midlecture. "Would've, too, if not for the goddamned shyster queers in the ACLU. At any rate, Wells, other than by using the Psionic Impotence Helmets, how're you keeping these hyper-freaks from staging a coup on this hell-rock?"

"Well, Mr. Squirrel, sir," said Wells, anxiously huffing steam onto his spectacles and cleaning them with his tie, "the Psionic Inhibition Helmets do their job on all the most, well, dis*turbed* cases, especially the psychics. But intensive use of psychoceuticals, mostly from Piltdown-Sorus-RX, keeps the bulk of our patients from hurting others. Or themselves."

"Mighty nice racket for Pilty, Wells," said Kareem, just as we entered the Political Villains Unit and glimpsed the Leninoids and the Eiffel Terrorists through the door monitors. "Piltdown-Sorus-RX created half this villain epidemic in the first place when it invented Nouitol—like we *needed* a cross between LSD and thalidomide—"

"Shut your crack-hole, Edgerton, when you don't know the first thing about what you're braying about—"

"Your company made the damn drug that got half these fruit bats addicted, mutated, and mind-smacked in the first place, Fasces—"

"So blame the goddamned FDA, not my company! If that gaggle of pink-eyed Poindexters can't conduct a simple double-blind study—"

"—not when you've got a thousand lawyers and lobbyists hammering them and the kot-tam administration to fast-track all your junk into the veins of old folks and babies—"

"Mr. X-Man," attempted Dr. Wells, "while it's true that Nouitol can induce intense feelings of entitlement, superiority, megalomania, and homicidal rage, it can also push the very limits of mental acuity in otherwise limited intellects—"

"No wonder Festy had it invented. Must be injecting himself twelve times daily—"

"Why, you filthy little—"

Dr. Wells: "To this day, carefully monitored doses of Nouitol are a regular part of our treatment here."

Kareem stopped dead. "You mean you're still injecting people with that poison? Are you insane?"

"I assure you, Mr. X-Man, that all safety protocols—"

A technomusic dancebeat erupted down the corridor, bulging with raunchy samba-salsa-mambo-rumba "samples." I rushed back to find the music blaring from Syndi's bustier woofers and crotch tweeters. Through the door monitor, I could see the target of Power Grrrl's HEAT Ray—she'd turned every member of the aging Mongoose Men, the Anti-Castro Cubanitos Crew who destroyed much of Florida during the Götterdämmerung, into dancing versions of herself. In their cell they were gyrating in sync to her music, all twelve of them howling out her Top 20 hit from the previous year, "La Vida Cola."

"Now Syndi," I said, "we talked about this, and I said no."

"Oh, ga-awd," she whined. *"Fine."*

Released, the Mongoose Men resumed their ordinary appearances, blinking at one another in dawning comprehension before turning away to slump in their respective corners.

Before I could catch up with the group, a frantic Dr. Wells ran back to me, telling me that Mr. Piltdown and Kareem had broken off on their own after insisting that they interrogate their intended targets immediately.

Rushing me along to the Secure Room, Dr. Wells signaled the guards to let me through, and I dashed in past the security checkpoint to see the Squirrel and X-Man staring through the letho-glass at two of the most beloved—and most feared—figures of the twentieth century.

When Heroes Go Bad

ven sans their glorious armor and clad in simple orange jumpsuits with faces ravaged by their decade-long sedation, these two superbeings were unmistakable.

Francis Ford Coppola was often compared to the elder of the two, given his wild beard and eyes, although, to my knowledge, the talented director never reached a height of eight feet, achieved arms like a bodybuilder's thighs, or had a mouthful of teeth like gleaming metal rail spikes. His younger companion, while shorter at a mere six feet, was every bit as remarkable, with his opalescent ram's hooves and horns, his golden body-fur like the mane of a California model, and his smell pungent enough that even through the letho-glass I felt as if I were bathing in coconut milk.

Heroes and villains in the same bodies.

Gil Gamoid and the N-Kid.

Of course, there were obvious changes. The N-Kid no longer carried his heralded Grail Pail, and both ex-champions were fitted with specially designed Psionic Impotence Helmets to accommodate horns or oversized head. Their psionic restraints looked like football helmets made of black glass, detailed with silicon circuits and frizzed out with flickering, brain-draining psiber-optic filaments.

With nothing on their side of the glass to sit on but the floor of the featureless white cube, they stood, their faces rigid with faltering self-control.

Mr. Piltdown stepped forward, opening his hands in anxious supplication.

"If there's anything you need, Gil, Kid, just name it," he said quickly. "If it were up to me you'd be at the Squirrel Tree being tended to by my personal physicians, not up here in this ghastly—"

"Get out get out get out GET OUT GET OUT *GET OUT*—" screamed the N-Kid, leaping from his seat and hurling himself against the glass, kicking his hooves against the barrier, while at every contact the glass seared his fur with awful purple arc light.

Dr. Wells yelled, "This isn't going to work, Mr. Piltdown, sir! I think we should leave—"

"NO, HUMAN," intoned Gil Gamoid, his voice like it was in his glory days, a love child of tuba and gong.

Even the N-Kid stopped long enough for us to focus. Gil said, "DR. WELLS. GO. FESTUS. GO. OTHERS, STAY."

Dr. Wells gestured toward the door as would a maître d', but Mr. Piltdown refused to look at him, glaring instead at his former teammates. Finally, he said, "I just want you both to know . . . that I forgive you. Both of you. We're even."

The N-Kid emitted a horrible goatlike *b-a-a-a,* a *b-a-a-a* of rage, a *b-a-a-a* of vengeance. Mr. Piltdown backed out of the room so slowly as to be almost comical, but the mood was nothing short of tragic. Dr. Wells sealed the cubic chamber on his own way out.

I leaned toward Kareem, whispering that he should beware; while he might have gained personal satisfaction by seeing the Flying Squirrel ejected, he needed to remember that the two converts to sociopathy before him were master manipulators. Ejecting their greatest defender, the man who had paid their multimillion-dollar legal fees and refused to denounce them for conspiring to kill him and blow up the Fortress of Freedom, seemed calculated not only to wound Mr. Piltdown, but to create the illusion of alliance between them and Kareem.

To my surprise, Kareem actually whispered back, "Good call, Doc. Thanks."

"Why you here?" jabbered the N-Kid. "What you want?"

Kareem sat in one of the two chairs. "Information."

"About what, X-Man-man?"

An eyebrow from Kareem. "So you know my name?"

"Of course know your name. Who you think you dealing with? Celebrity nitwit? President of country? No. You X-Man-man, *for*merly of League of Angry Blackmen-men, *cur*rently seeking information."

"Okay. You're obviously as insightful and intelligent as your reputation suggests," said Kareem, sliding into the trick-bag of the interrogator. "So why don't you tell me . . . why *am* I here?"

The N-Kid *b-a-a-a*ed a chuckle, horribly. "Gil, him try flatter me. Think that get him information."

Gil Gamoid narrowed his eyes at his smaller companion. "TELL HIM ANYWAY," rumbled the voice that roared inside my skull as if it were a dragon chick hatched and trapped there, booming like a sledgehammer slamming into girders. "WITH-OUT WASTING TIME."

"You want know," said the N-Kid, wincing from the rebuke, *"how Hawk King die."*

Kareem leaned back, both eyebrows creeping up before he returned them to default position. "Well then?"

"DENIED RIGHT TO ATTEND FUNERAL," gonged Gil. "HUMILIATING. EMBITTERING."

"That wasn't my call," said Kareem. "But you—you *wanted* to be there? Despite your two-man conspiracy to murder Hawk King and the rest of the F*O*O*J in 1985? Why? So you could finish what you started?"

"EARTH YEAR 1985, UR-PRIME YEAR BILLION-AND-SEVENTEEN, WHAT ALL MEAN? CROSS ALL THAT SPACE-TIME TO CAUSE HURT? WHY? TOO CREDULOUS, X-MAN."

"So why'd you want to come to the funeral?"

"PAY RESPECTS," said Gil Gamoid. "AND FINISH WHAT STARTED, YES."

Grasping at Straw Men

So you're admitting—"

"Ad*mit*ting nothing, X-Man-man! Separate issue! Never want hurt Hawk King. Never! Wouldn't!"

Kareem leaned forward. "So you're saying . . . you had a different target? You weren't trying to kill Hawk King either in 1985 or last week?"

Silence.

"Then who—"

"Enemy among you . . . not what seems."

"Who? How? A shape-shifter? Mind control?"

Silence.

Kareem stared at the two prisoners, trying to out-wait them.

A minute clambered past, like an ant across a salt heap.

Then a second minute.

And a third.

The glitter in the eyes of the two aliens had disappeared; their faces were calm enough to appear waxen.

Finally Kareem leaned toward me, whispering, "I thought they were refusing to talk, Doc, but . . . is it just me, or are they actually zoned out?"

"I think you could be right, Kareem."

"Their speech, their grammar, the difficulty with pronouns— they haven't talked like that since they first came to Earth. Is it the drugs? The P-Imp hats? Both?"

"Both, I suspect. Their charts indicate substantial decline in language and social skills since incarceration here ten years ago . . . but that could be part of a long-term deception, Kareem. Be careful not to—"

GONG! GONG! PING!

The sound was like someone hammering the pipes of a cathedral organ, but it was Gil. Having broken free of his momentary catatonia, he'd begun flicking his metallic fingernails against the iridescent horns of the N-Kid. One horn maintained its basso drone, while Gil flicked the other one into trilling treble.

> WHERE'ER BLASPHEMING LIARS RAIL
> TO SMOTHER TRUTH BENEATH LIE'S VEIL . . .

chanted Gil Gamoid, the crispness of his language once again what it was in his prime:

> . . . LET INNOCENTS REFUSE THEIR TALE
> FOR JUSTICE MUST ALWAYS PREVAIL!
>
> UNFURL THE SAIL!
> SEEK OUT THE GRAIL
> SO GLORIOUS HOPE
> MIGHT NEVER FAIL!
>
> FOR EVERY BREATH THAT WE INHALE
> LET EVERY VILLAIN E'ER BEWAIL
> THE POWERS STRONG OF HEROES FRAIL
> WHO DRINK THE MILK FROM N-KID'S PAIL!

The gong-and-chiming ended, but hung in the air, like a cruel sentiment.

Once upon a time, millions of cape fans and cape card–collecting schoolchildren knew that oath by heart as well as Gil Gamoid did. Upon reciting that creed, the uncanny N-Kid would be transformed into a Q-939 creature resembling an Earth goat, complete with teats protruding from the apertures of his goat armor. Continuing his incantation, Gil would kneel, and taking the N-Kid's Grail Pail, "milk" his companion, the rhythmic motion resounding like an underwater didgeridoo.

Thus was produced the awesome ultraviolet Q-ichor that, drunk, would grant the two titans twenty-four hours' worth of their cosmic Q-powers or, refined into Q-cheese, a week's worth.

But for ten years both the Grail Pail and the star-emblem armor of the duo had been locked far away from Asteroid Zed inside the armory of the Fortress of Freedom, while prison authorities daily injected N-Kid with lacto-suppressants. And despite Gil Gamoid's invocation of his pledge, the N-Kid stood in front of us untransformed, a humanoid goat-man with a perpetual young child's/old man's face, gouged by the aching tragedy of a life consigned to nothing but the long, long wait for death.

"Milk-milk's *gone,*" whimpered the N-Kid. "No more cheese for me."

"AND POOR GIL'S COLD," rumbled the elder. "ISHTAR CRIES FOR US ALL."

"N-Kid, you said," Kareem tried again, "that there's an enemy among us. Who is it?"

"So far from home, X-Man-man. Understand? Been gone so long, been gone so long, been gone so long—"

"SO LONG," echoed Gil.

"Fabled city of Uruqanthl, capital of Ur-Prime. Old Gil and me . . . children there. Ancient here. Everything small here. Small planet, small distance to sun. Ur-Prime orbits Quasar Qanthl from one hundred thousand light-years away. Even at that distance, radiation would burn humans into slices of toast—"

"N-Kid, please, I'm asking you to focus. You said you'd never want to hurt Hawk King. So help me find out who did."

"How can us help inside here? *You* the detective, out there."

"Your Q-perception—they say it's strong enough for you to see into the future, or the past . . ."

"Hat-hat hate perceiving," said the N-Kid, pointing toward his P-I Helmet, holding his fingers at a cartoonishly far distance that suggested he were feeding piranha. "No Q-ceiving in, what, eight years, Gil?"

"TEN. TEN YEARS."

"Even so, maybe . . . Look, have you observed anything else? Anything here out of the ordinary? Other inmates acting unusually?"

The N-Kid and Gil Gamoid laughed awfully, like grave robbers joking about bloated corpses in suggestive positions.

"Okay . . . I mean unusually for *here.* Anyone been asking you about your visions, like if they relate to Hawk King? Anyone asking questions, asking you about Hawk King's defenses, or his weaknesses, or the defenses of the Blue Pyramid?"

"Asking questions, X-Man-man? Years and years and years and years of questions-questions-questions—"

"POOR GIL'S COLD . . ."

"—and filling Gil and me with druggies, can't-thinkies, P-I-shitties . . . Done something to old Gil, so he can hardly talky-thinky. But never forget truth, X-Man-man. *Never.*"

"Which is what?"

"Bad moons rising—"

"TROUBLE ON THE WAY—"

"—serpent's egg a-hatching, dragon's unfurling, talons scraping, knives sharpening, bloody tide rising, leviathan rising from the deep-deeps, slithering and slouching forth, hungry-hungry-hungry—"

"Who, N-Kid? Who is it?"

"Secret! Mystery! Twilight of the century! Midnight of the millennium! Sky rains, stars darken! Butchering of the prophets! Burning of the scriptures—"

"KILL THE KING—"

"—and disappear, watchers with slaughtering knives and fingers cruel, into night, to butcher children with parents' own blades—"

"AND THE KING FALLS, NEVER AGAIN TO GLIMPSE

THE MOON, AND DOES NOT FLY LIKE A BIRD, NOR ALIGHT
LIKE A BEETLE—"

"Gil, N-Kid, help me out here! Who did or who's *gonna do*
what you're saying? Who killed Hawk King?"

"Mystery! Mystery wrapped inside enigma, wrapped inside
tortilla, wrapped inside light, fluffy nan bread, wrapped inside
flaky phyllo pastry!"

"Was it Menton?"

Instantly, Gil and the N-Kid ceased their ranting. Kareem
had asked the ultimate question, played his highest face card.
Whether or not Hawk King's death was from natural causes,
this question revealed Kareem's yearning for a pat and simple
answer. As an interrogator, he was now at his moment of greatest vulnerability to a mad prisoner's manipulation.

"Hard to say," leered the N-Kid, cocking his head. Then,
slowly, he said, "Who's . . . Menton?"

Kareem's lips parted, then nearly closed.

"Kot-tam," he mumbled. "We're done here."

"No! No-no-*no! Listen,* X-Man-man!" said the N-Kid, kicking the letho-glass with his hooves, ignoring the arc shocks.
"Who's Menton? Who's Menton? Understand?"

"FOOLED, X-MAN? FOOLED TO DEATH? DEATH TO
FOOLS? WHOSE? A PLAN, A PROSPECT, A PROJECT—FOR
A NEW HEROIC CENTURY OF DEATH DESCENDS, LIKE THE
BULL OF HEAVEN UPON THE WORLD, TRAMPLING TOW-
ERS LIKE GRASS, CRUSHING SKULLS BENEATH ITS
HOOVES LIKE GRAPES—"

"Listen, X-Manny-man! Listen!" Kick, arc shock, kick, arc
shock. " 'Whose?' Understand? *'Whose?'* "

Kareem shook his head and pushed himself out of his chair
while the electric shocks strobed the room into blinding white-
ness. "C'mon, Doc!"

"WHOSE, X-MAN!" Gil Gamoid plastered his massive palms
against the glass, arc-shocking his body into a giant humanoid

fireworks display, his rail-spike teeth turned into a panpipe of awful electrical music. "WHOSE MENTON? WHOSE X-MAN? WHOSE MENTON? *WHOSE X-MAN? WHOSE*—"

To Face the Devil Himself

Exiting, we found Iron Lass waiting by herself down the corridor, agitatedly stroking her cheek, ear, and neck with an index finger. An insignificant gesture for anyone else, the fidgeting was practically a panic attack for her.

I caught her eyes, but only for a moment before they flickered away. There was dread in the black of her pupils but far more guilt in the whites of her scleras. She'd always been close to the two heroes of Ur-Prime; by some accounts, she'd never forgiven herself for her role in their incarceration.

When I asked Hnossi where all the other F*O*O*Jsters had gone, she said that the Flying Squirrel had ventured into the biocontainment Unit X to interrogate the Devolver, who'd once attempted to devolve Hawk King into a tuna. André and Syndi, on the other hand, had retired to the staff commissary.

With Dr. Wells's guidance, Kareem, Hnossi, and I proceeded with growing trepidation to Unit Z, what was sometimes called the M-Wing. Past numerous security checkpoints, EEG/EPG monitoring stations and ever more obvious and numerous psi-dampeners, we descended to the cell-within-a-cell-within-a-cell wherein dwelt the Destroyer.

Passing through multiple metallic bank vault portals and rumbling scanners, beyond anxious armed guards, we arrived at the penultimate chamber. Dr. Wells reviewed with the three of us the psychic safety protocols he'd outlined when I contacted him the previous day, techniques to use in an emergency to stop Menton from terror-shackling our minds. Wells made us sign our final waivers, indicating next of kin and checking off the DNR boxes.

I reminded Kareem that if he wanted to turn back, there was nothing stopping him.

His glare, a costume of bravado and contempt, couldn't disguise his fear.

"We're ready," said Dr. Wells into the wall comm. "Release Unit Z Door 1, code delta-epsilon-alpha-theta."

Instantly, brutal blue light screamed into our vestibule through the retracting iris door until blue enveloped us, until blue was thick on our tongues like the taste of blood, until blue clogged our nostrils like the stink of gasoline.

We stepped through the circular doorway.

The prisoner was shackled into a massive P-I chair, wires and cathodes and tentacles sucking every psion of phagopsychotic energy from his body. His head was crowned with a specially designed P-I Helmet, its diodes drilled directly into his brain. Despite the chair's imprisoning purpose, I couldn't help but notice how much its technological grandeur had turned it into a throne, how much the modified helmet resembled a crown of silvery spikes, the tip of each twinkling like an electric ruby. And so as I looked at him burning in the center of the chamber, an ultraviolet star at the center of an ultrablue nebula, I was forced to remember Milton's description of the Fallen One who disdained service in heaven for rule in hell.

I'd studied the manifold clinical and mental techniques of this "man" once known as Dr. Napoleon Orator, corresponded with him, even published articles and books about him. But this was the first time I'd ever stood in the presence of the villain who'd murdered ten thousand people in a single, awful day in Las Vegas in 1983: Menton the Destroyer.

My bones felt like eggshells. And I was cold.

"Welcome, Iron Lass," stage-whispered the Destroyer.

The Valkyrie said nothing in reply.

"It's been a long, long time," he continued. "Especially for me. But of course, I have you to thank for my stay here. And I've been . . . longing . . . to express my gratitude."

Beside me, Hnossi stiffened, swallowed.

"And at last we meet, Doctor Brain," he said. "I've enjoyed our epistolary conversation over the years, some of which informed my article on therapeutic addiction for the *Journal of Clinical Psychiatry*."

"Yes, Doctor. Dr. Wells showed it to me. Quite impressive."

"And you," he said, his lightbulb eyes flicking onto Kareem. "You must be the uncanny X-Man."

"That's right," said Kareem.

He clearly intended defiance in his voice, but the words stumbled and tripped their way out of his mouth, rendering them almost inaudible.

"So . . . you've ascended to my realm. Supplicants seeking my counsel, obviously."

"Ve don't vant your 'counsel,' Destroyer," hissed Iron Lass. "You are not in charche here. *Ve are*."

The man formerly known as Dr. Orator emitted a sound that was probably supposed to be a chuckle.

It drilled into my skull like a mosquito piercing my eardrum.

Standing for lack of chairs, Hnossi and I watched while Kareem began his interrogation. Painstakingly he waded through Menton's ominous sarcasm and the events of his criminal career, both the matters of public record and the details sealed in F*O*O*J files.

But Kareem's self-proclaimed status as the world's *new* greatest detective soon revealed itself as self-delusion. Throughout his ping-pong evocation of Menton's life, he mixed up numerous facts, from the number of patients Dr. Orator "treated" at his clinic during the first known year of his criminality to the number of days he subjected Princess Astra and the Supersonic Snail to the unspeakable horrors of his *phagopsychosis.*

Yet for reasons surely unfathomable to any human mind, the Destroyer humored Kareem, allowing him to disgorge a steaming puddle of inaccuracies that caused even me a profound sympathetic frustration. Whatever evils Menton had committed, surely the very diabolical brilliance of his villainy merited an investigator's astute attention, rather than the dithering dilettantism of Kareem's detection.

"Kareem," sighed Iron Lass at last, "vhere are you goingk viss ziss?"

He flashed angry eyes at her, his entire body tensing visibly, and immediately resumed his inquiry.

"So lemme get this straight, Destroyer—you're saying that the only thing that kept you from mind-chewing the entire F*O*O*J in 1983 was the Flying Squirrel's Hypothalamic Scrambler?"

"Yes, yes, yes," muttered Dr. Orator, audibly irritated at last. "Why are you wasting my time with such inane queries, you cretinous—"

And then the X-Man clutched his head, releasing a burbling cry and collapsing, as if he'd been struck in the teeth with an ax.

Running Away from Answers

Menton!" yelled Iron Lass, her hands instantaneously clutching her eldritch black and white blades. *"In ze name of ze late Princess Astra, I commit you to ze grafe you deservedt twelve years ago—"*

"NO!" screamed X-Man.

Struggling to get up, he barked into his wrist comm, "All F*O*O*Jsters: emergency evacuate! Repeat: emergency evacuate!"

"Vunce I strike down ziss Loki-bastardt, Kareem, z'emer-chency vill be over—"

"There's no time—Asteroid Zed's about to be—"

Suddenly I collided with the bulkhead. Everything was sideways, then upside down, and sound exploded in my head like a locomotive's engine, wheels, and whistle screeching all at once. Even Menton howled, his lightbulb eyes blazing blue horror. Kareem reached up, yanked on the upside-down door-release without effect.

Iron Lass sliced through the foot-thick steel of the iris door as if it were made of aluminum foil.

"Kareem—get Doktor Brain to safety!"

Kareem grabbed me, helping me up and through the ravaged doorway. Iron Lass howled, "Miscreant!" and everything around me burned into agonizing blue supremacy while Kareem pulled me along the up-ended corridor.

And then the angle of gravity shifted again and we plummeted.

"Pillow!" yelled Kareem, falling, and just before the impact could grind our bones to pebbles, we slammed into the soft embrace of a ten-foot-thick black cushion.

While sirens squealed and flashed, Kareem yanked me along behind him. Guards and technicians were yelling and dashing all around us along the ceilings-turned-floors while prisoners screamed from their inverted cells. Kareem was pouring out smoke, but before I could ask him if he were on fire, I saw a dark cloud spilling from his mouth like a legion of black-flies in a breeze. Muttering over and over to himself, Kareem suddenly stopped and yelled into his wrist comm, "F*O*O*J squad! Come in! What's happening to the Asteroid?"

"Kareem!" crackled Syndi's voice. "Thank God it's you! Are you all right?"

"I'm all right, Syndi! You okay?"

"Yes, I think so—"

"What's happening?"

"They're telling me the Asteroid's been, like, hit or attacked or something! They're trying to evacuate, but—oh God, no!"

"What?"

"The Space Elevator's been destroyed, Kareem!" she said. "We're trapped up here!"

"*All F*O*O*J units!*" yelled the comm voice of the Flying Squirrel. "Converge on . . . on the Crystal Module, forthwith!"

"Squirrel, what's going—"

"I said 'forthwith,' you missionary-boiling grunter! *Forthwith!*"

Kareem resumed his muttered whisperings while pulling me behind him, and I finally heard what he had been saying. "*Find! Find! Find!*" he chanted, and for the first time I saw what the smoke was composed of: tiny logoids, none larger than a snowflake, and each one must certainly have read *find.*

The cloud dispersed itself into the walls, floor, and ceiling, while the explosions grew louder by the second.

X-Man scrambled up the tiers of a shelf bolted into the wall until he came eye-to-screen with an upside-down display. After punching keys, he jumped down and yelled, "Follow me!"

We raced toward the Crystal Module through the madness of evacuating personnel, sirens, flashing lights, and the overlapping overhead voices announcing the double-doom of Asteroid Zed:

> *Facility breach on tiers ten,—Lockdown breach! The prisoners—nine, eight, seven! Rupture—are escaping! Lockdown breach!—and vacuum protocols! The prisoners are escaping!*

Staff and prisoners trampled one another in the strobe-lit race for life-pods, while screaming and the stench of charcoaled meat meant that inmates had begun exacting vengeance from their guards.

My heart hammered kettledrums in my ears, but Kareem didn't even slow down, yanking me into the stairwell and down to the sixth story—the last unbreached tier of the tower—where we scrambled into the spherical observatory called the Crystal Module. Iron Lass ran in behind us. André and Syndi had already donned void suits, and through her helmet Syndi beamed at my arrival while looking at Kareem.

And then Mr. Piltdown burst in, pointing what looked like a personal cannon right at us, and yelled "Close your eyes!"

We heard an explosion.

Kareem, Hnossi, and I were knocked over and bubbled inside a canvassy-aluminum sack hiss-filling with air and choking with the reek of gunpowder. Through the bubble's porthole I saw Mr. Piltdown press a button on his belt, and then the Crystal Module's outer wall disintegrated into flaming shards before belching out into space.

We were all sucked out into the void like Pinocchio into the belly of Monstro the whale.

Escape pods piloted by surviving staff fell into the darkness all around us, like jellyfish fleeing the moonlight at the roof of the ocean . . .

And then I saw it above us: a Squirrel Shuttle descending upon us, its robotic bushy tail scooping us up into its underbelly.

As soon as the airlock pressurized, Iron Lass ripped open our emergency bubble. Through the window and across the chasm of the vacuum, we witnessed the prison asteroid convulsing, sprouting tumors of blue and purple fire before finally cracking and spilling rubble and debris and wriggling bodies into space.

"So do you *f*inally see what I was talking about?" yelled Kareem at his fellow F*O*O*Jsters. "You think I don't know what you were saying about me? And now somebody blew up the whole kot-tam asteroid! Why? To stop my investigation, or wipe us all out, or both!

"Any of you freaks wanna call me paranoid *now*?"

Paranoia: When the Underworld Is So Dark You Can't See Yourself in the Mirror

Paranoia is, ironically, a defense mechanism. Learning to deal with pain, disasters, and the loss of loved ones means accepting that we can control neither life nor death. Because they control us.

The self-delusion that mysterious forces and persons unknown are conspiring against us is, surprisingly, a *comforting* belief, because it means we're significant enough in this anarchic world to warrant someone's enmity. That delusion saves us from the far more difficult to accept reality: that we're not that important to anyone. That the universe just isn't "into" us.

Paranoia is the emotive-psychestructure's response to feeling ignored, unloved, or forgotten in an existence filled with random acts of destructive indifference emphasizing the inherent futility of life and struggle. If you're ever to achieve serenity, ultimately you must accept that in such a vast cosmos, you simply don't matter very much.

The F*O*O*Jsters' journey to the archetypal Underworld, and the chance to employ their enemies' faces as crystal balls to their own future, should have been enough to show all my patients how they could end up, unless they renounced their failed vision and bankrupt misconceptions about the meaning of their "heroism." At the moment of our return to Earth, it still was not clear whether any of them had learned their lesson—and in the case of Kareem, it *was* clear that his condition was actually deteriorating.

So unless you too want to devolve emotionally to the deranged, desperate, degraded depths of a Gil Gamoid, an N-Kid, or an X-Man during their final days, you need to make peace with your finitude.

Visualization and trance-work can help. Try picturing yourself as a single grain of sand inside an hourglass. You are not the first grain of sand through the spout, nor the last, but the middlest. But once the hour is up and all the sand has fallen, the hourglass is smashed to pieces and left on the floor, and no one will ever clean it up. When you can trance-contemplate that image for an hour without sobbing, you'll know you've successfully suffocated the influence of self-grandiosity and that you're well on the journey toward psychemotionally integrative recovery.

Unfortunately, as I was about to discover, my F*O*O*Jsters, especially the X-Man, were going to eschew integration in favor of paranoia . . . which ultimately led to a terrifying tragedy for everyone.

CHAPTER SEVEN

WHO ARE YOU, REALLY? SECRET ORIGINS AND SECRET SHAMES

TUESDAY, JULY 4, 3:59 P.M.

Fallout

oddamned coach-class StarCase™ Corporation!" growled Mr. Piltdown while piloting us back to Earth.

"If man were meant to conquer space inside a goddamned dumbwaiter he'd've been born looking like a room service tray and laundry! If not for me, all you ninnies would be vacuum-roasted and gut-burst right now, you hear me?"

By that point, the tenth minute into our rescue, Mr. Piltdown had already explained to everyone several times the mortal debt owed to him for having a Squirrel Shuttle standing by on remote, and how the Space Elevator was not a dependable means of transit, whereas Pilt-Dyne Scramjet-Rockets held the proprietary "future of mankind" in their Pulsar-class engines.

But our brush with asteroidal immolation wasn't my focus. I was worried about Kareem, who was sputtering in zero gravity through the labyrinthine warps of his conspiratorial delusion, raving that Menton had orchestrated everything from the "assassination" of Hawk King to the destruction of Asteroid Zed itself.

"What," said André, "and get his own ass smoked?"

"Menton," snapped Kareem, "wasn't even *on* Asteroid Zed!"

Syndi exploded with the manic laugh-cry of having narrowly escaped death. "Really, Kareem? Like, who exactly were you *in*terviewing, then, huh? Dracula?"

Kareem snorted haughtily. I'd noticed his tendency to delight in moments like these: hoarding what he considered critical facts, like a dragon leering from atop a mound of cubic zirconia. "Figure it out," he sneered. "That wasn't Menton."

"Really. Like, who was it, then?"

"I don't know—yet. I haven't gotten all my *medu-kem* back," he said, referring to the logoids he'd dispersed in his frantic mantra of *Find! Find! Find!* "Probably stuck on the outside of the shuttle. But when we're on the ground and I open the hatch, I'll know for sure."

"Strap yourselves in and cut the chatter, scatterwits," said Mr. Piltdown. "We're entering the atmosphere."

Everyone complied with the strapping-in, but none with the command for quiet.

"Kareem, uff course ze man I dispatched vuss ze Destroyer!" said Hnossi. Her face was flushed and puffy, the flesh under her eyes like raw steak. For a woman who'd seen combat on a global scale, she was taking these events much harder than I would have expected. "You yourself shriekt horribly in hiss cell unt collapsed ven he vuss usink his phagopsychosis on you!"

The lights shut off, and our only illumination came from the flames beyond the portholes as we hurtled planetward.

Kareem claimed he'd collapsed not due to any Mentonian attack, but because of a desperate telepathic gambit by Gil

Gamoid and the N-Kid to warn him—an effort, he said, which had to have cost them the ultimate price.

Their message: that Asteroid Zed was about to be destroyed.

"They combined their Qosmic Qonsciousness," he said, "and pushed right through their P-Imp hats. And it killed them. I smelled it inside my own skull, their brains burning into briquettes. Tasted like a tray of lasagna left in a kot-tam furnace."

The portholes were orange disks in the darkness while the heat shield ripped through the superheated air around the plummeting shuttle.

"Even if you're mistaken about how zey diedt, zey are det," said Hnossi, her eyes heavier than dumbbells. She touched her mouth with quivering fingers. Noticing the shaking, she grasped the digits with her other hand and tucked both hands between her thighs. It was an incongruously girlish, vulnerable image for a steely, immortal woman.

"At least, at last . . . zeir Q-souls are hettet beck to qvasar Q-Nine-Sree-Nine, beck to ze Ur-Prime vich produced zem."

"Yeah!" yelled Kareem, his voice nearly swallowed by the roaring engine deceleration. "Hope that's a comfort for all the families of the guards and the technicians! Looks like half the life-pods didn't even eject! Last five minutes on the Asteroid was the dance called 'prisoners' revenge,' and the band was on fire! So what we've got is an attempt to shut down my investigation and kill *more* heroes—*us!* Not to mention wiping out all the remaining villains!"

"Kareem, is you crazy?" shouted André through the descent. The portholes were bright red heating elements atop a black stove. "You sayin Menton not only wanna kill Hawk King, he wanna destroy us an *villains,* too? Why? What's in it for him?"

"My god, doesn't anybody have a kot-tam brain up here? Look! Hawk King's dead! Omnipotent Man one day just up and resigns? We almost get slaughtered up there, and almost every remaining rival for anyone who wants to take over is wiped out in one shot!"

"Take over what, Kareem?" howled Syndi.

And Kareem shouted one last sentence before reentry wiped out his voice: "What do you *think*?"

Inside the Fortress of Fear

Conversation was dead until we'd landed safely inside the Fortress of Freedom, where scores of heroes crowded round their comrades to make sure they were all right. Outside the Fortress wall, dozens of camera crews awaited interviews, since by then satellite photography had beamed images of Asteroid Zed's destruction around the world.

Although I'd been inside the Fortress of Freedom several times, I was—even then, even after having survived the orbital disaster—awestruck by the stained-glass windows depicting the tragedies and triumphs of the F*O*O*J's history, the vast 2.5-D mural churning with the chaos of the Götterdämmerung, and the titanic, soaring gold and platinum statues of the founding F*O*O*Jsters and the Flying Squirrel holding up the ceiling. (Although the Flying Squirrel didn't join the F*O*O*J until 1946, he was able to add his own colossus to the Fortress's Age of Heroes caryatids because the F*O*O*J was, in fact, his tenant. Mr. Piltdown not only paid for the construction of the Fortress, he remained the owner of the building and the land beneath it; to this day, the F*O*O*J pays rent from its federal operating grants to the Piltdomain Group.)

I was about to enter Heroes' Hall when the guards held me until Syndi vouched for me and I was let inside, where I saw a storm swirling with Kareem as its eye. F*O*O*Jsters, novices and veterans alike, seemed to have decided that the X-Man was the answer man. Mr. Piltdown looked none too pleased at the gravity wielded by his front-running rival for the post of Director of Operations.

I scanned the assembly, sensing these heroes' seething anxiety. At the back, Syndi was twirling and tugging at her hair hard enough to yank it rootless. On the far side, André affected detached cool while leaning against the wall, but he could not stop glancing upward constantly as if anticipating the collapse of the ceiling. I couldn't see Iron Lass anywhere.

Kareem eventually took to the stage, framed by a backdrop mural of F*O*O*J martyrs such as Captain Manifest Destiny, Doctor Patho, and Lady Liberty.

"Menton the Destroyer," said Kareem into the microphone, employing the profane name to shock everyone into shutting up, "was not on Asteroid Zed. I believe he had been replaced by an imposter. Specifically, Zee-Roks the Imitator."

With all eyes rapt on him, Kareem reported what we saw in the space prison and laid out his "evidence," such as it was: that he fully expected Menton to be a terrifying figure, yet he felt no fear of the man whatsoever; that his interrogation plan was to state incorrect knowledge about Menton's career and crimes to lure the egomaniac into "correcting" him, yet his subject affirmed Kareem's inaccuracies without hesitation; that his last-minute logoscopic investigation of Asteroid Zed's computers revealed microgaps in the data—so small only his logoids could find them—indicating an attempt to erase all record of at least two unauthorized prisoner transfers: one to and one from Unit Z, three years ago; that the "comatose body" occupying the cell assigned to Zee-Roks the Imitator in the Biovillains Containment Unit was actually synthesized from a combination of medical waste, rhinoplasty, and Swanson's Hungry Villain Dinners™; that contrary to early supposition, Asteroid Zed wasn't destroyed by any outside force, but instead annihilated by a malfunction in its gravity reactor, "unquestionably" due to sabotage; and that since Gil Gamoid and the N-Kid proved they

could overcome their P-I Helmets, the more psionically powerful Menton could have developed the same skill, without burning out his own brain . . . and if he had, only he would have had
the means, motive, and opportunity to overcome prison authorities, escape, kill Hawk King, terminate Omnipotent Man's career, and wipe out his enemies, his potential rivals, and his
tracks all in one shot.

It was a thrilling, intoxicating, highly speculative, totally
circumstantial concoction Kareem had brewed, and the hundred or so terrified F*O*O*Jmates in attendance, still reeling
from the loss of Hawk King and Omnipotent Man, were all too
willing to snort it up by the mugfull. But unfortunately for
sanity's sake, Asteroid Zed's destruction (which by Kareem's
own admission was due to a structural defect) meant no one
could verify X-Man's claims. And lack of verifiability was a
paranoiac's playground paradise.

But what happened next stunned even me.

"I agree with the X-Man," announced Mr. Piltdown, taking a
step onto the stage.

Every head swiveled toward the Flying Squirrel. Kareem
was agog.

"Our organization is under threat," called the Squirrel,
moving toward the microphone. "Perhaps its gravest threat
since the Götterdämmerung itself. And whether we're facing an
escaped Destroyer, or person or persons unknown of similar
threat level—my own investigation, which for reasons I'm not
yet at liberty to reveal, points to none other than Warmaster
Set—we are clearly being hunted by a shadowy foe of enormous cunning, power, and danger."

With greater delicacy than I'd ever seen him employ, Festus
Piltdown wedged himself between Kareem and the micro-
phone, saying, "On the authority of F*O*O*J General Security
Order Number One, we are now at Defense Condition Cyan."

With that, he clicked a button on his glove and the auditorium plunged into deep cyan.

Confused mumbling flooded the hall. Mr. Piltdown shook his head, finally shouting at the questions only he could hear: "No, no, no, you shankshaft, you put on scuba gear for Def-Con Mauve, not Cyan! Are you color-blind?"

"Why couldn't it be L-Raunzenu?" shouted somebody, slicing through the din.

Mr. Piltdown flushed darkly while the challenger railed on.

"Everything Kareem said about the attack, the plot against us, all of it could've been carried out by L-Raunzenu. Which you know better than anybody, Squirrel, since Piltdown Psychotronics synthesized the damn thing outta ten million neurocorded nightmares—"

"—at the cost of a billion dollars of defense-contract taxpayers' money," said Kareem, grabbing the microphone. "Look— Heli-Cop, isn't it? Listen, I hear where you're coming from, but L-Raunzenu has no need to free Menton, right? And I'm telling you, I was up there on Asteroid Zed, and Menton *wasn't.* If you wanna pursue that as a complementary investigation, we can continue this conversation in camera. But for now," he said, appealing to the crowd, "this is the angle I'm working."

"That *we're* working," said Mr. Piltdown, glaring at Heli-Cop. "Def-Con Cyan, everyone! Action stations! Action stations!"

And off they all shuffled beneath cyan lighting. By then there wasn't a hero in the Fortress who hadn't been swept up in Kareem's cyclone of neurotic panic. And when those heavyweights eventually hit the earth, inevitably the innocent would be crushed where they stood.

When the Hall was clear, I was alone in the cyan light except for one man. At six-five, he was hard to miss, but it was as if he'd been invisible until that point. Yet at that moment he was a lightning bolt of a presence in his dark blue suit and red tie, with his coal-and-silver hair greased into a single e-curl in front. His face looked as if it'd been dipped in tempura and yanked from the deep-fryer five minutes too soon.

"Doctor Brain, sir, ma'am," he whispered, shuffling toward me as if his every bone ached. "I . . . I need y'hep."

What Type of Sandwich Are You?

One glance into Wally's eyes communicated an epic of disorientation and dysfunction. If *you've* ever looked yourself in the mirror at three A.M. and seen such distress, felt so out of control, and been so desperate for answers, maybe it's time to stop looking around you, and start looking behind you. Your pain and life-disorientation may seem to be the products of your present, but they're not; your present is merely the effect of your past.

Just as a ham sandwich is composed of ham, bread, and condiments such as mayonnaise, mustard, and relish, and occasionally a slice of lettuce, avocado, or sweet pickle, every human being is formed of experiences. Some of them are supplemental, while others are primary. The tastes and textures of a smear of emotional relish and a leaf of psychic lettuce change drastically in relation to the bread and ham of your primary development.

Ask yourself honestly: are you two slices of rich, multigrain whole wheat sandwiching a fresh serving of organic country ham? Or are you two easily torn white wafers of over-processed flour mass-cooked into a lifeless loaf, trapping the fatty, cold, red-dyed sinews of a factory reconstituted swine product?

Only when you've answered that can you start asking the questions that will unlock the mysteries containing your misery. And if Wally couldn't do that for himself, there was no telling how far he'd plummet, or if he'd even survive.

Paying the Power Bill

isten, Miss Brain—are you listening to me? Because so far I don't think you've heard a goddamned word I've said about anything."

I assured Mr. Piltdown that I was indeed listening, knowing how oblivious he was to the irony of his insistence, since he rarely listened to anyone. Because I sensed that Wally needed the comfort of meeting with his agemates, I'd sought out Iron Lass, who was unfortunately unavailable; the normally steely heroine had been so psychically fatigued by the events of the past few days that she'd been returning nobody's telephone calls. And so I invited Festus Piltdown to join Wally and me.

Having reconvened at my Mount Palomax offices, I quickly tucked away the *Elect X-MAN Director of Operations, F*O*O*J!* pamphlets Kareem had somehow managed to leave around— whether for electioneering purposes or simply to antagonize Mr. Piltdown, I was not sure, although by then it was clear that antagonizing the Flying Squirrel was difficult to avoid, even for someone with my training.

"You were expressing," I mirrored to Mr. Piltdown reassuringly, "your reservations about Wally's performance in the Id-Smasher® simulation we ran last week."

"Expressing my—did you say *express*ing my reser*vat*ions? I was detailing the eight hundred and twenty-three reasons why that man is an unapologizeable cock-up!"

He tugged at his neck straps, removed his squirrel mask and put it on the leather of the sofa seat beside him, then ran his fingers through the chalk streaks of his blackboard hair.

"He's a *fraud,* Miss Brain. Earth's greatest superhero, my colon. He's a panty-willed, 'aw-shucks, ma'am,' unmitigated ultraninny. Times got tough, he resigned. And at Hawk King's funeral, no less, stealing the spotlight for himself. He's a serial spotlight-stealer, I hope you realize—has been for decades. And now that the destruction of Asteroid Zed is capturing the head-lines he wanted for himself, he's back here whimpering to *un*-resign himself—"

"I didn'*un*resign, I'm still resigned-ified, an you're just sore cuz y'almost got blowed up t'day an I couldn'be there t'save ya for the eightieth time on accounta m'health!"

"Save me?" yelled the Squirrel. "*Me?* I'm the one who saved the entire mission! But go out to any tin-kettled flapjack shack and ask Charlie Spam Sandwich and Edith Dishsoap who's saved this *republic* more times than there are stars on the flag and *your* name'll be the first on their slack-jawed lips . . . So if that assembly of brain-stemmed dinklewits that dares call itself the F*L*A*C wants to address efficiency and diminished morale in this time of Cyan-level crisis, they might first try ad-dressing the profound misallocation of credit foisted upon the galactically undeserving. That'd be one man's modest pro-posal."

Throughout Mr. Piltdown's venting, Wally sat surprisingly placidly, as if he was listening to delightful, faraway oompah-pah music only he could hear—of course, with his omni-hearing, he might very well have been doing just that. I returned him to our world by asking him how he felt about what Mr. Piltdown had just said.

"Wellsir, I respect Festus's opinion, and I respect his right to have an opinion, ma'am. Which is what makes our country great."

"Yes, I see, Wally. However—"

Mr. Piltdown: "Do you even *listen* to the pap that dribbles out of your mouth, Wally? You respect my opinion? My opin-ion just burned you down to a primary-colored cinder, and you respect it? Is there so much as the *smell* of a thought inside that high-density skull of yours?"

For the first time, Wally smiled, opening his hands in concession.

"Wellsir, Festus, you've got me there. I'm still an old-fashioned man. It's how I was raised. I b'lieve you should be able to disagree without being disagreeable, and, wellsir, I admit, I'm a might taken aback when you start, well—"

"No, Wally. You're not taken aback. You're weak. And stupid. You were a liability to this team since it formed, and in the years since then you've only deteriorated, and, QED, you've cast this country into jeopardy, including through your capricious crybaby resignation—"

Suddenly Mr. Piltdown shuffled himself in his chair, reaching inside a utility pouch at the armpit of his left flap as if he were itching from ants.

"Good goddamnit! How in the hell did that Congo coon—"

"Whatcha got there, Festy?"

"I take my cape off for two minutes at the Fortress to use the damned rest room and that sociopathic sleeping-car porter stuffs it with one of his mau-mauing election pamphlets! If that switchbladed *Australopithecus* gets on our F*L*A*C, I'm telling you, we'll all be speared in our sleep!"

"Mr. Piltdown," I said, "let's stay focused on—"

"He's got no respect for private property! This is my *cape,* for God's sake! You don't touch a hero's cape! My life depends on this thing operating properly—"

"Festy, calm down—it's just a lil ol' brochure—"

"Wally, while illiterates such as yourself may not care about the power of the written word—"

"Mr. Piltdown, let's focus on what you were saying about Wally. The words you chose carried an intense . . . certainty, and by your own description, they defy common wisdom. Why do you feel that Wally hasn't earned his fame? He was, after all, a founding member of the F*O*O*J, whereas you joined only after the original seven members had returned from Germany."

"Actually, ma'am, Festus tweren't a member till the next year—'46."

"Thank you, Wally. Yes. So what is the nucleus of your concern?"

Mr. Piltdown laughed, coldly. "Ah, Miss Brain. Further proof that initials after one's name mean nothing insofar as intellectual credentials, or even a child's capacity to peer through the viscous veneer of venerability. During the war, Earth's champion, there—"

"The war—you mean the Götterdämmerung?"

"World War Two! Two seconds ago you were talking about Germany, so why would I be talking about the Götterdämmerung? I don't expect you to keep up with me, but at least muster the cognition to keep up with yourself, if you don't mind."

I paused, allowing him to continue.

"—*As I was saying,* this man is celebrated for having somehow put the kibosh on that mustachioed Austrian misanthrope in '45, when in reality, as a result of his staggering incompetence, before Wally even got to Berlin he'd already destroyed a dozen Allied refueling ships and actually protected a U-boat by mistake!"

Omnipotent Man chuckled. "Well now, that there's kind of a funny story—"

"A funny story—helping the Nazis. Here's a funnier story, Miss Brain. Wally's entire origin is a sham. You've got yard-chimps from Bangor to Buckskin Falls collecting trading cards and memorizing statistics about this atomic-powered flatworm, and every last one of them knows the messianic story of his origin: baby Karojun-Ya, rocketed to Earth from the exploding planet Argon by his philosopher-king father Jobuseen-Ya and gaining powers over mortal men—half Hercules, half Jesus.

"But has anyone ever actually *seen* this planet Argon?"

He let the question smolder, his baleful eyes burning like heaps of garbage.

"No, you see," he resumed just before Wally could defend his origin story, "because it just happened to be destroyed before anyone on Earth could ever take a picture of it, even though his rocket got here faster than the speed of light. Nothing but snake-milt.

"Wally, there—what's the expression?—he's 'sexed up' the truth. He's no extraterrestrial. He's nothing but white supertrash. Have you ever seen a picture of his real family, Miss Brain? They're trailer-trolls from Fried Possum, Kentucky!"

"Wellsir, if I'm not from the planet Argon, Festus, then where'd I get my omni-powers?"

"People acquire powers for any number of reasons, Wally! Genetics, childhood trauma, cell phones . . . Maybe you got yours in one of those Mexican clinics—I really don't know. Some of us don't depend on powers to do our damned jobs— which you don't manage to do anyway—we actually have to *work*, understand? Be productive? Actually possess our own working testicles?"

"I'm a—now, you see, Doctor Brain, sir, ma'am, this is where Festy has a tendency to take his horsing around a bit too far outta the barn—"

"You know what this keen little patriot did during the OPEC crisis?"

"—I'm a very hard worker, always have been, been working hard since I was nothing but Omni-Lad—"

"—eating omni-grits, no doubt. During the *OPEC* crisis—"

"—been savin folks in this here country since I was old enough to—"

"*During the goddamned OPEC crisis* Wally promised Carter he'd use his 'omni-power' to create a new energy source to free us from the tyranny of those tablecloth-headed hand-choppers.

You know where Wally tested his brainchild? You recall a little gem of real estate called Three Mile Island? To this day the entire country still believes that was a nuclear power plant, instead of the argonium processor it actually was. Now *that's* PR, when the president himself covers up for you. Covers up for you being a filthy junkie!"

"Now Festus, you wait just a gollyshocking minute! I aint never had no problem with argonium—"

"What she ever saw in you, I'll never understand—"

" 'What she'—? Who ya talkin bout, Festy? Princess Astra?"

Mr. Piltdown shut his mouth, his eyes flashing at me and then away as if he was afraid he'd said too much. Then he regrouped and regained my gaze, thumbing his accusations toward his colleague.

"Those same hero card–collecting urchins who believe his rat-excrement nonsense about being from the planet Argon are true believers in his idiocy about argonium. That meteor fragments of his 'exploded homeworld' are the only substance that can kill 'Omnipotent' Man. Brilliant bit of logic, there, by the way, being allergic to his entire home planet. Just how does a species like that evolve, hm? *Gloves?* When the truth is, he's as addicted to argonium as a common coolie is to opium!"

"Festus, now dontchu be, be spreading any a your, your . . . exagge*r*ations again," said Wally, as if the word were the foulest curse he'd said in years.

"*Look* at him, Miss Brain," continued the Squirrel. "We've been trapped in your therapeutic clutches for more than a week now. Could even you be so dim as to've failed to notice how often he excused himself to go to the little cretin's room, and how when he came back, his nostrils were dusted with a fine blue powder?"

I glanced at Wally nipping at the nail of his right index finger. Given the omni-density of his nails, his chewing sounded like a boxcar locking into place in a train.

"This man," said the Squirrel, thumbing again, "so successfully hoodwinked that peanut-harvesting huckleberry of a president that he managed to turn the entire Department of Energy into his dealer! Three plum-sized glowing blue crystals per day back then. I haven't a clue where he's getting his supply now. Perhaps from somewhere out in the asteroid belt, which would explain all those 'exploratory missions' he's been on of late, and probably explains his resignation itself! Instead of being up on Asteroid Zed today making himself useful, he was probably out getting his fix—"

"Doggoneit, Squirrel, y'all better hush now—"

"Did you know, Miss Brain, that this apple-gnawing rum-donkey doesn't even restrict himself to *one* secret identity? He has at least five that I know of, presumably so he can be an utter failure in as many places as possible. How about it, Wally? Did you know *I* knew? Junkies tend not to hide things very well, but neither do they often realize what nakedly strolling emperors they actually are."

Wally's eyes became twin sunny-side-up eggs on the plate of his face, his lips an *O* of two crispy-curled slices of bacon.

"Wally," I asked, "what does Mr. Piltdown mean when he says you have more than one secret identity?"

"Festy, you nuthin but a lyin, steamin heapa goat shit, j'know that?"

"Oh ho! The monkey *finally* finds his mouth. But which of the three monkeys? Nothing but a disgrace to Hawk King's entire legacy—"

Suddenly the Flying Squirrel was flailing backward across the room because of a whipping, screeching tentacle of blue-white brilliance extending from Omnipotent Man's mouth to the center of the Squirrel's chest. Smashing into the opposite wall and crashing to the floor, Festus clutched the blackened, flaming hole in the tunic above his armor, gasping awfully.

I glimpsed myself reflected in the glass of a framed Munch

print—my hair static-charged, upright, and stiffened into the shape of an upside-down daddy longlegs.

The entire room reeked of ozone.

"Festus," said Omnipotent Man, electric sparks spraying out between his clenched teeth like neon spittle, "you'd better tuck-tail on outta here 'fore I lose my temper . . . suh'm fierce."

Achilles' Real Heel
Was His Whole Body

If you're like Omnipotent Man, you may have spent much of your career, if not your life, hiding behind the fig leaf of your physical indestructibility. But having a diamond-hard body doesn't guarantee you freedom from having a costume-jewelry soul, or that the gold of your mental health won't oxidize into an unsightly green.

Achilles, the "invulnerable" hero of the Trojan War, was vulnerable supposedly because of his very mortal heel. But a cursory reading of *The Iliad* shows that Achilles maintained very weak interpersonal relationships and was frozen at a child's stage of ego development, sulking in his tent even while war raged around him. Clearly, Achilles' true vulnerability was actually his *in*vulnerability, or what I call the *Achilles Threefold Folly of Superior Ability*.

The Achilles Threefold
Folly of Superior Ability

1. *Achilles believed in the myth of his own invulnerability,* so he never attempted to understand the meaning or ramifications of others' vulnerability.

2. Achilles' inexperience with physical pain meant that he *never developed a common lexicon of misery,* the key ingredient necessary for human connection.

3. Achilles, believing in his supposed inability to feel pain, and because of his lack of compassion, *never grew to understand his own or others' emotional pain,* which imprisoned him inside an inescapable confinement of existential solitude. When the poisoned, flaming Trojan arrow struck him, Achilles as likely died from heartbreaking loneliness (the narcissistic fantasy that he alone could feel such pain) as from toxins, infection, third-degree burns, and massive blood loss.

Unless Wally could rise to the challenge of confronting the reality of his own essential fragility, particularly during a time of such instability for the organization that gave his life meaning, he would never be able to achieve true strength and would instead die a broken, embittered, delusional man.

Secret Origins and Secret Shames

Without exception, every family keeps a veritable mausoleum of skeletons in its closets. Innumerable patients of mine have discovered only in adulthood that they're in fact adopted, that they're abuse survivors, that they're human-alien hybrids, or even that they're shaven, cerebro-boosted globus monkeys.

So when Mr. Piltdown attacked Wally about his origins, I couldn't help but ask myself some questions: Were Wally's parents extraterrestrial quasi-gods of powers surpassing our "awe capacity" and of intellect impenetrable to mortal men? Or were they salt-of-the-earth country folk from America's deep-fried gristle belt? Did Wally invent a myth of grandiose origins to overcompensate for his personal mediocrity? Or is it something else entirely? Or not?

In order to help Wally feel truly comfortable exposing himself, I dismissed Mr. Piltdown to seek medical care and resume his "independent investigation" into Hawk King's death. To aid in getting to Wally's inner truth, I brought out my DynaScan Reflective Spectroscope Junior®, and, while giving Wally a few hours to compose himself, I pored over the "Omnipotent Mess" chapter from Jack Zenith's *Two Masks of a "Hero,"* and contacted Mr. Piltdown to have him courier me his own Squirrel Intelligence files on Wally. And, as a precaution, I arranged two lightning rods on either side of my desk.

If Mr. Piltdown's claim about multiple secret identities had any truth to it, Wallace W. Watchtower was in far greater pain than I could ever have guessed.

Excavating the Ice Age of Jobuseen-Ya

So, Wally," I asked, while sunset sweetened the room into a glowing ketchup smear, "how does it feel to be out of the F*O*O*J? Sitting on the sidelines, watching the accidental destruction of Asteroid Zed and the by-election for the F*L*A*C?"

He gazed at me glumly, slumping in his chair like a mound of mashed potatoes.

"Wellsir, asteroids are always blowin up somewhere, y'know?" he mumbled. "An's far as th'lection, well . . . never really cared for thet administrative guff. I like doin thangs. Actin. Not fussin over forms an such."

I flipped through my file and the file Mr. Piltdown had sent me. "Hm. But . . . yes, you did serve on the F*L*A*C for a few years in the late forties and early fifties when the F*O*O*J was still new. There were some . . . problems . . .?"

"Tweren't really my thang, like I said, ma'am. Gil Gamoid stepped in for me, an Hawk King—may God rest both their souls—suggested I retire from the F*L*A*C so he could hep me keep refinin m'powers. The King hepped me find m'*real* callin: rescuin, savin, inspirin. I'm a 'big pitcher' sorta feller, not a dottin *t*s an crossin *i*s man, y'know. Hnossi, Festus, they're better with thet sorta stuff."

"I see. Would you say then, Wally, you've taken seriously, or not seriously enough, your history of failure?"

"Wellsir, ma'am, I'd like to say that I always never *don't* fail to take serious things seriously. I mean . . . wait a minute. Uh . . . yes?"

"So you agree then, that—"

"Now hang on, ma'am . . . You kinda rattled me there a minute with that question. So no, I don'think that I haven't taken . . . I mean, I have taken—look, I never said I was a failure. That's just not true. You know it, I know it, th'entire 'Merican people know it. They call me a hero. Now, I don'call m'seff a hero, but that's what they call me. And two hunnerd and fifty million people can't be wrong, no sir, ma'am."

"Now Wally, it's interesting to me that you phrased your response the way you did. Because I didn't say you were a failure."

"What? I coulda sworn you jess—"

"No, I asked you to characterize, or reify—*measure,* if you will—how seriously you've taken your failures."

Wally looked back at me with his eyebrows knitted into a muffler of confusion, until finally scratching beneath his right armpit. "Now maybe you didn'hear me right, ma'am, but I jess said I'm not a failure, I'm a hero. Herofyin is what I do. It's what I'm good at. Always have been."

"Wally, how realistic, really, is it to think that you're perfect?"

"I never said I was perfect, ma'am-doctor. Nobody's perfect. Even Hawk King, and I adored the man, so don'get me wrong, but even *he* wunt perfect, though you might think so, listenin to Festus. Okay, no one 'cept maybe my daddy's perfect. An he's passed on."

"So how did that make you feel, when Festus referred to your parents as—and I'm quoting from my notes here—as 'nothing but white super-trash . . . trailer-trolls from Fried Possum, Kentucky'?"

"Wellsir, twasn't nice, 'course, but I'm a big boy. But I was talkin bout m'*real* daddy, not m'step-pa."

"You mean . . . Jobuseen-Ya, from the planet Argon."

"Yessir, ma'am."

"Now, we had a bit of an incident here, when Mr. Piltdown started questioning whether Jobuseen-Ya and Argon actually existed."

Wally wrinkled his nose, turned to his side, sucked in a deep breath, then let it out over the course of a full half-minute. Frost formed a huge white circle on the window in the path of his breath, and even the Spectroscope next to me scummed over milkily. I couldn't stop myself from shuddering.

"Sorry bout that," he said.

"That's fine, Wally." I crossed my arms for warmth, noticing how my skin had pimpled like a plucked chicken's. The air temperature had to have dropped twenty degrees.

Omnipotent Man leaned forward, pushed himself up and out of his chair, and ambled over to the window he'd just made opaque. He put a fingernail into the frost, which I could see then was at least half an inch thick.

"Don'much care for people suggestin, Doc," rumbled Omnipotent Man, "that I ain't tellin th'truth."

Cold Reality

Y ou listen to Festus long enough," he whispered, maybe more to himself than to me, "y'start not even knowin what's true about y'*seff*. He c'n tear a strip off ya long enough to make a runway. On'y three or four people in th'world he don'never talk like that about. One's Hawk King, who he thought was doggone infalalal . . . in*fab*bubull . . . in*flab*bubble—"

"—infallible?"

"Right. Then there's Ir'n Lass. An I spose . . . yeah, Chip Monk, his ol sidekick, even though they had a powerful fallin out, but he still don'never say s'much as a bad burp about him.

"But me, he's always ridin me like a fat jockey on a poor man's pony. Sayin Argon don'exist, that I done wrong by 'Merica, that I'm, ha-ha, that I'm addicted t'argonium. I mean, don't that jess take jake-all?"

He glanced up at me for affirmation, while his fingernail continued cutting shapes into the frost field on the window, whether randomly or by design, I wasn't sure.

"So . . . all these accusations are false, Wally?"

"Yes'm."

"Let's take it that they're false, then. On a scale of one to three, with one being 'quite a bit,' and three being 'one hundred percent,' how much truth would you say Mr. Piltdown's claims contain?"

His fingernail stopped on a downward diagonal line. "Well, I . . . I mean . . . I guess then I'd hafta say . . . one? Wait, wait a second, is there a zero?"

"No. How relieved do you feel that you've been able to release yourself even a little bit from the burden of these self-deceptions, Wally? With one being 'very relieved,' and three being 'extremely relieved'?"

"Now, I didn'say that I was relieved, ma'am—"

"So how much do you wish that you had not let me know how relieved you are, with one being—"

"Now, Doctor Brain, sir, ma'am, what I'd, I'd, I'd really like to talk with you about is how goshdurn unfair it is for Festus t'be stompin on m'good name like that. An not just, like, a hour ago but for the last dad-blasted fifty years!"

I tapped the device next to me. "Wally, do you know what this is?"

He resumed drawing his frost image, his finger cutting and dancing faster than I could see and raising a cloud of snow. Without even looking back at me, he said, "A DynaScan Reflective Spectroscope Junior®."

"Very good. Do you know why I have it with me?"

He stopped, silent, his finger suddenly stuck in mid-draw.

"I've set it to scan for a rare substance," I said quietly. "Do you know which one?"

"Listen, ma'am, in my work I fly through solar prominences, planetary cores, Cirque du Soleil shows—I could have any number a things stuck to my suit an cape—"

"According to the scanner, this substance isn't on your suit, Wally, and you're not wearing your cape. It's on your fingers, teeth, lips, and nostrils."

He turned to face me, stepping away from the window. Only then could I see he'd drawn three startlingly detailed portraits, each slightly different, but all clearly versions of the same face.

His own.

And then he turned back to the window and expectorated a gob of electrons onto the glass, and the images *pfft!* into steam.

"I aint no junkie!"

Grateful I'd taken the precaution of wearing a rubber under-suit and wooden shoes, I adjusted the lightning rods on either side of me. "Wally, I never referred to you as a—"

"I aint!" he said, pointing at me, and without any warning his fingers fell off his pointing-hand and hit the floor.

"Ah, H–E–double oil derricks, not again," he said, stooping to pick up his scattered digits with his other hand.

" 'Not again,' Wally? Are you saying this has happened before?"

He nodded, holding his fingers up against their stumps, spitting electrical fire upon them to weld them back into place.

I got up to pat the chair across from me to encourage him to sit down when he'd finished with his hand. He didn't budge. "Wally, tell me about your father. Your real father. About Jobuseen-Ya."

"Y'mean, you don'believe Festus's foolin? You think I'm tellin the truth?"

"Wally, I know you're telling the truth. At least, part of it. Now let's see if together, we can get the rest."

The Original Golden Age, or the Age of Fool's Gold?

My daddy, m'real daddy, was the greatest official on th'entire planet Argon," said Omnipotent Man after a long, long silence in which the Los Ditkos night began to flow through my bay window like a cola beverage into a crystal decanter.

Wally hardly looked at me, staring instead into the twinkling Bird Island skyline and the neon-metallic phallus of the Tachyon Tower rising above it.

"Daddy was a genius," he said eventually. "Knew our whole planet was in danger."

"What type of danger?"

"Oh, all kinds. Aliens, 'specially. And traitors. Plus, Argon was gon explode if we didn'keep relieving the planetary pressure of all its excessive energy, which Daddy was a pioneer in removing."

"I see."

"So anyway, he realizes one day thet the whole planet's gon implode—"

"—explode?"

"—right, splode, like that very week, an he wants t'warn the public, but the damn gubment says he's jess causin panic is all, an they orders him to shut up or else they gon throw him in jail. So they won't let im say nuthin, he caint do nuthin, except one thing: save me. So he up and puts me in a rocket ship f'Earth."

"You were how old? In Earth years, I mean?"

"I reckon round eight."

"Now, Wally, what about the rest of the family? Your mother, siblings—you had two brothers and a sister—and everyone else in the extended -Ya family . . . didn't he try to save any of them?"

"Naw, see, he could only spare the one rocket, so he couldn'send any a them. Else he mighta got noticed and got in trouble."

"But if he were going to die with the planet anyway, then wouldn't jail time be a rather empty threat?"

His forehead furrowed into a farmer's field.

"So why," I probed, "do you suppose your father saved you alone, out of your entire family?"

His bright eyes blinked onto mine, glittering in the lamplight like two big drops of Windex. "Well, I . . . you know, I never actually . . . I mean, nobody's ever asked me that before."

"Wally, I want to show you something, if I may."

Drawing him over to my desk, I selected some images on my computer while he stood behind me.

"When you resigned, I was very worried about you and your processing of these recent experiences. Because I hoped we'd continue our sessions, I asked Gagarina Girl to search through some of Hawk King's galactic records for me—do some astronomical detective work, if you will. And she's come up with some very interesting results.

"It appears that you've been a bit off regarding the location of Argon, which you always said had been *here*," I said, pointing to the screen. "But if we look *here,* we get an entirely different story."

A high-resolution image of an alien world appeared, a Christmas tree of a planet with thousands of tiny lights, like fireflies orbiting a foolishly wrapped and rotting Yuletide ham.

"You . . . you're sayin . . . that's Argon? *It's still there?* No, that dun't . . . now wait, ma'am," he said, breaking into a relieved grin, "the light to take this photograph cain't travel faster than the speed of . . . of light! Which means this image is from before Argon exploded."

"But Wally, Hawk King invented the Khu-Kheperi imaging technology that makes these photographs possible. This is a picture of Argon as it looks *today.* And this," I said, clicking farther, "is a picture of the capital city, what you've always called Nietchion."

I clicked open an image of a giant tower shaped like a man hefting two massive weapons of indeterminate use.

"And this, assuming Gagarina Girl's translation is correct, is the Citadel of Galactic Security. And if we take a closer look," I said, clicking again, "on the top floor, in the office on the side facing us, is a man who looks like an older version of you, drinking what looks like a mug of something hot, what with the steam coming off the top, and he's dropping in something and stirring—perhaps an Argonian low-calorie sweetener of some sort, since he's in such good shape. And there, on the desk behind him . . . let me bring up the magnification, yes, a nameplate, which the translation says means *Jobuseen-Ya, Director of Argonian Security,* and right there on the side of the desk, that's a holograph of what seems to be him, a wife, and two grown boys and a girl."

I looked back up over my shoulder.

Before I could see his face, Wally W. Watchtower had turned around; he was trying to muffle the snuffling sounds he was making.

Pulling his expandocape out of his jacket and tying it around his neck, he began flying slowly around the room at less than walking speed. His cape was drooping sadly at his sides like the jowls of an aged hound dog; tears dropped from his face like that hound dog's melancholic slaver.

The Icon Trap had imprisoned Wally with even greater power than I had realized, but with a twist: the icon splintering Omnipotent Man's psyche into fragments was made of two persons fused into one dominating demon of disapproval: Jobuseen-Ya, and Festus Piltdown III.

The Inner Abandoned Child

Wally, please, it's better to talk this out."

"Why bother?" he said, flying snail-speed laps around the room. "Argon never was under no threat! You done jess proved that! M'daddy jess wanted to get ridda me! Like tyin up a big ol sack fulla kittens an droppin em in a dirty ol' creek!"

"Now, Wally," I said, rotating in my chair so I could keep him in sight, "Earth isn't exactly a 'dirty old creek,' and your father didn't kill you, now did he? Maybe originally he thought there really was a threat."

He turned to look at me. "So why didn'he try an get me back, then? You know what he *did* do, though?"

Distracted, Wally made a low-speed collision with my fig tree, knocking it over. "Aw, pig-snickers," he said, surveying the dirt. "Sorry bout that."

Before I could coax him into sitting with me, Wally was in

flight again, but he hadn't made it five yards before he hit the floor like a pelican flying into the engine of a DC-10.

I rushed to help him into a chair. It was like trying to lift a sack of bowling balls. I asked him to tell me about his father.

"That ol' bossy such-an-such!" he choked. "You know what he left me? This here cube," he said, producing a glinting black box no bigger than a large sugar cube. "Had it since I was hip high to a mule, when I was a kid growin up in Mannsfall, Kentucky, and confused as all jolly on accounta I couldn'member anything bout who I was before age eight. But I had this here necklace, see, which Ma and Pa said I was wearin when they found me in th'swamp. An when I got older an walked to An'ar'tica—"

"You *walked* to Antarctica?"

"Yeah, an this here box started tellin me how our planet'd been destroyed an how the box was the sum a m'daddy's intelligence an it was gon guide me throughout m'life in his stead."

He shook the device in his closed hand, next to his ear, as if he were about to shoot craps. "Even has Daddy's voice," he said.

He opened his hand, gazed. "But all this durn thing ever did was insult me. 'Karojun-Ya, how can you be so stupid?' an 'Karojun-Ya, you failed again, liver-brains' an all that kinda guff."

"Do you think . . . maybe that's why you put up with Mr. Piltdown's insults?"

He fixed his eyes on me again.

"Because the whole world calls you a hero, yet you let Festus talk to you like that constantly, as if you're worthless."

"I don'know."

"How did all your father's comments make you feel?"

"I don'know."

"Did they make you happy?"

"I don'*know*."

"When you swore at Mr. Piltdown and then electrospat him across the room, do you think that in some part of your mind you were spitting at your father? Was that the saliva of 'You can't hurt me anymore'? Or was it the albumin of a frightened little boy who was angry that his 'daddy' had rejected him?"

He looked down, mumbled, "I'ont know what kinda hork it was, ma'am."

"Because saliva—the water of life in your body—"

"Actually it was a beam of electrons, ma'am—"

"But the deeper truth of the saliva behind the electricity is what matters, Wally. Look at the rage you released in that single thousand-volt expectoration. You're the most mild-mannered man I've seen in this practice in decades. But then, one remark too many—"

"Yeah," he chuckled grimly. "Fried squirrel. Courtesy of m'omni-gob."

"Exactly. Being rejected by your father like that, believing that you're never good enough . . . Do you think that might have something to do with your stunning achievements in anti-success?"

"Well, I mean, I *spose* that . . . what?"

"Tell me about walking to Antarctica."

The Black Box of the Soul

Yeah . . . when I was sixteen. Ma an Pa, well, they's Jehovah's Witnesses, but I didn'know what I b'lieved. I was gettin inna trouble, drankin an messin around an such. I still didn'know bout m'powers, y'unnerstan. An Ma an Pa, they was always talkin about doomsday—seems every time a doomsday come up an didn'happen, they always had another one waitin.

"So I stopped wannin t'listen to em, specially when they wannid me t'go out witnessin, farm-to-farm an door-to-door an such. So they was fightin with me suh'm fierce t'go, an I up and decided to spite em by gettin as far away from em as I could.

"So I started walkin, an I member being s'prised by how far an how fast I could walk without ever gettin hungry. An before I knew it—like, on'y a coupla months'd gone by, an I was at the south end a Chile. And the cold didn'bother me neither, which I never knew before on accounta Kentucky always bein so hot. An I was jess so fulla spite I had to go th'whole distance, so I decided I'd swim over to An'ar'tica, which wun't the smartest thing to do, I admit, considerin I didn'know bout my powers yet, but I was always a good swimmer an figured why not? So I did. I made it.

"But I musta lost m'necklace with the black cube on it or suh'm, cuz when I came out the water, it was gone. But I looked behind me an all th'penguins an walruses were swimmin away cuz a big black iceberg or suh'm was comin up out th'water like a mountain bein born.

"On'y it wun't no mountain. It had a huge blue doorway glowin like one a them neon signs, an it was *willin* me to go through it! So I walked on inside an there was all sortsa blinkin machines, like chairs an beds an treadmills—like, like a big ol health spa from the future or suh'm. An I felt this powerful urge to sit inside one a them chairs, an when I did, suddenly I could feel all kindsa powers surging in me.

"An then I looked up and seen right on top a this pedestal— it's m'black box! Beamin out a ghostly image of m'daddy— that's what it said to me, that it was m'daddy—talkin to me bout how he sent me to Earth to save m'life an so at least I could be a success somewhere."

He sat across from me, chewing his lip. "Guess I never really paid attention to how he worded that before."

"Go on."

"Well, I got up outta m'trainin machine to pick up m'box, but I'd become so strong, I accidentally ripped the machine

outta th'floor an knocked th'pedestal down an then, well . . .
pretty much after that was a blur on accounta th'whole black
iceberg commenced t'comin down. An so I flew back home—I
could fly now, see?—an all th'while my box-daddy was tellin me
I was a complete nimrod, though that wun't th'word he used.

"I got back to Mannsfall, an I went to see m'step-pa an -ma
t'tell em all what'd happened, but I still hadn't quite got
th'hang a m'powers, so I accidentally burned down half
th'town and then when I was trying to use m'frost breath to put
out the fire I accidentally shrank th'whole place with some
other power I didn'even know I had. Still don'know how I did
it, actually . . . so I been workin ever since then to figure out
how to *un*shrank em."

"The whole town just disappeared? And no one noticed?"

"Well, it was a small town to begin with. An the war'd just
started. So anyway, I went over into Cloverport, bought me a
aquarium, an put the tinier town of Mannsfall inside it."

"And you just left it there?"

"No, I took it with me. It's in my condo, now, right on top
the toilet tank, so at least once a month I member to bring in
fresh food and water, which I crumble up and dribble down on
em like manna and drinks from heaven."

"Are your stepparents still alive inside the aquarium?"

"Yessir. Time seems to've slowed down on accounta the
shrankin. Or suh'm . . . don'rightly know, akchully." He
chirped up, "I can bring in the tank, if you like, to show ya."

"If you'd like to, Wally. For now, tell me more about what
you did after you returned home."

"For a while I did some herofying as I was learnin m'powers. That's when I was Omni-Lad. Then the war got worse, an
the call went out from Hawk King. I mean, akchully from his
hawk legion, which was searchin th'whole country lookin for
superheroes to help fight the comm'nists—"

"The Nazis."

"—right, an that's when I hooked up with him, Iron Lass, Captain Manifest Destiny, Lady Liberty, Gil Gamoid an th'N-Kid—"

"Actually, Wally," I said, leafing through the heavily redacted contents of the OMNIPOTENT FRAUD folder Mr. Piltdown had couriered to me, "I meant, what did you do when you weren't performing superheroics? Tell me about the jobs you held, the friends you had, the kind of life you led in your secret identity."

"Course, y'already know m'secret name, ma'am. An I expect y'already read Jack Zenith's book, since durn near everybody in creation did. So y'know I led a quiet life as a grade-school teacher."

"But what about writing, Wally?"

"What about it?"

"You also—as I've learned," I said, flipping through the files, "worked at a small newspaper in Blandton—"

"Now where in tarnation j'ever hear suh'm so silly?"

"—where you were apparently known as a shy and awkward proofreader named Willis Nesbin. But Nesbin was secretly the writer behind the popular syndicated advice column 'Ask Aunt Edna.' Which means this additional secret identity of yours was actually a two-for-one."

"Who toldj'all that?"

"You even rented an apartment under this Nesbin persona. Your neighbors there describe Nesbin as—I've got it here: quote, Quiet and polite, but not in that creepy serial-killer way, end quote."

"What, Doc, you been spyin on me?"

"So you admit it's true."

"No, consarn it! I mean, you been spyin on somebody else but *thankin* it were me, when in reality—"

"In fact, Wally," I said, taking out a set of photographs from Mr. Piltdown's folder, "you seem to have a great number of secret identities." I held up photos one at a time, each one paper-clipped with relevant news printouts on its back, and then set them on the coffee table between us.

"Billionaire playboy *Ricky R. Bustow* . . . pious conservative televangelist *Jebedai 'Crawdad' Crocket,* ruthless fight promoter *Francis 'The Musk Ox' Miller.*

"Since your resignation, Wally, no one's heard a peep from any of them."

He stared back at me emptily.

"And earlier today," I continued, "you carved portraits into the frost you made on my window. Portraits of these men, who, despite slight differences in hairstyles, glasses, and so forth, all look remarkably like you."

"Doc, you'd hafta have a sweater th'size a Kentucky t'pull that much wool over th'eyes of th'Merican people. How could I be all those men an still be me?"

"Only someone with powers beyond those of mortal men *could* do such a thing."

"Well, why would I even wanna?"

"How terrified are you of rejection, Wally? Mercilessly esteem-hammered by Festus, rejected by your own father who cast you out of his entire world, a misfit in your adopted hometown, a fraud in the field of superheroics, no known romantic relationships to speak of? So if you can hide who you really are and become something that is appealing to enough people—"

"Doc, I'm loved over this whole tadpoled planet! Why should I need any more adulation than I already got?"

"You tell me, Wally. Tell me why it's never enough."

"I never said it wun't! Now you jess quit all this crazy talkin! *So what* if I look like summa them fellas? Jess a coincidence! I'm Wally W. Watchtower, Karojun-Ya, last son of Argon . . . well, okay, maybe not th'last, but—th'invincible Omnipotent Man. That's it, that's all, no more!"

"Wally . . . are you saying . . . are you saying that you actually don't know about these other identities?"

"Doc, I jess said—"

"Maybe . . . originally you had yourself in check, this craving of yours for validation, but the more the public fed you, the hungrier you got—as if you had a tapeworm burrowed in your psychemotional gut—and the emptier you felt. So you found something you thought could fill you up. But what you didn't know is how much that very something would fracture you further."

At that moment, I reached beneath the coffee table to produce a leaden gray lockbox no larger than a lunch box. I opened it and placed it on the coffee table between us.

Wally blinked, his nostrils flaring, his lips crimping inside his mouth.

The stench of ozone wafted from the interior of the gray box, which glowed electric blue.

"Obtained courtesy of the F*O*O*J laboratories," I said. "Fifty-five grams of powdered argonium."

"I'd reckon it," he said after a taut twenty seconds, his eyes nailed onto the box, "more like fifty-four."

Supervillains Might Be a Reason, but They're Never an Excuse

I reached to close the box. Wally jerked nearly all the way out of his chair before he looked at me and stopped himself; his eyes locked on the box and then came back to me. He settled himself back, his face looking as if the iconic masks of comedy and tragedy were battling upon it for supremacy.

I waited with the powdered argonium open and available in front of him, counting out the seconds and then the minutes on the clock beyond his shoulder.

All the while, Wally's face and body clicked and contorted through a chaos of tics and spasms.

Finally, his lower lip trembling, he almost begged me. "Doc . . . y'know—*please*—"

"I *will* help you," I whispered. "Wally, did you know that one of the effects of argonium use is personality fragmentation?"

His eyes flickered over me, over the photos arranged before him, over to the window where his frost portraits no longer were.

He sniffed and nodded, defeated.

"And I can't help but wonder whether it might also induce delimbification in Argonians. How long has argonium use been affecting your work?"

"I'ont thank it affected m'work, ma'am," he growled. "I always showed up, I always—"

"Was that why the attack on the Allied ships, and saving the U-boat?"

"Naw, naw, naw—back before the war I aint even ever heard about no argonium. That was jess a mistake is all."

"So when did you first begin using—"

"Rex Mirthless," he said.

"The Vocabularian?"

"One an th'same," he said, drawing in a long, ragged breath. "M'first real superopponent . . . a true archvillain. We'd been havin these off-an-on melees for about a decade already, him always managing to slip away, like a coon dipped in bacon grease. Now Rex, he were this snootified, citified, sissified N'Englander. Wore a, whaddayacall them thangs—a cravat, c'n you b'lieve it? Wellsir, this was back in '58, an he were threatnin to take control a th'energy market, introduce some sorta sun-powered thang. It woulda destroyed th'whole economy. So I stormed his fortress—he had this base inside a volcano, an he was wearin one a them Beatle-type jackets, on'y it were white—"

"A Nehru?"

"Right, a Nero. He was th'first guy to do that, by th'way, th'whole volcana an white jacket dealy. Evr'body after that was jess copyin im. So he tricked me, knocked me out with some kinda cosmic beam, an then when I woke up he started goin inna all his plans, splainin em to me like he's braggin. I figured, heck, let im talk, right? Every second he gave me was time to plan an escape.

"But what I didn'know was that his cosmic ray-beam couldn'kill me physically, but he could kill me brainwise, jess by talkin. I mean, he was planning to bore me to death *literally*. He had some sorta thing funneling his goldang voice straight inside m'brain, wipin out m'memories, makin me all crazified . . . an th'whole time, like, days, he was standin in fronta me takin little sniffs offa his flouncy sleeve collars, from some kinda blue powder he kept puttin on there from his snuffbox."

Wally's eyes were far away, slipping from the window to me to the box.

"So he forced you to snort argonium?"

"Naw. Rex'd always been real jealous of me, see? Fraid I was more manly'n him, which is why he tried to neutralize m'powers." He chewed his lip, pausing. "So I told him, now thet your machines done wiped out m'omni-powers, whyonchu an me duke it out, mano-a-mano? And zap, for the first time in three days he'd shut his yap, and jess like that he had me outta his Zero-Chair or whatever it was."

"So what was it like, for the first time in your career, to have to fight a villain without being able to use your powers?"

"Well akchully, I still had em, see? Rex thought his cosmic beam's effects were permn'nent, but no sir, once he got me outta the chair, I jess ripped his arms and legs off."

"I see. So how did you save him? Cauterize his wounds with your omni-breath?"

"Naw. He bled to death pretty fast after being delegged. But he'd dropped his snuffbox. Now, you gotta unnerstan—I hadn't slept or eaten or had anything to drink in three days, an thet blue powder, wellsir, it smelled powerful nice . . . like wakin up and goin t'sleep at the same time."

His eyes were superglued to the strongbox, blinking so rapidly I almost couldn't detect it, while his nostrils repeatedly flared and his fingers clenched and strummed like white tarantulas undergoing seizures.

"I asked you before how self-medicating with argonium has been affecting your work."

He glared at me. "I'ont know!"

"Has anyone ever said anything to you about it?"

"Maybe . . . maybe Hawk King, once or twice . . . an, well, Ir'n Lass . . . an Gil Gamoid fore him an th'N-Kid up an went kernuttified an hadda be locked up on Asteroid Zed . . ."

"So your colleagues, your oldest friends . . . how does it feel, knowing that they know about this weakness of yours?"

Omnipotent Man leaned forward, gripping his skull as if he were about to rip into a fortune cookie.

"Wally . . . do you want to be able to wake up and go to sleep on your own, without any blue crystal to help you do it? Do you want to be yourself, and not billionaire Bustow, Reverend Crocket, 'Musk Ox' Miller, Willis Nesbin, or Aunt Edna? Just plain old Wally? I mean, omnipotent new Wally?"

As if trying to drown out my voice, he was muttering to himself, rocking and rocking and rocking in his chair.

"Listen to me, Wally! Hear what I'm saying! Do you want your life back?" On and on he rocked and muttered.

Finally I shouted, "Answer me, Wally! Do you want to be one sane man instead of a half-dozen fractured ones?"

And then I put a hand on his shoulder, and both his arms slipped out of their sleeves and rolled across the floor. He keeled forward face-first, his left leg ejecting from his pants like a slippery weiner squeezed out of a bun. What remained of contiguous Wally was sprawled out before me like a giant flesh tennis racket.

"Wally, goodness, let me help you!" I said while struggling to turn him faceup. I scrambled for his limbs; he moaned awfully. Opening his jacket, I ripped open his dress shirt and attempted to reconnect his detached right arm to its shoulder stump.

What I saw shocked me: the wound was no bloodier or bonier than a sliced-open tube of liverwurst, as if Argonian flesh were nothing but undifferentiated tissue. But the arm wouldn't take. "Wally, can you try welding your arm back on, like you did with your fingers?"

Keening, he tried spitting out an electron burst, but all he could manage was the sparks that a spent lighter could produce. He wailed, "I'm all out, Doc!"

Helping him to be as comfortable as I could manage, I had my secretary, Ms. Olsen, retrieve the containment suit I'd employed during my treatment of the Detached Man, whose body began crumbling into pyramids, cubes, and dodecahedrons without his conscious command. After opening the armor, Ms. Olsen and I hefted Wally and his parts inside it and sealed it shut, tightening the connections with everything in place except the boots and neck collar.

Just as I was calibrating the penultimate settings, I heard the telephone ringing in the other room. After running to answer it, Ms. Olsen informed me that the call was urgent. Since Wally and I had already been interrupted, I pressed the ERECT button on the containment suit so Wally could at least stand while I took the call. There was no point leaving the room for privacy, given Wally's omni-hearing—assuming he still possessed it.

"Miss Brain," said a voice as raw as a freshly killed deer, "it's Festus Piltdown."

Ordinarily I would have avoided using the man's given

name, but taking into account the direness of his tone and the fact that he was calling past eleven o'clock at night, I asked, "Festus, what is it?"

"It's Hnossi," he finally begrudged. "She, she wants you. To talk to you."

"Why? What's wrong?"

"Apparently . . . the, the immortal Iron Lass," he said, clearing his throat, "is dying."

I heard and felt the clap of thunder. I spun, finding Wally back on the floor like a tipped mannequin, his feet detached and upright a yard away from him as if his legs had simply stepped out of them.

It's Always Darkest Before the Dawn (or When You're Blind or Dead)

What will it mean for your life, and for your view of yourself, if the glory days never return?

Omnipotent Man: "For the first time I can remember . . . I'm totally afraid."

One of life's greatest paradoxes is that only when we see ourselves at our most naked, weak, foolish, ugly, disappointing, cowardly, broken, repulsive, selfish, and stupid, can we really appreciate just how special we are. For Wally to fill up the tank of personal reintegration, he was going to have to pull into the filling station of exhaustive self-assessment. And so will you.

Get a quiet space and writing tools, and block off enough time to write out all the occasions in your life in which you've been weak, foolish, ugly, disappointing, cowardly, broken, repulsive, selfish, and/or stupid. A day should be enough. Don't hold back. Total honesty is absolutely necessary.

When you're done, ask yourself the following questions:

1. *Who else other than I is to blame for what I've done?*
2. *How did I personally choose to be a victim of myself?*
3. *How did I enable myself to become a perpetrator against myself and everything I hold dear?*
4. *How many of the psychemotional barnacles attached to the ship of my consciousness am I willing to burn off in order to sail freely across the ocean of well-adjustedness? And why am I too cowardly to burn them all off at once and be done with it? Is it because I'm confusing the barnacles with the ship?*

As you're about to see, the challenge to Iron Lass's immortality would threaten not only her own survival, but Wally's recovery . . . and Festus Piltdown's soul.

CHAPTER EIGHT

UNREQUITED HATE

WEDNESDAY, JULY 5, 9:16 A.M.

The Roots Beneath the Tree

I sat upon the immaculate silver sofa in the immaculate bronze room across from the palace-owner, who was wearing his immaculate ivory suit and golden cravat. Festus Piltdown had no inkling of the reconnection—or confrontation—I'd already set in motion to bring him the peace he so desperately needed from a man he considered an enemy.

Yet the desperation and fragility Festus felt at that moment in his life demanded that I act, in secrecy, to bring to him a one-man intervention.

While Festus and I watched highlights from the 8:30 A.M. Fortress of Freedom press conference on the wallscreen, his aged manservant placed a cappuccino on the marble coffee table beside me before disappearing.

NBC reporter: —believe the destruction of Asteroid Zed to be in any way connected with the death of Hawk King?

X-Man: I can't confirm that, no. Not yet, anyway.

CBS reporter: There are reports that Iron Lass is dying from un-named causes, possibly connected with the orbital prison disaster. Can you comment?

X-Man: That's true—there *are* reports.

CBS reporter: Yes, but, but what about them? Are they true? Is her condition connected with the bombing of Zed or the death of Hawk King?

X-Man: I can neither confirm nor deny that at this time.

ABC reporter: Are you investigating Iron Lass's condition to see if there *is* a connection?

X-Man: . . . All I can say is—and I'm not saying she even has a "condition,"—but I will follow to the ends of this solar system any lead that points to a threat to the F*O*O*J, to this country, or to our planet—

PNN reporter: Following the destruction of Asteroid Zed, a Knight-Ridder poll put you fifty-five percentage points ahead of the Flying Squirrel for Director of Operations. How do you respond to those who say you're exploiting the death of Hawk King, the resignation of Omnipotent Man, and allegations about Iron Lass's health to advance your own personal political aspirations?

X-Man: My—! Look here! My only *aspirations* . . . are truth, and justice! And let truth and justice prevail though the heavens fall!

"Can you be*lieve* that hyperactive hypocrite?" snapped the Flying Squirrel, and then, as the image switched, he moaned, "Oh, not this again!"

Onscreen rolled the by then infamous funeral footage of Festus punching Kareem and Kareem hitting him back, with the anchor's voice-over about X-Man's "meteoric rise."

"Meteors never *rise,* you subcretinous discombobulators! They only fall, crash, and burn out!"

At that moment, Festus's butler Mr. Savant, so ancient and withered he might conceivably have been an unbandaged mummy, returned to say, "Madame is ready to receive visitors now, Lord Piltdown."

Noticing my reaction, Festus shrugged and said, "I acquired a peerage a few years back. Thatcher owed me for all the good press. Come on."

As Mr. Savant led us on the motorized pedway like a guardian mummy through its pyramid, we wound our way through the labyrinthine corridors of Festus's legendary crime-fighting headquarters, the Squirrel Tree. Every hallway was actually the interior of one of the Tree's "branches," and each chamber the interior of a giant "leaf." Vast hydrogen-powered magnetic counter-gravity generators kept the entire assembly, minus the trunk, suspended aboveground. With the facility's "smart garage," Trashbots™, Lawnbots™, air traffic dominance, and DETHscan security system coordinated by the Squirrel-Brain 9000X, the Squirrel Tree made Bill Gates's "smart house" seem like a Fisher-Price play set.

Passing through the cavernous Vehicle Hollow containing the Squirrel Copter, Squirrel Sub, and Squirrel N-ICBMs, and a fabulous five-story-tall replica of the one-dollar bill, we finally entered the Medical Hollow. Mr. Savant led us to the room, pulled back the curtain, stood aside.

From her bed, Hnossi Icegaard looked up at us.

The whites of her eyes were like filthy old pennies. Her face and neck were splotched ashen red and brown. In the worst sections, her skin was flaking off like the scales of a dead rattlesnake dropped into a campfire.

"Rust poisoning," muttered Festus. "Advanced."

"*Ja,*" rasped Hnossi, chuckling out of a bravura smirk. "But you shudt get a look at ze uzzer guy."

"When the cells opened on Asteroid Zed," explained Festus, "the Desiccator attacked her, that goddamned bastard."

"He dit not suffer long—" she said, only to pitch forward in a hacking fit, grating out a sound like someone repeatedly hitting the ignition on a running car. Finally she slowed, cleared her throat, and finished her sentence: ". . . vizzout his torso."

I approached her, gingerly touched her wrist. It felt like phyllo pastry. I told her Festus had passed on her wish to see me.

Mr. Savant left the room. Festus sat in a corner chair.

"*Ja*, Doktor. I am a varrior deity. Ein Aesir gott. My people . . . haff no Apollo, no Sos," she said, I believe meaning *Thoth;* both were deities of science and medicine. "Unt Festus's human doktors, for all zeir learnink, cannot heal vun uff *us.* So I am now facink my own personal Götterdämmerung. My own private tvilight uff ze gotts.

"Unt I haff been sinkink . . . about our sessions. About your qvestioning uff my, my relationships . . . viss my children. Unt now zat apparently . . . zere is no more *time* . . . I vant you to broker—"

Hnossi snapped forward and back, exploding her coughs like a car backfiring repeatedly. Festus leapt from his chair, yelled into his wrist comm for the doctor, then grabbed Hnossi's hand and roughly rubbed her neck and back to loosen her potentially lethal congestion. A doctor and nurse appeared, swept us out, and drew back the curtain.

Festus and I stood in the hallway not looking at each other.

Silence sandpapered a minute off the clock.

With his gaze nailed to his toes, the battle-hardened billionaire stooped before me, his six-foot-four frame fragile, faltering.

"She beat every villain on the planet," he whispered, then captured and released a long, hissing breath. "She's gonna beat this."

I stifled my professional duty to ask him *And what if she doesn't?* long enough for Festus to say, "And then, then, then that bastard . . . Warmaster Set . . . he'll pay for this."

"You're sure he's the one responsible?"

He glared at me. *"Everyone responsible will pay."*

The withered Mr. Savant appeared once more.

"Your . . . *other* guest . . . has arrived, Lord Piltdown."

"My what? I wasn't scheduled for any—"

"Master Festus," said the old man, his watery eyes trembling with sympathy, "it's Master Tran."

Festus straightened up. His spine crackled audibly. He swiveled his face to level his blast-furnace gaze upon me.

"Now why in God's good hell, *Eva,*" he growled, "would I be visited this morning . . . for the first time in fifteen years by my ungrateful . . . insubordinate . . . backstabbing . . . *renegade* of an ex-protégé, *Chip Monk?*"

Sidekicked: Prodigal Punishment

Beneath the grandiose high ceiling of the Allen Dulles room, Tran stood by the mantel examining a framed sepia photograph of a little boy wearing a suit and fire helmet and wiping away his tears. He turned his forty-five-caliber eyes on Festus as we entered.

"Hard to believe you were ever this young," said Tran to his former alpha-hero, putting the photo back on the mantel. "Or that you ever cried. For anyone."

"So," said Festus, his colossal frame regaining its lethal rigidity. His arms crossed his chest like battering rams. "You've returned after all these years just to abuse me, then? My, how your imagination has failed during your supplicant service to that Marxist menace."

Tran, although elegant in a cream-colored suit, was more obviously his fifty years in the full light of the drawing room than he'd appeared in the shadows of the Stun-Glas restaurant Dark

Star. Wince-lines crinkled the amber skin around his eyes; while he still had a swimmer's build, his movements were deliberate, as if he were consciously confronting arthritic agony. Given Festus's unusually youthful appearance, Tran appeared even older than his former mentor.

"I'm not here to abuse anyone," said Tran at last. "I'll leave the abuse to experts like you."

"This is pointless, Miss Brain! What possible good did you think would be produced by this pathetic pup's point-blank petulance?"

"I'd hoped, Festus, to see you finally able to aim the extinguisher of healing upon the kitchen grease fire of your relationship with Tran. And you can only do that when the sous-chef of your most important recipes—"

"I *get* it, all right?"

"All right, then. Let's begin."

I took a seat, gestured for both men to sit facing each other. Neither did.

"Both of you men are clearly suffering," I said anyway. "You were once the most celebrated superhero partnership on the planet. For the entire 1960s, no duo got more magazine covers than you two. You were the model. You took down Pauli the Living Mafia, Black Mamba, the Iron Eunuch, the Monitor Lizard, Standing Buffalo . . . The list goes on.

"And then the 1970s came, and slowly news dimmed of your brave biumvirate; before long all your busts were solo efforts. And then 1980 came and you were finished. Kaput. No more. The media—"

"The media!" snapped Festus. "Lying, distemperous pack dogs! Rabid, mangy curs who spend more hours tongue-bathing their own scrota than investigating the truth!"

"Spoken like the true media mogul of PNN et al. that you are."

"You haven't lost a nanogram of your snide superciliousness, boy."

"And you haven't gained an iota of introspection, *milord*."

"Gentlemen, please. As I was saying, the media implied that you two—"

"I don't need to hear from you what those filthy—"

"—were lovers."

Silence. And glaring.

"And," I continued, "that after Tran's four-year disappearance and resurfacing to work at Human Citizen, your falling-out was the result of Festus's having discovered that Tran was having an affair with Jack Zenith."

More silence. And more glaring.

"Well?" I finally prodded my way into their staring match. "To what degree were those claims true?"

Further silence.

I leaned toward the younger of the two men. "Tran?"

"Jack Zenith is a brilliant, dedicated man," said Tran, sculpting the air with his balletic hands, hands so deceptively delicate-looking one expected to see a cigarillo dangling smolderingly between their slender fingers. "And he is beyond question the finest American of this century—"

"Bah!" said Festus, making him the first human being I'd ever heard use that interjection. But Tran batted not so much as an eyelid.

"—but Jack isn't gay, Doctor. Not that he's straight, either. He's just . . . he's *just.* In a decade of working with him, I haven't seen him so much as smirk a randy thought toward man, woman, animal, or alien. All he does is write, organize, eat tabbouleh, and sue."

"You haven't answered my question, Tran. Why did you two split up?"

"I was ten years old when . . . when *Lord* Piltdown 'adopted' me from a South Vietnamese orphanage. Took me into his home. And trained me in his cult—"

" 'Cult!' "

"—his cult of hero-worship. Him worshipping Hawk King, and me expected to worship *him*. And, God help me . . .

"I *did*, Doctor. If that isn't the most sickening truth I could ever divulge. Everything about him. I identified with my master more than my master identified with himself. Even used his Squirrel Erasing Spray to try to whiten my skin, if you can believe it. It just rotted off all my body hair and left me with first-degree burns from brows to balls. I was fourteen when I did that. And all to become like this man. Did he ever tell you his secret origin?"

"No. But I'm familiar with the story."

"The official story, I'm sure. I only heard it, what, a thousand times . . . a month? How about the *real* story?"

Tran produced the very cigarillo I'd imagined he would smoke, made a show of lighting it, and blew decorative smoke trails and twirls in between holding his cigarillo upward as if balancing an invisible plate upon its tip. He seemed to be waiting for Festus to fight back.

"Yes, the real story," he finally said, lacking any verbalization from Festus. He began pacing and smoking. "How in 1942, when he was only eighteen, his blue-blood bee-baron father, Fountroy Prescott Piltdown V, sicced Hinkleton leg-breakers on the Okie, Mexican, and black migrant laborers trying to organize on his bee fields? How a young public interest lawyer led a class-action lawsuit against Fountroy to get redress for these men, some of whom were stung into hospitalization after the Hinkletons fed poppies and coca blossoms to the bees? How this same public interest attorney investigated Fountroy and discovered he was selling honey by the megaton to the Nazis?"

"This attorney was Jack Zenith?"

"Yes, Jack Zenith. By the time Fountroy's collaboration made the cover story of *The Wall Street Journal* he was so mortified he played a round of PGA roulette."

"What's that?"

"Golf in a minefield. Grenades instead of balls. Daddy Piltdown didn't make it to the first green."

I looked over to Festus, half expecting to see steam shooting from his ears, but he was as silent as his heroic namesake, perched and waiting for the precise moment to strike with deadly, nut-gnawing accuracy.

"So orphan, heir, and Republican Festus, suckled in the pouch of luxury, swears unholy goddamned vengeance against Zenith and the wretched of the Earth he represents. I must've heard him ten million times on the poor: *Parasites, leeches, tapeworms, foreskin-fleas* . . . as if *the poor* had killed his father, rather than his own greed and Nazi-trading treason."

Once again, I looked toward Festus expecting an explosion. Yet he offered nothing but his cold blue eyes glinting like sapphire ice picks.

"So what does he do with his daddy gone and the war on, you ask?" said Tran, pacing, smoking, and gesticulating. "He retreats to his family's Floridian properties in the swamps, a southern manor on a not-so-former plantation. All by himself in the spooky bayou, except for an army of butlers, maids, and indentured lick-spittles.

"So during a moonless midnight of the autumn equinox, while he was reading Nietzsche or Blumenbach or de Molay, a *Glaucomys sabrinus*—a northern hemispheric flying squirrel— plowed right through the twenty-foot-high bay window and showered him with glass, bloody fur, and squirrel musk. Making the young Master Festus soil his silks, I'm sure."

"Your mawkish, mocking attempts to provoke me, Tran," whispered Festus, "will be fruitless. But after you're finished ripping into me with your Zenith-certified rib-spreader, I'd suggest you reread *Lear,* Act One, Scene Four, for some self-description."

"And I'd suggest you remember, *Lord* Piltdown," said Tran, "that even while ranting about serpent's teeth, Lear was not only a foolish, bad, and stupid king—he was loopier than a snake in a garden hose."

Neither man spoke until I asked Tran about the squirrel collision with the window.

"Yes," said Tran, "that, apparently, is when the light goes on over young F.P.'s noggin regarding the power of the flying squirrel to instill terror in the reptilian brain, the 'dominant portion,' he said, of 'your typical urban phrenological reprobate.'

"And he also told me, as I recall, that he identified with squirrels because they're 'so productive . . . they collect nuts and store them while lazy animals freeze to death, as befits their miserable existences.'

"Somehow he never bothered to notice the obvious: that the trees are the ones making the nuts and all the squirrel does is take them. Parasitic, not productive. Like his family."

The Truth About Squirrels and Chip Monks

Tran's tirade, unsolicited, uninterrupted, and unanswered, proceeded for several minutes. And whereas I'd assumed Festus had been lying in wait for the perfect opportunity to destroy his former apprentice, I soon lost that certainty. The elder man, who'd finally sat down, looked less like the poised hunter than the felled hunted, like an aged hound dog on its side, breathing shallowly and awaiting the ripping teeth of rats.

Then Tran shifted to a new topic: hypocrisy. Tran said that

Festus had spent years of their time together exhaustively de-nouncing Wally W. Watchtower's argonium addiction. But the seventy-year-old Festus had the body and looks of an athletic forty-five-year-old for a reason no one was ever intended to know.

"He's," said Tran, shaking his cigarillo at his ex-mentor, "been riding on his argonium high horse like English royalty on a foxhunt, when he's a goddamned junkie *himse-e-e-elf!*" He elongated the word as if he were kissing it. "Addicted to GI Juice, Doctor. Ever heard of it?"

"That's . . . Hyper-regenerative Growth Hormone?"

"HGH, the one and only. The steroid of the long-underwear world. And ten thousand times more expensive." Tran blew an *O,* then shredded it with a spear of smoke. "The army stopped using HGH after Lance Lanternman was the only living GI to survive the trials—"

"That was Captain Manifest Destiny?"

"Yes, yes, Cap. Another addict, thanks to the army. Took HGH until his death in '56, when, according to the newspapers of the time and the history books of today, the Iron Kross killed him. But you can thank Piltdown Propaganda News for that. Why don't you tell her, *Lord* Piltdown? Tell her!"

After ten seconds burned away, Tran answered for him.

"The Iron Kross," he said, tracing the air with his figure-skating hands and jerking agitated strides across what must be the largest Persian rug anywhere in the world, "*had already been dead a year* when he supposedly assassinated Captain Manifest Destiny! He'd died in Argentina, on the F*O*O*J's secret-ops payroll!

"Yes, he hadn't even lived long enough to finish crush-ing the Arbenz Avengers in Guatemala, the very project the F*O*O*J had commissioned him to do! But thank heaven the Iron Kross's body could be journalistically exhumed and resus-citated long enough to frame him for an assassination . . . so that nobody would ever know the Captain had died a needleplunger. Nobody except for the World's Greatest Detective, of course, who found the corpse.

"Don't believe me, Doctor? I read the sealed medical report in the Squirrel files myself—oh, trust me, he's got secret files on everyone, including you, I'm sure, better than the FBI, SWORD, and the Church of Spyontology all rolled together. But the pathologist, yes, the pathologist at Fort Detrick who autopsied Cap said he was so deformed by tumors he looked more like a potato patch than a man. His wife'd had nothing but miscarriages—something else you'd never read in any newspaper.

"Now, the *human* reaction to this is to want to expose the government for what they did to the man and get compensation for his wife. That's what a *real* man, a man like Jack Zenith, would do. And it's also what a self-proclaimed enemy of Big Government should want to do.

"But not the delightful 'Lord' Piltdown, no! He took one look at the scene, found the drugs, figured out what they were for, arranged the cover-up, and he's been injecting ever since that night! Go ahead, Doctor—swab his mouth. Get a blood sample. Hell, take his cappuccino cup to a lab! That was his little joke, you know—he called it GI Joe when he put it in his coffee! This man—"

"Tran, I'd like to ask Festus—"

"Look at him sitting there! He doesn't even deny it!"

"Tran, just a moment, *please!*" I said. The ex-apprentice stopped rigidly in midstep and half-gesture, like a live shrimp flash-fried.

"Festus, I have to ask you—I've seen you emit devastating verbal attacks against anyone who even so much as raised an eyebrow in a manner you considered challenging. But you've just allowed Tran to upbraid you almost without interruption for ten minutes. Please . . . share with me what you're processing right now—verbally integrate it. Own your feelings!"

Festus let out a long, low sigh, like a zeppelin deflating from a penknife's puncture wound.

"He," said Festus, "was an orphan."

I wait. Finally I said, "Go on."

"Like me."

"Yes."

"I took him in. Gave him a home. Treated him like a son—"

"Like a *son*?" spat Tran before shutting up again. I initially assumed he had because of my cautioning glance.

But then I saw the look on Festus's face.

"I never . . . *never*—" He swallowed heavily. "Do you know what it feels like to have people write appalling, sickening lies about you, Eva? I've endured such filth being sprayed on my family's name ever since I was a child. I knew what it was like to be alone, vulnerable, despised. My own mother died when I was a boy, and my father never remarried. I found this child, afraid and alone, a refugee from a traveling Vietnamese circus. I took care of him. Trained him. Taught him everything I knew.

"Loved him."

Tran's eyes opened so wide they looked as if they'd fall out.

"Tran," I asked, "you look . . . as if you've never heard Festus say those words."

The former sidekick was frozen. He'd trapped his flapping, fluttering hands inside their opposite armpits. His cigarillo dangled limply from his lips. Not a word slithered between them.

Festus continued, "And so when those scandalmongering filth-rags accused me of, of 'touching him' because of some antiacademic 'repressed memory' idiocy in that 'abuse-recovery' necronomicon called *The Courage to Fly*—mythology packaged as science!—I sued every one of those libeling lycanthropes into an early grave.

"But it was too late, Eva. To this day, go ahead—look in

any book, any article, any 'Web page' on my career or on the F*O*O*J. All of them cite that toxic spew, even though there's not a syllable of supporting evidence. *Because the controversy itself became news.* Save a country, save a world, save a child— it doesn't matter. You don't need proof or even evidence to burn down a man's soul. All you need is accusation.

"So to answer your question at last, Eva, to answer the world's question at last, my . . . *association* with this young man didn't end because *I* made homosexual advances upon *him*."

Tran was turned to face out the window. His eyes were closed. He sniffed continually as if trying to read the flowers on the Piltdown estates with his nose.

"So, Festus . . . you're saying—"

"I'm saying, Eva, that as much as I tried to help this boy . . . there were things he wanted that I couldn't give him. And maybe if I'd . . . if I'd done a better job . . . he wouldn't've wanted them—"

"Stop it, Festus," choked Tran.

"I'm trying to tell you that it's not your—"

"Stop it! Just don't—"

"Lord Piltdown," wheezed Mr. Savant, shuffling his way inside the vast room. With obvious agitation he said, "Ever so sorry for the interruption, sir, but a third guest has arrived—"

"*Another* one? Eva! What baffle-gambit are you trying to pull?"

"Festus, I didn't—"

"No, sir, it's a Mr. Zenith, sir—"

A lanky, soil-and-ash-haired septuagenarian marched in behind Festus's centegenarian butler. Opening his jacket, he revealed a chest strapped full with explosives, like a smokehouse wall of dynamite. And it wasn't bad dentures distending his mouth, but a detonator clamped between his teeth. I noted with a certain detachment two things: my second brush with explosives in forty-eight hours, and the complete relaxation of my sphincter.

"Jack!" yelled Tran. "My God, what are you doing?"

"Zenith!" yelled Festus. "Have you completely fallen off your bean?"

"Gmph-KWUH!" shout-mumbled Zenith. "Wruh-*NNMMR!*"

With deadly acrobatic fluidity, seventy-year-old Festus vaulted from his chair, reached inside his jacket, and hurled something at Jack Zenith before he landed and rolled toward the wall to smack a hidden panel. Whatever he'd thrown at Zenith erupted into a cumulus cloud of something like shaving foam which apparently hardened on contact, immobilizing Zenith.

"Out, now!" yelled Festus, grabbing Tran, Mr. Savant, and me and launching all of us through the opening of the retracting window. The four of us spun plummeting toward death on the zen-garden boulders five stories below, when at the last moment nets shot out from tree-mounted launchers to break our fall—

—and above us, the Squirrel Tree drawing room from which we'd just escaped erupted into orange, flaming death and raining, burning rubble.

Collateral Damnation

ecurity!" yelled Festus into his wrist, jumping up. "Get to the Medical Hollow *now*. Status on the patient!"

Within seconds, a battalion of gliding, cybernetic Squirrelbots descended to secure the area and protect us while flame-defense mechanisms choked the inferno above. Less than a minute later, Festus's human security guards had scrambled to our location, providing first aid for Mr. Savant and taking me inside for a change of clothes from the extensively stocked manor.

I emerged within minutes and found Tran sitting at the stone enclosure base of the smoking remains of a massive topiary squirrel. He was an agony to behold, his body shaking in utterly silent sobs.

I put my hand on his shoulder. He went rigid. And then, in the random association grief begets, said, "We just . . . we just lost the only man alive . . . who's fit to be president of the United States." He sniffed back mucus wetly. "Not that he'd ever've been even . . . allowed to debate . . ."

Across the grounds, Festus was loudly excreting abuse into his wrist comm. ". . . I don't care, Doctor! You goddamned get her whatever she wants or I'll have you shipped to the Congo to spend the rest of your career harvesting Pygmy organs, you understand?"

Absorbed as he was, Festus hadn't even noticed the arrival of an unlikely partnership: the X-Man and the Brotherfly, there to investigate the near-assassination. Kareem was heading toward Tran, so I intercepted him and explained that he needed to allow the former Chip Monk time to process his psychemotional state.

"Of course, Doc," whispered Kareem. "Poor freaking guy. To finally have replaced *that*," he chin-wagged toward the invective-lobbing Festus, "as your 'father' with someone as great as Zenith, and then only to lose him, too."

He shook his head after another outburst from the lord of the manor. "Look at that—I mean, I've seen him flip out on people for bringing the wrong shade of orange juice," he said, "but thousands of people've been trying to assassinate him for decades. Why's this attempt got him so spooked now? Does he think this was the work of Menton or Warmaster Set?"

I explained to him Festus's concern over how Hnossi Ice-gaard might be reacting to the sounds of the explosion.

The X-Man surveyed the elder hero. "Who woulda thought?"

"What do you mean?"

"That he actually could give a demi-damn about anyone other than himself. Hm. If I didn't know better—"

"Good God," groaned Festus, no longer speaking into his wrist and having finally fixated on Kareem and André. "Dinosaurs, buffalo, the dodo . . . and merit-based hiring. All truly extinct." Then he shuffled off to examine the burned remains of a narcissus flower bed.

"I'm a bit surprised," I told Kareem, forestalling the inevitable fight, "to see you and André working together."

"Call came in. We were both at the top of the duty roster. Anyway, Doc, what hap—"

"Oh, *bzzzt,* Squirrel-dawg! Yo house is da *bomb*!" André howled laughter at his own commentary. He sang, *"The roof! The roof! The roof-is-on FI-YAH!"* Then, shifting into a Joe Friday voice, he said, "What happened here, ma'am? Just the facts."

"I'm the Primary here!" snapped Kareem. "Why don't you buckdance on over there and try not to contaminate the crime scene?"

" 'I'm the Primary!' " mocked André, flying up to examine the smoldering drawing room charcoaling out the midday sun. "Looks like the HNIC got a big ol stick up his Primary ass."

I asked Kareem to explain yet another F*O*O*J acronym. "HNIC," he said dryly, "means Head Nigger in Charge."

Kareem said into his wrist comm, "André, locate the butler and find out whatever you can about when Zenith pulled out the detonator, his state of mind, whatever." He clicked off without waiting for André to respond, just as Tran walked up. After the former Chip Monk had composed himself enough for the two of us to brief Kareem, Festus strode up and said, "They actually put *you* on this, Edgerton? Investigating a bombing at *my* house? Isn't that a conflict of interest?"

Kareem chuckled, apparently enjoying the sight of Festus's distress. "Look, Fasces. You gonna obstruct the investigation, or are you gonna be helpful for a change?"

"Just don't fuck this up. Do you think you can handle that? This is my home, for God's sake. My headquarters!"

Kareem closed his eyes, breathed in deeply, and enunciated the word *kheperi.* Around us, a hundred or more glistening black beetles—from the size of my fingernail to the size of my palm—shadowed into existence. For a few seconds they all crawled about and tested their wings with a sound like an orchestral string section warming up. Then up and off they flew, half of them zipping across the zen garden and grounds, the others flitting into the interiors of the Squirrel Tree.

"The forensics are covered, Pilty. Now I've got some questions for you."

Looking aghast at the insectoid investigators, Festus said, "Questions about that ACLU anarchist who tried to assassinate me, I hope!"

"No, but about Jack Zenith," said Kareem dryly. "About why a distinguished lawyer and civil libertarian would suddenly transmute into a suicide bomber."

For several minutes Kareem drilled Festus, demanding to know precisely what happened and what if any recent interventions Human Citizen had taken against the Piltdown Group, or vice versa. Throughout Festus's response, the X-Man dug into him repeatedly with one of Zenith's most persistently devastating charges: that the Flying Squirrel had pushed the F*O*O*J into starting the Götterdämmerung, and then into prolonging it, because Pilt-Dyne Defensive was its sole supplier of arms, exoskeletons, vehicles, and matériel throughout the war, leaving the American taxpayer footing the F*O*O*J's multi-billion dollar appropriations budget. Even the mid-1980s retrofit of Asteroid Zed was a Pilt-Dyne project, "when according to Zenith," said Kareem, "two dozen other contractors could have done this stuff for a tenth of the price. Or less. C'mon, fifty-thousand-dollar shower curtains? A half-million-dollar bidet? Who's gonna use a bidet on Asteroid Zed?"

"*I* made regular trips up there to supervise reconstruction, Edgerton, and those of us on the winning side of evolution *care* about matters of hygiene. I wouldn't expect you to understand."

Before Kareem could counter him, Festus's security agents ushered in a contingent of the LDPD. Before the tycoon could say a word, the X-Man stepped into the path of the lead detective.

"This is F*O*O*J jurisdiction, officer. So why don't you take your little men back to your brother-shooting clubhouse while we solve this case? 'Bye," said Kareem, turning his back.

The lead detective flushed borscht red. "Now you listen up, 'X-Man'—"

"No, you listen, Detective McDevil," said Kareem, facing him, "I've got full jurisdiction here, and you're standing on my crime scene. So unless you want *me* to arrest *you*, get out of here now. André!" he yelled into his wrist comm. "Get down here!"

The detective, outraged at being trumped in front of his men, looked toward Mr. Piltdown for support. Festus shook his head in sympathetic disgust and shared impotence.

"Don't look at him. Look at me." Kareem smiled. "The one ordering you to get your ass out of here."

"You better watch yourself, Edgerton," said the detective. "The bigger you get, the harder—"

"—the harder I'll kick a fool in the ass. *See* ya!" said Kareem, walking away and waving bye-bye over his shoulder at the retreating LDPD.

"Edgerton!" snapped Festus, sticking a finger in Kareem's face. "Leaving aside how you treated those peace officers, you've wasted ten minutes berating me about a man who tried to murder me in my own home as if *I* were the bomber when the real criminal blew himself to bloody burning bits! Maybe you should be leaving this investigation to someone who isn't conflicted by pursuing a personal agenda—or a political one!"

"Irony—cute. Might want to reflect on that irony yourself, Festes. So you'd have me believe that out of nowhere, one of the most brilliant investigative litigators in the country—"

"Maybe never being able to finish his vendetta against my family finally got to him, and he snapped! Maybe he had terminal cancer and this was his last chance to get me! Maybe—"

"Maybe Menton got to him."

Festus stopped, placing a thumb and crooked finger to his chin.

"May*be*. But . . . Menton wouldn't've been able to mindmaster the Tree's bomb-sniffing technology. It'd take someone like the supreme *khemist* of ancient Egypt, Warmaster Set, to do that. He'd be eminently capable of devising an explosive my sniffers wouldn't be calibrated to detect."

"But why would Jack Zenith work with Set? I mean, Menton could've mind-chained Zenith, but Set doesn't have—"

"The Scepter of Typhon. Obviously you're not the Hawk King authority you think you are."

The blackboard of X-Man's face chalked with exasperation before he wiped it clean.

"The Scepter of Typhon," said Festus, "discussed in the papyrus *The Book of Lesser Portals* as a staff of mental domination. It was lost around 1400 B.C.—but perhaps now found and used again." He snorted. "Not that I disagree with Set's choice of tools in this case."

"You son of a bitch!" said Tran, suddenly at our side. "Jack Zenith wasn't like all us, us *clowns* in the F*O*O*J prancing around in our three-color lingerie. He changed America more for the better than all of us combined. Combined a thousand times!"

"Well, evidently," quipped Festus, "the author of *Unsafe in Any Cape* was unsafe in his final suit."

And with that, Tran spat on Festus's cravat and stormed off.

Toward a Total X-Sanguination

What're you smirking at, Edgerton?"

"Admiring your spit-shine. Focus, Fes-face! There's another angle to the Menton lead—I've finally finished analyzing all the data my *medu-kem* brought me from Asteroid Zed's computers.

"Turns out Menton wasn't the only prisoner missing from Asteroid Zed. Sarah Bellum should've been in lockdown since 1972. But she never made it! With her powers, she could've mind-scribed everyone concerned into believing she was up there. For all we know, she could've been the one who catalyzed Menton's powers—"

The Brotherfly swooped down, brushing his feet on Kareem's shoulders and head.

"Get the hell off me, you moron!" yelled Kareem. "What took you so long? I called you down here five minutes ago!"

André landed, ignoring the question. "Yo, Kreem, you gots a *army* out there, son. Army of reporters. Looking to talk to *y'all*."

Kareem turned his back on Festus without so much as a word. I followed him toward the entrance with André flapping directly overhead.

"Got some fine-ass newsladies out there, K-dawg," said

André. "But what with your 'investigation' making you the Zulu flavor of the week, André gon hafta work his *bzzzt!*-mojo extra hard to get any attention, specially since you light-skinned negroes always get all the play—"

"What kinda bullshit have you been drinking, André? You and I are the exact same color! And you're the one who was on the cover of *The Source,* on *Essence,* you were *People*'s Sexiest Superhero Alive, so don't be giving me your—"

"Whoa-whoa-whoa! You redbone dodecaroons are so touchy! André gots to be calling you Detective *Defensive*! Don't worry, bruh—soon you can be releasin all the tension you got to with them repor-*teurs.* They's a fox from FOX out there with *ta-dow* who's bi*zang*ing!"

"I'm in the Forty-Two Chambers, André! Vow of chastity, remember?"

"All that means is more for André, dawg!" he said, rubbing his hands together and grinning. "All-you-can-eat *hoes*!"

At the gates of the estate, cameras and reporters swarmed X-Man, demanding answers about the status of his investigation and his reaction to polls showing him with a 60 percent lead over the Flying Squirrel. And then a reporter in a pinstriped pantsuit and push-up bra shouldered her way to the front of the throng, holding up a book with the face of an angry hyper-muscular woman on its cover.

"Jaylene Dander from FOX, Kareem. This is an advance copy of Billi Biceps's tell-all autobiography, *Butch Like Me*—"

"I don't know anything about Billi Biceps, Jaylene—she was never in the F*O*O*J, she doesn't—"

"Billi said she was the victim of a cruel lie—that her year-long relationship with Power Grrrl was nothing but a heartless sham—"

"—I'm here to investigate an attempt to assassinate one of this country's most esteemed superheroes, part of an ongoing investigation into the assassination of *the most* esteemed superhero—"

"—a heartless sham designed to cover up the fact that Power Grrrl was never a lesbian, that in fact she was having a secret affair *with you.*"

Suddenly every camera and microphone was shoved in Kareem's face, and for the first time since I'd met him, he was speechless.

"How do you explain this, Kareem?" said Jaylene. "You, the radical, militant, antiwhite, Black Power crimefighter, sleeping with someone that *Hero Threat* calls 'a skanky, white, cryptosexual, pop-tart heroine-poseur'?"

André howled from above, buzzing his wings in hilarity. "And he aint even supposta be sleepin with no ladies at all, no how!"

Cameras swung up toward the Brotherfly. "Him an all his Forty-Two-Chamber-havin blackocentric homies, they all *supposta* be 'chaste,' an now it turn out he been doin the *chasin,* an that he been lying down on the job to be eating off th'blond rug?"

"Shut up, you *mak*-head! Look, Jaylene, your allegations are a complete, utter colostomy bag! I—listen, I never, *ever*—"

"How do you respond to newly surfaced documents, Kareem," said the newswoman, "showing that you actually hated Hawk King?"

"*WHAT? Are you NUTS?*" he shouted. "What kind of insanity is that? Hawk King was my hero! My teacher, leader, and mentor—"

The statuesque reporter took out a thin newspaper. "This is a 1984 copy of *Mama Said Punch Whitey in tha Throat,* the Langston-Douglas underground newspaper you used to write for under the pen name Anavidge Blackman. You wrote, quote, Hawk King . . . is a stooge for F*O*O*J-led white domination of

the planet, end quote. And in another article," she said, producing that issue, "you wrote, quote, I've been proudly hating
all my life, hating the nation of millions holding us back. We
opposing jive turkeys."

Cameras were clicking, whirring, and whining faster than
ever. Kareem's face had drained to beige.

"Because your allegations about Hawk King's secret identity," said FOX's Ms. Dander, "and the alleged 'secret connection' you supposedly shared with him have been the key to
your electoral legitimacy—"

"Tomorrow, look, tomorrow, everyone—listen! I'm
scheduled—I told you all at Hawk King's funeral that I would
be revealing the contents of Hawk King's final papyrus, contents which will—"

"—a papyrus whose authenticity, given your molecular
word-powers, will be impossible to prove, I'm sure," said Jaylene Dander, who then shook the newspaper articles in the
X-Man's face. "But how do you rate your chances of being elected
Director of Operations, Kareem, now that these extreme documents showing your extremist views have seen the light of day?
How can you expect voters to trust a white-hating extremist?"

"How do I—I don't hate white people! You just used the word
'extreme' or 'extremist' three times, you freaking Hyksos—"

Kareem spluttered to a stop while cameras clicked all over
him like a plague of crickets.

"No kot-tam *comment*!" he yelled.

He shoved himself into the choke of reporters, trying to
wedge his way back inside the grounds and through the gate.
Blocked by photographers, he finally started shoving and curs-
ing and got shoved back and cursed at, which made him
counter-counter-shove and -curse. Every moment of it was im-
mortalized in photographs and news video that soon would be
beamed around the nation.

"You'd better back up off me, punks!" Kareem yelled, swinging blindly and punching a coiffed white reporter in the throat, knocking him to the ground gasping.

In the ensuing chaos, Kareem scrambled up the wrought-iron fence, but while clearing the top spikes, he snagged and ripped his pant legs with a cartoonishly extended tearing sound while he fell. He bounded back to the Squirrel Tree with his torn black trousers flapping like pirate flags while the cameras recorded every second of his ragged retreat.

When Distraction
Becomes Destruction

Left unchecked, the quixotic and paranoid paradigm so typical of superheroes can become self-destructive at even the cellular level. In fact, the awesome psychic weight of believing that others depend on you for their very lives can be lethal. For instance, new mothers suffer from postpartum depression not only because of tectonic hormonal shifts, but because of the juggernaut realization that motherhood will be a lifelong, relentless burden of worry, moral (and mortal) responsibility, and embittering power struggles.

Iron Lass had labored as protectress for two thousand years, but the protector burden had finally crushed her immortal-immune response, giving rise to a lethally opportunistic infection from an otherwise minor attack. X-Man's Herculean yoke was his Racialized Narcissistic Projection Neurosis—his irrational urge to view all phenomena as the effects of a vast, encompassing, imaginary "white power structure," rather than recognizing the inherently orderless nature of human societies, the fundamental indifference (or seen another way, impartiality or justice) of the world, and the inescapable ennui that ultimately euthanizes all joy, satisfaction, and human connection.

When dysfunctional self-distraction devolves into delusional self-destruction, neurosis turns into psychosis. If Iron Lass and the X-Man could not discharge their neurotic need to be needed and their yearning for vengeance against nonexistent enemies (whether Menton or "the Man"), their psychotic *mortiquaerotic* (death-seeking) urges would seal their doom . . . and the F*O*O*J's with it.

PART THREE

APPEALING TO A HIGHER POWER

CHAPTER NINE

PARANOIA:
IT *CAN* DESTROY YA

MONDAY, JULY 10, 3:57 P.M.

X-Communication

t was the morning of the press conference, Kareem's first statement to the press since the previous Wednesday's shocking revelations. At the back of the Fortress of Freedom's Hall of Proclamations, I was standing beside the Brotherfly looking at a veritable herd of journalists awaiting their chance to graze upon a fallen hero's next words—perhaps the final words of his career.

While some of Kareem's comrades had turned out to show their support, including attorney Tran Chi Minh, Original Fabulous Man, and the L*A*B's Shango and the Player Hater, the absence of the majority of F*O*O*Jsters was a death-knell indictment of his credibility, and of his bid for the directorship of the F*O*O*J's operations.

Polls shunted him down from 75 to bottom out at 15 percent of decided voters. The Flying Squirrel had glided up to 50 percent. Even Spoiler Man at 18 percent had pulled ahead of Kareem.

In the five days since the story had plopped into the fan, the media had subjected Kareem's life and career—his every article, utterance, deed, failure, and foible—to a public colonoscopy. The only division in the electorate seemed to be over which of Kareem's "betrayals" was worse—violating his own vow of chastity to prosecute a "racially hypocritical" relationship with a white woman, or his racially paranoid denunciation of Hawk King.

(Shockingly, the media-ravenous Syndi Tycho had completely vanished from journalistic sonar screens; not even X-ray paparazzi had been able to snap a shot of her emerging from a trendy bathhouse or a four-star Kabbalah temple. Her publicist had issued only a single statement in the face of the Billi Biceps autobiography and Kareem scandal: "Ms. Tycho wishes to express her profound sadness at the lack of happiness being experienced by her colleagues at this time.")

In the previous day's edition of *The Langston-Douglas Crisis,* two of Kareem's former comrades from the League of Angry Blackmen had accused him of being a "super sellout"; on the AANT program *Oh No She Didn't,* Ms. Thang of the Supa Soul Sistas had demanded "the return of X-Man's race card." And Civil Rights–era icon the Spook had called Kareem "a militant negro threat to democracy as great as that of a Kyklos the Imperial Grand Dragon."

Amid editorials describing Kareem as a "black supremacist" and "race-fixated head case," *Sentinel-Spectator* accusations that he belonged to "a black hate group called the L*A*B, an 'Ebonics' acronym translating out to 'Lots of Antiwhite Blacks,' " and a shocking editorial cartoon depicting Kareem as a bell-bottomed pimp wearing a KKK hood while soliciting Power Grrrl on the streets of Langston-Douglas, came the calls for Kareem to drop out of the election, recuse himself from investigat-

ing Hawk King's death, and even resign from the F*O*O*J itself. The turkeys of Racialized Narcissistic Projection Neurosis
had come home to roost, and were laying their eggs all over Kareem's face.

Flashbulbs erupted like mortar fire when Kareem stepped
awkwardly onto the stage at precisely four P.M. X-Man took his
place at the table arranged with microphones from two dozen
news outlets and was shortly joined by other members of the
so-called X-Slate in the impending election: Gagarina Girl, candidate for Director of Personnel, and Dynamiss, candidate for
Director of Finances, as well as their allies, the current Director
of External Affairs, Shockra, and Director of Investigation, the
Spectacle.

Flashes illuminated the emptiness of the final seat behind
the nameplate for the X-Slate's candidate for Director of Research & Development, the Periodic Man.

Kareem's neck rocked side-to-side in the by-then loose collar of his ubiquitous white shirt, while his skullified eyes
stared straight ahead, a poker face for facing the Grim Reaper.
He looked as if he'd hardly slept or eaten in days.

Having escaped the labyrinth of Langston-Douglas to fly
within tanning distance of the sun inside the F*O*O*J's leadership nucleus, Kareem had allowed the wax of his racial hyper-
rage to melt and scatter the crow's feathers of his afro-paranoia,
leaving him to plummet into the seat—and fate—he'd taken at
that very moment.

"Time to watch this muthafucka squirm," giggled André,
grinning and literally rubbing his hands together.

I tried to catch André's gaze, hoping to glimpse some of
whatever could motivate such an intense psychemotional response toward the X-Man. But he was as fixed on the proceed-
ings as a Roman senator in the Colosseum about to watch a
Christian become cat food.

Kareem's sole opportunity to salvage his career and psychemotional wellness from the Minotaur of his own delusions, and to flee the maze of his own misjudgment, was to accept full responsibility for his grievous errors and beg the public for forgiveness. Only by throwing himself on his sword, battle-ax, dagger, and pocket-knife could he excise the cancer that was consuming his very soul.

Meet the Press, Beat the Repression

Complaining that he'd been "quoted out of context" and citing his need as a young hero "to shock a deaf, dumb, and blind public into consciousness," Kareem gave an opening statement that fell desperately short of the apology for which the press had clearly come looking.

His defensiveness intensifying during the "media analysis" section of his rant, he threw back into the reporters' faces his by-then infamous quotation "I've been proudly hating all my life, hating the nation of millions holding us back. We opposing jive turkeys."

"What I actually wrote," he said, reading, "was, quote, In the 1960s at least we knew we were fighting the Man. We should've called him the Punk. But then in the 1970s, we lost sight and got obsessed with opposing 'jive turkeys.' By the 1980s, we'd whittled down our objective to battling sucker MCs. And by the nineties, the best we could do was oppose 'playa haters.' Well, I have been proudly hating all my life, hating the fools, suckers, and liars with expensive amplifiers who are blinding, deafening, and dumbing us down, and so I've been emphatically opposing the nation of millions holding us back, which sometimes—guess what?—*is us.* We spent too much damn time getting down. Now it's time to get up. End quote.

"So listen, press. If you people're going to attack me for

what I wrote, at least have the intellectual integrity and the professionalism to quote me in full and attack me for what I *actually* said—"

Reporter #1: "Kareem, if you're saying you don't really hate and want to destroy all white people, why did you say you did? If you didn't mean it, why did you say it?"

Reporter #2: "Is it true you own a spear inscribed with the words 'I'm Gon Git You, Whitey'?"

Reporter #3: "Why, after Professor Hnossi Icegaard's declaration of the Götterdämmerung, did you say that, quote, The world might be a whole lot safer if Iron Lass had a husband, end quote?"

Reporter #4: "Kareem, do you lust after *all* white women, or just Power Grrrl?"

Reporter #5: "X-Man, will you offer a complete and unqualified retraction and apology?"

"Listen, listen!" he said, and when he lifted his hands in a gesture of *quiet,* flashbulbs erupted like a prairie lightning storm, capturing his every gesticulation in images that would later be given meaning through captions.

"Let's get this in perspective, all right? The F*O*O*J is under attack, do you understand that? Hawk King is dead, quite possibly murdered, Omnipotent Man has resigned under mysterious circumstances, somebody destroyed Asteroid Zed, someone tried to assassinate both the Flying Squirrel and the hero formerly known as Chip Monk, Iron Lass is dying—"

Kareem froze, wincing with the realization that he had not been authorized to release that information.

Every reporter screamed for verification and elucidation of his slip.

"—and, and, and meanwhile you people have derailed my investigation for five days because of something you ripped out of context that you don't even understand that I wrote *years* ago, when meanwhile a murderer, possibly one of the worst supervillains in history, is systematically wiping out our most powerful champions! And by focusing your attack on me, you people are playing right into his hands, while the *real* enemy—"

Questions inevitably and correctly called for Kareem to address his own delusional paranoia. Angrily battling the questions, he tried to shift focus onto his Five-Point Platform, his proposed "Götterdämmerung against Corporate Crime and Ecological Evil," and his slate's whimsical schemes to use the F*O*O*J to promote their "Mission for Quality of Life."

But as Kareem dodged weakly, reporters tossed stageward the literary bones they'd exhumed from Kareem's corpus of writings, seeking his reactions if not retractions: his rage against white people who wore "dreadlocks" or who used the phrase "ghetto blaster," his charges that "the Beatles had less talent in four voices than James Brown has in a single scream" and that "Elvis was a talentless chicken-fried steak–gnawing junkie thief who should've been charged with grand larceny for stealing black music and executed for the treason of taking the title 'King of Rock and Roll,' " that Civil Rights–era pioneering hero the Spook was "a Driving-Miss-Daisied, ham hock–swallowing, yassuh-bossing, friendly-firing, stealth-flying, five-star general house negro," and that Kareem had once said that "the only position for a woman in the F*O*O*J is sixty-nine."

"Kot-tam it, how many times do I have to apologize for that 'sixty-nine' remark? I said that eleven years ago—when I was *drunk*—at a Stun-Glas wake for Maximus Security when the F*O*O*J was on the wrong side of the Atlantean war that killed him, and some pretty-boy reporter from the *Sentinel-Spectator* was there—"

A reporter: "Isn't it against your black power religion to drink?"

"I wasn't even in the L*A*B or the Forty-Two Chambers at that time—and it isn't a 'black power religion'—and I told the reporter right away I didn't mean it, but he still up and printed it anyway—"

And on and on went the media melee, with André cackling beside me at every drop of Kareem's blood.

Reporter #113: "—hate *all* white people, or just *most* white people?"

Reporter #98: "—and so how soon will you resign from the F*O*O*J?"

Reporter #141: "—initiated the relationship, you or Power Grrrl?"

Reporter #72: "—still in love with Syndi Tycho or just using her for sex?"

Reporter #122: "—did Hawk King know what you said about him and did that break his heart and if so do you think that may have killed him, Kareem?"

Reporter #37: "—true you repeatedly had sex inside the F*O*O*J Fortress's Mission Simulator, leading some F*O*O*J-sters to nickname it the 'Emission Stimulator'?"

Kareem rocketed to his feet, flipping the table and scattering the microphones. His slatemates backed up, stunned. The lashing of a hundred flashbulbs bleached him white. *"All y'all can KISS MY MUTHAFUCKIN BLACK ASS!"*

The Desperate Need for a Chum When the Sharks Are Finished Dining

By the time André and I squeezed through the crush of reporters to enter the greenroom, the then-anorexic-looking Kareem was still as haggard and harried as he'd been onstage. He didn't even raise his head from cradling it in front of the vanity mirror.

His wrist buzzed, petitioning him hollowly: "X-Man, some

reporters from *Jet, AANT,* and *The Crisis* are insisting you speak with them—"

He smacked his wrist, crushing the voice.

I pulled up a chair beside him, sat down, and asked him how he felt.

"That," he muttered, not even looking up, "was a galactic fucking disaster."

The sigh he let out was so heavy, deep, and cold, it merited its own frost warning.

"Whole kot-tam world's falling apart, asteroids exploding, Squirrel's a corrupt corporate-welfare bum, people of capes dead and dying, and the conspiracy to bring down the F*O*O*J is working on hero number *four.* You got Wally the junkie jonesing for glowing blue crystals—"

"Kareem," I asked, "what makes you think that Wally—"

"Give it a rest, Doc! Half those kot-tam reporters out there've known the story for years, but do y'think they'd ever report it? You're never gonna see Wally on the cover of the *Urinal-Expectorator* with his nostrils and fingertips dusted blue an looking like a kid fiending on powdered blueberry Tang! Wally coulda single-handedly stopped Asteroid Zed from being destroyed if he hadn't quit his job while fucked up on argonium, and then Iron Lass wouldn't be dying—"

During his diatribe various logogenic apparitions from his speech flashed into existence, including disembodied nostrils and fingertips. The black body parts rotated around his head, disintegrating randomly into black silt-shadows.

"—and damn in a can," he railed on, "the man was caught flying under the influence how many times? And the argonium exacerbating his MPD? That's a bigger kot-tam scandal than anything I supposedly wrote, said, or did! That's a matter of kot-tam planetary security! Where's the kot-tam press on *that* shit?"

In the corner of the greenroom, a large, steaming, malodorous pile of logogenic feces manifested itself, at which point André said, "Whatever you do now, Kareem, *don't* say the word *muthafucka. Bzzzt!*"

Kareem looked up in exasperation, his black irises like two Rolos dotting twin scoops of vanilla ice cream.

"Can you be serious for one stinking minute, André? What if . . . look . . . Wally, right? He's cracked, MPDed, strung out on argonium . . . What if—I mean, Menton's powers were always strongest on people hiding secrets—maybe he puppet-mastered Wally into killing Hawk King! Wally's one of the only beings with enough power to do it, and then, even if Menton suppressed his memories, guilt from that could be seeping into his conscious mind, which motivated his resignation—"

"Tha fuck you talkin bout, Kreem? That got to be the stankiest heap a Tyranno*saurus* shit André ever took a whiff of!" The Brotherfly affected his trademarked hiss-laughter despite his obvious rage. "Evrabody, *e*vrabody in the whole world guilty a suh'm but *you.* Reporters didn'quote you right, Festus is a corrupt rich man, Wally killed Hawk King, an Hawk King worked f'the white man! *But what about Ka-REEM?*" said André, grabbing X-Man by his face and shoving it back like a tetherball.

Kareem snapped back and leapt up out of his chair, staggering to stay upright, swinging back at André who danced out of the way, causing Kareem to pitch forward and nearly hit the floor.

"Don't you get it?" spat Kareem. "You've gotta put all that you-me shit aside, *Andrew,* long enough to see this attack's bigger than me! This's about my investigation! I *should* be pursuing this Sarah Bellum angle, tracking her connections to Menton! Maybe they've been working together all along . . . or maybe *she's* Menton! Brother, the timing of that smear-job on me was no kot-tam coincidence!"

"Don't 'brother' me, punk-ass nigga! You de*serve* this shit. Biggest accuser who ever shit on somebody he don'like now gettin the shit he dumped, dumped back on him. Where I come from, that's called justice, dawg. *Natural* justice."

He stepped forward to lean down his six-three frame and shove his face in front of Kareem's, close enough for each man to smell the other's breath, to see the sleep (or lack of it) in the other's eyes.

"I hope they rip your ass in two, Kareem," he said, "which's maybe the only way t'finally clear all the shit outta you!"

"André!" I said, shocked for a moment from my professional detachment. "Why do you hate Kareem so much?"

He didn't shake his gaze from Kareem for a moment. "I don't hate *anybody,* Doctor," he said crisply. "Unlike *this* person."

How will you face knowing that you will never exceed, or even equal, the accomplishments of your predecessors?

Brotherfly: "Glory's a hole. Gimme that mo-nay! *Bzzzt!*"
X-Man: "I don't give a fuck about glory. Give me truth."

Denial and Delusion: Always Unhelpful?

Kareem demanded I leave him to his greenroom solitude. I spent the next two days at the Hyper-Potentiality Clinic anxiously awaiting his call. Beyond the fright-show skullishness of his looks, it was the crumbling desperation in his voice, so striking in a man ordinarily so strident, that worried me. Polls showed him crashing through the basement of his previous disapproval ratings. I hoped that wherever he was, there were neither pills nor rope.

And there was no word from Syndi either, the target of her own backlash after having been "inned" by Billi Biceps. There had been a public tearing-up of her membership papers for

GLAAD, and the weekly *SuperherOUT* had denounced her for "pimping queerness to advance her shallow career through poseuristic lesbian chic."

Iron Lass had been too sick to see me, and neither Festus nor André had anything to say outside of anti-Kareem gloating. And so the only person left attending therapy was Wally.

As Argon's only son on Earth continued to integrate the experiences of his many personalities (or *alters*) into his central persona, his powers continued to malfunction and fade. It was as if his hyper-capacities depended on his own lack of self-awareness to function. And the picture that had emerged of Wally's alters wasn't pretty.

As playboy Ricky R. Bustow, Wally had left a trail of businesses he'd plundered, insider-traded, or plunged into the ground; as fight promoter Francis "the Musk Ox" Miller, he'd built his Vegas sports book and his fortunes entirely on Omnipotent Man's battles—not whether he'd win, but how long it would take to defeat his foes, which powers he would use, and which buildings he would destroy; as Reverend "Crawdad" Crocket, he'd built a televangelism empire exploiting his congregation's fears that the Götterdämmerung was Armageddon, but behind the scenes he'd left collection baskets full of broken hearts and at least one very reluctant abortion.

Fascinatingly, the alters possessed qualities of shrewdness, discernment, and intellect that Wally had not yet manifested in his own life. Perhaps a rural upbringing had wilted such capacities in the young Wally, and the overbearing influence of Festus Piltdown III had stifled them afterward. But argonium had stimulated them and set them free. If Wally, free from his destabilizing argonium addiction, were able to harness the alters' mental faculties and awaken them inside a unified Wally-prime personality, he might be able to save his sanity and himself.

But we were nowhere near such a dynamic integration.

Even the existence of Wally's retreat, his Stronghold of Standing-on-My-Own-Two-Feetitude, had come into question, when satellite telemetry in Flying Squirrel's Omnipotent Man file challenged the Stronghold's Antarctic location by showing no such edifice had ever existed there. In fact, the real Stronghold was in the Andes. Faced with such photographic proof, Wally confessed, "I never was no good at d'rections."

Every session, Wally's powers failed further, his panic escalating the closer he got to realizing that his extraterrestrial hyper-abilities might be at their end. I encouraged the desperate Wally to use visualization and the serenity affirmation to picture himself without his powers, but completely at peace. But my request only drove Wally into such deep despair that he began regularly articulating suicidal ideation.

Desperate for a solution, I asked Wally if he would be willing to go along with a last-ditch gambit for his survival.

"Yes!" he wailed, rocking and sobbing in front of me, cradling his head between his knees, pounding his fists into the back of his head heavily enough to elicit gongs. "But how, Doc? I feel like I'm dead already!"

Locking Wally into the Id-Smasher®'s psi-mulated environment for a continuous session stretching over a week, I induced in him the mental experience of having all his powers back. To restore his confidence in his own character, I created a psi-mulated Hawk King who walked with him, talked with him, and flew with him, who constantly reminded him to assert ownership of and become a stakeholder in the Hawkish qualities he so admired, to own the target of his own admiration.

It was a grave risk. Such an auto-belief in his career and his powers required Wally to activate vast mental energies into a delusion of his own competence and the fantasy that the future would unquestionably see the return of his powers to their original magnitude. My dangerous strategy was predicated on the psychestructure's enormous capacity for denial, an evolutionary defense mechanism intended to preserve the sapient organism against overwhelming odds.

Given sufficient time, Wally might eventually have come safely to integrate full awareness of his failures and accept his imomnipotence. But that time had not yet arrived.

THURSDAY, JULY 13, 9:59 P.M.

Self-X-Amination

A t last, on the third night following the press conference, while Wally was still contained inside the Id-Smasher® for his ongoing personality reintegration, Philip Kareem Edgerton showed up at the door of my Hyper-Potentiality Clinic.

He was unshaven, appeared to have lost even more weight, and looked and smelled as if he hadn't changed his clothes since Monday.

"How'm I supposed to do my job when *I've* become the story?" he said by way of greeting. "That's not a rhetorical question, Doc. I'm *asking* you."

"Kareem," I said, showing him into the Encounter Room and frothing him a whippaccino, "what these people are all expecting from you is a statement of accountability. All you have to do is accept responsibility. Then they'll let you do your job."

He sat, looking out the window into the distance toward the hundred and fifty stories of neon called the Tachyon Tower. Based on his sneer, I doubted he was pondering the cosmological-dimensional research being undertaken there.

"Re-spon-si-*bil*-ity . . ." he drawled. "You know, that's the one word Hawk King used in his *Instructions* papyrus more than any other. For all the good the papyrus'll do anybody now. Might's well seal it back inside a canopic jar, let some brother try again with it in a thousand years . . . when the world's ready to listen. To believe. No—scratch that. *To think*."

Disconnecting, Kareem asked me if I'd seen the latest press on him. The stories had mutated into a public version of the childhood game of telephone, with various sources alternately claiming that Kareem's brief article on Hawk King was in fact an essay, a thesis, a dissertation, or even a two-volume set called *Ofays Aint Shit*. *Esquire*'s apparently last-minute cover story, featuring a file photo of Kareem crossing his forearms into an *X*, was entitled *X-Man Hates Your Cracker Ass*.

"You see what that chai-sucking, subintellectual yuppy pinhead wrote?" asked Kareem in reference to Shauna Slyming's column on him in the *Sentinel-Spectator*. "She ignored everything I explained, and then wrote that I 'used words like bullets'—never mind who's using actual bullets against black folks, which apparently doesn't concern her—and then she denounced, quote, *all black radicals*, and accused me of being sexist!"

"Kareem, can you blame her for being upset with you? You must've hit her in the head with a microphone when you flipped the table. Did you see her photo? She's got a huge lump on her face—"

"Naw, she always looks like that. You know she actually phoned me later that day before she wrote her 'opinion piece'? Told me that when I'd written this one article a couple of years ago saying, quote, There should be more female superheroes, that—get this—*that* was somehow *sexist*! Slyming's a crypto-conservative supramoron, Doc! And you know what else she said? She tells me . . ."

The hour wore on, with Kareem frantically spewing out his elaborate theory of self-justification, which, because of his severe RNPN, he could not recognize as proof of his subconscious acknowledgment of his own guilt and the fundamental irrationality of his black-panic paradigm.

"Kareem," I finally interrupted, "what about when we were at the Squirrel Tree, and you called that policeman Detective 'McDevil'? That's a racial slur. That's the kind of thing the public and the press expect you to take responsibility for. You claim you're against racism, and yet you're guilty of exactly what you accuse others of doing."

"First of all, that isn't racism—I can't deny McDevil or his people their jobs, their homes, or their lives. Second, that punk deserves the name. Wanna know why I call him that? Back before I had my powers, he was a patrolman at a Stun-Glas demonstration after Maximus Security got killed in New Atlantis. Punk's worse than a cracker—he's a kot-tam saltine. He *beat my legs,* Doc, beat my legs like he was tenderizing rhino meat!"

"For someone whose very powers are based in words, Kareem, you're employing a double standard on hurtful language. The children's rhyme about 'sticks and stones' isn't true—hurtful words hurt, Kareem, no matter who's using them."

"The cops *have* sticks! What do you think McDevil was beating my legs with?"

"Kareem, when life gives you lemons, make Lemon Pledge! And then take that Pledge and clean up your act! You're losing an opportunity to see yourself for who you really are and therefore to self-actualize—"

" 'Losing an opportunity'? Have you opened your eyes once in the last week? Have you seen what's happening? A conspiracy to murder one hero and neutralize three others, destroy an asteroid, get two supervillains disappeared without a trace—"

"Look inside yourself, Kareem! What opportunity for yourself are *you* missing?"

"This is not about *me*! Why can't you shrinks ever get that, that the world is bigger than the kot-tam individual? The

F*O*O*J is nothing but Lost Opportunities, Inc.—doesn't do a damn thing to solve actual problems. Best it ever does is put out fires, but it's spent way more time settin em.

"You know what Colonel Strom Flintlock spent his whole career as Director of Operations doing? Trying to keep black, female and gay heroes out of the F*O*O*J, stick the Ten Commandments inside every hero's oath, and overthrow the government of New Atlantis. That paleoconservative's a hundred and seventy-three years old, did you know that? The only dead soldier the GI Juice experiments successfully revived from—as he loved to call it—the War between the States. He wasn't fit enough to fight in World War Two, and he didn't join the F*O*O*J until 1946, but he's occupied the DOO chair ever since. A kot-tam joke! That swasti-fossil's so right-wing even a supersellout like the Spook was too black for him! That's what I'm up against!"

"Kareem!" I snapped, standing up. "Listen to yourself ranting about and casting blame on everybody but you! Here's a question to which you have still not given a straight answer to anyone yet, which is at the heart of your current calamity! Did you or did you not have an affair with Syndi Tycho?"

He shoved himself out of his chair and raged out of the room like a zephyr in a rumpled black suit and tie.

The X-Files

According to the F*O*O*J's psychological profile, Philip Kareem Edgerton was, to say the least, a complicated young man. At thirty-four years old, highly intelligent and with a corrosive personality, the X-Man had gained (and had just lost) enormous public standing, an ironic indicator of his interpersonal isolation. In a survey, not a single member of the F*O*O*J had described him as "a very close friend" or even "a

good friend." And despite Kareem's "good old days" affirma-
tions about the L*A*B, I had seen little indication of those hal-
cyon times when I'd visited the Dark Star restaurant and he'd
appeared only marginally more welcome than André.

Facing black racist accusations of "lily-diddling," Kareem
found himself denounced by almost every member of the L*A*B
and the Supa Soul Sistas. A would-be leader without followers,
a lonely man alone inside a mob of his making, the secretive Kareem was a fascinating contradiction: for one who'd railed so
long against white society, he'd immersed himself in the nearly
all-white F*O*O*J, and apparently conducted a secret affair
with a scandal-magnet white heroine. Although he screamed
that he was drowning in it, Kareem apparently loved the tub.

Unlike his fellow L*A*Bsters, Kareem had never been a
street tough, but a quiet, bookish political science student at
Langston-Douglas's Robeson College. Finding a voice through
his writing, Kareem had grown in confidence enough that his
development of superpowers had led him almost instantly into
crimefighting and a subsequent recruitment into the L*A*B,
providing him what he'd never had before: comrades, a base,
training, and technology.

But despite the enormous destructive capacity his logogen-
esis afforded him, the X-Man rarely got into melees; he'd pre-
ferred to devote himself to becoming, in his words, "a thinking
man's hero, and the world's greatest detective, but for real."

Yet his own awesome anger had continued to plague him,
causing fractures between him and his editors, within his first
superteam, and later within the F*O*O*J itself. If Kareem failed
to destroy his own anger, that anger would finish destroying him.

n the days that followed, despite uninterrupted therapy
being a condition of maintaining active member status,
most of my F*O*O*Jster patients stayed away. I did receive up-

dates on two of my sanity-supplicants: Hnossi had declined further, while Festus kept vigil at her side, leaving only to pursue leads in his investigation of Warmaster Set.

Only two F*O*O*Jsters continued their therapy: Wally maintained his feelings-work, sealed inside my Id-Smasher® for uninterrupted reprogramming. And André continued seeing me, splitting his session time between bragging about his sexual conquests and condemning Kareem. Once, for variety, he informed me that he'd visited Syndi in her undisclosed location, and that "she be doin all right."

The only subject that slowed down André's leering litany of lust or his cantankerous anti-Kareem catechism was the death of Hawk King. At any mention of the fallen mentor's name, André's smile turned inward; he chewed his lips, nodding and staring at the floor, saying only, "Ain't no justice in this world, Doc. No justice for nobody."

SATURDAY, JULY 15, 8:30 P.M.

Lame by Blame

When Kareem finally returned to the Hyper-Potentiality Clinic on Saturday evening, he was calm but sullen. He opened our session complaining that his investigation had been all but destroyed since he couldn't gain access to the "crime scene" of the Blue Pyramid (sealed by the Ka-Sentinels ever since the funeral), and because wherever he went he was mobbed by reporters, yelled at by angry citizens, and stonewalled by uncommunicative witnesses. But that tirade soon gave way to his obsessive attempts to convince me that his recent reversal of fortunes was the result of a "white power structure" bent on destroying him.

"Is that really true, Kareem? I mean, take that editorial cartoon in the *Sentinel-Spectator* that made you so upset. That was by Melvin Moal, and he's black, I believe."

I pulled the cartoon from my file, but he refused even to look at it. I glanced at the image of the Klan-hooded Kareem in a "pimp suit" prostituting Power Grrrl on the streets of Stun-Glas, with its embittering caption X-CONTENDER.

"Melvin Moal," sneered Kareem. "The kot-tam Moal-man. Never even stepped foot in Stun-Glas. That Tobytron belongs to the Cartoonist Council of White-Gloved, 'Yowza'-Howling, Tomosexual House Negroes. It isn't just *me* he sold out—you should see the racist shit this guy drew about the Crimson Kafeeyah, the Palestinian crimefighter. Drew him like a mad dog, actually used the words *Arab, animal, savage,* and *killer* in the background—I mean, no wonder he's fucking with me like this! This sellout punk Moal, I swear, he got named Tom of the Year by *Tom Magazine* three years running—"

"Now, Kareem, we both know there's no such thing as *Tom Magazine*—"

"Well there should be!"

"You can't heal yourself of your toxic, boundless rage if you don't admit some culpability, Kareem. Are you really saying that everyone is to blame but you? That this is all the result of some vast white conspiracy to, how did you put it, 'keep the black man down'?"

"I never said that!"

"I think you did, Kareem."

"Wouldn't I know what I said?"

"So I'm wrong, the media is wrong, the F*O*O*J is wrong, Hawk King was wrong, the L*A*B and the Supa Soul Sistas who denounced you are wrong, everyone is in on this vast white conspiracy and they're all wrong except you, the very person who wrote the words that are now coming back to destroy you?"

"This is bullshit! You're setting up a freaking *battalion* of straw men! I can *hear* the quotation marks you put around every political term you spit back at me! And whatever book you plan on writing about all this, I hope you announce yourself in the foreword as being the most unreliable narrator since Jonah went deep throat!"

Feeling the frustration of battering the impenetrable wall of Kareem's X-rhetoric, I decided it was time to allow him a break.

How will you face knowing that you will never exceed or even equal the accomplishments of your predecessors?

X-Man: "I don't give a fuck about glory. Give me revenge."

The Parable of the Two Dogs

After Kareem had discharged some of his anger through a journaling session, I shared with him a Native American parable. It was my hope he'd be able to use the story in visualization to help him contain his raging self-destructive tendencies.

"There once was a tribal elder who found an anxious young brave," I told him, "who was perched atop a butte beneath a moonless night sky. It was the night before the young brave was to begin the trials of his manhood initiation, his 'vision quest.' The brave told the elder, 'Medicine Man, every night I dream that there are two wolves fighting inside me. In the morning when I wake up, I feel as if I've been ripped apart during the night. What does it mean?'

"The shaman told the young brave, 'Inside everyone there are these same two wolves. One is white, and one is black. The white one is Joy, Hope, Courage, Loyalty, Justice, Honor, and

Love. The black one is Rage, Despair, Fear, Selfishness, Revenge, Cowardice, and Hate.' The brave asked him, 'Really? That's what these wolves are inside me? Then which one will win?' You know what the medicine man answered, Kareem?"

He shook his head.

" 'Whichever one you feed.' "

Kareem argued with me at length over the colors for the wolves, but I refused to budge on the deeper truth of my story, and throughout his dinner break he ate his bean pies quietly, his every munch a munch of intense, self-actualizing introspection.

Chaos X Machina

After supper, a mellowed Kareem still refused to discuss Syndi, but neither did he launch himself out of the room when I asked him about that relationship. Instead, the ever highly strung Kareem suddenly uncoiled like a black mamba on muscle relaxants, waxing nostalgically on the first hero he'd ever wanted to emulate—not Hawk King, but the Langston-Douglas legend Maximus Security.

Rising to prominence as a crusader against neighborhood drug dealers and the "corrupt police" supposedly in collusion with them, Maximus Security left America in 1975 to fight alongside the MPLA in Angola. The young Kareem, then known only as Philip Edgerton, had idolized the maverick crimefighter throughout those overseas adventures and even more after his return to the neighborhood in 1977, following his every move and filling scrapbooks with everything he could find on the man.

"Old people used to look at Brother Max and shake their heads," laughed Kareem, imitating their scowls. "They thought he was gay. See, he used to wear this shiny yellow disco shirt open down to his navel, these tight blue pants, and this huge, oversized chain around his hips—"

"Would that bother you? If he were gay?"

"What're you talking about? I don't give a frosty freak about any gay/straight yah-yah. Coulda been gayer than Oscar Wilde and Felix Unger for all I cared. He was my hero, understand? He had his own style. Man was always using weird expressions like 'Holy ship!' and 'Jesse H. Chimpmas!' and saying to the cops stuff like 'You jive turn-key'—I mean, corny as all hell, but he'd wink and all us kids'd laugh, and he'd toss us some goat jerky. Man was so popular, they actually based the movie *Shaft* on him, and *Schoolhouse Rock* even did a cartoon that everybody in Stun-Glas just knew was really supposed to be him: 'Verb! That's what's happening!' I mean, you know you hit it big time when they start making cartoons of you!"

"There was a cartoon of you, Kareem. Do you feel fulfilled to have 'hit the big time'?"

"Editorial cartoons depicting me as a Klan pimp and drawn by step-and-fetching, massa-sucking, porch-monkeying, professionally hamboned ultra-Toms don't count, Doc. And you already knew that, so quit talking shit," he sniffed bitterly. "Like I was saying, Brother Max, he was every ghetto kid's hero. So when he up and joined the New Atlantis International Brigades against Reagan's terrorists, we all wanted to go off with him, be his Stun-Glas junior troopers. He was so tough that if we could be like him we'd never die, cuz *he* could never die. And then it was 1984, and he did."

"Did what?"

"Did die," he said darkly. "So yeah, you've been blasting me, blasting me, blasting me about being angry, that I have to 'take responsibility' for what I wrote about Hawk King. Yeah, I was angry. And I had a right to be angry. I wrote it and I was right: from Guatemala to Congo to Iran, the F*O*O*J were, quote, agents of global honkification and leucogemony. And yeah, that included Hawk King, going along with all this shit about truth, justice, and the American way. I wrote that you could have truth and justice *or* you could have the American way, but you couldn't have em all together. And you know what happened? After I wrote that?

"Hawk King, who'd supposedly exiled himself inside the Blue Pyramid almost every day and night for the last nine years, he came to visit *me*."

"You? Personally?"

He nodded slowly and heavily, as if the power of his claim were in the mass of his chin. My wristband buzzed three quick vibro bursts into my skin; I subtly tabbed the ACKNOWLEDGE key to let Ms. Olsen know I'd received her message.

"I was sitting up on the roof of my apartment building drinking coffee," said Kareem, unaware of what I had waiting in store for him, "pounding out my column on my manual typewriter like I did every Sunday night. Every once in a while I'd look around . . . maybe at all the network transmission towers, at the lights of the Hermes Theater, or over at the Tachyon Tower, wondering what kind of astonishing discoveries they were finding in their dimensional research labs, scanning out past the edge of the galaxy, spelunking black holes, gazing at quasars . . .

"And while my head was all whirling inside those mysteries, suddenly the moonlight went out.

"I looked up, and I was staring into the moon-frosted silhouette of a man-hawk.

"He swooped down, landed in front of me—six-four, golden beak and gold-rimmed eyes glittering, flapping his huge black-and-gold wings with enough strength in em to crush me like a ripe tomato.

"I thought . . . I thought he was there to kill me, Doc."

He shook his head again, got out of his chair to gaze through the window across the Bird Island skyline.

"But he'd come to tell me he'd read what I'd written," said Kareem, ". . . and that he thought I was *right*.

"I couldn't believe it. I was completely in awe, humbled that he'd even read something I'd written, that he'd been moved by something I said. And somehow I managed to cough up the guts to ask him why he'd come to me.

"And then he invoked a spell . . . and transformed himself. Into a man, an old man, maybe five-seven, in a crummy, crumpled suit looking like something my grampa would've worn in maybe 1945. He was sitting there in front of me, a black man. In a wheelchair. Told me his name was Dr. Jacob George James 'Jackson' Rogers. That he wasn't a god, but a man from the dawn of civilization who'd gained his celestial powers by leading a war to avenge his slain father, the ancient Sudanese mystic named Lord Usir.

"I mean, it's a Sunday midnight and I'm sitting at the feet of the man Hawk King's turned into, who's revealing to me his life story underneath the city lights and the moon and the stars. He told me that after ruling over the lands of the Nile for a century as its Hawk King, he felt empty . . . Except for great-grandchildren, he'd outlived everyone he'd cared about: wives, mother, friends, cousins . . . and in all that time he'd never gotten over the loss of his father, which happened even before he'd been born. So he left. Went up into the stars to try to find his father's souls. Found himself still in battle against his evil uncle, Warmaster Set, and holding back the chaos of the cosmic serpent Ããpep.

"Sometimes he'd come back for a while, rescue Egypt when she was in trouble . . . and after Egypt fell, he helped out in other places where people still knew his secret names, in Meroë, in Namoratunga, in Timbuktu . . . but he'd always go back out into the rolling deeps of space, searching for his father.

"And then, one time, after searching for he didn't even know how long and still not finding him, he came back. But everything'd changed. He realized it'd been seven thousand years since he'd been born, and he hardly even recognized the world anymore. But he saw a war going on—World War Two—took a side, raised his own army. The F*O*O*J.

"But when the war was over he wanted a life, not as a *hawk* man but as a man. So he transmuted himself back into his human body. It'd aged—not seven thousand years, of course, but still. And when he went looking for a place to live, he made a discovery: most places in the city wouldn't rent to a black man.

"He knew what it was like to be a persecuted refugee—that's how he'd started his life, since his uncle'd murdered his father and he was raised by his single mother, a warrior-woman on the run. So he decided to blend in. Got an apartment in Ellison Heights in Stun-Glas. Practiced medicine for people who couldn't afford it. Got his doctorates in archeology and cosmology and taught at the university and tried just to live as a man by day while guiding the F*O*O*J as a mystic-philosopher-king by night.

"But Dr. Rogers . . . he was devastated by what he saw in the world. And he just . . . he couldn't figure out what to do with his powers that wouldn't involve conquering the planet, killing and destroying to impose his will, and he didn't wanna solve things like that. Said it wasn't right and that it wouldn't work in the long run anyway. So he'd decided to bide his time, do his research, figure everything out.

"He told me, when he came to see me that night, that he'd finally figured it all out. Partly because of the death of Brother Maximus Security. And partly because of what I wrote.

"He told me he was reaching out to what he called 'the virtuous young' to become his *Shemsu-Heru*. That he would entrust us with certain powers, his to enhance and his to take away depending on what we did with them. And then he gave me a papyrus roll, what he called *The Book of Doing Knowledge*. Told me to search out the canopic jars he'd left around the city, across the Americas, across Africa . . . and write down whatever words I found in them.

"Within a few months I'd found a dozen jars, mostly in Stun-Glas libraries and in the Schombro Center. They were like glowing turquoise, and after you opened 'em, they spoke their words to you and then—*whoof!*—they just disappeared. And because I was searching for them, I met a bunch of other young brothers and sisters looking for them, too. That's how I met the people who'd end up forming the L*A*B and the Supa Soul Sistas. It was like a, a, a Hawk King affirmative action program.

"At last, deserving people weren't gonna be held back by where they were born, or what they sounded like on the phone, or looked like when they showed up for the interview. Brother Grimhotep, he found so many jars and gained so much wisdom, he was the one who created the Brotherhood of the Forty-Two Chambers and initiated the rest of us. We connected, selected, directed, and defended Stun-Glas. And waited for the day Hawk King promised when we'd be trained enough and ready for him to reveal to us all his celestial, revolutionary vision."

"So," I asked, "with all that success and what you saw as an inspiring vision, Kareem, what happened? Why did the L*A*B to which you were so devoted decide to excommunicate you?"

He looked back toward me, his lips parted, not even trying to hide his shock.

"I *am* a psychiatrist, Kareem. We don't get our degrees for being completely dim, you know."

I got up, joined him at the window, noticing how the street-lights turned into stars in the blackness of his eyes. "Did the L*A*B kick you out . . . because they found out?"

He looked down. His jaw muscles bulged visibly around the base of his scalp as he ground his teeth against one another.

"So this is it, huh?" He chuckled grimly to himself. "This is how my career ends. Not because some dickwad's laser beam cuts me in half, not because the Ammit Monster chews me to bits, not because the Turner Diarists blow me up in the Los Ditkos Federal Building . . . but because of the kot-tam lie that I hated Hawk King . . . and the truth that I . . . that I—"

"—that you *did* have an affair with Power Grrrl."

He stood, still as a statue.

"Yeah," he said finally.

I touched my wrist. "Ms. Olsen, would you please show in Ms. Tycho now?"

Kareem looked up at me, eyes bulging as if he were choking.

Syndi walked in. Gone was all her glamorous glitteralia, the look-at-me paraphernalia and the outrageous temporary tattoos, all replaced by a simple black PG!-logo T-shirt and jeans. Even her trademarked blond mane had changed—faded to black.

"Hello, Eva," said Syndi, her mascara drenched into raccoon smears. "Hello, Kareem."

The Long Kiss Good Morning

T he two black-garmented heroes sat as far as possible from each other on opposite corners of my wide white leather chaise loungue.

"This is bullshit!" rumbled Kareem. "I *should* be investigating a murder case! Hawk King's dead, Jack Zenith's dead, Asteroid Zed's destroyed, Iron Lass is dying, Menton and Sarah Bellum are missing—"

I cut him off. "Syndi, how do you feel about what Kareem's just said?"

She shook her head. "It's just, like, sad, Eva? Because Kareem was always, like, *afraid* to look inside himself. Which is why he was always looking 'out there.' But snap, like, let the world save itself? You've gotta save *your*self, you know?"

"So you don't believe Kareem's claims about the Destroyer being responsible for this current crisis?"

"Gawd, no. Even when we were together, Kareem spent half the time talking about these, like, elaborate conspiracies. This Menton-thingy's just the latest one."

"So, Syndi," I asked, "why did you lie about being a lesbian?"

She twirled her hair, rolled her eyes at the ceiling and then back toward me, indignant at being questioned. "I didn't, like, *lie,* Eva."

I produced the advance copy of *Butch Like Me* that Festus had acquired for me, flipping through the ghost-written Billi Biceps autoherography until finding the first of many passages I'd marked. " 'In eight months together, Syndi never even let me get past first base. Or maybe second—I never really got that whole baseball thing. That's a man's game, anyway, what with all the phallic crap. So let's just say volleyball. Well, I never spiked her or anything like that. Just overhand serves. But regardless, the point is, she's no dyke, you understand? I don't think she's even bi. She's just the world's biggest poser. Everything is all about appearances with her, and it's *always* all about her.' "

I closed the book and kept my hand on the cover image of Billi as a steroidal Rosie the Riveter. "Well, Syndi? Is Billi lying? Or are you?"

"I never, never said, *Eva,* that I was a lesbian. Never! I just created provocative imagery and let people think, like, whatever they wanted to!"

"You joined GLAAD."

"You don't have to be lesbian to join GLAAD. They got something they wanted out of it, and I got something I wanted out of it. Everyone profits. What's your hyper-damage?"

"So your profit was more albums sold, a possible film deal, more makeup endorsements, and more sales of your books, perfumes, breast enhancers, Power Grrrl Dental Dams™—"

"And they got to use me for *their own* PR. Everyone wants to use me. Even these men who think I'm lesbian and buy my posters and videos and go to my movies . . . I mean, how insane is that? I'm more popular with men because they think they *can't* attain me?"

"You lied to Billi."

She looked back at me, her eyes blue radiant rage inside the black halos of smeared makeup.

"According to this book," I said, tapping the cover, "you broke Billi's heart. Did *she* profit?"

Deformed into its trademarked pout, Syndi's mouth suggested indignation far more than photogenic lust.

"How does it make you feel . . . to know what you did to her?"

"I feel ashamed, okay? Are you happy? Is that what you want to hear?" she yelled. "I never meant to break her heart. No one was supposed to get hurt. It just . . . things got out of control. Like they are now. Kareem won't even talk to me, for months he's refused to even look at me, he won't even say my fucking *name,* people are dying left and right around me and I'm gonna be left alone . . ."

"Tell me," I said, "about your relationship with Kareem."

At that, the two former lovers finally looked at each other, their faces crawling with the crabs of conflicting emotions.

When neither broke from their eye war, I finally asked, "Which one of you initiated the relationship?"

Kareem raised a black eyebrow with all the menace of a Jolly Roger, but Syndi didn't flinch.

"*I* did, Eva," she whispered, her voice puckering with melancholy. "I first saw Kareem in the press, like, five years ago. I thought he was hot. And dangerous. And hearing him speak . . . it was like watching a panther run after a gazelle. I'd catch stories on PBS's *Langston-Douglas Black Journal* about him and his L*A*B patrolling Stun-Glas—"

"*You* watch PBS?" I asked. "*You* watch *Langston-Douglas Black Journal*?"

"Yeah," she said, flitting her head in an unspoken *no duh.* "So then they got their HUD contract, and Kareem was this up-and-comer, sexy, angry, successful, going places. So, like, this was four years ago and I was still an up-and-coming singer/heroine myself, and I was the opening act for Salt-N-Pepa's *Let's Talk About Sex* tour at the Hermes Theater in Stun-Glas, and the L*A*B was doing security that night—"

"Four years ago . . . so Kareem, you would've been thirty, and Syndi, you would've . . . been only fifteen?"

Kareem's and Syndi's eyes faxed multipage documents to each other in text too small for me to read.

"Uh . . . *yeah,*" she said. "Anyway, I arranged to meet him backstage after the concert. And I thought we, like, had this chemistry, but he was all, like, 'Aren't you a lesbian?' and I was, like, 'Don't try to put me in your little box, baby. So are you down or what?' and he was, like, 'No, I'm a black nationalist, I'm chaste, and even if I weren't I don't do white girls, and plus you're just a kid,' and I was, like, 'Whatever! You're a man! You really think you can resist me?' And so I started tracking him down, and he was, like, 'Stop following me,' and I was, like, 'Nuh-uh, you stop following *me*—' "

"*Damn,* Syndi," groaned Kareem. "Would you please give it a rest with all this 'like, like, like' shit? We're here, all right? Doctor-patient privilege? And after everything I've been through . . ."

She looked at him, suddenly even softer.

"I think that's the first time you've called me by name since . . ." She sighed. "All right, Kareem."

I said, "You're not nineteen, are you, Syndi? You're older."

She nodded at my statement.

"And not a lesbian, either. So what else isn't real? The bubblehead act, obviously. So you really did write all those books, then."

"She's a marketing genius, Doc," said Kareem. "And one of the smartest women I ever met. That's why . . . why I started liking her."

Syndi glowed like an aromatherapeutic candle.

"So who was driving the bus?"

Kareem scrunched his face disgustedly. *"What?"*

"She's asking who wore the pants in our relationship, Kareem. I'd say . . . it was pretty fifty-fifty in the driver's seat, Eva," she said, nodding to encourage him to agree with her.

He laughed bitterly at her nonverbal request. "I'da been happy if it'd just slowed down long enough for me to get *on* the bus! I spent the whole time running after it with my coat caught in the kot-tam door!" Syndi wince-smiled abashedly. "She came on so strong, Doc. Wouldn't leave me alone, kept following me, until I couldn't get her out of my head. I knew I shouldn't've, but . . . kot-tam it, I was lonely. I've always been lonely. Wasn't like I'd ever had women chasing me. I'm not made of stone. She wore me down. So finally I agreed to meet her—incognito."

He sighed, deeply.

"I told her to drive out and meet me in San Sebastiano at the only Ethiopian restaurant in town, a little place called the Emerald Lion. She wasn't all tarted up that night. She was elegant. Wore a long black skirt. Her hair . . . it smelled like saltwater and hot sand. And we just . . . talked. For hours. About music, food, books, comedy, art . . .

"I'd been angry so long, serious so long . . . and suddenly there I was laughing, reminiscing about cartoons, toys, games, things I hadn't thought about since I was a kid. And feeling . . . totally free. In my life, I always had to set a conscious example, come correct, what we used to call in the L*A*B, *be blackified.*

"But with . . . *Syndi,*" he said, visibly forcing himself to say her name again, "I didn't have to do that. Or need to do it. It was like, suddenly, all I had to do was just one thing: be happy. When I was with her, suddenly it was like there was no world, no politics, no mission, no duty. It was just us."

"And you so fell in love with her."

His mouth opened angrily, as if he were about to spit denial. But then he softened, looking at Syndi, then at me, and finally granted a single nod in defiance of himself.

A sigh almost broke into a sob in Syndi's throat. But she was smiling enough to crinkle her eyes.

"But then the L*A*B found out," I pushed. "What'd they do?"

Kareem glared out the window.

Syndi leapt in: "They told him to stop seeing me! What the hell business is it of theirs?"

"Why's this gotta be the big bad fetish—black man, white woman—like it's the end of the kot-tam world?" said Kareem. "You see these newspapers? These punks'd happily be printing headlines like 'Nigger B&E's into Whitey's harem' even if the planet were plunging into the sun!"

"But didn't you used to feel the exact same way, Kareem? Isn't that what you said in one of your articles?" He said nothing. "And you were denounced by whites for your *hypocrisy,* not your transracial eroticism. Those denunciations were almost all by blacks." He wouldn't answer. "So the L*A*B kicked you out. How did that make you feel?"

"I talked with Dr. Rogers," he said, "asked him what to do. The L*A*B was already under fire—we were about to lose our HUD contract, and now I was in the middle of a relationship I shouldn't't've been having at all, for several reasons . . . He said that everything was unfolding as it was meant to, that my destiny was ultimately to lead the F*O*O*J.

"I laughed. I mean, I figured he was yanking my spear, trying to cheer me up. But he wasn't kidding. So before the L*A*B could force me out I quit. Syndi'd already been in the F*O*O*J a year by then, done her probation, was already a made member, so she sponsored me. No one made the connection. But I'd already shocked the hell out of everyone just by asking to join."

"So what happened? Clearly you were both passionately in love. What went so wrong between you two that you even stopped saying Syndi's name?"

This time, instead of their eyes sending faxes to each other, the two turned toward opposite walls, my question rebuffed by their receivers being taken off their hooks.

Little White Lies and Big Black Secrets

nraveling the bandages covering Kareem's and Syndi's psychemotional wounds was exhaustive work, since their bloodied psychic linens were so crusted together they'd congealed into experiential gore. As the night deepened, we baby-stepped our way through the basic facts toward what I'd sensed was a devastatingly destructive betrayal.

We established the basics: that the relationship was passionate but rocky, its secrecy deemed necessary by both but frustrating to each; that over time, Kareem saw Syndi as selfish, shallow, vain, and narcissistic, whereas Syndi came to see Kareem as obsessive, deluded, impersonal, and emotionally retarded.

And as was generally the case, the sexual problems that erupted during such a contrapersonal disconnect were misdiagnosed by the couple as cause rather than as effect.

From Kareem's perspective, Syndi had grown sexually unresponsive in the second year of their secret trysts, "after the kink wore off," he sneered, and also, according to him, because she was terrified that he was finally seeing through her multiple layers of deception and self-deception to gaze upon the real Syndi. The more she shut down verbally, psychemotionally, and sexually, the more frantically Kareem inverted their preset roles of hunter and prey, driving her farther from him and him deeper and deeper into chasing after connection with her and drowning himself in self-loathing.

And then, one night, in a desperate attempt to restart their physical passion and emotional intimacy, Syndi made a snap decision that shattered something in Kareem which apparently had not healed one iota in the two years that had followed. And the closer we moved toward gazing into that smoldering crater, the more Kareem's body stiffened and his face splintered.

"It'd been two *months*, Eva," said Syndi. "Since we'd. You know. Made love. I mean, we'd sleep in the same bed, but we wouldn't even hold each other.

"I was desperate, just . . . terrified it was over. I mean, I *loved* him . . . but all we did anymore was go through all the cloak-and-dagger bullshit just to see each other and spend the night together without any witnesses connecting us, and then we'd just argue! All night! Or sit in silence! Or sleep together without even touching each other. I just . . . I wanted to feel close to him, for the sex to be good again, for everything to be like it was in the beginning."

"So what did you do?"

Kareem's eyes flared. "So, great, not enough I'm humiliated in front of the kot-tam world, now I get humiliated here, too?"

"Kareem—" she said, reaching out for his knee or arm or shoulder or cheek, but he shoved himself off the chaise longue and walked to the farthest point in the room from her, pretending to read a book he'd pulled from my shelf.

I forced her to look at me. "What did you do, Syndi?"

"I . . ." she said, trying to decide whether to confess, and finally: "I used my HEAT Ray on him."

"Your . . . your hyper-emulation beam? You . . . turned him into a copy of you? Which you controlled?"

She nodded. Kareem looked angry enough to bite through the wall.

"And it was amazing," she said. "I'd never felt anything like that in my life. Ever. It was so good . . . the best—"

"Kot-TAM!" snapped Kareem. "Can you *hear* yourself?"

"Kareem, please. Let Syndi process this. Continue, Syndi."

"That's it. I mean . . . what else can I say? It was really that good—mind-blowingly, Richter scale fantastic. But after I relea— . . . when we were done . . . Kareem, he was shaking. And he . . . he cried. For an hour. And he wouldn't let me touch him. I'd never seen anyone react to the HEAT Ray like that before, but—"

"Had you ever used it in sex before?"

"No, but . . . no."

"Syndi, don't you think it's odd that although you've told me you're not a lesbian, you've presented yourself to the public as one for years, and that after finding yourself sexually unsatisfied with a man" (even without looking at Kareem I could *hear* him react) "turning him into a woman reignited your erotic energy?"

"No, Eva, you, you don't get it—that wasn't it at all. It's not that I turned . . . I mean, that Kareem became a . . . look, it's not that I was making love to a woman—"

"It's that you were making love to *you.*"

She swallowed, looked away from me, then down at the floor. "Yes," she whispered. "Yes."

"Kareem . . . you obviously had a strong psychemotional response to this sexual engagement—"

" 'Engagement'!" he hollered at the roof.

"You're verbalizing a great deal of antihappiness. Could it be that you're actually manifesting this antihappiness toward yourself?"

He turned to me. "What in the hell are you talking about?"

"Are you 'angry' at yourself because you liked the experience so much? Of becoming a woman?"

Kareem's arms and legs slackened, and he slumped against the wall, his jaw seemingly unhinged. He was literally panting with speechless rage.

"Gender confusion is a common experience, Kareem, and nothing to be ashamed of."

"I don't *have* 'gender confusion'!"

"Not to mention the psychic clash with your pronounced homophobia of being suddenly transformed into a lesbian—"

"I am *not* homophobic and I didn't *'transform'* into a lesbian—"

"Well, a clash of your becoming a woman against your deeply held sexism—"

"For fucking out loud, *I AM NOT SEXIST!*"

"Well, whatever label you choose to affix, you were frightened by this experimentation—"

"It wasn't 'experimentation,' *Eva!* It was *ex*ploitation! Complete kot-tam hum*i*liation! So I got angry—to use a word you fear so much—angry because someone who said she loved me could make me her puppet, her toy, her kot-tam *slave,* and then have the gall to expect me to like it! To expect me to willingly throw up my wrists for her to lock the cuffs on again! And because she couldn't muster up a gram of shame or face a milligram of my righteous rage at her betrayal, she, can you get this, *she* dumped *me!*"

"But look at your every word and gesticulation, Kareem," I said, gesturing gently to reassure him of the liberating truth of my diagnosis. "It's not her you're angry at. It's yourself."

He howled at the ceiling. "Do you ever listen to anyone but yourself, Eva? Ever think an original thought that hasn't dripped like toxic sewage out of one of your head-shrinking, misanthropic pseudoscience textbooks? Man, *Stalin* could've paid you to write copy for him!"

"So you're telling me you're not angry at yourself? Not even a little?"

"If I'm angry at myself, it's not because I 'liked' what she did to me, but because I put up with her as long as I did. I'm angry because she had the means and motive and I still gave her the opportunity to fuck me over like she did, literally! And because I didn't dump her ass before she could dump me!"

"Kareem, anger isn't the opposite of joy any more than hate is the opposite of love. Both are manifestations of intense attention, focus, preoccupation: your anger and hatred toward Syndi are proof of your joy *in* her and your love *of* her."

"So you're telling me that if a woman is raped, her obsessive anger and hatred prove she loves her rapist?"

"Kareem, the effort you devote to dodging obvious realizations proves my point. The very intensity of how much you deny having enjoyed your experience as a woman—"

"I *didn't*! How many times do I have to say that?"

"—case in point—are simply denial. Obviously you loved being dominated by Syndi, and your enjoyment in becoming a woman is directly proportional to the effort you expend bearing the awesome psychic yoke of rigid African American machodeterministic phallarchical gender roles. It's been amply documented in studies of heterosexual African American drag queen subculture that many black men harbor psyche-fragmentary 'lesbians' inside themselves—alternate sexual personalities or 'sex alters,' if you will—a condition referred to on the street as being 'on the down-low, sideways.' Do you deny that?"

"Deny what?" guffawed Kareem. "That you're psychotic?"

I waited. When he refused to say anything else, I shifted angles.

"Kareem, Syndi . . . do you hate each other . . . or do you still love each other?"

Again, each one turned to the other, glaring in agonized aggravation, anticipation. Desperation.

"Well?"

Suddenly Syndi was sobbing.

I offered her the box of tissues.

Kareem, against his will, staggered toward her, finally sitting on the end of the chaise opposite her.

I asked about her tears.

"Because, because," she wailed, "because everything's falling apart, because he hates me, because everyone's leaving me . . ."

"That's the second time you've said that, Syndi," I said, gesturing for her to take another tissue. Her cheeks were channeled with black lines, a white porcelain sink dirtied by a child's playground mud. "What do you mean, 'everyone's leaving me'?"

She shook her head again and again while blowing her nose. "My mother," she said at last.

"Yes? What about her, Syndi?"

"My mother . . . my whole life, she always, always put me last. I was like a dog, you know? Waiting on the couch by the window the whole day for its master to come home, but the master never does, and so the dog practically breaks its fucking tail off wagging and whimpering and whining alone . . . That's why . . . when Kareem was always so obsessed with his job instead of bothering to spend time with me, focus on me, take care of me, I just couldn't take it. I got scared, and I pushed him away. Because *he was already pushing me away,* don't you get it?" She hiccuped her sobs. And while the exhaustion on Kareem's face suggested he'd heard her story before, the pain in his expression was as real as hers.

"I'm surprised, Syndi," I said, "because from everything you've ever told me, you and Bianca have an excellent, close bond, not to mention the most famously successful—and lucrative—mother-manager/daughter-talent relationship in either showbiz or in superheroics—"

"No!" she choked, looking up and moaning. "No! Bianca's . . . she's not . . . she's not my *mother*, Eva, she's just my agent. That was just a cover story. I'm crying . . . because my real mother's *dying*."

"What?" said Kareem. "Syndi, then who's . . . kot-tam, Syndi, are you saying—"

"Yes," she said, choking back a sob and visibly making a decision. "My real name is Inga Icegaard. My mother is Iron Lass."

And suddenly there it was.

With her hair now raven-feather black and her eyes bright sapphires on the black felt of smeared mascara, the ax-blade of her cheekbones and the taper of her chin—it had been hidden right in front of us all along.

Looking into Kareem's pinballing eyes, I could see he was as stunned as I was. His face was a sorting machine, visibly reevaluating his every experience and conversation and fight and sorrow with Syndi, not to mention his workplace relationship with Iron Lass and her witness of the last two years of his behavior toward her daughter.

And then something else suddenly stormed into his eyes, like a vision of thundering horses and a chaos of lightning.

The X-Man bolted out of the room without so much as a glance good-bye.

"Kareem!" shrieked Syndi, crying again. *"Kareem . . ."*

How will you face knowing that you will never exceed or even equal the accomplishments of your predecessors?

Syndi: "I never *asked* for glory. Just unconditional love."

Does Your Heart Come
Wrapped in Your Cape?

Now that the age of heroism is drawing to a close—and even when it was at its peak—if you've found yourself spinning from one frantic come here/go away relationship to another, it's time to start owning your role in creating your own misery, loneliness, and feelings of worthlessness.

As a superhero, you may have told yourself that your central purpose was saving lives and protecting the public peace. But now that your apartment is empty, your bed is cold, and your freezer contains nothing but Lean Cuisine Single Heart Entrees™, it's time you took ruthlessly courageous action.

Ask yourself: while donning the cape and tights may have seemed to you to have been about helping others, was it really all along about helping yourself? Were you actually connecting in your heart and mind the applause of the crowd with Daddy throwing you in the air and saying "Attaboy!" and Mommy nuzzling you to her chest and telling you that you'll always be her "bestest widdle girl"?

Now that the world has gone quiet around you, you have the time to face the ultrafoe who's been stalking you all along: your fear of being forgotten, unloved, and alone.

Don't back off from the challenge. Don't surrender. In the jungle of your unfolding developmental path, don't let yourself sink beneath the psychemotional quicksand of alcohol, drugs, cybendorphins, serial sexual conquests (or surrenders), or cryptosuicidal reckless adventurism. You need to capture the destructive nemesis known as Dr. Despair, because he's holding in his cold cobalt claws the two powers you've always truly needed but never known how to attain: self-awareness and, through it, self-actualization.

CHAPTER TEN

THE BATTLE OF ALL MOTHERS, THE MOTHER OF ALL BATTLES

SUNDAY, JULY 16, 10:00 A.M.

Yearning for Détente on the Eve of War

t was a Sunday morning. And quiet. A family reunion in the hospital.

Festus, Syndi/Inga, and I were sitting in silence in the Squirrel Tree Medical Hollow suite of Hnossi Icegaard.

The dying goddess was writhing in tortured sleep.

Once raven-haired, she now had a mane of oxidized hospital green; once creamy, her skin was now a minefield of festering red-gray craters. She was covered in sensor pads feeding biometrics to the machines counting out her final days on the planet, like a female Gulliver roped down by med-tech Lilliputians.

Festus, who'd never hidden his contempt for Syndi, had maintained an undeclared truce since we'd arrived at nine A.M. and she'd explained her genealogy. His face betrayed no surprise; perhaps the self-proclaimed "World's Greatest Detective" had already known, or perhaps his affect had been steam-rollered into a parking lot by recent events. Either way, he'd accepted Power Grrrl's "new" civilian name, dark hair, and altered clothes and speech without comment.

Syndi/Inga looked especially tragic that morning. She was clad in a tight black leotard shirt and skirt, and her white pancake makeup and black lipstick and eyeshadow were framed by her black hair, the "Neo-Orc" look she'd popularized on the cover of her first multiplatinum album, *Jagged Little Pudenda*.

The quiescence splintered when Festus suddenly whispered into his wrist comm while cupping his ear. "How long was he there? . . . Well, if he comes back . . . Yes—like a hawk. The *second* that recidivist reprobate—yes, exactly."

"What's going on?" asked Power Grrrl.

"It's your boyfriend," growled Festus.

"He's *not*—What about him?"

"After he fled Miss Brain's clinic last night he went to the Fortress. Spent all night on the computers."

"So what, Festus? He's a F*O*O*Jster. He's got a right to be there. But now you've got someone *spy*ing on him?"

"Apparently your ex-lover was hacking into private F*O*O*J personnel files, 'Inga,' and focusing his search on the known weaknesses of his colleagues."

He leaned forward, narrowing his eyes and scanning her frame as if deciding on which of her limbs he should barbecue first. *"Any idea why?"*

Indignantly, she said, "How would I know?"

"I expect you might know, you little—"

Wet hacking—a sound like the plungering of a soup kitchen sink—drowned the proto-fight. Festus rubbed Hnossi's back with rough gentleness, holding an emesis bowl beneath her bowed face. Wiping the bright copper sputum from her lips, he asked her what she wanted him to do for her.

"Nussink, Festus," she whispered. "You'ff been grandt."

Turning to Power Grrrl, she said, "Miss Tycho. How nice uff you. Sank you for comink—"

"I told them, Mother," she said. "They know."

Hnossi fell silent, her face a *Mona Lisa* of melancholy, a Klimt of *verklempt.*

"Come on, Miss Brain," said Festus, standing. "These two need to be alone."

"No, Festus," snapped Hnossi, raising her hand in *stop* and dragging tubes, wires and sensors with it. "I tried asking Frau Doktor ze uzzer day . . . to help me . . . to help *Inga* unt me . . . put behindt us all our discordt. Before ze ent. Vhich now . . . is almost here."

Shutting off the Current of the Past

If your family contains intergenerational hyperhominidism, then whatever dysfunctional tendencies exist inside your relationships are magnified by the proportional strength and agility of the powers you collectively manifest. In order to discharge the psychic voltage between mother and daughter, as in the case I had that morning, we first had to shut down the breakers whose power had been convulsing Hnossi's consciousness into an id-confrontation loop for decades.

"To help both of you sort out this mother-daughter contra-dynamic, especially given the . . . shall we say, 'time constraints' involved," I told them, "since we don't have the option of years of therapy, we need to delve immediately into your relationship, Hnossi, with your own mother."

Staring at me with her icy amethyst eyes, Hnossi reached weakly for her emesis basin, loosened her lower lip, and let drip a long, viscous purple-green cord which plopped into the pail, which she rested back on her side table.

That was her only response.

"Hnossi," I tried again, "without examining your mother's template, which you inherited and which formed you—the same one you used unconsciously to draw the contours of your relationship with Inga—we can't reformat it so that you can re-draw your relationship with her now."

"Surely, Doktor," she rasped, "you haff more to help us in our hour uff needt zan zese barkain-basement Freudian clichés about muzzer-blamink!"

"Eva," said Inga, holding up a warning finger, "don't listen to her. She's trying to knock your arm away because you've got your arrow aimed right at the bull's-eye."

Hnossi glowered at her daughter, a look cold enough to freeze sunshine and shatter it on the pavement.

"Ze real proplem for me, Doktor, is ze pain of realizing zat my daughter hass vasted her talents unt her career gallivanting arount in front of ze cameras for nussing uzzer zan fame, for-tune, unt scandal, like a golt-luffing little slut—"

Jutting her head forward, Inga scalded out the words: "You mean. Just. Like. *Gramma?*"

I waited for Hnossi to deny the charge. Instead she main-tained the killer frost of her glare.

"My mother, Hnossi Icegaard," said Inga at last, "is the acci-dental feminist icon who secretly spent her career trying to keep women *out* of the F*O*O*J or from climbing the ranks and is maybe the most sexually repressed woman I've ever known."

"Inka! You shut your mouse! You don't know vut you're talkink about!"

"And all of it," said Inga, "because she's disgusted by her own mother! Did you know her own father left them? She's spent her whole life looking for a powerful man to pull her wagon. Why do you think she was so devastated when Hawk King died? But then, when whatever man she'd finally tricked into falling in love with her eventually, inevitably turned out not to be strong enough to reach her stratospheric standards—because, I mean, who could ever be as strong as the strongest woman in the world?—she'd crush him like a monk stomping grapes and then go on a bender with the wine. And that's," said Inga, "what she did to my dad!"

And so with Hnossi's eyes spraying liquid nitrogen all over her daughter, Inga-Ilsabetta Icegaard revealed the neurotically distorted prunings of her family tree and hinted at how her mother's problems with love resulted in a failed marriage, damaged children, and a terrible fate for her daughter that Hnossi did nothing to prevent.

Curdling the Milk of Human Kindness

From the contents of Hnossi's F*O*O*J personnel file, and from my own observations of her and her daughter's interaction, a three-dimensional image had begun to emerge: the Hnossi who stood beyond—or lies behind—the iconic warrior-goddess and the type A professor of Military History, Political Economy, and German and Scandinavian Literature.

Clearly, Hnossi Icegaard was a woman who'd been upset about many things for many centuries and was, no doubt, sexually repressed, quite likely in reaction to the extensive coita-lambulation of her own mother, for as Inga/Syndi put it, "Gramma Freyja was a major ho."

Content for millennia to be mistaken as the daughter of the Aesir goddess Frigg, wife of Odin and queen of Aesgard, Hnossi hid her shame at her true genealogy as the daughter to the Vanir goddess Freyja, who was commonly mistaken either for the regal Frigg, or for Idun, keeper of the Apple of Youth. History recorded Hnossi as having only one sister, Gersimi. But according to Inga, "Gramma" Freyja actually had nine hundred and ninety-nine daughters, all of whom she raised on Mount Snafulnir near the "party halls" of Folkvangar and Sessrumnir.

By all accounts, Hnossi's mother, Freyja, was exceedingly beautiful; but her marriage to the god Odur ended when he "disappeared." Distraught to the core, Freyja wandered Midgard in despair for him while crying tears of purest gold. Intensely vulnerable, Freyja engaged in tens of thousands of dalliances with gods, humans, elves, dwarves, giants, and sundry other magickal beings, all the while sinking into the disreputable practice of *seidr* magic.

Eternal scalawag and Ragnarokian rogue Loki went so far as to accuse Freyja of sleeping with every god in Aesgard, every elf in Alfheim, and even her own brother Freyr; although the trickster deity and storm giant was forced into a retraction and a sealed settlement in Aesgard's Hall of Judgment, the victory was purely Pyrrhic for Freyja ("her only purity," quipped Loki famously) since her own actions had already ruined her reputation.

But Freyja was also a goddess of combat and death whose lust for men was equaled only by her lust for war and gold. Possessing a feathered cloak that she used to transform herself into a falcon, and a chariot drawn by two iron cats, Freyja sometimes wandered the Earth at night disguised as a goat, and, when not transporting the souls of the slain to Valhalla, she was adding to her jewelry collection, as when she famously acquired the necklace Brisingamen as payment for sleeping with the four Brising dwarves.

Witnessing this sad, pathetic carnal crusade for love, and embittered by the booty of shame and humiliation she'd amassed as a result, young Hnossi sought recruitment into the sorority of battle-maiden Valkyries, clutching at the hope that by joining an organization she equated with purity, she could escape one aspect of her family history while embracing another.

Historical accounts list Hnossi as an unflinchingly brave warrioress who personally dispatched untold thousands of elves, dwarves, giants, and monsters back to the Niflheim damnation of the nethergoddess Hel; in the modern era, Iron Lass masterminded the Götterdämmerung, conceived its strategy, issued its battle cry, and even wrote its manifesto.

Having broken from what she saw as her own mother's lack of control, Hnossi Icegaard became the quintessential controller, a strategist supreme of global affairs. But lacking a model for wife-and-motherhood, the control she so desperately wielded could not but cause chaos inside the family she was about to create.

As Inga/Syndi said, Hnossi—perhaps to replace the father whom she never knew and to repair the psychemotional damage caused by the mother she did—pursued extremely strong men. In the twentieth-century she fell in love with and married the human mortal Hector "Qetzalcoatl" El Santo, HKA Strong Man. Five months later, Inga-Ilsabetta El Santo y Icegaard was born, followed two years later in 1964 by younger brother "Lil Boulder" Baldur.

Strong Man was indeed a strong man. Having risen to prominence in the Mexican wrestling circuit, Strong Man claimed to have derived his powers by ingesting the miraculous "Maize of Chac Mol"; his strength increased with every year of his life until he could pick up entire oil tankers with his gloved hands.

But Strong Man's powers weren't limited to physical deeds; he invested his profits from wrestling and crimefighting back into Mexico's wrestling and film industries. Capitalizing upon his own reputation and the putative source of his powers, he invented Corna Cola (which despite its Anglo name became

Latin America's third most popular soft drink), created the Yucataxi Cab Company, bought out the entire Volkswagen manufacturing base in Mexico, and founded the popular fast-food "Milk Chac" chain in the USA.

The union of two such attractive, dashingly heroic figures led to a decade of magazine covers and idolization; the storybook couple of the hyper-hominid world was considered *the* marriage to emulate.

But it was all a sham. Despite the passion of the relationship, by 1974 the milk of loving-kindness had curdled under the heat of acrimony whose causes neither spouse ever revealed. Separating from his wife, Hector El Santo returned to Mexico to raise both his children in a remote Mayan fortress in the Yucatán. From that familial stronghold he rebuffed her ever-increasing attempts at reconciliation and rejected her ever-greater declarations of devotion, devotion that burned far more hotly during separation than it ever had during their togetherness.

Finally, in 1981, after seven years of separation, El Santo filed for divorce.

One month later to the day, Iron Lass declared the Götterdämmerung.

"I always wanted more for myself," said Syndi, concluding her matriography, "than the barren, angry, cruel life my mother'd hacked out for herself. All she knows, Eva, is how to keep people away, keep people on the wrong end of her swords, how to keep herself cold and hard. Like iron."

I turned to Hnossi, expecting rage. Instead I saw exhaustion: rust craters dimmed her appearance as if she were fading into a red dusk, the medical webs strewn across her seemingly weighing her down like steel cables.

"Inka," said Iron Lass, releasing a sigh over thirty full seconds, as if the effort to form the words was a mountain-sized yoke, "grow up."

Inga glared at the ceiling.

"Alvays it is ze same viss you. Vut do you sink zis vurlt is made uff, hmm? Nussing but canties unt sugar cakes unt parties unt dencing unt booze-soaked sex?"

"Oh, right! Because there certainly were never any parties or drinking or sex in Aesgard!"

"Joy unt luff . . . zese are *illusions,* my daughter. If you luff a men he vill alvays hurt you—if you trust a friend she vill stab you in ze guts. Life is hard vurk, drutchery, boredom, exhaustion. At its finest it's honor unt devotion to higher ideals zan oneself, unt *ja,* higher even zan one's family, vhich you could never see! You're a demigoddess, Inka . . . You must rise to assume your true status. Beingk in an organization such as ze FOOCH means protecting mortal civilians, but not beingk like zem, not vallovink in zeir veakness unt self-pity unt ridiculous neet for 'luff'—"

"Like you did?" said Inga. "So why bother devoting your life to protecting people you despise, Mother? Why not just abandon them, like you abandont Daddy and us?"

"I dit *not* abandon any of you! You all abandoned me, remember?"

"Even when you were with us," said Inga, "you weren't!"

The Battle of All Mothers, or, Not F*O*O*J but FOOI: Family of Origin Issues

Throughout their argument, both goddess and demigoddess walked the brink of discussing what I suspected was the trauma that had caused the greatest tragedy between them. For a daughter to side with a father following a parental separation, and then to develop two nested secret identities to sever her connection with her mother, indicated a profoundly violent amputation in the body of mother-daughter connection.

Despite Inga/Syndi's paradigmatic divergence from her mother, Hnossi raised no objections to the biographical facts recounted by Inga. Nor did she say anything to rebut the charge that she both admired and despised the powerful males she pursued, squeezing from them whatever professionally nutritive juices she could before shoving them into the relationship composter, as her own mother Freyja had done before her and as Syndi would do after.

The sole counterpoint in Hnossi's behavioral script was her adulation of Hawk King. Because Hnossi's contempt for men had always become directly proportional to their desire for her, the Egyptian strong man's unavailability to any woman only magnified Hnossi's adulation of him, guaranteeing that the elder god's death would crack valleys into the lowlands of Hnossi's flattened affect. Arguably, the disruption of her immortal immune system that had led to her terminal condition could have been assigned in part to the psychemotional devastation caused by her true icon's death.

But Hawk King's allure for Hnossi went beyond his now permanent unattainability. Hnossi had inherited her mother's magical feather cloak; while she could not transform herself into a falcon, in her possession the cloak transmuted into giant *hawk* wings. Hawk King had been famous for his impartiality, wisdom, and strict but compassionate leadership and guidance. His epithet among the supercommunity as simply "the King" spoke to the esteem in which he was held by all.

Unfortunately for Hnossi and her family, even while she'd admired Hawk King's character, Hnossi had failed to manifest his kindly demeanor. She didn't deny Inga's charges that on their rare family "adventure" camping trips to Jotunheim and Pacari, Hnossi would become so enraged at her family's refusal to follow her strict camping protocols (for instance, prohibitions against sleeping late or intrameal snacking) that she would go so far as to throw things at her husband—things such

as boulders. Once when Hector failed to have the morning coffee ready at the instant of sunrise, she ripped down a butte and
struck him over the head with it, terrifying the children, destroying their chariot and badly denting their iron cats with the
resulting rubble.

Mothering had come no easier to Hnossi than had wifing;
despite his nickname "Lil Boulder," her son Baldur possessed
neither superstrength nor invulnerability. Instead, much to his
father's delight, he was a brilliant painter and muralist who
emitted scented paints from his fingertips as a spider would se-
crete webbing.

Considered by many to be a prodigy of Diego Riveran pro-
portions, the eight-year-old took it upon himself to paint the
entirety of Spectre Valley with a mural depicting the Mayan
story of creation and doomsday. Art critics from around the
planet flew at once to California to examine "the Work," as it
was called, some hailing it as the greatest single gigantic artwork
in human history, not to mention the best smelling. Hnossi dis-
agreed, ordering the boy to scrub off the entire work by hand
since he'd painted it without state permission and was facing
charges of vandalism, mischief and destruction of a state park.
Hector and Hnossi clashed bitterly over the incident, with
Hnossi ultimately denouncing "ze undiknified life of an artist"
to her former-actor husband before freezing and burning off the
mural with her twin swords. The wedge between them crept
deeper.

Hnossi's opinion of her elder child had been even less encouraging. While Inga's early powers didn't include hyper-
emulation, her singing was hypnotic—literally. But since Iron
Lass disliked rival F*O*O*Jster the Siren (the heroine whose
1968 lawsuit forced the Fraternal Order of Justice to change its
name to the non-gender-specific "Fantastic"), Hnossi was entirely unsupportive of her daughter having any similar power.
Desperate and lacking her mother's positive reinforcement,

young Inga soon began taking advantage of her hypnovocalism, singing to children and adults—especially males—to bend them to her bidding. The only people immune to Inga's powers were her kin. But her father and brother adored her because of their familial bond, not requiring any sonic manipulation for their experience of love.

"But there's something much deeper than this," I told Syndi. "Something your mother won't go near and something you're only hinting at. Something truly awful happened between you two which made you distance yourself from your mother so greatly that you created *two* secret identities with which to obscure your connection to her. What is it?"

Hnossi's ancient, deathly eyes fixed on her daughter like leeches, whether to shut Inga down or finally to open her up, I was not sure.

Inga/Syndi got up and excused herself to go to the bathroom.

The moment she returned, I said, "Tell me about Cassiopeia Rand."

"What?" said Inga, floored. She clutched her hands to her chest as if my question had denuded her. "How the hell did you know about her?"

"Festus," I said, showing her a folder from my briefcase. "He's been very helpful with supplying additional background material from his extensive files."

"My God!" said Inga, shaking her head and looking with disgust toward the ceiling. "How long has that old fascist been spying on me? On all of us?"

"Ach, Inga," rasped her mother. "Stop beingk so dramatic. Ze man is ze vurlt's greatest detectiff. Vut dit you expect him to do viss his information-gazzering apparatus? Answer crossvurt puzzles?"

"Duh, I dunno, how about, *catch criminals?* And not invade the privacy of law-abiding citizens?"

"Answer ze qvestion. Who is ziss Cassiopeia Rand?"

"Inga," I pressed, "tell me about Space Girl."

The Debut, Disappearance, and Downfall of Space Girl

had problems igniting my career, okay?" said Inga, glaring at me with all the toxic, self-indulgent angst of her Syndi Tycho persona, but without the incessant use of *like* and *gawd*.

"It was 1981. I was nineteen. So I tried making my debut as Cassiopeia Rand, HKA Space Girl. I was singing Latin pop-lite tunes—this was years before Gloria Estefan blew up—and fighting a little crime on the side with my hypnovoice, just to get some press.

"I was starting to move up, get noticed. I even had an HBO special with special appearances by Cher, Cheech Marin, and Tim Conway. But the day my special aired," she said, jutting her lower lip toward the hospital bed, "*Mother* up and declared her global war. Every channel was glued on her and her crusade for the next month! Debuts are delicate, Eva! And mine, thanks to her, was a complete dud! And unlike in heroics, in showbiz, you don't get second chances."

Believing her career was over, Inga-Ilsabetta exiled herself back east, eventually studying marketing, music production, and singing at the Alison Blair Institute for Advanced Disco Studies. Excelling in every course, by 1987 she created a brand-new persona through which to reinvent herself and forge her own second chance.

Dyeing her hair, and with the almost perpetually youthful looks of a demigoddess, she emerged as Syndi Tycho, HKA Power Grrrl, who in 1991 capitalized upon the need of the post-Götterdämmerung F*O*O*J to reinvent itself, too, in the wake of the promised "peace dividend." An angry, exhausted, and broke public needed happy, lively, pretty new faces if the F*O*O*J was to survive into its new postvillain era. Fast-tracked, the "seventeen-year-old" became a made member in 1991 after a mere six-month candidacy and, with her new legitimacy, immediately launched extensive marketing tie-ins.

"The government loved me, the F*O*O*J's corporate sponsors loved me," said Syndi, "the public loved me, everyone loved me. Everyone was happy. It was great."

"How about your mother?" I asked without malice, regretting the crumpling of her features as soon as I saw it. "How about you? Did you love yourself? Have you ever been truly happy?"

"Of course I loved myself! Of course I'm happy! What kind of question is that?"

"I think you didn't feel loved, Syndi. That you never felt you were getting enough love. That you had a hole in your soul. That you believed your mother'd never given you enough of what you needed. That you had to comfort your heart-shattered father and raise your little brother by yourself, depriving you of time just to be a girl. You feared Kareem would never put you first—"

"Is that a crime, Eva? To be more in touch with my need for love than other people are?"

"It's not a question of crime, Inga, but dysfunction, and of causing damage to others. You seduced Kareem *emotionally,* not just sexually. And the ramifications for him have been gigantic. Scandal might help *you* sell more albums, but this could quite likely be the end of Kareem's career."

"Unt you hat no right to treat Fraulein Biceps like zat," said Hnossi. "She vuss a gut varrior. She deservt better. Regartless of her uzzer . . . you know. Her . . . liebenschtyle."

"After you felt your mother'd rejected you," I said to Inga, "you determined you'd never be rejected again. By anyone. Every

relationship you've ever had—familial, platonic, romantic—
you ended before *they* could."

"God!" she said, pacing the tiny room like a black rat in a
white box. "This is completely wrong, Eva! We're supposed to
be talking about what my mother did wrong! She's the reason
I'm so messed up!"

" 'Messed up'? Earlier you claimed you were happy and felt
loved. Syndi . . . Inga . . . anyone as desperate as you were, as
you still are, to avoid rejection—I mean, your entire career has
been about attracting the attention you equate with love so as to
guarantee yourself a never-ending 'fix.' Anyone *that* terrified of
rejection has unquestionably harmed or debased herself in
ways she isn't proud of. Ways she may never have told another
living soul . . ."

Inga froze, focusing on me tapping the cover of my POWER
GRRRL folder. Her blue eyes paled into water.

"Vut is it? Vut's she talking about, Inka?" said Hnossi. "I
don't understandt . . . Vut are you getting at, Doktor?"

"You really should tell your mother, Inga."

"This is so unethical of you, Eva!"

"Inka," said Hnossi heavily, "*tell* me."

Inga scrambled up into a chair as if afraid of floor mice,
hugged her knees against her chest, her eyes looking like huge
balls of wet ice.

"I did *the capes*," she mumbled.

"Vut? Inka, you're not—you're not serious—"

Her daughter said nothing, saving her glare for me.

"Odin's eye," whispered the dying goddess.

The niche pornography industry called *the capes,* worth an
estimated $2.5 billion annually in the United States alone,
served those men and women who sexually fetishized superhero tunics and the people who wore them. On rare occasions
a genuine superheroine or hero (always a fallen one) gained

"employment" in the field, appearing in films, videos and holo-grams. Best known of these was the sole "success" story: Magna, the 1980s heroine and daughter of the Lodestone. At the height of the Götterdämmerung she'd left crimefighting to begin her own highly profitable pornographic production company in whose features she'd frequently "starred."

And the file Festus supplied me contained photographic proof. As Cassiopeia Rand, HKA Space Girl, Inga had appeared in "supporting" roles of "adventure" films such as *Magna: Pirate of Men's Pants,* "documentaries" such as *The Theory of Magnajism,* and "intellectual erotica" such as *Magna Cums Laudly.*

"But there's more, Inga," I said, "isn't there?"

"Mein todt, how can it get any vurse zan ziss, Doktor?" moaned Hnossi, clutching at whatever frosted-green crabgrass remained attached to her skull. "My own dottir! A whore for ze cameras! Ziss is all her fazzer's fault, ze filse of all his showbiz dreams—"

"Hnossi, please! Inga—all these years desperately craving attention, pursuing show business, and reinventing yourself and even manufacturing scandals to guarantee the attention your mother denied you and that you equated with love. Always being the one to end relationships first. All of it to ensure you would never be rejected and that instead you would be the one doing the rejecting. What's the ultimate way to ensure that?"

I looked at both women. Neither would look at me.

"Ladies, please," I said. "The signs are all there, as giant and unavoidable as sky-writing. Will one of you please verbalize what happened to you and your family after you, Inga, at the tender age of twelve, attempted suicide?"

Discovering—and *Healing*—
the Scared Little Goddess
Inside You

espite the younger Icegaard's propensity for blaming her problems on her mother, the suicide attempt was the sole damage zone even she had feared to retread, perhaps because once she began, there was no going back. If the "answers" her terminal mother gave her were insufficient, she would forever be denied her sole chance to heal, even the opportunity to wonder "what if?"

Recounting her years in and out of therapy, Inga/Syndi parabolically approached the issue of her preteen attempt at self-murder.

"For years, I thought I'd done it because maybe I'd been abused," she said. "I had all these recovered memories from my other therapists . . . memories of Mother . . . beating me. Cutting me with her swords, cutting my limbs off and magically reattaching them so the police wouldn't suspect anything.

"But then I had this one therapist, and he said I should talk with Daddy and Baldur about it, and, and . . . well, *now* I know it was just the therapists screwing with my head, planting these ideas in my mind. But I've always had this problem with, you know, depression? And I used to cut myself, throw myself off of buildings and cliffs and things, burn myself, try to hurt myself . . . My therapist said it was Munchausen syndrome. Said I was trying to get Mother to rescue me."

She smiled coldly, then reduced her expression to a corpse's repose.

"It didn't work," she concluded.

Of all memories, "recovered" ones are the most unreliable. According to Dr. Steve N. Strainge, the psychiatrist whose testimony interred Dr. Napoleon Orator on Asteroid Zed, Menton's career of manipulation began before even he realized he had such powers. For years during the therapy sessions he led, he had been implanting false memories of trauma in his patients, after which he was paid to supply expert testimony at trial for clients suing their former baby-sitters, coaches, pastors, teachers, siblings, parents, deliverymen, meter men, and aldermen.

But since Inga had successfully detached from her therapist-implanted pseudomemories, there was hope for her eventual recovery, even if we then had to descend deeper into the swamps of her dysfunctionally agonized adolescence.

I asked her to tell me what had precipitated her attempt.

"Mother," said Inga, "was out. Again. Always on some mission. She and Daddy'd been fighting for what must've been two days straight, and this was after two years of a downhill shit-slide with them. I mean, it was both of them, yeah, but it was her fault.

"So Daddy, he couldn't take it anymore, said he was going out and she was screaming at him and telling him that if he goes out now he shouldn't even think about coming back and he just said, 'Fine, maybe I won't,' and he rushed back in and packed a suitcase and I was trying to hold on to him and drag him back but he was almost as strong as Wally, and I was crying and begging him, 'Don't leave, Daddy, please don't leave!' and I was terrified, *terrified* that she'd finally driven him away and that I wouldn't ever see him again—"

"Ziss is outrageous!" said Hnossi, her red-gray pockmarks glowing like campfire coals. "Zat's not how it happent at all! She vuss a childt! She doesn't remember how it happent—"

"Hnossi, please," I said, forming my hands into a time-out *T.* "We all have our own truths—"

"*Ach,* vut sheisen you peddle!"

"Please don't interrupt. You'll have your turn. Inga, go on."

"And so Daddy's gone and I'm on the floor sobbing, and

like, two seconds go by and then her comm goes off, for Ymir's sake, and then she's all, 'I've gotta go fight the Gorgon Legion or some ice giants or whatever and you're in charge of your little brother until I get back' and *boom*—she's gone, just like that!

"So she's gone and Daddy's gone and Baldur and I are alone all night and all the next day and for the next two fucking days and nights after that," said Inga, plucking at her tight black long-sleeved shirt as if she were rehearsing ripping the skin and flesh from her skeleton. "I was twelve, Mother! Twelve!"

"You vere a bik girl, you vere oldt enough—people were goingk to be killt unless—"

"Unless *you personally* went and did your heroine-thing because it's not like you ever said no even though there were a hundred other F*O*O*Jsters who could've—"

"None viss my powers, experience, knowletch—"

"Sure, right, because it's all about proving how you're the toughest bitch who ever lived, that you don't need anyone and no one's better than you and that you have no weaknesses, not even a husband who couldn't take your shit anymore so he left you or two scared little kids you abandoned at home that you could never wait to escape at the very first buzz on your wrist—"

"People neetet me! How can you not unterstant zat?"

"*We needed you, Mother!*" screamed Inga, sobbing. "*I* needed you!"

I cut in: "So what did you do, Inga?"

"I was so tired . . . of being scared. And lonely. And then all of a sudden I just felt this, this *surge* of power, of bravery, like nothing I'd ever felt before. Totally, one hundred percent determined—the 'will to power,' Mother always called it—like I was drunk or stoned or on fire. I knew where Mother kept all her magical implements, the stuff we were never supposed to go near, and I knew the spell to open the lock. I took *Jörmungandrstooth,* this *seidr* blade she had at the bottom . . . and I invoked the name of Ymir . . . and then I, I just—"

Her lips shut. Her eyes shut. She mimed a fast motion over her wrist, eight times in total.

Her eyes opened, ablaze from reliving her truth. "And then my soul was ripped out of me," she said, "and sucked right down into the depths of Niflheim and into the hands of Hel."

And Hnossi, despite her reputation for never crying, who only two weeks before had sat across from me at Soup 'n' Heroes crying iron-ingot tears, sat upright in her hospital bed, seeping not liquid metal, but tears of pale, ordinary water.

"I came home," said Hnossi in a weakened voice, then, shattering, "as soon as Odin's ravens fount me, tolt me vut you't done to yourself. I fought my vay srough ze ice hordes of Niflheim unt zen against Hel herself to get you beck! Do you not remember ziss? I risked my life to safe you—"

"And what did you do the very next morning after you brought me back, *Mother*?" said Inga with sufficient acid to burn her mother's swords.

Silenced, Hnossi simply stared at her daughter with perfect vulnerability, that of the accused who'd just surrendered checkmate evidence to the tribunal, and who'd glimpsed the approach of the executioner.

"You went back to work," said Inga, her smile awful and vicious with irony. "You spent nine days in the netherworlds slicing the icicles off frost giants, but for your weak, stupid daughter who tried to kill herself out of loneliness, you could not sit for one lousy fucking day.

"After almost losing me forever, *you went back to work*."

Inga waited for her mother to speak.

Finally: "Nothing to say, woman?"

Everything was charged with emotion—even Inga's darkened mane and Hnossi's pale green tufts were puffed up, hairs splitting at their ends and vibrating in the tingling air.

"Inka," rasped Hnossi, "I'm . . . I—"

"Don't say it!" yelled Inga. "Whatever you're gonna say, it'll be all fucking wrong anyway, so just don't!" She stepped across to Hnossi's bedside, leaned down, and yelled some more, and the highly vincible goddess shriveled like a weed sprayed with herbicide.

"And don't call me 'Inga' anymore! Inga died that day in 1974 because your neglect killed her! So you can stop wondering— assuming you ever did—why my official bio and F*O*O*J file say I was born that day, the day I left you and Daddy left you and Baldur left you! All you have to know, *Hnossi,* is that on that day I gave birth to myself!"

SNAP!—It was a sound like a whip cracking, and Syndi reared back and slammed against the wall, clutching her cheek. White smoke leaked between her fingers. I reached for her but stopped at the sight of electrical firecrackers exploding all over Hnossi's face and arms and above the white blanket covering her torso.

"Stand back, Syndi!" I shouted, just as all the medical equipment shorted out in sparking mechanical death cries. My nostrils clogged with a burning stench. The air tasted like metal. "Doctor! Nurse!" I yelled out into the hall. "Code blue!"

The goddess who'd almost never cried, cried out her agony.

"Mummy!" said Syndi, releasing the burn wound and rushing forward to clutch her agonized mother. I tackled her before she could electrocute herself, knocking her against the wall beside the headboard and bouncing the two of us to the floor.

Her mother continued keening like an animal in a leg-hold trap. The only word we could make out, screamed over and over before the nurses dragged us out, was *"Vally!"*

Iron Fatigue, or Rust in Pieces?

The finest specialists money could buy scrambled past us in their rubber scrubs, ready for the final stage of the disease. But while the metals of Hnossi's body were breaking down, deteriorating even faster was the hope for psych-emotional reconnection between goddess mother and demi-goddess daughter.

"Did you hear that? Did you goddamned hear that?" spat Syndi, again clutching the arc-gash on her face. "Ymir's sake! Even now, even when she's dying . . . I mean, who's here with her? Not Gramma, not Daddy, not even Baldur—*me*. I am."

Crying without trying to hide it, she dragged her sleeve across her entire face except for her burn, smearing her already smeared black makeup across her white features until she became a blurred mime. Short of breath, Festus raced up to us and stopped, glancing toward Hnossi's room and back to us, his eyes demanding an explanation.

Syndi offered him no comfort. "Even when she's goddamn *dying*, Eva . . . the only person she calls out for is some super-powerful unavailable loser who won't love her . . . and who walked away." She singsonged bitterly, "*Sur*-fucking-*pri-ise*!"

For many second- or multigenerational hyper-hominids, the ability to achieve self-actualization is hampered by the incapacity of their supposedly heroic and self-sacrificing parents to verbalize self-shame.

All too frequently in my practice, I've seen that the reason superheroes neurotically deny their own needs to the point of risking their lives originates in family of origin: the parents who modeled monkish asceticism while forever failing to indulge their children's basic need to be the recipient of intimacy behaviors and the center of Mommy's or Daddy's affection and caretaking ideation. A parent who fails to recognize that a child's needs are distinct from and supersede her or his own is demonstrating a classic psychesituational signature of narcissism.

Because of the relationship Syndi had had with her mother, Syndi's relationship with Kareem was a paradox doomed to destruction. Far more than civilians, superheroes desire to change the past, some going so far as neurotically orbiting the planet at hyper-speeds under the delusion that they can reverse the Earth's direction and thus the flow of time, giving them a second chance—the most hoped-for boon in history.

So when Syndi selected a man whose workaholism, religion, and racial paranoia guaranteed he would be emotionally unavailable, she was assembling in the present a re-creation/rejection-cipher of her unavailable mother, thus giving her the opportunity to win his (and symbolically Hnossi's) love and attention. If she failed, she could preemptively reject him, therefore exerting the present-day capacity to deny the love that was denied to her in the past. Even her hedonistic hypersexuality/anguished frigidity demonstrated her paradoxical needs to defy and reconnect with her mother, an anti/sexualism whose ironies she could only rationalize/integrate through her HEAT Ray experiment in "self-love."

While Syndi probably did love Kareem as much as she was capable, her own narcissism amplified her need and destroyed her capacity for genuine self-love (the prerequisite for truly loving others), much as a burst of oxygen will engorge and accelerate the end of a fire.

Toward Resolving Paradoxes, and Paradoxical Solutions

For the first time since I'd met the man, Festus Piltdown III was beginning to look his seventy years.

Slumped against the wall, his cravat uncinched and asymmetrical, the wrinkles in his face suddenly as obvious as those of a suit that had been slept in, it was clear that no dosage of "GI Juice" could forestall his aging process permanently, especially when deeply personal agony was hastening the inevitable approach of his own death.

Inside the sealed suite, specialists tracked their bootprints of vocal mud all over the plush white rug of our silence, while Syndi and Festus waited in medical impotence with wan faces and tears.

The wall comm chimed.

"What is it, Mr. Savant?" said the old man, tabbing the wall.

"Lord Piltdown, I'm terribly sorry for the interruption, but a Mr. Fly is here to see you—terribly important news of some sort, he insists—"

"It's okay. Send him up."

Shortly we heard the familiar whine of André's approach, and then the man himself was flapping down beside Festus, his bright yellow visitor E-tag hanging from his neck, having prevented his incineration by the Squirrel Tree's DETHscan security system.

"What is it, Parker?" said Festus. "What's so important you couldn't simply use the comms?"

"Kareem's been acting crazy, Festus," said André, doing a double take at a Syndi Tycho he'd never seen before. And then, bizarrely enough for him, he employed standard American English and the first-person pronoun *I*. "First I caught him hacking into F*O*O*J personnel files. But then he started cross-referencing everything on Menton with everything on Sarah Bellum, and making the computer correlate all of that with the F*O*O*J's records on Doctor Brain—"

"On *me*?" I blurted, stunned by a development I had not foreseen.

"—and he's been accessing all available Hubble imagery, cosmological records, everything on the Nistan dark matter nebula, downloading everything he could on the molecular physics and pharmacology of argonium," he said in articulate, almost broadcastable English. "He's up to something, Festus. Something I don't like one bit!"

Syndi's raccoon eyes snapped up onto him. Festus put his massive hand on the younger man's shoulder. "Slow down. What're you talking about?"

"I think he's planning some type of terrorist attack," said André, his eyes wild, his posture bowed as if to confide a state secret. "And he didn't have time to completely wipe the computer of his work files before he figured out I was on to him. I unerased his notes—*he thinks Doctor Brain is actually Menton.*"

The words hummed in the air. The three F*O*O*Jsters locked gazes.

Then all their eyes turned on me.

"Well, *come on*, everyone," I reminded them, "*ob*viously he's paranoid. You know that. Right? Remember the whole scandal? Let's stay focused here—"

At that exact moment Dr. Singh, the specialist team leader, exited Hnossi's room. "What is it?" demanded Festus.

Remarkably, this middle-aged woman working for one of the most powerful magnates in the world ignored him and spoke directly to Syndi.

"Miss Tycho?" said the specialist.

"Yuh-yes, Doctor?" choked Syndi. "How's she doing?"

"Not well, I'm afraid. Your mother has perhaps two days to live."

The Mother of All Battles

acking external foes, one F*O*O*Jster was psychosomatically destroying herself, and collectively the remaining F*O*O*Jsters were turning on themselves in a psychotic downspiral of workplace-superpowered civil war. Most disturbingly, in their collective breakdown, the F*O*O*J's paranoia had plummeted even to the point of questioning the identity and integrity of their therapist.

Unless I were able to help my sanity-supplicants integrate the disparate lessons they'd gained from therapy into a new paradigm of postheroic psychemotional equilibrium, they would soon destroy themselves . . . and countless innocent people along with them.

CHAPTER ELEVEN

SELF-DISTRACTION IS SELF-DESTRUCTION

SUNDAY, JULY 16, 4:33 P.M.

Countdown to Armageddon

erhaps I should leave," I suggested, "and let you all work during this obvious crisis."

"You're not going anywhere, Miss Brain!" said Festus.

"Surely you don't believe Kareem's delusion about me being . . . I mean, that I could be—"

"It's not whether *I* believe it. It's that *he does*. Which means you're his target. So you're not only in danger and needing our protection," he said, stepping toward me and clamping his gigantic hands on my shoulders in a gesture I imagined was intended to be reassuring, "you're our bait."

After forcing me to offer multiple reassurances that I was not Menton the Destroyer, the three F*O*O*Jsters focused on the aforementioned frightening fracas soon to unfold. Not since the breakdown of Gil Gamoid and the N-Kid had there been the threat of terrorism by a member of the F*O*O*J.

After a moment of silence, Festus said, "How do we know *Edgerton* didn't kill Hawk King?"

Syndi's lips parted, curled into disgust accentuated by the electrical burn on her cheek. "Oh, shut up, Festus! Why not just accuse him of killing Kennedy while you're at it? Oh no, I forgot—Kareem was only a baby, but *you* were in Dallas that day—"

"Naw, look here, girly," said André, regaining his trade-marked urban drawl and swagger. "What if Squirrel-dawg be right? Check it: Major Ursa and the Spectacle said there were no signs of forced entry or teleportation at the Blue Pyramid. Whoever, y'know . . . *did* it, like, Hawk King had to've known im, right? So what if Kreem's tellin the truth about a special re-lationship with Hawk King? The King coulda let him in—"

"How, André? How would Kareem have enough power to kill Hawk King?" she said. "And more important, why would he want to kill his idol?"

"Look, girl, who knows how powerful Kreem really is? Think about what he could do with all his logo-magicalisms. He could send words down somebody's throat and clog their lungs or stop their heart, or inside their veins and explode their brains! F'all we know he could make poison gas or a nuclear bomb—"

"Why, André? You haven't said anything about why!"

"Why? Shit, P-girl, man's a Afro-paranoid! He prawly blieves Hawk King really was black, so maybe he went to im, said, 'Help me knock off whitey,' an when the King said *hell, no!* and got ready to lock im up, *BAM!*, Kreem up an *words* im to death—"

"—and then leads an investigation not only to boost his electoral delusions," nodded Festus, "but as a diversionary tac-tic away from himself and onto an absurd conspiracy theory about Menton."

"Absurd?" spat Syndi. "You yourself said that—"

"And worse," said Festus, "his goddamned plan worked!

That diabolical deviant is smarter than he smells. He wanted power on the F*L*A*C, power now denied to him—oh, you wouldn't believe how many transcripts I've read of his speeches to antiwhite agitators and melanin-maddened malcontents over the years—"

"Damn, Peej, Kreem be usin his word-things to do his spyin inside computers? He could track anybody, maybe *evra*body? Think about it! Combine that with what he could do inside people's cells, they brains . . . snap, he on his way to becoming the most powerful man in the world, you knawm sayn?"

"The man hates the F*O*O*J," said Festus. "And he never hid it. Hates the F*L*A*C, hates the membership, hates our history, our traditions, our values, our mission—the only thing he *didn't* hate—"

He stopped a second to rake Syndi's pelvis with his gaze.

"Fuck you, Festus!"

André: "People, people, eyes on the prize, here!"

"Obviously, Edgerton's aim," said Festus, "was to seize control of the F*O*O*J, by election if possible—remember, Hitler came to power by election—or by nefarious means if necessary . . . and eventually make the F*L*A*C all-black, contract all outsourcing services to black companies—"

"Do you have an atom of proof for *any* of this, Festus?"

"When you've been the World's Greatest Detective for fifty years, little girl, your instincts lead you far more than the evidence ever does. And you . . . weren't you the one who sponsored him to join the F*O*O*J in the first place?"

She rocked back. "Suh-so what?"

"How do we know you aren't spying for him right now and that your perfectly timed public 'outing' wasn't intended to distract attention from your continued collusion with him?"

"Now who's paranoid, *detective*?" she yelled at the exact moment something smacked her in the face and hovered above her head.

It was a black rectangle no larger than an ordinary envelope.

"It's from Edgerton!" said Festus, reaching for it, but Syndi got it first.

"It's got *my* name on it," she scolded, turning it over to show us. Opening what was not an envelope but merely a folded sheet, she flashed its contents at us: letter-shaped holes in the black substance formed text. Placing the logogram against the wall for easier reading, she shielded it with her body for privacy.

"How'd that get in here?" said André.

"Perhaps it followed you," I suggested.

"But if it's for her," said Festus, "how would he've known André'd be meeting up with her?"

"Brotherfly's more concerned," said André, "that Kreem can be trackin any*body,* any*where*. An next time he might not be sendin no letter, knawm sayn?"

"What's it say?" demanded Festus.

Syndi paused. "He . . . he wants me to meet him."

Festus glared an *A-ha!* at her.

"I'm not working with him!" she said. "He said he just wants to see me to tell me what he's figured out. He said," she choked, "that he's . . . he's worried about me. That he wants to protect me."

"Go to him," said Festus. "And we'll be right behind you with a hammer the size of his skull!"

"You think I'm gonna help you kill him, Festus?"

"For someone who said she's not working with him—"

"I'm not, but I'm still not gonna lead you to him like a Judas-goat—"

They shouted at each other for minutes, Syndi refusing even to take a holographic imager, tracking device, or microphone along. "And I'm not going anyway! Unless you forgot, my mother's sick and dying in there!"

"Oh, and you've always been such an attentive, devoted daughter!"

After she'd drenched Festus in a steaming spew of profanity, he reminded her that saving others was what her mother would want her to do.

"If you're going to live with yourself after . . . *after*," he stage-whispered, even touching her forearm with a gentleness of which I hadn't thought him capable (and even more shockingly, she didn't flinch at his touch), "then you know that having carried out what would've been your mother's final request will be what you'll need . . . so you won't spend the rest of your life with that regret crushing you like a fallen building."

André and I were as shocked by Festus's reasoned delicacy as Syndi seemed entranced by it.

Quietly denying a final request to bring Festus along to the rendezvous location, Syndi said she'd reveal any plans Kareem had on the condition they posed a threat. After Festus made one last effort to divine the location of the meeting, Syndi conceded only one piece of information: that Kareem had asked her to meet at a place only the two of them would know.

"Where I first kissed him," she said, choking up, covering her face and dropping the letter.

Just before she could leave I grabbed her arm.

"Be careful, Syndi. The Kareem you fell in love with . . . he's suffering. And when people are suffering, they usually hurt the people closest to them, because those are the only ones left around."

She showed me her white-and-black smear of a face, her eyes cold and deathly. "Kareem . . . my mother dying," she said. "This is all a wake-up call for me."

The Intoxicating Ambrosia of
Old Hatred (and Older Love)

The moment Syndi exited the Medical Hollow, Festus stooped to retrieve the letter but reared back when it broke up at his touch and its pieces scrambled away like cockroaches. "Disgusting!" he said.

"That's Kreem fuh ya," said André. "Just like a cockroach: a low-down, dirty scavenger who runs when the light's on im."

I hung back a few steps with the Brotherfly while Festus led us to his crime lab. "André," I said softly, "I asked you once before, but your answer was clearly hiding more than it was revealing. So tell me at last, why do you hate Kareem so much?"

"Damn, Doc, fool be threatenin *mad* havoc an you aksin me why *I* hate *him*?"

"Yes, but André, you felt this way about him long before today, which is partly why you ended up being ordered into therapy in the first place."

"André's whole life," he said, fussing, fidgeting, even fluttering his fly wings, "fools like him be all up in André's face, hatin, hatin, tryinna put they cleats all up in my ass—"

"Are you sure you have an accurate picture of your relationship with Kareem? At one point you even suggested you were jealous of him for, as you claimed, having fairer skin, when you're both obviously black. Truly, André, you seem far more antagonistic to him than the reverse."

"Only cuz he be reservin his best behavior f'when he know he bein watched by you. Him an all his L*A*B-holes—nuthin but muhfuckin haters, fuh real!"

I tried probing further, but André was as agitated then as he had been the day in therapy he'd thundered at Kareem to cease investigating Hawk King's death for evidence of a conspiracy. "Naw, Doc! Don't be defendin him! Punk aint nuthin but a bigot, knawm sayn? He a hatin muthafuck who gone crackhead on his own pipe fulla hate, an he deserve whatever he gon get when we put a superstomp on his ass tonight!"

"But Syndi said she wouldn't—"

"Trust me, Doc. You cross Festus, you gots to pay, an he *always* got a way. Thass how it is. André get hisself some side action for free, he aint complainin, knawm sayn?"

In the center of the Surveillance Hollow, Festus sat like a king bee in his hive, surrounded by an encompassing honeycomb of hundreds of hexagonal monitors beaming images of city streets, boardrooms, industrial facilities, public parks, elevators, libraries, mosques, bedrooms, and more. He was tracking Syndi's path using a far more extensive network of cameras than I think anyone realized the Flying Squirrel possessed or could access, one even greater than the F*O*O*J's own intelligence-gathering techweb.

"Damn it!" said Festus, pounding his console. "That tricky little tramp's smarter than she lets on."

On several hexagonal screens focused on the nearest Ditko-Train station, a knot of people suddenly melted into a contingent of shapely, black-skirted, black-haired, white-pancaked young women, each of whom headed off in separate directions for various trains heading everywhere.

"That little bitch," growled Festus. "Doesn't have a trusting bone in her body."

I pulled up the only other chair in the lab (a dusty one, its back monogrammed CM) and sat beside Festus. He glared at me as if I'd used a piece of the True Cross for kindling.

I was struck again by how weary and worn he looked, slumped in his chair, his thinning hair whiter than ever and matted to his forehead. Perhaps he'd been skipping his "GI Juice" injections, or perhaps the psychemotional stress had been diminishing their effectiveness. Even inside the center of his superheroic sanctum, his legendary yet no longer "undisclosed location," Festus Piltdown III looked like an aged farmer gazing impotently at the hailstorm thrashing toward his fields.

"This is a very hard time for you, isn't it, Festus?"

"I can see why," said Festus, his eyes scanning his scanners without so much as blinking toward me, "you need the PhD after your name, Eva. You certainly wouldn't drum up business with anemic banalities like that." He snapped, "Of course it's hard on me! It's hard on all of us!"

"But on you personally. Only Syndi is bearing Hnossi's condition as heavily as you are."

"That's because I've known her for five decades, twenty years longer than even her no-account daughter has. And now I've got to worry that these leads I was pursuing on Warmaster Set were all black herrings. Which means that even the destruction of Asteroid Zed—my God!—even *that* was the work of that Beelzebubian bastard Kareem—"

"Let's focus on your feelings, Festus—your worry for Hnossi. To see her in this state—"

" 'This state'? Dying, you mean? In bed, the way no warrioress would ever want to go?"

"*And* before she can resolve her family troubles, her distance from her children, not to mention any other . . . unresolved interpersonal issues—"

He cut me off. "I was never married, so I can't relate to that. But missing your children—that I understand. I have compassion for that pain. And as her comrade."

"I'm not seeing comradely loyalty alone here, Festus," I said, touching his hand. I expected him to yank it away, even order me not to touch him. Instead, he was frozen, his eyes unfocused amid the flashing images from his surveillance honeycomb.

"I've been reading up on your noncaped careers," I said, anxious to maintain the opening. "You two not only worked together in the F*O*O*J, but elsewhere. For decades, Professor Icegaard was a paid consultant of your defense contracting corporation. Pilt-Dyne built the B9 bomber, which you christened the *Iron Lass* class; because of you, Pilt-Dyne's nuclear submarine was named the *Icegaard* class." I squeezed; his hand trembled. "For a hard-boiled industrial magnate like you, Festus, those were practically love poems."

He looked over at me, his eyes wet and glossy and twinkling from the honeycomb lights. Sitting there in his chair with his whitened hair, he was no longer the frightening, furry one-man war on crime, and no longer even the towering tycoon of technology.

He was just an old, lonely man facing the truth of his own powerlessness.

"And yet," I said, probing this rare vulnerability to examine the psychemotional damage that was crushing the life out of him, "for all your devotion to this woman, now that she truly needs you and there's no one else in your way, you still can't do anything to protect her . . . or save her."

"What?" he whispered, too horrified to be furious.

"Festus, you were up on Asteroid Zed with her, but when she was attacked by the Desiccator, where were you? Even now, with all your wealth and influence, and the awesome power of the surveillance you have at your fingertips right here, the woman you've loved for fifty years is dying, and there's nothing you can do to stop it."

His lower lip quivering, the spindly old teeth of his lower jaw exposed like a skeleton's, Festus leaned back in his chair, clutching his chest as if to keep his heart from exploding.

"Festus," I whispered, leaning toward him, *"how does all that make you feel?"*

His eyes were huge, his pupils swollen blackly, his face drained of all its color.

Suddenly the high-pitched buzz-whine in the background noise climaxed to buzzsaw anxiety that ripped through Festus's misery. I glanced up and spied an agitated Brotherfly crawling the Hollow's ceiling in endless circles while fluttering his wings at just below take-off speed. Festus shook his head as if to wake from sleeping at the wheel, then shoved his chair back away from me and stood.

"Get the fuck out of my crime lab!" he yelled, flipping back the sides of his dressing gown, his hands hovering at the holster level of his exposed utility belt. "And take that wall-crawling parasite with you!"

At Festus's behest, Mr. Savant, employing a crutch and with one arm in a cast, showed André and me to a drawing room. I offered André a tranquilizer, but he still wouldn't sit down, leaving his hand- and footprints all over the walls, windows, and ceiling.

Finally, following my special instructions, Mr. Savant left and hobbled back pushing a cart with a bowl of luxurious, exotic fruits, placing it on the grand marble coffee table at the center of the room.

Lured down by the sweet scents and tropical colors, André perched on the coffee table to ingest the fruit, doing so by expectorating rancid yellow digestive juices all over the oranges, bananas, mangoes, papayas, and grapes which dissolved the produce—peels, stalks, seeds, stones, and all—into a steaming, stinking pool that spilled all over the marble table. Opening his mouth, André unfurled his well-endowed proboscis and began sucking up the bubbling soda-pap he'd created.

Suppressing my gorge with an act of supreme will, I sat, taking out my ANDRÉ PARKER, HKA THE BROTHERFLY F*O*O*J file as well as the MORRIS ANDREW PARK, ALIAS BROTHERFLY file that Mr. Savant had brought me.

"You're twenty-six, André, correct?" He slurped and nodded, still sucking up the revolting stinking slime on the table. "And you've been in the F*O*O*J how long?" He held up three fingers.

André was a fascinating set of contradictions. As the hip, laid-back, fun-loving Brotherfly, he could not be a more profound counterpoint to the militant anal-retention of the thirty-four-year old X-Man. In one session, Kareem had described André as a "hyper-womanizing, antiintellectual, willing slave . . . enough of a collaborator with every racist stereotype about young black males that he should be a PR man for the Klan," and he'd denounced André to his face at the Dark Star soul food restaurant as "a slack, slick, loose-dicked, willingly-no-self-control . . . senseless, thoughtless, shiftless, aimless, brainless, oversized pants–wearing, forty-ounce-loving, penis-fixated, self-underrated supreme champ*een* of galactic niggativity."

But as the real man beneath the André Parker construct, *Morris Andrew Park* had so much in common with Philip Kareem Edgerton that the toxic enmity they shared became all the more shocking.

Glancing through the file's photos, I was struck by how severely André deviated from Andrew: tiny four-year-old Andrew in glasses on the back of a huge, shaggy dog; petite eight-year-old Andrew as chess wizard; puny sixteen-year-old Andrew in thick eyeglasses singing the role of Fortunato in his school's musical production *The Cask of Amontillado* . . . contrasted with several photos of muscular, tall, sexually turbo-charged twenty-two-year-old André "boogeying" in Bird Island nightclubs the Meet Market, Bone Dancers and Peacocks.

Undoubtedly Kareem would have approved of Andrew having attended the so-called "historically black college" Nat Turner U. It was there that the frail, awkward genetics student, the victim of a fraternity "prank," found himself forcibly gene-spliced with the dynamically altered DNA of a bluebottle fly.

After an astounding array of mutations, which saw Park autonomically spin a cocoon and retreat into it for the entirety of a spring break, Andrew had emerged with an enhanced genetic matrix that had imbued the brainy recluse voted "Most likely to Urkel" (whatever that meant) with the proportionate speed, strength, agility, and "flyness" of a fly.

After first gaining his powers, the shy young undergrad who'd never shone anywhere but onstage or on the dean's list looked for some way to employ his neotalents to help pay the bills of the elderly aunt and uncle who'd raised him. But as his acne dried up, his vision improved, his chest rippled, and his coordination soared, Andrew found himself winning stage roles as a leading man and attracting romantic attention of which he had never dreamed. After a fateful confidence-supercharging, career-advising meeting with Dennis Rodman, "André" began earning more money than he'd ever seen—as an exotic dancer. Although crimefighting as such had never been André's intention, the post-Götterdämmerung F*O*O*J was recruiting fresh faces for its own face-lift, and as André said in his job interview, "The benefits are good."

Perhaps beneath the André-bravado and underlying the anti-Kareem rage was the awkwardness of young Andrew, the tiny boy lacking in confidence everywhere but in the theater. This frightened inner-child Andrew likely confused the hyper-verbal, hyper-confident, hyper-aggressive Kareem on a psych-emotional level with all those who had ever bullied him—from the children who shoved his face in the urinal until he ate the cake to the "frat boys" who so cruelly spliced his genes.

Yet there was more driving the Brotherfly's overcompensating humor, erotic aggression, and anger—another deeper node of sadness, pain, and, I suspected, guilt. Ordinarily André would have been far too attention-deficited for me to probe into his deeper psychemotional workings, but as Mr. Savant had followed my instructions to inject the liquid tranquilizers I'd given him into the fruit, André was opening up like a can of soup.

"My uncle," he said when I inquired about the pain I knew he held in his psychemotional reservoir. "Poor ol Uncle Benteen."

"What about your uncle, André?"

" 's dead," he slurred sleepily. "My fault."

"Why would you say that?"

"I'd . . . y'know . . . *changed* . . . a lot. When I. Went offta school. 'Slot ferimmta handle. Went away a liddle boy. Came backaman. Never toldimmabout my, my, my mutation. Shun. That I wuzza supereero, that I joindaF*O*O*J. N one day, I, I, I didn'know hewuzzome. An I's getting into it . . . an he—"

"Getting into what, Andrew?"

His eyes telescoped on me as if I were a million miles away. But as he picked up speed, his hands and wings fluttered with ever-greater agitation, his face and voice rending themselves with ever-greater tragedy.

". . . gettin inta my *uni*form," he said. "An Uncle Benteen, he juss walks right into my damn bejjroom an sees me there with my armzanlegs half innannouttuvvit . . . an he grabs his heart, an he, he, he juss drops over! An therewuzzn't fuckall I couldoabouddit! Dead's dead. *Dead,*" he said, cupping his face in his hands, snorting and shuddering and wailing.

There was more, I sensed—something even more painful that André had yet to disclose. But before I could probe further, Mr. Savant appeared next to me.

"Madame," said the ancient manservant, "Ms. Icegaard is awake and is requesting your presence."

Stroking André's hair and straightening out his antennae, I assured him I'd be back as soon as I could. I hurried off for what in all likelihood would be Hnossi's final session.

When Good-bye Is the Only
Time to Say "I Love You"

D oes Hnossi know, Festus, how you've felt about her all these years?"

He fixed his furious eyes back on me, already enraged that Hnossi had insisted on my presence during his last remaining hours with her. After he refused to acknowledge my question with anything other than rage, she spoke for him.

"*Ja,* Frau Doktor," she whispered.

By then her skin was almost entirely racked with seeping red craters and brittle white plates. Even her scalp was a tortured moonscape, with what had remained of her hair burned off during her electrical discharges.

Yet when Festus turned to look at her while she struggled to talk, there wasn't a hint of horror or disgust in his eyes.

Only love and pain.

"Of course . . . I knew," she said.

"Was there ever anything between you? Sexually?"

Festus's back stiffened, but neither of them answered.

Finally Hnossi said, "It vuss 1961. Five munse before I vuss to marry Hector. Unt Festus unt I vere vurking longk hours, heading up ze anti-Treemason task force . . . unt, vell, zere hadt alvays been ziss . . . ziss *potency* betveen us, betveen me unt Festus. Unt vun night after a battle, ve came back to ze Fortress, unt ve'd bose been drinking . . ."

She sighed so heavily I feared the onslaught of another hacking fit—possibly her final one. But then she resumed.

"I felt so guilty . . . I couldn't even look at Festus, unt our friendship . . . vell, it never vent back to vut it hadt been. Never. Unt me . . . my *self*-respect . . . after all zose centuries uff svearing I vud never be like my own muzzer. But it vuss like a curse. I vuss no better zan zat whore."

She gnarled her fingers together, gazed toward the ceiling with eyes almost entirely scummed white. "All my talk. About honor! Nussing but vurmvoodt."

"And so," I asked as delicately as I could, "you said this was five months before you married Hector. And five months *after* your wedding . . ."

"Ja. Inka vuss born."

"And is she—?"

"She's Hector's," said Hnossi. "Sank Odin for zat. I put ze man srough enough pain. But Festus . . . venever ve hadt FOOCH family picnics, I'd catch him staring at Inka ven he sought I vuzn't lookink . . ."

Festus's eyes went wide. He'd apparently never known that the watchman had been watched.

"Staring how, Hnossi?" I asked. "At what?"

"Like . . . he vuss tryingk to see if somehow ze test hadt been wrong . . . or if I'd lied to him about ze test, maybe? I don't know. And zen after she got to a certain age, he stopped lookink at her altogezzer, I sink, because . . . she remindtet him."

"Of what?"

She looked at me, twin tears glistening in the shock of her frosted eyes, apparently stunned that I could not figure it out for myself. "Of vut couldt never be!"

She beckoned in Festus's direction. He was at her side instantly, holding her crumbling hand with the delicacy of cradling a newborn.

"Festus . . . I vant to tell you sum sings . . ."

"What, Hnossi?" he croaked, his throat a tuba of mud.

"I'm sorry . . . zat I made you suffer srough all of my, my—"

"This isn't the time for *sorry*s, Hnossi—"

"Let me finish!" she snapped, then instantly softened. "I'm sorry for hurtink you, rejectink you . . . for all my . . . vut does Frau Doktor call it? Ze 'crazy-makink' behavior, *ja.*"

"It's okay, Hnossi," he said, clearing his throat and swallowing heavily, twice. "It's okay."

"Nein," she whispered. "It vuss never okay. But at least now, at ze ent, I can say to you vut I shudt haff said back zen, back in 1962 . . ."

He waited, stooping, clutching her hand to his cheek. When she said nothing, he begged, "Yes, Hnossi?"

He looked down into her eyes.

They were pale gray, motionless.

Her chest fell as softly as snow.

Red, rust-scented smoke was drifting from her mouth.

The medical monitors screamed as one.

"Hnossi!" shouted Festus. "Dr. Singh! Nurse! DR. SINGH—"

The door swung open, and a suited and caped Omnipotent Man strode in.

"Wally, you idiot! What the hell are you doing here? Get Dr. Singh!"

"Step aside, Festus," he said. He clutched Festus's shoulder and plucked him out of the way like a mother dog retrieving a puppy by the neck.

Wally reached into the bed, sifted out Hnossi, and clutched the red-ravaged body in his arms.

And then he kissed her.

Electricity crackled from Wally's mouth into Hnossi's, streamers of it whipping frenetically around the room and overloading the machines and exploding the lightbulbs, plunging the room into flare-strobing darkness. Festus screamed at Wally to stop while Hnossi's limbs danced and jerked and her chest sucked closed and inflated outward violently again and again, and still Wally welded his kiss onto her, and when the scorching blue luminescence brightened to the point of blindingness, Festus and I scrambled from the room in fear for our lives.

"HNOSSI!" screamed Festus from the hall, while light seared our eyes even from around the rim of the door for what seemed like forever.

And then there was silence.

The door swung open.

Standing beside the steely, confident Omnipotent Man was Hnossi Icegaard.

Reborn.

Her skin was gleaming copper, her hair was returned miraculously to its full thick blackness and luster, and her eyes were shining like halogen amethysts. Wrapped only in a white bedsheet, she looked more Greek goddess than Norse, glowing before us and smiling with secret, joyful knowledge, as if listening to celestial music only she and the divine could hear.

"Wally," gasped Festus, relief and horror fighting for control of his face, "what did you—"

"All th'little gal needed, Festy, was a little galvanizin. Course," smirked Wally, "not every man knows how t'perform that."

Back in therapy after the excursion to Asteroid Zed, after Hnossi had already developed rust poisoning, Wally had fallen to pieces and electro-welded his own fingers and limbs back on. But none of us—not I, not Festus (whom Wally'd electro-blasted across the room), and not Wally himself—had realized how that power might be applied to transforming others.

I complimented Wally on his apparently successful transformation of Hnossi and, of course, of himself. He turned a sunrise smile on me, saying, "I couldna done it without ya, ma'am-doctor."

"And your alters? Ricky R. Bustow, Reverend Crocket, Musk Ox Miller? Are they—"

He tapped the side of his skull, eliciting a soft bell tone. "Wellsir, they's still all up here—but now, they's together. *Uni-mah-fied*." Even Wally's voice had been transmuted, expanded, as if the multiple "voices" inside him had harmonized soni-cally into a melodious choir, powerful and hypnotic.

"I did like you told me, ma'am," said Omnipotent Man. "I cogitated suh'm fierce upon who I *wannid* t'be, steada all the thangs I weren't an that I was a failure at. I put all m'short-comins in th'closet an put on m'best Sunday-go-t'meetin suit, an fixed m'self to bein like m'mentor. An th'more I did, the more I realized the truth." His eyes shifted toward the ceiling, as if gazing past drywall and plaster and up into the majesty of the revolving, evolving galaxy.

"And what truth is that, Wally?"

"That I have a personal relationship with the Ka of Hawk King," he said, his voice riding a rhythm. "That I have accepted the Ka of Hawk King as my own personal superhero. That the Ka of Hawk King has *saved* me—"

"*Ka*-ka," mumbled Festus.

Wally's eyes flashed tiny electrical arcs, twin bolts of light-ning, but he did not stop.

"—and that in his celestial crusade for justice, he has made me his knight. His *Hawk Knight*."

Draping herself from his shoulder, Hnossi stared up at Wally, her eyes sparkling as if his dynamic current were still surging inside her. Her flesh renewed, her muscles taut and de-fined, I'd never seen her look more powerfully beautiful or beautifully powerful.

And I had never imagined I would see the dark matter of dis-dain so disintegrated from her demeanor that she would shim-mer like a nebula from the light of a hyper-masculine supernova. Wally's omni-belief in himself, and the resulting growth in his own superstrength, had proved an old maxim: for many women, even goddesses, power is the greatest aphrodisiac of all.

And then Mr. Savant returned with Syndi, who was agog at the sight of her radiant mother. Mother and daughter embraced in a death-averted hug with more warmth than they'd likely ever shared before.

Festus Piltdown, on the other hand, slumped against the wall, looking as if he'd just been punched in his soul.

Graffiti from the Ghetto of the Mad

Gathered with us back inside the crime lab, Syndi, flush with relief at her mother's recovery, divulged all the information she'd received from her rendezvous with Kareem, even revealing the location, since it no longer mattered: the now-abandoned Hermes Theater in Stun-Glas.

"He told me to save myself. Because he said that you, Eva . . . that you're either Sarah Bellum, or Menton, or both."

Grimacing as if swallowing a pill the size and shape of a horseshoe, Syndi was clearly pained to be revealing her intelligence—whether from a wish to protect me or Kareem, I wasn't sure. The luminous Hnossi and Wally stood flanking her, each with a comforting hand on one of her shoulders.

Festus stared anywhere in the room but at that trinity.

There was a sudden whining buzz about my ears. I batted away the distraction.

André asked, "Why do that nutjob think she Menton or Bellum?"

Syndi shook her head. "Oh . . . it's . . . it's so sad. It's crazy. Paranoid. He was all over the place—because Eva'd written all those books on Menton, like she was the Earl of Oxford to Menton's Shakespeare."

I found myself startled by Syndi's reference, still integrating my comprehension that nineteen-year-old celebrity puffhead

Syndi was actually thirty-two-year-old intellectual Inga. "Why else, Syndi?"

She carefully laid bare the layers of Kareem's paranoia, as if opening a set of nested Ukrainian dolls. Apparently, Kareem was accusing me of being Sarah Bellum; he said also that I was originally the minor heroine Right-Brain Girl, rejected for F*O*O*J membership in the early 1970s; that he'd seen photographs of the "real" me standing in front of bookshelves full of Ayn Rand texts; that in the late 1970s I'd "assumed" the identity of Dr. Brain, and as therapist for Tran Chi Hanh had driven a wedge between the Flying Squirrel and Chip Monk, destroying their partnership; that I either had caused Dr. Napoleon Orator to become Menton so I could have the perfect mate, or had "doubled" my mind, placing half of it in Dr. Orator as the first fiefdom of my geopsychic empire; that, imprisoned on Asteroid Zed, I had evolved my *phagopsychosis* to absorb psinergy from the planetary unconscious itself, eventually enough to wreak murderous revenge on Hawk King; that I had used deceptive, destructive therapeutic techniques to initiate Omnipotent Man's breakdown; that I had manipulated my F*O*O*J patients into going up to Asteroid Zed where they could be mass-murdered, and, barring that, where a Plan B could initiate the death at least of Iron Lass, which in turn would weaken Syndi and Festus; that I had accessed secret, comprehensive files on X-Man and Syndi, leaking the information to the press to destroy him in a scandal; that by establishing myself as the F*O*O*J's chief confidant, I had placed myself in the perfect position to gather supreme intelligence on them, exploit their weaknesses, and destroy them one by one—or to manipulate them to my further end of taking over the planet for a never-ending *phagopsychotic* feeding frenzy on the collective minds of the human race.

When Syndi was done, a cold silence clutched the crime lab like the metallic fingers of Count Speculum.

"It's tragic," I said, "that a young man so bright, with so much promise . . . Ah, well. Now. Given the threat to public safety that Kareem's psychosis clearly poses, we need to focus on what all of you are going to do."

"Oh, and there's one more thing, Eva," said Syndi, taking out and handing me an ordinary paper note addressed to me. I swatted at the insects whining in my ears before taking the note.

"What's it say?" demanded Festus and André in unison, rushing me.

I scanned it, and then read aloud:

First, "Doctor Brain," or whoever you truly are, my final ten-word answer to your recurring question about what I'd do if I could never equal the glory of my predecessors is as follows:

"Pursuing glory is what created this mess. I'll take justice."

Second, contrary to your psychobabbling parable intended to "heal" me, I want you to understand that I don't have two wolves inside me and never did. Just a single black dog with four paws: one of fear, one of hope, one of rage, and one of love.

And he's a good dog.

Festus snapped, "What kind of Congo-jumbo is that sambo sociopath dithering on about?" André shushed him violently, and remarkably Festus obeyed.

And finally, before the end of this day, I intend to expose the real assassin of Hawk King and explode an even more diabolical conspiracy that would otherwise leave thousands of American citizens dead, thus subjecting the country, if not the planet, to a never-ending war on freedom. And I swear by the Udjat, *I will do so by any means necessary.*

> *Dā-f xu, us em maāxeru!*
> The X-Man

"Y'hear that?" slurred André, still sobering up. "How he gonna . . . 'explode' a 'conspiracy . . . by any means necessary'? We can't wait any longer! If we don'put the smackdown on that psycho now, who knows what he gon do? An how many people he gon hurt?"

"Where do y'all think he's gon strike?" asked Wally. His voice echoed in the Hollow beyond its solitary sonic power. In the shadowy chamber, he, Hnossi, and Syndi seemed to be glowing.

Festus addressed his computer array rather than look toward the golden triangle. He swatted flies away from his ears. His voice was ice.

"Since Edgerton's attempting to blame the good doctor here for everything wrong in his misbegotten life, clearly he's going to attack her wherever he thinks she could be—which means her home, the Squirrel Tree, or her Hyper-Potentiality Clinic. Don't worry, Doct—"

"Now don'tchu worry, lil lady," said Wally. "We'll protect ya."

Festus bit his lower lip, hard, then keyboarded his console like Bach playing his organ. The honeycomb monitors flared, fluttered and flashed with millions of random images, and while we watched, the data flood began channeling into select motifs.

"Good goddamn," said Festus. Then, distracted by the buzz whining in the air, he turned around to glare at André.

"Hey, it ain'me!" said the Brotherfly.

"Vut is it, Festus?"

He shook his head disgustedly. "I should've caught this, but with everything going on, the conspiracy, me taking care of you—I can't keep absolutely everything under control, I never claimed to be a god, just a hardworking—"

"*Festus!*" snapped the Iron Lass, the syllables evoking the slash of a whip. "Vut. *Is* it?"

Still without looking toward her, he pointed at various monitors while electronically highlighting them.

"Here," he said, clicking on a hexagon of a black man and an Asian man in an office. "Footage recorded several days ago. Our X-Hero's retained legal counsel. *With Tran.*" He snorted heavily enough to dislodge his pancreas. "Quite a turnaround for an ambulance-chasing backstabbing barrister employed by an antisuperhero watchdog agency!"

Click. A desert canyon in searing daylight. The image scoped down to a network of drill holes. One after the other, four black baboons emerged from the holes, carrying tiny sacks and running. "Yucca Flats. The abandoned mine sites."

"So?" said Syndi, swatting at and missing the insects buzzing in the Hollow.

"That's where th'gubment was drillin f'argonium," said Wally, his tabernacle voice Pavarotting my brain. "I always told 'em there hadda still be some left down there."

I asked Festus why Kareem would send his shadow creatures to retrieve argonium.

"Who knows? A dirty bomb? Insurance against . . . someone who might finally bother to return to active duty? Combine that with the argonium data he downloaded . . . We've seen close-up how addictive it is. What if Edgerton could shadow-extract it or shadow-synthesize it, combine it with something else, and mass-produce it? That racist reprobate has sworn revenge for the F*O*O*J 'denying' him his 'rightful place.' What if he's planning to drown white America in a tidal wave of argonium-crack?"

"That's complete bullshit, Festus," said Syndi, "and you know it!"

"*Ja*, Festus . . . Kareem may be a schwarzextremist, but still, I caun't believe—"

"Oh no?" he said, trying and failing to swat the insect buzzing near his ear. "Then what do you make of these?"

Festus clicked several hexagons: multiple angles of Sunhawk Island and the Blue Pyramid, time-jumping imagery of a black falcon entering and later exiting the Pyramid from the aperture of the mysterious shaft on the forty-second tier.

"The Ka-Sentinels *sealed* the Blue Pyramid," growled Festus, "three days after Hawk King's death. The drones wouldn't even let Major Ursa or the Spectacle back into the crime scene. And after the divine apparition at the funeral, no one wanted to risk trying to break in. And yet *here*," he said, pointing, "we see that Edgerton's been sending his shadows inside! For what purpose? What's he been doing?"

Suddenly Festus hammered his fist into his console. Syndi, André, and I jumped in reaction. Festus looked down at what he'd crushed: glistening black fragments. Which then *poofed* into nothingness.

"That bastard! He's been monitoring us this entire time! I should have crushed him with my bare hands!" he yelled, his voice resounding in the Hollow: *BARE HANDS BARE hands barehands* . . . Panting with rage, he muttered almost inaudibly, "But that would be messy. *Gas* is neater for bugs."

A comm call came in from the Fortress of Freedom. Festus stabbed the HOLD key on his console.

I confessed to Festus that I failed to see why the situation was as dire as he seemed to think.

"How can you fail to comprehend this, Miss Brain? That fanatic's been sending his word-things *inside* the Blue Pyramid! *He* killed Hawk King! And if he could do that to a god, how long do you think a defenseless human being could last against one of his nightmarish creations? And why murder Hawk King at all, unless he'd gone to the King under this delusional negroid–Hawk King theory, shared his plans with the King and expected support, and when the King refused him any further access to the Blue Pyramid and its technology and threatened to turn him in, or attempted to capture him right there—"

"Technology? Inside the Blue Pyramid?"

"The ancient technology inside Hawk King's fortress, Miss Brain, could incinerate half the United States. If the X-Man were to use the Pyramid as his command and control center, he could prosecute a one-man global race war . . . and possibly even win it."

Psychesituational Presentation of X-Tremism

Determined to go into battle immediately, Festus sketched out his strategy, accepting as-brief-as-possible interventions from Hnossi and fitting Wally with a device he called an "OM Meter" so he could monitor Wally's health in case the X-Man had acquired sufficient supplies of argonium to pose a threat. When I pressed him quietly on the "OM Meter," Festus conceded that he was more concerned that this "brave new Wally" was unstable, and he "refused to risk the success of the mission on the cultic conversion of any Kentucky-fried fanatic."

The monitors beeped impatiently with the call Festus had forgotten was on hold. He tapped his keyboard, and the central hexagons of the honeycomb united into a single image: the black-furred Major Ursa, surrounded by a hundred F*O*O*J-sters, gathered inside the majestically muralled auditorium of Heroes' Hall.

"What is it, Major?"

"Uh, well—we've, we've all been waiting for you, sir."

"Waiting for *me*? What are you on about?"

"Your speech, sir—you were supposed to begin your speech ten minutes ago."

"Speech? I'm not giving any speech, Major!"

"But you used the Alpha-One channel, you asked us to—"

"I certainly did not use the—" He stopped. His eyes grew tiny. *"Major Ursa, evacuate the Fortress forthwith! Condition Red! REPEAT, EVACUATE ALL PERSONNEL FORTHWITH—"*

The honeycomb flared with sound and fury, and then went null, into default blue.

Festus stammered, "Good God—even *I* didn't think that madman would—"

Everyone gazed at the empty blue, dumb with horror.

Festus dialed into his hexagon-screen comm system, patching into both the Alpha and Zeta Channels.

"Ah . . . attention . . . cuh-calling all F*O*O*Jsters," he said. "Calling all retired F*O*O*Jsters and all independents. This is an Alpha-One and Zeta-One priority message, invoked under the authority of FEMA Protocol SH Two. The Fortress of Freedom has been bombed. Everyone inside has been . . . everyone is presumed dead."

"NO!" cried Syndi. "Kareem would never do that! It must just be, like, knockout-gas bombs or something—"

Festus muted the comm to face Syndi. "You *still* believe that fanatic isn't dangerous? You heard him in therapy, in his note to Miss Brain! That he'd 'explode' a conspiracy! Well he's done it! With bombs!"

He unmuted his comm. "Stand by for scrambled mission strategy. Converge as outlined. Flying Squirrel out."

Festus turned, facing his troops. "Professor Icegaard. Contact the Spook directly—try him at Langley; I think he's speaking to the graduating class. He'll want a piece of this bastard boiled and dipped in butter. Wally. Try using your omni-hearing to locate Edgerton. We have to assume he's heading to the Blue Pyramid immediately—assuming he hasn't taken it already.

"Everyone: the only people we can count on now are us. We in this room may be the only surviving active members of the F*O*O*J. We have one mission, perhaps our most important ever: to neutralize the X-Man and his L*A*B fanatics tonight before they neutralize us all."

Failing to Fight the Supervillain Within

Still unsure of the extant conditions and locked inside a psychemotional grand mal seizure of their own combative, antagonistic paradigm, the F*O*O*Jsters were determined to defeat their former colleague—not with reason, visualization, feelings-work, journaling, or an intervention—but with naked, brute violence.

Even if the F*O*O*Jsters could somehow manage not to destroy one another, their capacity for psychic healing would be all the more diminished by their refusal to engage the most important hyper-battle of all: against the supervillain within.

CHAPTER TWELVE

SUPERHEROES NEED SUPEREGOS

SUNDAY, JULY 16, 7:12 P.M.

Processing Unresolved Issues

n the bowels of Langston-Douglas, terror was growing like a radioactive polyp. With news helicopters ratcheting overhead in the choking 110 degree smog and the streets bloodied by sunset, the QRIB HQ of the League of Angry Blackmen stood in dark defiance of the noose tightening every second around it.

Having divided all responding heroes into attack squads for three separate targets, the Flying Squirrel waited at ready with his own strike force from an undisclosed location, monitoring the shrinking cordon around the faux–Egyptian temple of the QRIB.

Including Power Grrrl, Red Squad was composed of eight trained and armed fighters, warriors straining at the ropes to begin combat, valiantly ignoring the shouted curses and tossed garbage of neighborhood residents: fifty-three-year-old *Kid Kombat Sr.* with his wrecking-ball arms, buzzsaw "wings," and missile-launcher backpack; forty-three-year-old *Saber-Tooth Beaver,* scourge of Treemasons and environmentalists, and champion of the nation's forestry industry; fifty-five-year-old *Smithing Wesson,* lord of firearms; fifty-one-year-old *King's English,* the superbobby; the sixty-four-year-old *Rock Breaker,* armed with his mystic hammer John Henry; thirty-eight-year-old *Super Bastard,* half lawyer, half trailer park; and the commander, legend among legends (despite lingering court cases surrounding a few dozen friendly-fire deaths), the sixty-three-year-old military master, the *Spook.*

Safely ensconced inside the Squirrel Tree's crime lab, I was able to observe the approaching melee two ways: visually through the honeycomb of monitors, and empathically through the OM Meters the Flying Squirrel had ordered everyone to wear so he could coordinate the battle. Perhaps due to a malfunction, I couldn't pick up Festus's own cognistream, but I could experience the unfolding crisis from as many other psi-POVs as I could handle.

"I can't believe, like, what a bunch of pathetic, fossilized old geezers I'm stuck with," complained public-persona Syndi, perhaps having forgotten that her comm was active (or perhaps not forgetting).

"Cut the chatter, Red Two," snapped the Spook.

"Quit calling me that, Sanford! My name is Power Grrrl!"

The Spook: "Red Squad, lock weapons and prime powers in attack readiness."

Kid Kombat Sr.: "Red Three, standing by."

Saber-Tooth Beaver: "Red Four, standing by."

Smithing Wesson: "Red Five, standing by."

King's English: "I say, old chap, Red Six, standing by."

The Rock Breaker: "Yessuh, Red Seven hyah, stannin by-an-by."

Super Bastard: "Red Eight, frickin ready to *rawk an ro-o-oll,* good buddy!" (Pause) "Stanning by."

(Pause)

The Spook: "Red Two, confirm readiness!"

Power Grrrl (sighing): "What*ever.*"

Still monitoring visuals only, I watched as the Spook, suddenly lit by red and blue lights stroking him and the buildings around him, stood to address those bunkered inside the QRIB.

"ATTENTION, PHILIP K. EDGERTON AND OTHER L*A*B MILITANTS!" boomed the amplified voice of Red Squad Leader. "SURRENDER IMMEDIATELY. WE HAVE YOU SURROUNDED! COME OUT WITH YOUR HANDS UP AND YOU WILL NOT BE HARMED."

Seconds gouged into everyone's nerves. There was no response.

After forty-six seconds, Saber-Tooth Beaver asked, "Are we even sure they're in there?"

"Yes of course we're sure!" said the Spook. "Hold your positions, and your tongues!"

On the honeycomb hexagons haloing the combat theater, video unfurled from the helicopters of the local and national news stations. Reporters explained that they were "live at the Stun-Glas standoff" (seconded by onscreen titles proclaiming the location as "KRIB Headquarters" [*sic*]) where "black L*A*B cult militants are under the command of disgraced F*O*O*Jster the X-Man"; PNN's story proclaimed Kareem an "antiwhite fanatic turned terrorist and superpredator" against whom the "dusk raid has been launched following a terrorist attack on the Fortress of Freedom where assembled F*O*O*Jsters are presumed dead . . ."

Once sixty seconds at full alert had expired, the Spook ordered Syndi to deploy her HEAT Ray against the L*A*B to "dance them out." Syndi reminded the field commander that her beam worked only on line-of-sight, useless against the L*A*Bsters trapped inside.

The Spook: "Then hit the music, Red Two!"

Instantly:*BUHM-BUHM-BUHM-BUHM . . . BUHM-BUHM-BUHMti-BUHM . . .*

Ripping her bustier speakers up to full volume, Syndi opened her mouth to unleash a sonic tsunami upon the neighborhood, a herd of auditory woolly mammoths trampling over tepees:

"I wanna SHOCK you, BABY
ROCK you, BABY
TALK you MAYBE
Into GOING
DOWN, DOWN, DOWN, DOWN
DOWN on ME-E-E-E . . ."

Rushing to their windows, ghetto dwellers leaned out, screaming inaudibly against the aural assault; soon they disappeared only to return to their sills throwing bottles, forks, and burning trash—

The Spook: *"Take 'em out, Red Two!"*

Syndi's HEAT Ray bathed the tenements in intense swirls of disco light, and instantly the dozen window terrorists were transmuted into twelve individual Power Grrrls, all of them harmonizing with her choral invitation to cunnilingual fury. When other residents emerged to pelt the Syndis in their own building with garbage, they too were flash-HEATed into singing submission.

When five minutes had passed and still no one had emerged from the QRIB, the Spook patched into Syndi's sound system to declare his ultimatum:

"ATTENTION MILITANTS! THIS IS YOUR FINAL WARNING! IF YOU DO NOT SURRENDER WITHIN THE NEXT SIXTY SECONDS WE WILL OPEN FIRE! YOU WILL *MOVE* OUT OF THAT *HOUSE* OR YOU WILL *FACE THE CONSEQUENCES*!"

QRIB Deaths

When the sixty seconds ended, the Spook ordered in the Rock Breaker.

With remarkable speed for such a massive sixty-four-year-old man, the Rock Breaker leapt over the barrier and sprinted across the street, his mystic hammer John Henry in front of him like a sword.

At the final second before his strike could rip out the corner of the QRIB temple, dark tentacles tore out of the soil and tripped up the elderly black man, knocking him to the ground and seizing the fallen John Henry. Rising from the soil with his tentacles like a giant black daddy longlegs spider, the Dreadlocker closed on the Rock Breaker to rip him to stumps.

And then a twenty-foot battering ram of an arm smashed the Dreadlocker into a smear on the sidewalk.

Super Bastard, piloting his giant "Transformer" suit of linked robotic trailers, stood to his full six-story height, scraping the gore and dreadlocks from his arm before displaying evidence of his kill for the Spook.

"HOW'S SHE LOOKIN, PARTNERS?" he boomed, before the QRIB's roof exploded from the emergence of a six-story-tall Arnold Drummond, Esq.

For terrifying seconds it was giant lawyer against giant lawyer, prosecutor against defense, locked in lethal litigatory combat, until Arnold Drummond got the upper hand and knocked Super Bastard down with one swing of his massive supersubpoena. The trailer-Transformer fell, crushing the Rock Breaker into the potholed street. Drummond jeered, *"Whatchu talkin about, Bast'd?"*

The Spook: "Red Five, take him out!"

Kid Kombat Sr. knelt, bowing his head for clearance, and smoke trails streamed six hundred feet diagonally upward from his back to sear Arnold Drummond's face, turning the left side of his giant skull into a cratered ruin of ravaged, sagging, burning flesh. An abattoir's worth of meat and bone pelted the ground like human hail.

Roaring in his death throes, Drummond charged the line before another tendril of smoke exploded through his midsection, dumping him dead overtop the struggling megaskeleton of Super Bastard.

Seconds before Kid Kombat could fire into the QRIB temple itself, his backpack exploded. Aflame, he fell to the ground screaming and flailing, dying like a crab dropped into a pot of boiling fat.

The Spook: *"What the hell—"*

I switched angles on the monitors. Charging across the street was Aunt Ester of the Supa Soul Sistas, who must have aimed her chemotrophic powers into the unarmed missiles on Kid Kombat's back. Still advancing, she transmuted five of Smithing Wesson's bullets into blossoms of steam before the sixth one punched a hole through her sternum big enough to reach through.

The scene devolved into chaos: Onyx Fox, another Supa Soul Sista, executed a hundred-foot arcing wire-work side-kick into Smithing Wesson's back—the King's English hurled his bobby hat, which transmuted midtumble into a vicious, scrabbling badger that chomped on to Onyx Fox's leg—the Diva emerged, shooting her Look, and everyone in range dropped to their knees in worship until she and Syndi locked eyes and powers in diva-to-Diva combat—Saber-Tooth Beaver dashed across the smoking, flaming attack zone to start gnawing a new entrance into the QRIB—Anita Hill waded through strafing fire, her shield-law protecting her while she inched ever closer into range to unleash her power of discovery—

And then three giant silver-black wedges flew screaming overhead and dropped incendiary "eggs" on the QRIB.

The temple roared flame into the sky like Vesuvius.

Arcing out of their first bombing run, the Spook's terror-dactyls circled wide, aligning for their second attack vector.

Having leapt all over the surrounding tenements, the fire transformed the entire block into a massive, multistory bonfire. The QRIB's walls fissured and burst, and what remained of the roof crumbled and shattered through the four lower stories until all that remained was a rubble inferno.

For just a moment I activated Syndi's OM Meter, seeking an empathic survey of the situation. Beyond her horror, what I felt from her was a hammering heart, a throat raw from singing and screaming, and a nose scorching with the stench of smoke and burning meat.

The Spook: "Attention all units. This is Red Squad Leader. The target has been pacified. Repeat: The target has been pacified."

Regardless of what the adrenaline addiction of superhero-ism may afford you, if you're serious about "pacifying" yourself, you'll need to look past such easy solutions as immolating those who spin you into a shame spiral or body-check you into belligerence. Remember: No one can "make" you "feel" anything.

The power is yours—and yours alone—to actualize yourself, to create your own reality, to free yourself of the illusions that imprison you more completely than could any malevolent mastermind. Had either X-Man or the Spook remembered such basic truths for achieving psychemotional equilibrium, they could have saved themselves not only lethal, destructive combat but substantial consternation.

Final Lessons at the Alma Mater

By the time I scan-switched over to Sunhawk Island, Blue Squad had engaged its enemies. In the inky indigo dusk over the Blue Pyramid, orange flares and sparks lit up the combatants. But otherwise beyond those light sources I was blind, so I patched my OM Meter into Wally's cognistream:

~~What is all this crazy junk in m'face? M'team's gettin clobbered an I caint hardly see nuthin—better comm Festus. He'll know what t'do . . .

"Mission C'mmand, this here's Wally—"

"Copy, Blue Squad Leader. Over."

"MC, I'm getting blindeded out here—some kinda black cloud fulla lil ol squares is followin me—"

"Look carefully, Blue Leader—are the squares tiny words? Over."

"Uh, well now that y'mention it, yes, yes they is—"

"All right, then—they're logoids! Have you seen Edgerton anywhere? Over."

"No, not yet—"

"Blue Leader, White Squad's engaged his word-creatures at the Hyper-Potentiality Clinic! He's overextended—there's no way he can keep manifesting so many apparitions at once for long without completely draining himself. Hang in, Blue Leader! Over and out!"

"Over and out!"

~~Cain't keep this up f'ever. Better spit on em. Now that's a sight! Fry, you stupid lil words! Golly, I always loved that smell—like burnin hair. That's better—now I c'n get me a clearer look-see. Golldangit! Lookit the size a them boys, them whatchacallem—Ka-Sentinels? Like a football team of tar black Goliaths with hawk faces. And who's that fightin alongside em? Whoever it is, they's beatin the stuffin outta Ivory Giant!

~~My gosh, it sure is a lovely night; stars all a-twanklin. Sunhawk Island'd be a nice place t'go campin sometime. Think maybe when we're done t'night I should grab me some dinner at th'Olive Garden. They give ya extra breadsticks gratis if y'ask for 'em kindly. Maybe I should get me that collie dog I been thankin about for a spell. They shed suh'm fierce, though . . . Hm . . . Is they reruns of *Rockford Files* on tonight? Always like that there Jim Rockford . . .

"Blue Leader! Blue Leader! This is Cathode Girl, do you copy?"

"Cathode Girl, this is Omnipotent Man, the Blue Leader. Over."

"Blue Leader, we need your assis—"

"Say, Cathode Girl, who's that fella leadin alla them Ka-Sentinels—the one wearin the golden skirt and whippin around that scepter? Over."

"Blue Leader, that's the L*A*Bster, Grimhotep the Living Ka! Blue Leader, please engage! We are currently having the sweet shit kicked out of us! Over!"

"Cathode Girl, this is Blue Leader—please keep th'profanity off this here channel! Over!"

"Blue Leader, Eldritch Cleaver has cut off Atomic Giraffe's legs, Ivory Giant's being kicked to death on the ground, and it's all Zed and I can do to shatter these Sentinels! We need your help, Blue Leader!"

"Don' get y'drawers in a knot, lil lady, I'm a-comin!"

~~Gotta plow through another cloud a these word-dealies. Worse'n Mexican skeeters. Lookit alla them animals runnin around down there—so dark out, it's tough to . . . what're them, crocodiles? An hippos! An a elk or suh'm? Hawk King shore had hisself a fine preserve here. Okay, let's deal with these Sentinels.

~~Hm—skin feels like marble, cool and smooth. Still—*uhn*—they aint so tough. Just like crumblin crackers in yer soup. Ten-foot-tall black crackers with golden beaks, anyhow. How many left—okay, got those two. Get them over there—done and done. Spit down these six. Where's Grimhotep? Fightin Cathode and Zed the Livin Phoneme. They'll be fine. Okay, smash this one. Crack them two. Spit these five down to—

~~*DMMMF!* M'dadblamed skull feels like I jess been quarterback-sacked in a minefield! Where am I? Up to m'neck in th'water—Sunhawk Island's way in the heck over there an I'm a-bobbin in th'Bay—

"Who sucker punched me? C'mon, show y'self, unless yer yella! Don'make me smoke ya out!"

~~*NFFF!* Like takin a missile in m'midsection—an whoever's plowin into me is shootin us up outta th'water now—

~~Kick him away—watch that crumb-bum spinning end-over-coffeepot. "Who are ya, y'no-good sucker-puncher?"

"You don't know me, Argonian?"

~~Somebody's hovering out there with his back to th'moon, all shadowed an I cain't see 'im fer squat—'cept he's got a cape an he's holdin some kinda oversized double-sided ax or suh'm.

"Sorry, buddy? Could y'all turn on a light or suh'm? I'm guessin y'all don'get many offers t'play basketball at night."

"Taunt all you like, *Im*potent Man! For I, Shango, will be the *orisha* of your doom!"

~~OW! Betty *Crocker,* that smarts! Put his lil ol ax right in my turnstiled *knee*cap! Let's see how he likes a little spit-shine! That's better, son—*now* I can see ya, lit up like a 'lectric Santy Claus on Bustle Avenue at Christmas!

"How ya like that, Shangy-Man? You talk tough for some-body wearin such a funny little tiara!"

~~UHFF! Tough sumbitch, all right! Better shock him some more—still keeps on coming—burnt off most of his hair an clothes, an he's still swangin, grabbin me, wrastlin me like a Florida king gator hopped up on funny-beans—hokay, gots

to choke im—gon be tough—his neck's tougher'n m'thigh—
practically huggin im he's so close—

~~Now, there she goes, throat's finally crackin—

~~DAMN, he up an *smoked* me in th'eye with a head butt—

~~What's all this sand or dust or whatever—hey, smells
like—

~~Everything's foggy an spinnin . . . World's gone blue an
black an blue an black an blue—like I'm swimmin in Windex
and crude oil, all hot an cold at the same time, I'm all tinglin
an singin an laughin an m'heart's a-throbbin . . . Why's the water
rushin t'ward me like that? Okey-dokey, I'll take a little soaky . . .
Nice a Shangy to go fer a dip with me, even if he's lyin facedown an all. Looks powerful peaceful. Think I'll try it—

deselected my OM Meter link into Wally's mind and checked
the honeycomb for a visual scan of what was happening, but
I could see nothing except darkness interrupted by flashes.
And if a night-vision setting existed, I didn't know how to activate it.

I dialed up an audio link. "Anyone, anyone, can you hear
me?"

"Miss Brain! This is the Flying Squirrel! Get the hell off this
mission channel!"

"I'm sorry to interrupt, Festus, and I'm sure you're busy, but
Wally's been incapacited somehow—he may be drowning—"

"I was OM Metering the whole affair! He's been hit by an
A-bomb!"

"An atomic bomb? Are you sure?"

"Argonium, you nitwit! Probably laced with Edgerton's
shadow-synthetic version. And I seriously doubt Wally'll
drown . . . his brain can survive without oxygen for decades—
hadn't you noticed? Now get the hell off this line and stay off!"

I hung up and spoke to the computer directly. "Where is Philip Kareem Edgerton, HKA the X-Man?"

The honeycomb flitted through thousands of camera-sights on Los Ditkos—the mainland, the Bird Island borough, and Sunhawk Island—sorting and filtering until dozens of urban angles lit up on the same image: a black car streaking at what must have been more than 140 miles an hour, racing from Ellison Heights over the Rubicon Bridge and the Mantlo River, bypassing the clogged traffic of Bustle Avenue and ripping along River Drive beside the elite Bechtburton district, burning straight toward the northern plateau of the island—

But why was X-Man headed there? And why had the rest of his confederates thrown away their lives elsewhere? What had they been protecting? Or had it all been nothing but a diversion?

Flying Squirrel: "White Squad and all remaining units, this is Mission Command. Converge on Tachyon Tower! Repeat: Converge on Tachyon Tower!"

When We Lose Our Delusions, We Must Not Lose the Lesson

Zooming every available city security camera I could, I tracked the shadow car as it rocketed up the hills to the plateau and then—astonishingly—*straight up the side* of the Tachyon Tower.

The black blot further silhouetted itself against the scoreboard-style full-color advertisements coursing the tapering heights of Tachyon Tower. Decelerating rapidly, slowing to a crawl just before it reached the tower's apex, the car braved an upside-down ascent from the bottom of the giant faux-plasma globe, then inched up along the curvature until finally at the globe's equator . . .

Switching angles to an interior camera, I gazed upon a vast window, on the other side of which the X-Racer stuck to the glass like the world's largest refrigerator magnet.

Something extended from the underbelly of the vehicle, and then a neat circle etched itself in the glass, popping out a hole through which slid the cloaked L*A*Bster the Dark Fantastic, Chip Monk (in an altered version of his original costume—black tights instead of scaly green briefs), and the ever white-shirted, black-tied, and black-suited X-Man.

Kareem glanced back to the window. The X-Racer disappeared. Through the crisp circle in the window, wind instantly whipped their costumes and scattered brochures across the Sunday evening desertion of the observation deck. The Dark Fantastic raised his arm—

—and every hexagon scanning that gallery of the Tachyon Tower deck blinked not to null blue but total black.

I flicked at the controls to bring up another image, but the invading trio was completely blacked out.

Instantly another hexagon seized my attention: One floor upward, a wall shattered inward, and then a woman in shining armor landed on the debris of steel and reinforced concrete— Iron Lass, her black wings transmuting back into her cloak, her twin swords bared for battle. Scanning her surroundings, she dashed toward the vault door, on top of which a sign declared:

CONTAINMENT UNIT X
FULLY AUTOMATED FACILITY
EXTREME DANGER

ACCESS RESTRICTED TO
SECURITY LEVEL INFRARED
AND ABOVE

Shoving her swords into the massive metal mechanism, she was showered by sparks and instantly lit up by flashing bullet fire from a dozen angles and splashed by jets of a liquid spray that coated her and everything around her in icicles. Throbbing lights plunged the room into red and purple.

With her armor protecting her from whatever she didn't deflect with the nearly invisible speed of her swords, Iron Lass leveled both blades at the firing zones, emitting blasts of her own frost and fire until the entire room was a chaos of steaming and flaming destruction.

Vanishing her swords, she pried her way through what was left of the vault door, and I lost visual contact with her—apparently certain wings of the Tachyon Tower had no cameras in them, or required some further pass-code or override for me to access them.

By the time I patched into Iron Lass's cognistream—

What *is* this contraption? Like planetarium projectors—seven of them? They almost look like psionic inhibition siphons . . . but they'd be the largest ones ever built, all clustered and pointed at . . . is that a *person* inside that cube? Like a man sitting inside a washing machine! Is he asleep?

~~Ymir's blood—can it really be?

"Destroyer?"

~~Withered, depleted, a human apple core left in the sun—eyes shuttering open, twin blue suns—

"Menton! But . . . but I *kilt* you!"

~~His mouth slowly working, chewing and swallowing, dryly forcing itself to work, as if the man's emerging from a coma—

"Ah . . . Professor . . . *Icegaard*? Killed me, you say? Your delusions . . . of grandeur . . . are as cloying as ever . . ."

~~*Grendelsmuter, Darkalfheimsdottir,* to me!

"Surely . . . Professor . . . you have no need . . . of your weapons . . . against a desiccated corpse of a man . . . strapped into this . . . Torquemadan technology?"

~~Caution, Valkyrie—don't gaze into his eyes for too long at a time—he murdered ten thousand mortals in a single night, feeding upon their *minds*—

~~*Grendelsmuter*'s silver light upon the butcher's face makes him look even paler—

"How in Niflheim didt you get here, villain?"

"I believe, Professor Icegaard . . . I heard someone call it . . . Project . . . *Paperclip*? Transferred me on the CSV *Odessa,* if memory serves, from the Asteroid . . . I don't know how long ago . . . You'll forgive me . . . My mind's not what it used to be—"

"Haff you been behindt all ziss? Destroying ze Asteroidt? Murtering Hawk Kink?"

"Me? Hnnnh . . . hnnnh . . . excuse my, my wheezing, Professor . . . it's the only laugh I have left. I'm flattered, truly, but no . . . my glory days are long expired . . . Time to lift me on the pyre. These days . . . I'm nothing but a humble document . . . in the archives of power. To be filed, refiled, *defiled* at the whim of a higher power—"

"Zen be filedt in ze grafe by *my* power, monster, for now at last you vill die!"

~~Ach, *sheisen*! My sword—I've smashed one of the psionic inhibitors—his *eyes*—

"YOU WILL LET ME OUT OF THIS ABOMINATION, HNOSSI."

~~Must . . . fight him . . . but I can't . . . stop . . . myself . . .

"EXCELLENT WORK, WIELDING THOSE BLADES OF YOURS LIKE SCALPELS. THANK YOU FOR FREEING ME. AH . . . FORGIVE ME IF I DON'T STAND UP . . . AFTER SUCH A LENGTHY CONVALESCENCE, MY LEGS . . . YOU UNDERSTAND? AH, I CONFESS, THIS INTIMATE TIME WE'VE

SPENT TOGETHER HERE HAS GIVEN ME NOTIONS. WOULD
YOU BE A DEAR AND *SHARE WITH ME YOUR HEART*?"

~~No . . . my *Grendelsmuter*—away! Why won't you away?
Ah—no, not through my armor—NOT INTO MY—

H nossi's agony momentarily blinded me, shocking me right
out of her cognistream. I dialed through every camera I
could, then through every OM Meter feed I could locate, until I
clicked on to Syndi's.

"—How ya like me *now*?"

~~That's it . . . sing it with me, asshole!

"How's it feel being the one controlled, Menton? Oh, what's
wrong, legs weak? That's okay, you dirty old bastard—dance!
Dance anyway! You know this one? *Hey! MEN-ton! LEAVE my
MOM aLONE!*"

~~That's it, that's it—right on her goddamn sword, you old
fuck! . . . Look at that . . . hardly even bleeding. Like a mummi-
fied mental Hitler . . .

"Muzzer! Can you hear me?"

~~She's so heavy, all this armor . . . Odin, please don't let
her be dead—

"Can you hear me?"

"Ah . . . my daughter . . . you'f . . . safedt me . . . ?"

"Yes, Muzzer!"

"Such . . . a gut . . . girl—"

"Muzzer? *MUZZER*?"

"She'll be all right, Syndi!"

~~Who the hell? Chip Monk, Dark Fantastic, and—

"*Kareem!* Oh, Kareem—why? Why'd you do all this? Why,
Kareem? *WHY*?"

"What're you talking about?"

"All those, those, those *peo*ple, Kareem, all those F*O*O*Jsters at the fuh-Fortress—we *worked* with them! How could you just, just, just *kill* em all like that?"

"I didn'kill anybody, Syndi. Just hit em with the F*O*O*J's own knockout gas, that's all—they'll be fine!"

"Thank God, Kareem! I told them, I told them, I said you'd never—but *why*—"

"I had to put em outta commission until I could get here—the stakes are too high to risk them trying to stop us—"

"But what were you trying to do? Take out Menton? Because I just did that!"

"*That's* who that is? For real? Shit, couldn't tell when you got him all *you*ed up like that. Kot-tam, I knew it! I knew it! Yo, 'Tastic, didn'I say?"

"*Word.*"

"Syndi! Is Menton gonna die?"

"No, I don't think so—not if we get him to a doctor . . ."

"How do you know he's not dying?"

"I'd know—if I want to, I can feel what they feel when they're HEATed—but he's out cold . . . I should *let* him die—"

"No, keep him alive! We need him to testify! We need the whole truth out on this!"

"Kareem, does that mean it's all over? I mean, I captured him, right? So now he can stand trial for Hawk King's murder, Asteroid Zed—"

"No, Syndi—Menton wasn't behind any of this—well, maybe Zenith, but—"

"What the fuck are you talking about, Kareem? You're still fixated on Eva? Eva's not Menton! *This* is Menton! And she's not Sarah Bellum, either! Kareem, listen to me: You've been under a lot of stress! You're not seeing things as they really are. You need help! You need therapy!"

"Shut up, Syndi! I know Doctor Brain's clean!"

"Whu-what? But what about everything you told me at the theater?"

"Yeah, I had my suspicions at one point, but—"

~~Chip Monk's grabbing Kareem by the arm . . .

"X-Man, dam*n*ation, we've got *to move*—"

~~Can't let Kareem leave!

"But Kareem, you told me yourself, this elaborate conspiracy theory about how Eva had—"

"I just told you all that cuz I knew you'd sell me out to those freaks the second you got back to the Squirrel Tree!"

"What? You . . . you *used* me? Why? For revenge?"

"For a diversion!"

"So when exactly did you figure out this massive conspiracy, hm? And when were you planning to let me in on it?"

"It all clicked when you said who your mother was—everything fell together: Festus, Asteroid Zed, Menton—"

"That doesn't make any sense—"

"Who's the detective here? And besides, the proof is in the kot-tam pudding-pops! I'm tryin to save the planet here!"

"Always gotta be the one saving the planet, Kareem! How could you—just *use* me like that?"

"Even-Steven!"

"Oh *that's* mature!"

~~Dark Fantastic stomps his boot . . .

"Brother *X*!"

"Look, I'm not gonna argue with you, Syndi! How long can you keep Menton *you*ed up?"

"I don'know—hours?"

"Good! Get him and your mom outta here, and evacuate the building—"

"Why, what're you gonna do?"

"We're gonna blow this entire dome if we have to! Chip, 'Tastic—split up—stay off the comms except for emergency! Find a way to get up to that dimensional research lab!"

~~And now they're all gone, and I'm alone . . .

~~*Muzzer* . . .

Sibling Rivalry and
Oedipal Combat

switched cameras, clicking through until I could find one of the three invaders.

I spotted Kareem, covered in an Xoskeleton, smashing through a window and crawling out onto the exterior of the building.

I clicked again, finding a dozen camera angles on the outside of the dome from which to choose. And on Dome Camera Ext. 11, I spotted Kareem.

Backlit by the twinkling skyline, he was climbing up the dome with his clawed shadow-gloves, his shadow-cables keeping him from plummeting 150 stories to his death.

But above the whipping wind, I could hear the whine growing until it was like a band saw chewing into fresh pine. Kareem looked up—

"Okay, asshole!" shouted the Brotherfly. "Now you an me are gonna finish it for real!"

André opened his mouth wider than any human mouth should be able to and disgorged a steaming jet-spew of some type of corrosive, digestive juice onto Kareem. Kareem screamed, wiping at his exposed flesh, then reformatted his Xoskeleton to seal itself completely—even over his eyes. With Kareem stuck blind on the curve of the dome, André flew closer, kicking and kicking and kicking into Kareem's shadow-armor until Kareem was swinging on his tow cables from the impacts, his body and legs whipping side to side. Then one of his feet went right into a camera, and the hexagon went null blue.

Flipping and clicking wildly to find another POV, I hit something that brought onscreen the phrase TACHYON TOWER— UPPER DECK CAMERAS—SECURITY OVERRIDE—ACTIVATED, and then I found myself witnessing an interior shot of Chip Monk and the

Flying Squirrel smashing each other into the walls and across the chamber in a hurricane of weaponry and martial arts. In the brief moments when each man stopped to circle his opponent, they hurled fragments of cruelty at each other, horrible claims about disloyalty and hatred and paranoia.

The Flying Squirrel: "So, you're mixed up with that shine, now? He's doing for you what I wouldn't? Wouldn't Zenith be jealous?"

Chip Monk: "Zenith? The real hero that you murdered, Festus? Not that you'd do it yourself, that'd require you getting your hands dirty! You had your marionette Menton murder him for you!"

The Flying Squirrel: "How dare you question me! *Me!*"

The two men leapt, clashed, and the Squirrel fell onto his protégé. There was a loud crunch, and then Festus stumbled up backward, gasping, holding his hands in front of him as if to push away the sight of the motionless, costumed body on the ground.

E xactly at that moment, the exterior camera started working again.

André was still pummeling Kareem, but the X-Man wasn't even trying to fight back. Instead his Xoskeleton was growing something like a fiddler crab's oversized arm, a massive drill-like tool that chewed a hole through the dome wall until Kareem retracted his device and slipped through the gap.

Using the security override, I dialed up an interior camera view just as André followed Kareem inside the chamber, only to be smashed across the room by what looked like a massive black flyswatter. André careened off equipment, hit the wall, and landed on his side.

Given the angle of his impact, his body's contortion and his screaming, I guessed his hip was crushed and at least one of his legs was broken.

Sirens were howling, and speakers were automatically chanting *All personnel, this is a Level One emergency! Hull breach in the dimensional interface chamber! Initiating full system shutdown!*

Behind André in the cavernous technochamber was a huge, radiant iris, a three-story gold-silver blossom whose center shimmered with nebula and stars, vibrating with a disturbing violet luminescence.

Kareem staggered over to André, his Xoskeleton fading to gray and then to nothingness. Panting and groaning, he clutched his side as if his ribs were broken.

"Now listen . . . you superduper . . . killer house nigger! I know . . . *you* killed . . . Hawk King!" His chest was heaving. He tried and failed to catch his breath. "Tell me why . . . kottammit! *Why?*"

"You *crazy,* nigga!"

"My *medu-kem* . . . found dust . . . from the Blue Pyramid walls . . . on your costume, André. But you said . . . you hadn't been there . . . since you were a kid—"

"So your logoids are wrong!"

"No way in hell. I also had them . . . go through Festus's computers . . . Big Squirrel Brother . . . has got the whole city . . . under observation. Grimhotep . . . finally decrypted the file I retrieved. Shows you . . . flying away from the Pyramid the night the King was murdered. With a scepter in your hands. The Scepter of Typhon."

As his accusations grew in strength, Kareem regained his own.

"So how'd you do it, André? Mind-control him with the scepter into revealing his transmutation phrase . . . turn him into defenseless old Dr. Rogers in his wheelchair, and then kill him? And then . . . use the transmutation phrase to turn his body back into Hawk King's so no one'd know? Why, mutha-fucka? How much did that son of a bitch pay you?"

André yelled, "Fuck you, man! Ain'nobody pay me! I loved Hawk King! I loved him! He was my hero!"

Kareem put his foot onto André's pelvis and leaned.

The act—and André's scream—was so repugnant that even as a trained psychotherapist, it was all I could do to keep my-self from turning away.

"I aint fuckin around with you, André!" yelled Kareem. "Now you tell me why you did it, or next time I'm standing *up* on that muthafucka like you a StairMaster!"

When André's eyes drifted back into focus, he said, "They were blackmailing me, man!"

"Who? Festus?"

"I don't *know* who! Guy came to me, told me he'd tell my aunt Maybelle that I was responsible for my uncle Benteen's death! It'd kill her if she found out!"

"His death?"

"Because, because my uncle, he . . . I was in my room one mornin, an I didn'know he was home, an he didn'think any-body else was home, so when he heard somethin in my room he just came up an barged in an caught me changin into my cos-tume, an then he just had a massive heart attack—"

"He caught you fuckin a guy, didn'he, André?"

"What? No—no, that's not true, Kareem!" said André, or perhaps I should say Andrew, given his speech shift. "Who told you that? It's not true, whatever you heard!"

"No one told me—I figured it out days ago, after I bugged Doctor Brain's glasses. Your whole origin story—it didn't wash. All your 'womanizing'—I *saw* the photos from your file of you at those nightclubs. Just cuz Eva doesn't know what kind of clubs the Meet Market, Bone Dancers, and Peacocks are doesn't mean I don't!"

"No, Kareem, please, just . . . look, don't tell my aunt, all right? Whatever you think of me, don't tell my aunt—"

"You're a kot-tam *murderer,* André! You think I'm just gonna give you a pass cuz you don't wanna get in trouble with your aunty?"

"It'd *kill* her, Kareem! Don't you understand? Just like my uncle—I was trying to protect her, that's all! She raised me!"

"I don't let murderers walk for *any* reason! Let alone the Judas who assassinated the greatest leader we ever had!"

"Oh . . . sure," sobbed André, catching himself before he continued. "Fine. High and mighty Kareem. So perfectly just. Judging me! The homophobic, white girl–screwing hypocrite, judging me!"

"This aint about homophobia!"

"Isn't it? When I went to join the L*A*B when you mutha-fuckas were recruiting? Remember that? I went down to the QRIB. All I wanted was to protect Stun-Glas. And all your friends, laughing about these applicants you'd rejected, 'fag' this and 'fag' that, and the Dreadlocker saying how he'd put some 'battiman' in the hospital just for looking at him and how he'd 'put fyah' on the next one he found!"

"*I* never talked like that, André—"

"No, but you didn't fucking stop it, either, did you? Did you have Dreadlocker arrested for confessing to a horrible aggra-vated assault? Did you kick him out of the L*A*B? Even just fucking *talk* to him about it?"

X-Man looked down, opening his hands as if he'd left some-thing important in them. "You're right. André. You're right," he said, clearing his throat. "But that doesn't excuse—"

Kareem was smashed against the wall.

I zoomed back: the Flying Squirrel was reaching into his utility pouches—

And then the monitors inked into blackness.

A Fear-Filled Final Inventory

couldn't see anything. Even the eerie light of the dimensional portal had been snuffed out. The Dark Fantastic must've entered right behind the Squirrel. I clicked into the Brotherfly's OM Meter cognistream, but he'd passed out. Festus's link was still offline. My only means of monitoring was auditory.

"What's a matter, Festus?" called Kareem. "Night-vision goggles don't work? Even infrared is light, you know!"

"So we're *all* blind, then! I'll find you, Edgerton. And when I do, I'll snap you into kindling!"

"I don't think so, Festus. You're tired. Exhausted! I can hear it in your voice! And there're *two* of us!"

Sounds of tripping and falling—perhaps one man, maybe more.

The Squirrel: "Ah . . . but you're injured *and* exhausted. As soon as I take out your hooded hoodlum friend and his darkness dissipates, you'll be nothing but a lame black cockroach that can't even dash for the shadows. And injured as you are, I'm guessing you won't have power enough for many word-monstrosities now, will you?"

There were more sounds of crashing.

Kareem: ". . . Hey, that's a great gamble, Piltdown. Sure . . . I don't have any Words left at all. I'm defenseless!"

The Squirrel: "You're bluffing."

Kareem: *"Try me."*

Silence.

Kareem: "I'll give you this, Festus—you had me fooled for the longest time. Didn't even cross my mind that *you* were the one who'd arranged Hawk King's murder."

Festus: "You Liberian lunatic, so now you've shifted your roving delusions from Miss Brain-as-murderess onto me? What's next? Accusing Iron Lass of assassinating Lincoln? Or Caesar? Or Abel?"

"It took me a while to put it all together, Festy . . . but when I saw how totally broken up you were about Iron Lass—you haven't just been mourning her, you've been racked with guilt because you never thought your plot would get her poisoned!"

"That's why you went on this terrorist crusade of yours, you crackpot? Because I was mourning the impending death of a lifelong comrade?"

"No—because you, the world's self-proclaimed greatest detective, were dragging your feet on *two* investigations! I thought, Why isn't he out rousting everyone he can think of? He loves this woman, and revenge is that bastard's middle name! So why wouldn't you be attacking somebody, anybody, tossing whole neighborhoods for suspects . . . unless you knew there was nobody to hunt down, because *you'd* arranged for Asteroid Zed to be destroyed! Nobody wanted to go up there when Brain insisted, but *you* practically exploded a lung in protest! And then you wanted to take your own shuttle, but even when you finally relented and took the Space Elevator with us, you still had one of your ships standing by on remote!"

"You equate preparedness with homicide? Your lapses in logic have always been astonishing, Edgerton, but even for you, this is grand!"

More stumbling and crashing.

Kareem: "If I've got lapses in my logic, Pilty, it's funny how much your own computer records and surveillance footage helped form a picture of what you did, and what you're planning to do."

Silence.

"Nothing to say to that, huh? Yeah, I thought so. Even *I* didn't know I could do that until escaping Asteroid Zed gave me no choice but to send my Words inside the computers. But because of that crash course I realized I could search your mainframe, and that's how I found out the people you've had combing the Middle East had finally located the Scepter of Typhon months ago, after searching for it for years. And even though it's one of the only things that could make Hawk King vulnerable, you never turned it over to him, your supposed idol.

"Why wouldn't you? Unless you needed an ace up your sleeve—or a dagger? You had to destroy Asteroid Zed because my investigation would take me to Gil Gamoid and the N-Kid, and you had no way of knowing whether their Qosmic Qonsciousness might've picked up on what you'd done, or the attack that L-Raunzenu was planning, the one that no one but you and Hawk King knew about!"

"L-Raunzenu? What in God's—you're truly deranged, do you know that, Edgerton?"

"And you also couldn't risk me finding out that Menton and Sarah Bellum'd been moved. You were using them for your dimensional research, right? I mean, one of your holding companies owns Tachyon Tower! Sarah Bellum probably burned out or died, so you went back to the store for something with a little bit more kick. And who better to arrange the destruction of Asteroid Zed than the head of the company that retrofitted it after Gil, the Kid, and Menton were transferred there in the first place, and the head of the corporation that ran the Asteroid after the kot-tam thing was privatized? You'd think—"

A crash. Huffing. Cracking.

The lights seeped back on, emergency lights in red and the dimensional portal in purple.

The Flying Squirrel was standing over the cloaked body of the Dark Fantastic, all of whose limbs were pointing in directions they shouldn't have been. And right beside them stood the X-Man.

Kareem shouted something in an alien tongue, and four black baboons smoked into life and leapt on Festus, ripping at him, biting him, shredding his utility pouches and smashing whatever components they could find. The Squirrel whirled to fight off his attackers until he crashed into Kareem, knocking him down and sitting on top of him and reaching through the arms of his simian attackers to remove from his own neck the last item of Squirreltech he still had in his possession—a collar—which he locked around Kareem's neck.

The baboons disappeared.

Kareem punched Festus in the face, heaved, and shoved the old man off of him, struggling to get the shackle off his neck. He couldn't. "What'd you do to me?"

Barely able to push himself off the floor, the tattered, bleeding, and weaponless Festus, while panting, actually chuckled.

"Something . . . I whipped up . . . when you . . . affirmative-actioned your way into the F*O*O*J. Just in case. Scrambles your brain just enough . . . to stop you . . . from making your Words . . . come true."

Kareem backed away from the older man as far as he could.

"I don'care what it is," said Kareem. "Thing's got a battery—an since this is your first test, you don't know how long it'll last against me—"

"Oh . . . I don't need long . . . to kill you."

Both men were so injured it was remarkable that they could walk at all, yet still they stalked each other, pit bulls in a dog pit, waiting for the chance to rip out the other's throat.

"I found the footage in your mainframe, Festus. You're like Nixon—you're so paranoid, you even bugged yourself!"

"Keep talking, Stepin Fetchit. Keep on using up your breath—"

"Hawk King came out to the Squirrel Tree to talk to you personally, to get you to shut down Tachyon's dimensional research labs. I read his astronomical notes—my X-falcon found them. He'd been scanning the Nistan Nebula, and he found out that L-Raunzenu was planning to attack Los Ditkos . . .

using the Tachyon Tower's dimensional portal. But you wouldn't shut the portal down, would you? Because you had your own plans for keeping that attack secret . . . *and for letting it happen.*

"How many people d'you think an L-Raunzenu sneak attack from there could kill? Tallest building in the city, with nothing to block its nightmare-stream? I guess you'd know better than anyone, since Piltdown Psychotronics spent a billion tax dollars to create fuckin L-Raunzenu in the eighties. Your 'master weapon' in the War on Supervillains . . . but then L-Raunzenu didn't work so well in the Götterdämmerung, did it? Unless turning on us, killing us, and escaping into another dimension rank as high quality control in your estimation . . ."

The two men were now so close that they were stumbling and tripping to stay just out of grasping range, each one trying to fake out the other—or attack.

"So what did Hawk King order you to do?" said Kareem. "Shut down the portal in forty-eight hours or he'd shut it down himself? But hey! The F*O*O*J was collapsing, right? Letting in darkies, letting in gays, just before its most important election ever . . . Plus, you couldn't just stand by and let a little thing like global peace threaten the multibillion-dollar Pilt-Dyne defense contracts supplying the F*O*O*J, could you?

"So you needed something, something big, an interdimensional Pearl Harbor, to justify a new Götterdämmerung. A permanent one! With sweeping new powers for the F*O*O*J and for yourself, with *you* as Director of Operations! That's what Gil Gamoid and the N-Kid were trying to warn me about, only they were so fuckin cracked they could hardly string a coherent sentence together! And so what if a few thousand people'd die? I mean, they'd die anyway *someday,* right? And it's a small price to pay for Piltdown!

"But I'm gonna shut down this portal, Festus, if I have to use your skull like a fucking hammer to do it!"

Finally finding the right combination of buttons, I patched through on the speakerphone of the Brotherfly's belt.

"Kareem—please! You need help! Let me help you!"

"Doc? What the hell are you—"

The Squirrel leapt on him, and the two men smashed each other against the walls, the machinery, the floor. The large man rolled on top of Kareem, punching him and ramming his head into the floor. And then the collar snapped open and fell off the younger man's neck.

Kareem yelled, *"GIANT FIST!"*

A black fist the size of a tank arced down from the ceiling, smashing through the portal and destroying it, shearing through the floor and ripping open a huge hole in the wall extending to the level below and revealing the dark emptiness beyond. Ruptured by the impact, the metal floor buckled into an impromptu slide, and the two men, locked in each other's arms, shot outside into a 150-story plunge.

Exterior cameras caught strobing images of their descent:

145th floor: two bodies—

130th floor: tumbling feet-over-head in darkness—

105th floor: X-Man punching Festus—

70th floor: Festus doing nothing but gripping Kareem's mouth shut—

25th floor: *And a streak of light and one body still falling—*

And a sonic boom that erased the impact.

Reintegration

An hour later I was at the base of the Tachyon Tower in the hot darkness and the glare of emergency vehicle flashers and television cameras, watching three injured but still-standing members of the F*O*O*J issue their statement to soothe a concerned country and a worried world.

". . . and thanks to the superior strategic and defensive capacity of this organization," said Festus Piltdown III, scratched and scarred but no longer bleeding, "once again, the F*O*O*J has saved America from the threat of supervillainy . . . a sleeper agent who was among us for years, part of a diabolical plot to infiltrate the highest levels of F*O*O*J authority. A sleeper working for a previously unknown network of new supervillains, stretching across the planet . . . and right here in the homes of America—"

Festus broke off in midinspiration, visibly angry at the sight of a swaying Omnipotent Man (his face still tinted blue) who was alternating between flashing "thumbs up" and "double guns" toward the cameras. Covering the microphones, he leaned away from the podium and growled something to Hnossi, who steadied Wally.

Leaning back to the microphone, Festus said, "Understandably, we're all exhausted. But our exhaustion, our injuries, even the sacrifice of our fellow F*O*O*Jsters and other brothers-in-capes who perished tonight . . . this is a small price to pay for preserving the liberty of our great nation, the greatest nation on this planet. Thank you.

"No questions."

EPILOGUE

BE A PHOENIX, NOT A DODO

The Prize of Victory

As you have seen throughout *Unmasked! When Being a Superhero Can't Save You from Yourself,* the struggle to achieve psychemotional wellness is far from hopeless. If you can muster all the members of your internal superteam and rally under the strategic command of the methods outlined in these pages, victory can indeed be yours.

You have learned that the vulnerability you experience in the face of the greatest threats in your life originates in your own self-defeating behaviors. You have seen how your worst suffering originates inside your refusal to accept inevitable defeats. But when you choose to embrace such defeats, you will achieve prizes that no villain, external or internal, can ever wrench from your gloved and mighty hands: the shield of clarity and the sword of acceptance.

Avoiding Extinction When
the Food Supply Ends

As a superhero, you dared to devote your life to saving others. As a reader of this book who has borne witness to the case studies within it, you have come to see that the reward for superheroic public service is usually nothing more than public adulation.

So when, as all things must, that adulation disappears, you come to see that the far greater daring is in the effort to save yourself. However, if the world has changed around you, you may find yourself without an environment that can support you. If so, and if you fail to examine your psychemotional circumstances, you may go the way of the dodo.

Buy mythology teaches that even if you face total burnout, you can still be a phoenix.

Since the end of the Götterdämmerung, the heroes who have been entrusted into my care have come to me in two types, as distinguished by their attitudes: dodos and phoenixes. The dodos could not adapt to the new, exterior demands of a dynamically changing world and the intrinsic reorientation required to exist in that world, and therefore their own refusal to change led them to their ends.

But even those who were terrified by change, who nonetheless found the courage to seek psychic safety within, discovered their capacity to survive and even thrive in a world being re-created daily.

The Tragedy of a Fallen
F*O*O*Jster

Whether because of the fantastical, delusional ideation of Racialized Narcissistic Projection Neurosis, or because he was acting on the orders of his masters in the recently revealed Neo-Villain Network, Philip Kareem Edgerton, VKA the X-Man, posed a grave threat to the United States. His near-ascendancy to executive authority on the F*L*A*C of the F*O*O*J remains a cautionary tale, a dodged bullet whose *kablam!* still rings fear in the ears of the nation.

The F*O*O*J's special investigative task force concluded that Edgerton himself had murdered Hawk King, then exploited that murder to boost his electoral hopes. When his ascent to power failed, he exploded his Plan B in the July 16 Attacks.

For such a diabolical operative, Edgerton was ultimately incompetent in terror, surprisingly typical of one trapped in an id-reflexive conflict loop. The task force discovered that the bombs Edgerton had planted at the Fortress of Freedom were so shabbily constructed that the chemicals they contained had been improperly mixed, which resulted in them emitting only knockout gas instead of lethal fireballs, except for the "X-bombs" that destroyed the Fortress's comm system.

More worrisome was the task force's discovery of Edgerton's previously unknown capacity for mind control, a variant of his logoid power. Edgerton used it to bludgeon a false "confession" from the Brotherfly. Another victim of that power was Tran Chi Hanh, as disabled by dodo tendencies as his confederate was, who died hating the man who had given him a home and who had treated him like a son.

Ultimately, the task force was unable to find a shred of evi-

dence linking Hawk King to one professor Jackson Rogers of Ellison Heights, Los Ditkos, who coincidentally disappeared the
same day Hawk King died. While the task forced declared it
had insufficient evidence to link Edgerton to Rogers's disappearance, suspicions remain.

Fortunately for everyone, the containment of the QRIB was
accomplished with only minimal casualties; aside from the
members of the L*A*B, only a few dozen families died from
fire or smoke, a statistic all the more remarkable when compared to the far greater number of homes destroyed. More lives
might have been lost had firefighters not been ordered by the
Spook to stay clear of their equipment for fear that they, too,
could become targets of the L*A*Bsters.

Healing the Nation, Healing the Soul

ortunately for the plight of both freedom and mental
health, most of my F*O*O*Jsters did learn the lessons I attempted to impart to them in the Hyper-Potentiality Clinic.
Some, in fact, were learning those lessons before our sessions
began, recognizing the ways in which they would need to look
past old ways of thinking, to make embassies of peace to those
who previously had been adversaries, and to re-create themselves anew in a new world.

Explaining to the F*O*O*J special task force that Menton
had been clandestinely transferred to the Tachyon Tower to
serve in the highest level of Global Anti-Supervillain Intelligence, the Flying Squirrel demonstrated how the top-secret
new Menton Protocols of GASI had helped the F*O*O*J keep
tabs on all new developing hyper-threats everywhere, from
scanning the minds of seemingly innocent Americans to check-

ing what books they were reading and with whom they were socializing, all in order to preempt the development of the next generation of supervillains.

By Menton's analysis, the situation is disturbing.

There are somewhere in the neighborhood of six million Americans with protovillain tendencies, and hundreds of millions with such tendencies around the world, not to mention those who are already acting upon such malevolent ideation. A grateful public has embraced this new "Mentology" surveillance service, which ensures safety by stopping villainy before it can kill, so that, in the words of the Flying Squirrel, "the smoking gun is not a laser cannon burning down Los Ditkos."

The New Horizons of Psychemotional Stability

So how are my sanity-supplicants doing, now that they've completed the first phase of their therapeutic adventure?

POWER GRRRL continues to process her narcissistic ideation and behaviors but has entirely overcome her Munchausen tendencies. Having left the F*O*O*J and superheroics altogether, she has moved her entertainment career completely out of the pop/dance/techno field, and is currently delving into an edgier, angrier "rap/hip-hop" sound with a forthcoming album, *Straight Outta Virgins*. Since the events of July 16, she has refused to speak to the media about Edgerton.

THE BROTHERFLY, after several months of physiotherapy and a hip replacement, has returned to me for an expanded role of talk therapy in his life to address his Secret Identity Diffusion and to finish exorcizing the ghosts of Rudolphism-inspired pain. Currently remodeling his family home which he recently inherited, he's now hosting Ultra Power Network's hit *Brother-fly for the Regular Guy,* featuring André dispensing superhero chic for the fashion-challenged ordinary citizen.

OMNIPOTENT MAN, FLYING SQUIRREL, and **IRON LASS** unveiled their strategy for a revitalized F*O*O*Jification of global affairs. *The Prospects for a New Superheroic Century* calls for and maps out a vigilant stance against the new breed of super-menaces lurking beneath the illusion of peace like subtopical acne waiting to erupt on the face of an innocent adolescent.

WALLY W. WATCHTOWER has made astounding progress in overcoming his Crisis of Infinite Dearths, Mission-Identity Loss Disturbance, Icon Trap, Post-Power Stress Disorder, and Secret Identity Diffusion, integrating his manifold alters and powers into a unified, successful new identity. Like an eagle, Omnipotent Man has soared past his previous popularity to unexpected new heights, not only because of his triumphant return to superheroism and his victory in the July 16 Attacks, but because of a new development sweeping the nation. Piltdown Psychotronics has developed and mass-marketed a home consumer OM Meter, one which in these uncertain times allows ordinary Americans to connect empathically with one of their greatest leaders, one whom they feel confident is in direct, daily connection with the Ka of Hawk King himself. After only a few months of retail sales of the OMpathy Box, it's estimated that half of all Americans own or regularly use one and pay monthly subscription fees. Sales of OMpathy Boxes show no sign of slowing down.

HNOSSI ICEGAARD and **WALLY W. WATCHTOWER** are now happily married, and Hnossi has given birth to a baby boy. The product of combined Aeserian and Argonian genes, the fast-forming fetus gestated to full term in less than a month, with a birthday of September 12. Eager to celebrate their union in numerous ways, the couple toyed with the names "Hnally" and "Wossi," but arrived at a happy third option by naming their child Freedom.

PROFESSOR ICEGAARD has overcome her Savior Complex, removed herself from her id-crisis of scripted behavior loops, deactivated her narcissistic tendencies and Uranus Conflict with her daughter, countered her Mortiquaeroticism, and successfully disassembled her Icon Trap. In doing so, she's found a new life and new love, and has gone past mere consultation with Piltdown Dynamics to become its Chief Research & Design Officer as Pilt-Dyne's vanguard in the development of all new peace-delivery technology systems including the new B10 ballistic-pacification flight vehicle currently under construction.

MR. PILTDOWN, still unmarried, remains saddened by the loss of his former protégé, whom he still remembers as the happy, smiling child he'd once been. More pleasantly, he's processed his way through his own Icon Trap. Because of his role in protecting the public safety, he's been able to reduce his Mission-Identity Loss Disturbance, and he's made great strides in minimizing his id-confrontational tendencies, his Obsessive Defensive Ideation and Compulsive Fight-or-Flight Behaviors, and has addressed his own case of the Achilles Threefold Folly of Superior Ability. Buoyed by his newfound mental clarity and public acclaim for his heroic role in the July 16 Attacks, he was elevated by an overwhelming margin to the F*L*A*C as Director of Operations in the F*O*O*J election of September 12, with his Squirrel-slate swept in alongside him. Awarded the contract to build the Asteroid Omega penitentiary, Piltdown Dynamics is also constructing and will be operating a new network of high-tech criminal containment facilities around the United States, providing jobs and safety for the nation.

Festus Piltdown was perhaps my most reluctant sanity-supplicant, beginning as an angry, confrontational, embittered, and lonely man who was suffocating under the weight of his own past. Yet he employed our psychemotional processing more successfully than any of his comrades to undertake the greatest degree of self-actualization into the humble, correctly confident, serene, and wise leader he is today.

Because of that success, I'm going to give him the last word in *Unmasked! When Being a Superhero Can't Save You from Yourself,* quoting his final answer to my repeated question about how to face life if the glory days never returned. And because I'm giving him the last word, I'll even spot him a few more than the allotted ten:

"New days are upon us. We have no need for personal rewards or individual glory. We, a new F*O*O*J for a new century, have only one mission, and we'll honor that mission to our highest capacity: to serve Man."

—FESTUS PILTDOWN III, HKA THE FLYING SQUIRREL

ABOUT THE AUTHOR

DR. EVA BRAIN-SILVERMAN lives and works at the Hyper-Potentiality Clinic inside the refurbished Mount Palomax Observatory in Los Ditkos. She has been helping hyper-hominids for more than twenty years.

ACKNOWLEDGMENTS

To my longtime comrade Dengar Shafiq for indispensable advice on revisions, and to amazing poet, author, and friend Mark Kozub for his encouragement on this project.

To my agent, mentor, and friend Marie Brown, who continues to dazzle me with her knowledge, wisdom, and understanding: my eternal affection, gratitude, and respect.

To my fellow SF writers who've been especially encouraging and gracious to me and my work: Richard Morgan (*Market Forces*), and Canadian cohorts Nalo Hopkinson (*Brown Girl in the Ring*) and Robert J. Sawyer (*Hominids*).

To my little sister E-Beth for use of her line "punched him in the soul."

To all the wonderful folks who promoted and supported *The Coyote Kings of the Space-Age Bachelor Pad,* particularly the mighty Colleen Lindsay, and those readers and critics who understood that beyond the humor, *Coyote Kings* is a serious book.

To authors Dr. John Gottman (*The Relationship Fix*), Sandy Hotchkiss, LSCW (*Why Is It Always About You? Saving Yourself from the Narcissists in Your Life*), Dr. Elizabeth Loftus and Katherine Ketcham (*The Myth of Repressed Memory*), and Nafeez Mosaddeq Ahmed (*The War on Freedom: How and Why*

America Was Attacked September 11, 2001) for their often electrifying insights and case studies.

To my wife, Michelle, my best friend and truly a blessing from the Divine.

And finally, to the Creator, from whom radiates all splendor, power, and triumph, who is the great hope of the universe, the maker and master of the stars, and the love of all the worlds. All praise is due to You.

The mistakes are mine alone.

ABOUT THE REAL AUTHOR

MINISTER FAUST is a high school English teacher, community activist, and public broadcaster in Edmonton, Canada, where he lives with his wife and daughter. His writing has appeared in *The Globe and Mail, Alberta Views,* and *Vue Weekly,* and his fiction, poetry, and essays have been anthologized in *Fiery Spirits and Voices, Poetry Nation,* and *Edmonton on Location: River City Chronicles.*

Hailed for its language, humor, and rich characterization, Minister Faust's first novel, *The Coyote Kings of the Space-Age Bachelor Pad,* was a finalist for the Philip K. Dick Award, Compton Crook Award, and Locus Best First Novel Award, and ended up on 2004 top ten lists for *January* magazine (fiction), *Barnes & Noble* (SF&F), Amazon.com (SF&F), and *SF Site* (SF&F, Editor's Choice). *The New York Times Book Review* said of the book: "Faust anatomizes [the Edmonton setting] with the same loving care Joyce brought to early-twentieth-century Dublin . . . Faust's debut novel is a fresh and stylish entertainment."

Since 1989, Minister Faust has been a community broadcaster at Edmonton's CJSR FM88 and has freelanced for the CBC. His national award-winning Africentric and pro-democracy news program, *The Terrordome Afrika All-World*

News Service, and his cohosted music show (with Bongbiemi the Original Tribesman), *Asiko Phantom Pyramid: Global Afrikan Musics Led by a Headcharge of Hip Hop,* can be heard around the world at cjsr.com.

Minister Faust's website The Original BRO-LOG (ministerfaust.blogspot.com) hosts his commentaries on a range of social, political, and pop-culture issues. The BRO-LOG is also a portal to Minister Faust's extensive writings, with audio and video, and including podcast archives for *The Terrordome* and *Asiko Phantom Pyramid* and a vast array of links to Africentric, social justice, pro-democracy, and literary websites.

His superpowers include always being able to find an excellent parking spot and the infallible capacity to choose the slowest checkout line in any store.